SECRETS AND SECOND CHANCES

Anita Shirodkar was the creative director (art) at Mudra Communications and has spent twenty years in advertising. She is currently creative consultant to a destination management company that promotes tourism to India. She has also forayed into food writing, including writing content for a gourmet food store in Mumbai, and a cookbook which she has designed, photographed and ghost written for a nutritional specialist. Anita resides in Mumbai and Dubai, where she manages a business. This is her first work of fiction.

Secrets
and Second Chances

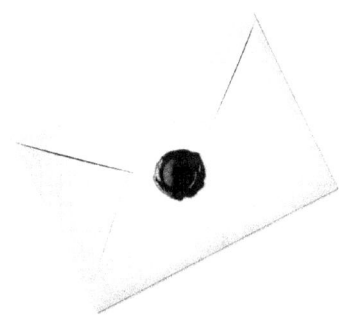

ANITA
SHIRODKAR

Published by
Rupa Publications India Pvt. Ltd 2014
7/16, Ansari Road, Daryaganj
New Delhi 110002

Sales centres:
Allahabad Bengaluru Chennai
Hyderabad Jaipur Kathmandu
Kolkata Mumbai

Copyright © Anita Shirodkar 2014

All rights reserved.
No part of this publication may be reproduced, transmitted, or stored in a retrieval system, in any form or by any means, electronic, mechanical, photocopying, recording or otherwise, without the prior permission
of the publisher.

ISBN: 978-81-291-3269-7

First impression 2014

10 9 8 7 6 5 4 3 2 1

The moral right of the author has been asserted.

Typeset by RECTO Graphics, Delhi.

Printed at Thomson Press India, Faridabad

This book is sold subject to the condition that it shall not,
by way of trade or otherwise, be lent, resold, hired out, or otherwise circulated,
without the publisher's prior consent, in any form of binding or cover
other than that in which it is published.

For Alisha and Sid…
one of the greatest joys in my life is being your mother

CHAPTER ONE
Mumbai, January 2013

Nandita Dharkar walked into the marble-laden foyer of Sea Breeze Apartments on a buoyant note. Finally something that looks half-decent, she thought, casting a quick glance around her. A pot-bellied security guard held out a register and a cheap plastic pen to Pawan Bhandari, the representative of Sai Krupa Estate Agents. Pawan, who was escorting Nandita, clearly believed that he was above such mundane formalities. He brushed the register aside, informing the guard imperiously that he was here to show the seventh-floor apartment. The guard did not seem particularly impressed; nonetheless, he looked at Nandita appraisingly. He ushered them in respectfully enough, though. Nandita stepped into the chrome-plated elevator, paying scant heed to the murmurings of the diminutive Pawan beside her. She was lost in a train of thought that had nothing to do with him. As he fumbled with the keys to apartment 7B, she drummed her fingers impatiently on her oversized silver tote. At least this place was clean and well-maintained, she reflected, surveying the cream marble corridor with approval. It had been a long, arduous and disappointing afternoon of apartment hunting, and she was just about ready to give up for the day. Nandita was seriously contemplating hiring yet another broker if this didn't work out. Who would have thought that apartment hunting in Mumbai would turn out to be such an exhausting task...it was enough to make one want to turn around and consider going back home!

Pawan Bhandari unlocked the door successfully and stepped back to let Nandita enter first. He was beginning to tire of this unpredictable client. He had guessed from the start that this picky woman was not going to be an easy customer. She looked young, but it was evident that she had previous experience and knew a lot more about what made an apartment attractive than he did. It was unnerving, the way she had pointed out flaws in buildings and flat layouts, making short shrift of his usually efficient sales spiel. His other clients generally swallowed these stories in good faith. But Nandita had detected leaky ceilings before they had actually begun to leak; she knew exactly which apartment would get unbearably warm during the day and which one would not be able to withstand rain. It was uncanny how she just knew.

At present, Pawan was showing Nandita a compact, 'two-bedroom-hall-kitchen' furnished flat in a shady by-lane in the much-coveted residential suburb of Bandra, and hoping fervently that this would be the end of her lengthy, critical search.

As Nandita stepped into the flat, she immediately sensed that it could be what she was looking for. She had always relied on her intuitive sense about living spaces, and her instincts had rarely proved her wrong. She loved, above all, plenty of light and open spaces, and the first thing that attracted her as she walked through the door was the presence of large French windows, almost down to floor level, through which the westerly evening light was streaming in. The living room was small but suffused with a warm glow that bathed the white walls in pale peach. The furniture was not chic but appeared comfortable. An enormous beige couch dominated the living room, which also boasted a white rug strewn with numerous large cushions. A rather grandfatherly armchair sat by the window, well-stuffed and covered in slightly worn brown leather. As she looked around, Pawan hastened to open the windows, letting in a gentle breeze.

Pawan was endowed with a disproportionately large moustache, ostensibly to make up for his lack of height, and he was presently stroking it to quell his agitation. He glanced at Nandita. It really couldn't get better than this, and if she thought it still wasn't good enough, she was just expecting too much. Such a young girl had no business being so demanding, he thought indignantly. Most working women her age were suitably grateful for modest one-room paying guest accommodation in the city. Or even the hostels. But not this one! Pawan thought he had every reason to be righteously aggrieved. There was something infuriatingly confident about the way she carried herself. She had reduced him to babbling incoherence more than once, and even now she had a list of demands as long as they were, in Pawan's opinion, grandiose. Why did a single girl need two bedrooms? He was curious about her profession but she had not been very forthcoming about personal details, and somehow he felt he could not ask. She was obviously making decent money, to be able to afford a place like this. He realized he was a little intimidated by this tall, glorious creature.

Nandita was oblivious to Pawan's disapproval. For the first time, she was not dismayed by what she saw. She tried to ignore his hovering presence and looked pensively around the little living room. It was definitely the nicest of the fifteen-odd places Pawan had shown her so far. In spite of living in a sprawling Delhi bungalow all her life, she was resigned to the fact that Mumbai's apartments were indeed matchboxes. Compact was just a euphemism for poky, she thought, but decided to console herself with cosy instead. But small or not, it was going to be hers, and hers alone. For a brief moment, a surge of panic threatened to engulf her, but she fought it down as quickly as it had arisen. Ridiculous! This had been her choice; it was what she wanted more than anything else. She wasn't going to chicken out now.

She opened the glass door at the end of the living area and stepped out into a miniscule balcony, breathing in the fresh evening air. She noticed with amusement the three sparse potted plants that went, according to Pawan, by the ambitious name of 'a garden', and resolutely put the image of her expansive backyard in Vasant Vihar out of her mind. The hirsute agent plucked at his moustache again, unconsciously betraying his nervousness. He ventured to suggest that it was practically impossible to get such a 'decent' deal off Mumbai's fashionable Carter Road, and that too with a sea view. He scoffed at Nandita's opinion that the small patch of ocean visible from the living room window could hardly be called a sea view. Did she think that she was going to live on Chowpatty beach? Really, the girl was impossible!

Pawan's quivering moustache strongly reminded Nandita of the pet rabbit she had owned at the age of nine. 'It is decent society, madam. All good phamilies. No gadbad. Also very near to Pali Market…so easy, no? And then, you are having office in Bandra Kurla Complex, very decent for commute! *Baarish mein problem nahi ayega, madam.* Very decent place!' Clearly, Pawan thought that decency reigned supreme in all matters. He stole a curious look at Nandita.

'Madam is *alone* staying here?' Nandita ignored this obvious but unspoken question about her marital status with accomplished ease and walked into the master bedroom. Oh man, she thought. Her practised eye swept over the decor, if it could be called such. The room was furnished with assorted pieces that were bought from the Jogeshwari version of Chor Bazaar at throwaway prices, newly made 'antiques', finished to look old and expensive. The bed was imitation antique four-poster, hung with a frilly pink lace canopy. Throw away the frill immediately, she decided. The carved dark wood closet didn't look like it would accommodate even half her things, but she'd deal with that. At least the curtains were a sober floral white-on-white pattern and not adorned with hideous purple and pink pansies, like the ones in Pawan's previous offering. The French windows made their appearance in the bedroom as well, and the huge wall-sized mirror that lined one side of the room made it look much larger than it actually was. The bathroom was a pleasant surprise, clearly newly refurbished, and with such good taste that she wondered what had happened to the person who chose the pink frill.

Nandita did a quick survey of the room. After mentally eliminating tacky embellishments like the fuchsia fur cushions and multicoloured embroidered wall hangings, she considered that the room could be made habitable. A small, serviceable desk stood before the window, and Nandita imagined it would make a fairly acceptable workspace for her laptop. A cursory inspection of the kitchen was next. Seeing that it had a spacious black granite counter and a modern cooking range, she decided to overlook the tiny cabinets and startling yellow paintwork.

Nandita was due to start at her new job in a week and realized that she could not afford to prolong her house hunt now. She took a final approving look around her. It was only a rental, after all. And it was definitely convenient. All her friends had told her that Bandra was the place to be…young and happening and so very central. She thought the rent being quoted was absurdly extortionate, but Pawan had assured her that if you wanted a 'decent' place, you had to pay decently too. She was getting accustomed to Pawan Bhandari's parlance! If she could get used to living with dark green marble flooring, she might even call this place home someday. And notwithstanding what she had told the Moustache, the miniscule sea view was charming to her, having lived all her life in a city far removed from the coast.

'I'll take it,' she said in a decisive tone. 'When can we finish the paperwork? I need to move in by Saturday latest, or there is no point in taking it.'

There she was, riding roughshod over him again. Pawan rushed in to placate her. 'Oh, yes madam, immediately! No problem. Madam is finally happy, no?' Nandita smiled and nodded, secretly ticking off the varying emotions that were flooding her mind. Happiness was not exactly the predominant one. Apprehension, confusion, perhaps ambivalence...happiness would come later, she hoped.

'Party is wanting eleven-month lease,' Pawan explained painstakingly. 'We can renew after…'

Nandita cut in imperiously, 'Yes, yes, I understand. Just let me know when I can sign.'

Pawan was reduced to incoherence once more, but the animated moustache bobbed happily up and down, and his mind dwelt for a pleasurable moment on the substantial brokerage he would claim from both parties. The Kohlis were moving to Singapore and they were anxious to let the place quickly. Mr Kohli was going to be very pleased at how efficiently Pawan had sealed the deal. Maybe that new car would be possible after all, and life would get easier. At least his wife would be satisfied; she could finally be on par with her snooty sister, and not have to feel ashamed of the rickety old Maruti 800. He promised to complete the formalities with alacrity, and then with a sigh of relief, sat respectfully on one of the carved dining chairs and allowed his mind to drift to the next day's clients.

While Pawan's mind was thus fruitfully engaged, Nandita got the uninterrupted time she needed to take stock of what she would need to buy, to make the place more livable.

Though Nandita had never set up an apartment of her own before, she was fast discovering that it was not rocket science. Thanks to her mother, she was far more knowledgeable about kitchen affairs than most girls her age, and the only other thing she actually cared about was closet space. She ruefully realized that she would have to send a large portion of her belongings back to Delhi, as there was no way even half her stuff was going to fit in here. She made a few quick notes in her diary and shut it with a decisive snap.

'Sorry to keep you waiting, Pawan. I'm all done. Please make sure I'm in here by Friday, I'd have to have at least two days to move in.'

'Yes madam, surely. Surely.' Pawan was obsequious to the point of almost bowing. Nandita felt a little guilty about her cavalier treatment of the man.

As she stepped into the elevator to leave, she was in a much happier frame of mind than she had been when she arrived. She was mentally going over her plans of what she was going to do in order to transform 7B, when the lift door opened and she was confronted by the sight of a matronly woman of generous proportions. The lady was eyeing her with undisguised interest.

'She is moving into 7B?' The woman addressed Pawan in what she mistakenly believed was a diplomatic undertone. 'I know the Kohlis are trying to rent the place out!'

Nandita pretended not to have heard and feigned an interest in the magazine she was carrying. When Pawan's moustache had twitched in the affirmative, the woman lost no time in putting out a chubby, exquisitely manicured and heavily bejewelled hand towards Nandita. 'Mrs Kulwant Singh. 8B. And you are?' Nandita was about to reply when the lift door opened again, this time to admit a lissome young girl sporting tightly fitted pink track pants and bleached hair, wearing an iPod on her arm. She looked like she was in her mid-twenties, in the pink of health. Wholesome, thought Nandita…she's not just pretty, she looks positively delicious, down to the last strand of her bleached blonde hair. The new arrival flashed a radiant smile at everyone in general.

'Oh, hello Arushi!' said Kulwant. 'Going for jogging again! You are too thin already, beta! Like Kareena Kapoor you look, that size zero type…no flesh only on those bones! In my day, girls used to be healthy, hatti katti…'

'Nonsense, Kulwant Aunty. I'm perfectly healthy,' quipped Arushi. She added, with a smile that robbed the words of offence, 'In fact, *you* could do with some exercise yourself… Why don't you come to Joggers' Park with me sometime?' She winked conspiratorially at Nandita before she shot out of the lift at a brisk trot.

'Always teasing, that Arushi,' said Kulwant with a sigh. 'Now what will an old woman like me do in Joggers' Park? *Zindagi mein kabhi jogging nahi ki, jo ab shuru karoon!*'

Nandita believed her. She reluctantly introduced herself to Mrs Singh, and was forced to spend the next few minutes listening to an abbreviated version of the comings and goings of the residents of Sea Breeze apartments. Kulwant Singh had the natural curiosity of an older woman with not much to amuse her, and was dying to find out more about Nandita. She told Nandita that she was a widow who lived with a paying guest to keep her company.

'*Bore ho jati hoon na,*' she said cheerfully. 'Always nice to have a young person around the house. My own son is living in Amreeka, too busy to come and visit.' She paused and eyed Nandita closely. 'You are not married?'

Nandita resisted the impulse to roll her eyes and tick the inquisitive Kulwant off. She made all the right noises and said a firm goodbye.

'You will need a bai!' Kulwant called after her as she stepped out into the beautiful sunset. 'Let me know, I will send my Gauri to you!' Nandita escaped as quickly as she could. Clearly, Mumbai had its own version of Simi Aunty, whom she had left behind in Delhi. She had no intention of being adopted the moment she had arrived.

Once out of earshot, Nandita reached for her mobile phone and dialled a number. 'Rajeev? Hello, it's Nandita Dharkar... Yes, the apartment is finalized, and I can start next week... Bandra, just off Carter Road... That's really nice of you, but I'll manage... Thank you, I'll see you on Monday... Of course, I'm more than ready to get to work! Bye, Rajeev.'

She walked out of the little lane on to Carter Road, breathing in the salty evening breeze. The upscale boulevard in Bandra was flanked by a long promenade along the seashore. A few stray dogs barked amiably at her, as if extending a lukewarm welcome to their neighbourhood. The evening strollers along the walkway were a varied and colourful lot. Chatty, energetic ladies in groups pounded the pavements to burn calories even as they exchanged elaborate recipes for dinner, while determined solitary joggers trotted by in disdain. Middle-aged enthusiasts walked their fluffy spaniels, and young couples blissfully lined the parapet, oblivious to the world. Maids with assorted perambulators and babies chatted coyly with chauffeurs, rickshaws honked shrilly, and teenagers with raging testosterone levels sped by, driving swanky cars with heavy metal music blaring out of the rolled down windows.

Nandita leaned back on a bench under a precariously swaying palm and shut her eyes. Nandita Dharkar, architect, abundantly talented and successful. That was how the world saw her. How did she see herself? Nandita Dharkar, twenty-nine, beginning a new phase of her life, unsure, hesitant and vulnerable. Single girl in Mumbai, living on her lonesome ownsome... Hey, that was what I wanted, wasn't it, she mused. Nandita was definitely off men for a while; at least, she amended, off the kind of men she'd known and dated till now. Her experience of the opposite sex so far had taught her that most men were intimidated by her professional success, her crisp, businesslike demeanour, her rather forceful personality and, she suspected, her complete lack of inclination to be a housewife and mother. She was the antithesis of her friend Shanti, Aditya had told her categorically.

'Nan, you are better off sticking to your designing stuff. You aren't cut out to be a freaking housewife. You'd drive the poor sod insane in a week.'

It was also true that Nandita had not actually wanted to marry any of the men she had dated. The 'poor sods' were all so...was it possesive? Or did she mean regressive? Why did men assume that a woman was willing to roll over and play dead the minute things got serious? Career must take a back seat, while husband, in-laws, kitchen and children squeezed demandingly into the front seat well before you could say 'I do'.

Case in point: Gaurav Mathur. She'd enjoyed his company—he was good-looking, a successful banker, all of the right things to make him a 'suitable boy'. Maybe she had even been a little bit in love with him. She wasn't really sure...she'd liked him a lot, but felt none of the uncomfortably violent feelings that her girlfriends popularly associated with being 'in love'. And though she did miss Gaurav, she was certainly not devastated by the break-up. She may have married him if things had been different.

But he had a mother, two younger sisters and a spinster aunt who were dependent on him, and he had expected Nandita to be more of a nurse cum major-domo than a wife, to give up a career she enjoyed and had worked hard at to excel in.

Nandita was not ready to give up her life and be a stay-at-home wife. Gaurav had been furious with her for refusing to conform to what he felt was not an unrealistic expectation. A man who was willing to provide his wife every luxury in exchange for taking care of his family was a responsible and considerate husband, so why the hell did she have to carry on about her career? How could that possibly be more important? She didn't *need* to work; all that 'double income' stuff was fine for couples with economic problems. Gaurav was abundantly well off, he could more than afford to keep her in style. Nandita realized that they stood at two opposite ends of a vast spectrum. After the breakup, Aditya had told her that unfortunately, Gaurav was out of sync with everything about her that was most worth loving. She knew her mother had been disappointed when the relationship fell apart, but Amrita Dharkar had understood, and Nandita had gone back to being single, if not happily, then at least without regrets.

The sun had set and the sky was incandescent with orange and pink. Nandita got up to look for a cab. Now that she was actually here, she thought it was destiny that had finally brought her to what had always been a dream city for her. Nandita had travelled a fair amount, if not extensively, within India and outside. But this city was completely new to her, as she had never actually visited for more than a day or two. And she owed her newfound independence to her dearest friend Aditya Arora. For all her strength and resolve on other issues, this particular move would not have been possible without his persistence and nagging. And here she was, finally, free of the fetters that she had begun to find so irksome. She had expected to feel nothing but soaring exhilaration, but sitting here in the deepening twilight, she was surprised to detect unmistakable feelings of apprehension. Her mind dwelled briefly on the blue sheet of paper at the bottom of her jewellery box, and the cryptic lines it contained... a few lines that may or may not define everything she was. There was so much to discover in Mumbai.

Nandita knew that her new job with Rajeev Sabarwal, the celebrity architect who had blazed his own unique trail in the field over the last few years, was an achievement that many of her peers would sell their souls for. Would she measure up? There was so much to do, so much to prove. Again, Nandita quelled the wave of alarm that was threatening to overtake her. She hoped that she had made the right decision by giving up her life as she knew it, and taking this plunge into deep, uncharted waters. Of course, it was too late to turn back now.

CHAPTER TWO
Delhi, October 2012

The dry, blazing afternoon was hotter than any she could remember in October, and Nandita determinedly adjusted her Versace shades as she got into her car. It was an unbelievable nuisance, but it had to be done. Her high-profile, almost-celebrity client had called with a desperate, 'Come right away, pleeeeeaaase!' It was a prestigious job, and though Nandita doubted that it was as urgent as it sounded, she knew she had to obey the summons. Such projects gave her a lot of exposure, and she did not need any negative publicity from a disgruntled client. Nothing else would have dragged her out of her air-conditioned studio in her Vasant Vihar home and made her drive to Qutub Enclave. That too today of all days. Her school friend Shanti was getting married, and the first of the major parties was scheduled for this evening. The preparations for the sangeet had kept Nandita occupied all week, and today, when the big event was to take place and she was expected to be there bright and early, she had been called to iron out a glitch in the new showroom she had designed for couturier Avantika Puri. She knew from experience that Avantika's starry tantrums could drag on forever if they were not nipped in the bud. Nandita believed that Avantika was in a permanent state of PMS, and appeasing her once she had descended into shrieking banshee mode was a superhuman task. Of course, she also dreaded Shanti's reaction if she failed to show up in time for the sangeet. Screwed on all fronts, she thought, as she pulled up outside the store, and mentally reviewed what could have gone wrong. Avantika's assistant had not been specific, but the summons had clearly been urgent. A babble of voices and utter confusion greeted her as she entered.

'Oh! There you are, thank god! I thought you would never get here!' cried Avantika breathlessly. 'I can't bear it!' Avantika was dressed in her signature loose white pants and white silk kurti, enormous earrings dangling down her neck, eyes heavily lined with kohl. Her hair was cropped short, close to her head, giving her an oddly boyish look that was at variance with her delicate jawline and her extremely feminine features. Around her neck, she wore an absolutely stunning necklace of antique silver, probably Tibetan, and at least a hundred years old.

'Can't bear what, Avantika? Do calm down!' said Nandita, with just a trace of annoyance in her voice. She was not taking the trouble to mask her impatience this time.

'It's that revolting wall. It looked wonderful as a swatch, but now it's looking so distracting… And don't you think it will clash hideously with the clothes? You know that a large part of my new line is sea greens and lime greens. What a disaster!' Drama was Avantika's forte, and she was playing up with predictable fuss.

She's dragged me all the way here for *this*, mused Nandita resignedly. She surveyed the long, glossy, perfectly painted peach-coloured wall critically.

'I hate to point it out, Avantika, but that was exactly what I had warned you against. But you insisted on the peach…'

'I know, I know! Nandita, do something, my opening is in two days, and I have to start bringing the clothes in this evening!' Avantika looked genuinely terrified, and Nandita relented.

She sighed wearily and sitting down on an exquisitely carved antique chair, she dialled a number on her cell phone. 'Vinay? Look, I need to see some paper samples immediately… No, no, I'm at Qutub Enclave. Yes, it's very urgent, and I need the wall papered by this evening... White and beige textures is what I require...by 4.30? *Kaise bhi karo, lekin aaj ho jana chahiye.* Great, thanks Vinay...see you!'

She turned to Avantika. 'We can cover it with some nicely textured white wallpaper for now; that should work. It won't look too plain, but won't distract from the clothes either. I'll figure out a more permanent solution after the opening. Now that I'm here, let's check the racks and go over the flower arrangements for the opening.'

'Nandita, darling, you're a lifesaver. I was just telling my client Pinkie Vohra about you yesterday. She's looking for someone to do her new farmhouse in Vasant Kunj. She's got heaps of taste, you know, and you'll have a blast working with her.' Avantika paused to take a breath and asked her assistant to get Nandita some tea.

'Heaps of taste' did not augur well, in Nandita's experience. By and large, socialites with 'taste' were much harder to deal with than those who were genuinely interested in the inputs of a professional.

'And darling, now that we're at it, just take a look at the fittings in the powder room. I don't think the copper sink works after all. And what about rethinking the metallic veneer on the exterior door? It's all making me so nervous, Nandita!' The PMS queen was on a rampage.

Nandita picked up the rosebud-patterned china teacup that had been placed in front of her, and felt revived by the fragrance of the chamomile tea. Taking a refreshing sip, she pulled out her laptop and decided she may as well settle down for a long afternoon. Avantika had been one of those clients who wanted exceptionally sumptuous interiors for her store; something she believed would enhance her brand. She was one among the new brigade of designers who took their brand image very seriously.

It had to be cutting-edge style, drop dead chic and 'personifying *Avantika*—after all, I'm the brand,' she had told Nandita earnestly. Of course, after all that rhetoric, she was quite indecisive about *what* 'brand Avantika' actually was. Nandita could deal with PMS, demanding and pretentious, but vacillation was a disaster. She was sick of the prima donna act.

For as long as she could remember, Nandita had wanted to design things. As a child, she had been besotted with the innumerable Lego sets that were gifted to her by those who knew her best. Even at that age, she was preoccupied with mass, space, form, volume, texture and structure, and she would spend hours crafting structures as diverse as they were fantastic. By the time she was ten, she owned thousands of colourful Lego blocks; they were her most treasured possession. She was never happier than when left alone with her imagination and her drawing board. Her mother had always nursed fond hopes of a fairy-tale marriage at the 'right age', of seeing her daughter settled in her own home. Nandita herself had not exactly been averse to these plans, but life had other things in store for her. Marriage had not happened to her so far, but her passion for design had certainly found its natural outlet. Amrita had always encouraged her artistic abilities—she had hoped that Nandita would become an artist and paint stunning canvasses. But Nandita had been set on architecture.

Nandita's mother was Maharashtrian by birth, but Nandita was born in Shimla. Amrita had told her that she had been widowed at twenty with an infant daughter to care for, and had moved to Delhi to make a living for herself and her daughter. Nandita had grown up in a milieu quintessential to the capital, with absolutely no memories of a father. A highly cherished only child of a besotted single parent, she was her mother's pride and joy. She had grown up shielded from every adverse wind and cocooned in maternal care all her life. Nandita's mother had tried hard to never let her feel the absence of a father, and as a consequence, Nandita had always pretended that the absence of the unknown Manav Dharkar had never troubled her. In actual fact, she missed having a father very much; it pained her not to have any photograph, not even any stories to remember him by. Her father was a totally unknown entity, and that cold fact always made her feel incomplete. But it was not something she could ever communicate to her mother.

Amrita had, surprisingly, not been visibly affected by her untimely widowhood. Her mother rarely displayed any sentimentality about her departed husband. In fact, Amrita did not display much emotion in general and was one of the most controlled people Nandita knew. She seldom spoke about Manav and discouraged questions about him. Nandita's enquiries had been kindly but firmly rebuffed on dozens of occasions, and her natural curiosity had escalated into a latent but burning desire to know about the past.

Nandita thought it odd that her mother had never considered remarrying. It appeared that she was happy to just be her mother. If she'd ever had any aspirations to play a role beyond that, they had long been buried under the carpet of time—dusty, neglected and all but forgotten. Amrita and Nandita were, as a result of their absorption in each other, an inseparable twosome. But lately, Nandita had begun to feel acutely tied down by this cloying interdependence. To keep the house fires burning, Amrita ran a highly lucrative catering business with tremendous success, but she was never the public face of her company. She employed a string of young managers to deal with most of her clients. Amrita was an intensely private person and took pains to remain so. Various sections of the media had approached her for an interview at different stages in her career, but to Nandita's chagrin her mother refused to either be photographed or written about.

From being a lanky, awkward teenager, lost in her own creative world and bordering on socially challenged, Nandita had blossomed into a self-possessed, professionally competent young woman, who lacked neither friends nor social life. A pair of luminescent green eyes (inherited from the stunningly beautiful Kokanastha Brahmin Amrita) was her most prominent feature, complemented by her silky complexion. Nandita had been told that her mother's community, somewhere down the ages, had acquired European DNA in their gene pool. She was not very impressed by this tidbit of information, but was quite happy to have been handed stunning eyes by these unknown benefactors. While she was not the fashionable size zero of a ramp model, hers was an enviably tall, full and shapely figure. Her luxuriant hair fell in abundant ringlets down to her waist. She would never be the serious, rare beauty her mother was, but could pass anywhere as a very attractive girl.

Nandita's career had progressed quickly after her graduation from the National Institute of Design, and with her kind of passion and dedication, she was fast being recognized as one of the promising young architects in Delhi. This translated into requests to design glossy stores and avante garde apartments. It had not been easy, and Nandita had been a bit startled when she found out that professional success in these circles was less about talent and more about how you presented yourself. She learned the ropes quickly enough; the need of the day was to be socially acceptable and not appear to require the work. In fact, if it looked like you were doing the client a big favour, so much the better! Personal style was crucial, and Nandita knew that many of her clients judged her more by what she wore and how she spoke than by her last job. It was a little disconcerting, but if that was the way she had to play the game, she was happily prepared to do it. Aditya more than took care of the social angle—it was right up his street—and he made sure she met all the right people and attended all the right parties. Nandita enjoyed it all at first, especially when she began to be recognized and recommended to the society queens. She charged a hefty design fee over and above her commissions, and the more she charged, the more demand she found she attracted. When she started out, her meagre budget did not allow for the style of society dressing that the Delhi divas favoured, but with a little imagination and ingenuity, Nandita was able to present a very individualistic style. As her business and clientele grew, Nandita developed a taste for fashion and brands, but still managed to keep her own eclectic style in place.

Now, years later, she had increasingly begun to realize that the honeymoon was over, and she was bored. She had been pigeonholed in the glamourous niche of a society interior designer, but she had no desire to remain there. She longed to sink her teeth into something more challenging than boutiques, farmhouses and Pinkie Vohras, but somehow did not feel the opportunity was going to present itself in her current scenario. Nandita wanted to be an architect, not just an interior designer. She knew she was capable of so much more than this, and if she didn't do it now, caught up as she was in this frenetic social haze, she wouldn't even notice time pass her by. Her restlessness had extended to her personal life after she ended a three-year relationship with Gaurav, and lately she had found herself growing increasingly disenchanted with her life.

'Nandita!' She was recalled to her surroundings by Avantika's plea. 'Will you wait here until Vinay's people finish papering the wall? I want you to see how it looks.'

Nandita looked at her watch. 'No, I have to run, I am just so late…but I promise I will be in early tomorrow, before the opening. It will be fine, don't worry. Vinay is the best in the business.' Avantika's theatrical pout said it all, but Nandita was in no mood to be conciliating. She said a quick goodbye and made a graceful exit.

By the time she reached the Taj Palace for Shanti's sangeet that night, Nandita felt the beginnings of what promised to become a blistering headache. Whether it was the tension of her aggravating day, or the pressure of the dozen hairpins that held her heavy curls away from her face, she would never know, but she pressed her palm to her temple to quell the throbbing. She paused for a moment to twitch her heavily embroidered ghagra into place and adjust her apricot-coloured chiffon dupatta. Summoning up her reserves of energy, Nandita took a deep breath and entered the ballroom.

Shanti had been one of Nandita's schoolmates, two years her junior, who had actually grown close to Nandita much after they had both left school. Their friendship had blossomed during a shared phase when tennis had become a ruling passion, so that they spent hours at the club together. The next chapter had been pottery lessons, followed by yoga. Their lives became intertwined over many such shared activities, as well as their love for shopping and eating, and before Nandita knew it, Shanti and she had become inseparable.

Never one to seriously consider a career, Shanti had flitted from one job to another without much interest—sometimes working as a boutique manager, sometimes playing secretary to one of her father's benign friends who wanted to indulge her, and once even serving as a flunky on a film shoot. She had finally found her calling as an ecstatic bride, and was now happily marrying her Mr Right and moving into a large joint family, replete with in-laws of varying ages and descriptions. Nandita was not surprised at how easily the affectionate Shanti had already endeared herself to the members of Varun's large household. Varun Khanna himself was pleasant and easygoing, not the type to be passionately in love or demandingly romantic, but this suited the practical Shanti perfectly. All that love-shove was too taxing, she maintained. What really mattered was the comfort level. Waking up in the morning to serve hot aloo parathas lathered in butter to an adoring family of eleven was not Nandita's idea of comfort or for that matter, marriage, but Shanti, she thought fondly, would enjoy it tremendously! Why not? Not everyone was lumped with Nandita's foibles, making life unnecessarily complicated. She envied Shanti her ability to enjoy the simple pleasures of life and to take everyone and everything at face value.

The wedding planner had, as promised, delivered a tastefully decorated hall. The theme was, quite predictably, Royal Rajasthan, and Nandita felt she had walked into a mini replica of the Meherangarh Fort in Jodhpur. A colourfully dressed girl was belting out a popular Hindi film song, while two lehenga-clad nymphets were performing a dance item to enthusiastic applause.

She slipped into a chair behind the bridal couple and was immediately accosted by Shanti, who turned around to whisper fiercely, 'Where on earth have you been? You missed the entire sequence by Varun's masi! Everyone has been asking for you!'

Nandita mumbled a hasty apology. Shanti looked so alien in her elaborate bridal attire that Nandita had to look again to ensure that this was indeed her habitually jeans-and-T-shirt-clad friend. Her mother had spared no expense to have her fitted out elegantly, arming her with designer bridal wear, numerous heavy jewellery 'sets' and a mind-boggling trousseau of sarees, salwaar kameezes, bags, footwear and lingerie. Shanti had confessed to

Nandita that she would never have occasion to wear even half of all that finery.

The whispered exchange between the two came to an end when the next item was announced. It was Shanti's sister Avni and her two friends, who were going to do a number imitating and poking mild fun at Varun's entire family. It was not malicious in any way, and the Khanna family was hugely amused at Avni's antics. Dadiji, the oldest member of the Khanna household, looked distinctly pleased as she tapped her feet to the rhythm of the song.

Nandita looked around idly at the array of colour on parade. Aunties in brilliant shades of peacock blue and rani pink, grannies in sober pastels, eligible young men in resplendently embroidered churidar kurtas, and marriageable girls on display, duly decked out in the latest in designer lehengas and jadau jewellery. The match-making elders watched with interest, mentally pairing off couples after comparing age, family, financial status, and of course, looks. After all, what better place to arrange a wedding than a wedding!

Nandita observed that Shanti's cousin Sheetal had been induced to sit next to Rohit Agarwal's mother, and was being gently 'interviewed', much to her discomfiture. Rohit was an uncommonly eligible boy; the eldest son of a prominent business family with an MBA degree, good looking, 'fair', he was considered a prize matrimonial catch. But Nandita was aware that Sheetal was dating a classmate from college, who had neither family credentials nor any major prospects, and guessed that Sheetal would eventually be advised, if not actually coerced, into marrying Rohit. And the funny thing was, she would probably be happier for it in the long run. It was odd, she thought, but in many cases, the so-called arranged marriages had equally good chances of success. The families were supportive, the young couple came from similar backgrounds and social milieu. At least there was no major adjustment to be made on any of those issues.

It wasn't long before Shanti's mother leaned over to Nandita.

'Beta, what about you? It's time you were thinking of settling down. You know, after a certain age, it's very difficult to get good boys.'

Nandita had heard this line enough times following her break-up with Gaurav, and was acutely aware that there was no occasion like a wedding to hear it repeated again and again. God knows, it was kindly meant, and normally she parried such intrusive comments lightheartedly, but tonight she was in no frame of mind to deal with it. Luckily, Shanti's mother was distracted by Dadiji who, by now wholly enticed by the music, was getting up to perform a dance number of her own. The onlookers cheered with gusto as she swung her seventy-eight-year-old hips with gay abandon to the beat of 'Sexy Lady on the Floor', and Nandita was able to get away to the buffet room. She was joined by Aditya who gave her a quizzical look.

'Down in the dumps, Nan?' he asked sympathetically. 'You look dreadful.'

'Thanks Adi, that makes me feel so much better! You, of course, are looking your extremely handsome, charming self, down to your boyishly ruffled new hairstyle!'

He laughed. 'Oh, you know what I mean. You don't look like you're enjoying yourself. The old biddies at you again?' He helped himself to a sizzling chicken kabab from a passing waiter's tray. 'And thanks for your lavish compliments, even though I am sure they are not well meant!'

She smiled ruefully. 'They're not! Why don't they get after you? Why is it that men escape the constant persecution on the marriage issue?'

'Actually darling, they don't,' he replied candidly, munching on the kabab. 'It's just that twenty-nine for a man is not as bad as twenty-nine for a girl, so they haven't started on me yet!'

'How can they?' she retorted. 'You, my friend, are with a new girl every week! But you're probably right. I know they mean well, but I swear to you, Aditya, the next time someone says something, I am going to explode.'

Another waiter passed by with mushrooms stuffed with cheese.

'Vegetarian?' Aditya asked. The waiter nodded, and Aditya promptly sent him off to procure some meat.

'You won't die if you eat the occasional vegetable, you know,' Nandita said acidly. 'And, as usual, your stomach is more important that anything else!'

'I get hungry. I played tennis for two hours this evening,' he replied in defense.

The waiter with the boti kababs appeared with miraculous speed, and Aditya helped himself liberally.

'Listen, babe, you've moaned enough about all this nonsense… why don't you just make a clean break?' he asked, deliberately casual. 'Go off on your own, do something different. You've always wanted to go to New York. Or Hong Kong. Whatever. It's time you stopped living in your mother's house anyway. Get out in the world, girl. How long are you going to hang on to mamma's pallu?'

Nandita pushed a wayward tendril of curly hair back from her face and looked at him, her expression unfathomable. 'How many times have we been through this before? Do you seriously think I haven't considered it?'

Nandita had, in fact, considered it several times. She longed to get out of Delhi, explore new avenues in her profession, meet new people and get out of the boring monotony that she had been living in for the last few years. She felt suffocated, trying to play the role expected of her, and would have given anything to stand in Aditya's shoes right now. Free, unencumbered and mistress of her own life.

Of course, Aditya had none of Nandita's discipline and focus. She adored him, and had known him literally from the cradle, but she was not blind to his careless and negligent ways. He had been born with the proverbial silver spoon to a family with generations of amassed wealth, and at almost thirty, he himself followed none of the good advice he gave Nandita. Orphaned at a very young age, he was restless, impossible to pin down and the bane of his exasperated aunt's existence. Income from ample family investments provided him with a lifestyle that was as lavish as he wanted, and he had no real motivation to make anything of his life. At present, he was indulging his passion for photography and trying to make a career as a fashion photographer. Nandita was sure he was doing nothing more than having a rollicking time in the process. Life to Aditya was a roller-coaster ride, and he was zipping through it without giving much thought to the future. Nandita had remonstrated, been caustic, wheedled, cajoled and tried every trick she knew to get him to take life more seriously, all to no avail.

'You worry too much about your mother,' Aditya said with a disapproving frown. 'She is much stronger than you give her credit for, Nan. You can't bury your head in the sand for ever, you know.' Nandita couldn't bring herself to reply. Aditya gave her a quick, comforting hug, and bore her off in search of a fresh drink and more food.

By this time the Khanna family was happily getting its revenge on the bride and her clan in the dance hall by threatening never to send Shanti to her maika, and suddenly, Nandita decided she was not going to ruin Shanti's evening with her own freakish mood.

She noticed that the purple aunty was whispering to the lilac one, both glancing furtively in their direction. The old dearies are matchmaking in vain, she thought in amusement. She and Aditya? Impossible! It was true that they had dated for three years after she had returned from NID and Ahmedabad, but that phase of their relationship had been an exhausting one. Their liaison had been turbulent and passionate, predictably ending in a volcanic row that had left them in a state of non-communication for six months. But they'd both realized that their lives were incomplete without each other, and somehow, defying all logic, they went back to being best friends. Nandita and Aditya were each other's crutch, and neither thought twice about it. It was just the way things were. She observed the lilac aunty bearing down upon her with unmistakable purpose in her stride, and decided it was time to join the revelry on the dance floor, which was steadily degenerating into graceless stomping.

As she swung to the tunes of Rabbi Singh and Group, she realized that her childhood friend was right. Why the hell was she being such a wimp? Gaurav Mathur was history, she had designed enough swanky homes and stores and she had more than outgrown her mother's protective nest. She was so, *so* done with Delhi. What in heaven's name was she waiting for? It was time to take responsibility for herself, and do what she needed to do.

And then, always lurking at the back of her mind, was her other reason for leaving Delhi. Nandita wanted more than anything to go to Mumbai, for reasons she would not divulge even to Aditya. Now was the time, she thought. She had to do it before she turned thirty. In Nandita's mind, that was the dreaded age of no return. She had to change her life before then, or she would stagnate forever.

Aditya watched Nandita, almost reading her mind from a distance, and knew that she would be gone before long, whether she herself realized it right now or not. Seeing her leave was not going to be the easiest of things for Aditya. He'd insisted that Nandita should not languish in Delhi, but it was not until now that he pictured the void that was going to be impossible to fill… Nandita had always been Aditya's top priority in life, and his numerous girlfriends past and present had all been reconciled to the fact that Nandita's needs always took precedence over theirs. It was just a simple fact of life. Aditya was certain that if he did not find something to do with his time, he would drive everyone around him insane. Most of his male buddies were now busy with their respective careers, and found very little time to hang out at the club or on the tennis courts. He wondered if that was yet another sign that he should begin to take his own life more seriously. But if that meant getting into the family business with Simi Bua, it was a definite no, thank you. He would be even more bored than he was now. And he was bored alright, though he never admitted it to Nandita, not wanting to confess that she had been right about his indulgent ways after all. So where did he go from here?

CHAPTER THREE
Delhi, November 2012

Amrita Dharkar woke on Sunday morning with a deep sense of foreboding. She couldn't pinpoint what exactly was making her uncomfortable, though. She didn't usually pay heed to her intuition, but today, it was telling her that something was surely amiss. No one but her friend Simi had ever seen Amrita appear frazzled or angry. She was the perfect example of a composed, graceful, exquisitely groomed, and above all, very beautiful woman. She looked, Nandita informed her regularly, too young, and altogether too ravishing, to be the mother of a grown-up daughter. Amrita routinely dressed much in the same way she had as a young woman; jeans, shirts, fitted churidar kurtas, and for work, austerely cut jackets and pants, with her long, silky hair left untied. At forty-seven, she did not have a single wrinkle on her delicate face, and was every inch the beauty she had been in her youth. In fact, age had only enhanced her, experience had improved her, and she was far more beautiful today than she had been at eighteen.

But she had shut her mind to what had happened in her earlier years, steeled herself to never think about what could have been. She had promised not to torture herself by ever going down that particular memory lane. Nandita knew nothing about that heartbreaking period in her mother's life, and Amrita was determined that she should never find out. She had made her mistakes, paid for them dearly, and in many ways, was still suffering the consequences. She would not allow the shadow of her past to cloud her daughter's happiness. She would have given anything to go back and change the course of her life, but that was obviously wishful thinking.

Amrita set about soothing her ruffled emotions by heading to the kitchen, her favourite way of easing stress. It was, Nandita always maintained, completely incongruous that a woman as beautiful as Amrita, clearly cut out to be a reigning diva on the silver screen, could be so happy in the anonymity of her kitchen. Amrita could cook anything under the sun and make it taste wonderful. She had, as her daughter often fondly told her, that certain something in her touch that could transform the most ordinary dish into a transcendent treat. Amrita had a passion for food, not in the sense people normally do, but in a mystical, divine way. She innately understood ingredients and coaxed them into blending to form exquisite flavours. Amrita's masterful culinary odyssey earned her the reputation of a connoisseur's delight—her fusion flavours of foie gras prepared with Japanese artichokes, mango, coconut and ginger had become the rage of Delhi's cocktail circuit.

After they moved from Shimla to Delhi, Amrita had channelled her talent into a boutique catering company, The Epicurean. She had experimented, improvised, gone abroad for short courses and, more recently, rummaged the Internet, until she had mastered traditional culinary techniques, which she then began to weave into her own original ones. She was now ardently sought out by select society hostesses to provide that special touch to their dinners in a way that only she could. Amrita's recipes were always superlative, beautifully presented, and above all, completely original.

Once Amrita had decided to mix talent with commerce, success had come very easily. It seemed that people could not get enough of good food, and when it was as good as Amrita's, there was no dearth of orders. She had started small, with dinner parties at friends' houses and ladies' lunches. Before long, she had moved out of her own kitchen into rented commercial premises, and had never looked back. She was eternally grateful that she had been able to give Nandita an upbringing that lacked nothing on the material front. Amrita's circle of acquaintances spread far and wide, but very few became her friends. She guarded her privacy fiercely and preferred to stay away from society events, earning the reputation of a recluse. She did not mind; it was far more agreeable than putting up a façade of being the life and soul of Delhi society. Her closest friend Simi was the exact antithesis, but the two of them accepted each other's way of living and managed to co-exist in perfect harmony. Amrita enjoyed nothing so much as the small get-togethers she sometimes hosted. Only her close friends were invited to these; not too many people were even aware that she even entertained at home. She would have been astonished and amused to know that her select parties were very much a hot topic of discussion in Delhi circles, and those who were lucky enough to be invited were the object of a good deal of envy—as much for the privilege of being invited to Amrita Dharkar's home as for the joy of eating a special meal cooked by her.

Not surprisingly, several offers of marriage had come her way over the years. Amrita had refused all of them without explanation. When Nandita was younger, she had been blissfully unaware of this; when she reached an age where she could understand, she had watched her mother rebuff two genuinely nice men who would have made good fathers. She said nothing to her mother, because Nandita could never let Amrita know that she missed having a daddy. It would have broken her mother's heart.

Amrita decided to skip her Sunday morning plan to go gourmet with poached pears in lemon sorbet and Eggs Benedict, deciding instead to indulge Nandita with her favourite ricotta cheese pancakes with raspberry coulis for breakfast.

Nandita's preoccupation with some ongoing inner battle had not escaped her mother's keen notice. It was obvious to Amrita that her daughter was not her usual sunny self. At first, she put it down to the break-up with Gaurav. Upon closer observation, she decided that Gaurav was not the cause of her angst. Last night, she had watched Nandita at dinner while Shaila Bhatia, their neighbour, had quizzed Nandita about her marriage plans. She had appeared supremely unconcerned, and all Amrita could detect in her daughter's demeanour was faint annoyance. The mother had quickly fired up in her daughter's defense, informing Shaila in no uncertain terms that Nandita was enjoying her work immensely and had plenty of time to think about getting settled. But her own heart was full of misgivings, as she wondered what exactly Nandita wanted for herself and what would make her happy. Aditya was less concerned when she voiced her fears to him later.

'Amrita Aunty, let the girl be. We don't live in the twentieth century anymore, there is more to life than just getting married. Let her figure out what it is she wants from life.'

Amrita had bristled angrily. Aditya could be so blasé sometimes. Didn't he realize that…well, it may sound old fashioned, but twenty-nine was past the official marriageable age. Why, Nandita was almost on the shelf!

'It's all very well for you to say that, Aditya, but just think straight, for once. I don't want to force her to do anything. I just want to protect her from being hurt, and lonely!' And who better than Amrita to know how deeply inundating that loneliness could be?

Aditya was not so sentimental. 'You can't protect anyone,' he had told her with his characteristic bluntness. 'You have to let people make their own mistakes…even your own children. Don't tell me that you never made any mistakes yourself, Aunty,' he had added brutally, silencing Amrita at one stroke, little knowing that his arrow had found its mark.

Amrita, though her thoughts were in overdrive, was exceptionally gentle with her ricotta pancake batter…it had been sitting for half an hour since she'd made it, and she was careful not to stir it as she ladled small spoonfuls into the sizzling butter on the hot griddle. Why couldn't people like that Shaila Bhatia mind their own business? And Aditya. He probably knew Nandita better than anyone did; shouldn't he be more responsible about the advice he gave her? She was just flipping the golden pancakes over when she heard Nandita call out.

'Aai! Where are you?'

'In the kitchen, baby! I hope you're hungry… it's ricotta pancakes!'

Nandita bounced into the kitchen, sniffing in appreciation. She was wearing soft yellow pajamas and looked, Amrita thought wistfully, young, vulnerable and utterly childlike. Her curly hair was tied up with a yellow band, and her mother thought she looked no older than a schoolgirl.

'You spoil me too much, Aai. What will I do when I have to fend for myself?'

'Oh, you'll manage well enough.' Suddenly, Amrita read a new meaning into her daughter's remark. She turned around quickly. 'Fend for yourself? What could you possibly mean?'

Nandita looked guiltily at her mother. 'Sorry, Aai, I didn't mean for it to come out like that.' She paused to collect her thoughts before she spoke again. 'I don't know how to say this so that it will make sense to you.'

Hiding her misgivings, Amrita removed the pancakes from the pan, and drew her daughter's arm through her own. She led her to the dining table. 'Sit down, Nandi,' she said with surprising gentleness. 'And just say whatever it is you want to, straight out.'

Nandita realized there was no easy way to do this. 'Aai,' she said abruptly, looking her mother straight in the eye, 'I have accepted a job in Mumbai. As soon as I finish my commitments here, I am leaving Delhi.'

She waited for the explosion, the shock, the accusations, and braced herself for the hurt and anger her mother was bound to feel. She had taken this decision without so much as informing her mother, much less consulting her. In truth, she had done so because she could not deal with the possibility of Amrita persuading her to change her mind. It had taken her days of soul searching to get to this point, but once she had made up her mind, she was determined to go ahead with it. Never in her life had she wanted anything as badly as she wanted this, and she was prepared to stand her ground, even go against her mother's wishes, if need be.

Amrita felt like she had been punched in her stomach. 'Is *that* what has been cutting up your peace of mind for the last few weeks?' she asked, hiding her shock under the guise of mock surprise. Mumbai! Not Mumbai, please god! She quickly gathered her wits about her, and masked her turmoil with the admirable skill she had acquired through years of practice.

'Nandi, I actually thought you were pining for that lame Gaurav of yours…what a relief!'

Nandita was dazed—had her mother actually understood what she had said? Why was she reacting like this? She should have been ranting against her daughter, pleading with her not to go, trying to make her see sense! Oh god, had she sent her mother into shock?

'Aai, have you registered what I just said?' she demanded, her voice urgent. 'I am moving to Mumbai. Away! Away from home!'

Amrita flinched, a knife twisting in her heart. 'Yes darling, I have understood exactly what you are saying. I'm not exactly thick. You have found yourself a job in Mumbai and want to move out of this house… Are you expecting me to freak out or something? What makes you think that would make me sad? Don't you think I want you to be happy?' She sat down beside her daughter. Nandita was taken aback when she detected a rare hint of tears in her mother's luminous eyes.

'Nandi, I would love to see you married and settled, and no one knows that better than you, but I also want to see you happy. I want you to achieve your goals, to realize your dreams, and I am aware that your dreams for yourself are not the same as my dreams for you.'

Nandita couldn't believe what was happening. Amrita loved her daughter dearly, but she was not the sentimental type, and almost never showed her emotions or made soppy speeches. For once in her life, stunned and bereft of words, all Nandita could do was to hug her mother with tears of gratitude streaming down her cheeks.

With superhuman effort, Amrita reverted briskly to her practical self. 'Are we going to cry and waste the hot pancakes, or are we going to eat breakfast together?'

'Eat, of course,' said Nandita, recovering from her shock slowly. She looked at her mother with a surge of guilt. 'Will you manage to live alone in Delhi? Does it scare you, Aai?'

'Hey, probably better than you will manage to live alone in Mumbai!' Amrita spoke lightly, but she was having a hard time concealing her feelings. She had accepted Nandita's decision with apparent equanimity, but inwardly her thoughts were in complete turmoil. Her daughter had ideas of her own, had planned a future for herself that did not involve the consensus of her mother.

Amrita had known that this moment would come sooner or later, but now that it had, she was finding it surprisingly difficult to deal with. Nandita was a very mature twenty-nine, and had been working for the last eight years. She had faced and solved many problems on her own, and was more than capable of moving to another city, of looking after herself, of carving out a niche for herself in Mumbai. Of all this, Amrita had no doubts. She had been mentally prepared to lose Nandita to a husband, and quite ready to part with her if a suitable marriage was on the cards. But this! Was she ready for this? Why did it have to be Mumbai? Mumbai was where Amrita's world had fallen apart, and how could she believe that cruel city would be any kinder to her daughter? She knew that Aditya was right. Nandita had been slowly suffocating in the predictable confines of her life, on the professional and on the personal front. Though she did not blame Nandita for anything, Amrita had been upset when the relationship with Gaurav Mathur had ended. The marriage would have kept Nandita in Delhi for a few years at least, and her daughter would have been financially and emotionally secure with Gaurav. She certainly hadn't expected anything like this to follow.

Amrita was not focusing on the fresh batch of golden pancakes she was frying, but instinct and practice ensured that she served them to Nandita with just the right amount of crispness while retaining the soft fluffy centres. She ladled the bright scarlet berry coulis over them and placed the plate in front of her daughter.

Nandita ate a heaping forkful of the light, delicious pancake and sighed in ecstacy. 'Aai, you are a culinary goddess!'

'Nandi, you have actually accepted a job? Already? How did this happen? You've obviously been thinking about it for a while.' Amrita carefully kept any note of censure out of her voice.

'To tell you the truth, it practically fell into my lap,' Nandita replied, quite eager to discuss her plans, now that she saw how composed her mother was. 'It was Aditya who put the idea of moving out into my mind, and I was mulling it over. You remember the evening I went with Varun and Shanti to that opening at the art gallery? Of that new artist from Mumbai?'

'Oh, yes! You said he was very talented, and you wanted your client, Mala Goel, to pick up some of his work.' Aditya's idea, she thought savagely to herself. Hmm. Amrita might have known it. Aditya was always egging Nandita on to 'spread her wings'. Bloody cliché! In fairness to him, he had been Nandita's biggest supporter when she decided to set up her own studio, and had pulled every string among his Delhi high society contacts to introduce her to the right people. He seemed to be more interested in Nandita's welfare and career than his own.

'Ma, are you paying attention?' Nandita saw that her mother's mind was elsewhere.

At that moment, Amar Singh, Amrita's major-domo, came in carrying two steaming cups of masala chai, a favourite of Nandita's. *'Khane me kya lenge, memsaab?'*

'Nako, no lunch for me, Aai. Can't afford to keep eating like this... this stuff is absolutely sinful.'

'Hum bahar ja rahein hain, Amar.' The manservant retired, looking forward to watching the cricket match on TV in uninterrupted luxury. 'I am going to Simi Aunty's for lunch. Her friend Sonia Lal is here from London. Will you come?' asked Amrita with a mischievous smile, well knowing the answer.

Nandita grimaced, and picked up her cup. 'You're not serious! Sounds like one long gossipy afternoon. That Sonia spins stories by the second... I don't know how you stand it. And Simi Aunty encourages her, she's as bad!' Simi Arora was Amrita's confidante and constant companion, and the two women shared a close relationship. Nandita loved her dearly, but was sometimes overwhelmed by her gossipy, overbearing nature.

Amrita bit her lip in displeasure. 'Don't be so harsh, Nandi. She is not malicious, you know. She has been an extremely good friend to me.'

Amrita didn't elaborate, but Nandita wondered, for the hundredth time, why her mother was always so protective of Simi. Of course, they were friends, but she'd always suspected there was something her mother had not told her. Even though Nandita knew that Simi would have done anything for her and for her mother, she was resentful of the fact that she rubbed Aditya the wrong way. She knew she shouldn't be, and that Simi had put her personal life on hold to raise Aditya, but their bickering really troubled her. Simi had never married, but Nandita knew, through the occasional bits of overheard conversation, that there was a married lover in the wings, discreetly concealed. She never asked, knowing instinctively that the topic was taboo. Well, why ever not, she thought. Simi was unattached, and unobtrusive, at least where the lover was concerned. She was a pleasant looking forty-nine, her short hair elegantly styled, cut to the perfect length to suit the shape of her face. Her cattier friends called her fairly well preserved. As if, Amrita often voiced, distressed, she was shalgam pickle or guava jelly. Simi never wore salwaar kameez, the prescribed mode of dress among the more conventional Delhi ladies, preferring to flaunt her well-preservedness in sophisticated Western attire. She had devoted her life to raising Aditya after his parents (Simi's brother and his wife) had died in a plane crash when he was barely two, and to looking after their chain of sports equipment stores. She lived with her nephew in the most fashionable part of Delhi, and enjoyed an active social life. Nandita and Aditya obviously knew the identity of the married lover, but had never been permitted to comment on him or discuss him openly.

Amrita picked up her cup and headed to the garden. 'Let's sit outside and have our tea. The weather's been so much cooler this week. Tell me what happened at the gallery.'

Nandita followed her mother into the spacious garden. Amrita did not really have a green thumb, but her trusty mali certainly did, and his hard work was evident in the lush green lawn and bunches of casually planted flowers. Amrita hated structure, so the effect that had been achieved with so much effort was charmingly careless. By Delhi standards, the bungalow was not huge, but it was too large for a family of two. The Dharkars had lived there since Nandita was a baby, and it was the only home she could remember. Summer holidays were spent in Shimla, where Amrita had grown up with her mother and grandmother. On the whole, Nandita's little world was predictable, orderly and comfortable.

Nandita plonked herself down on an enormous white wicker chair, lined with fluffy cushions covered in deep turquoise blue. 'Have you heard of Rajeev Sabarwal? The celebrity architect who was featured in last month's *Architecture Today*? He's the one designing that new seven-star hotel in Gurgaon, and also the new Starling Lotus in Mumbai.'

Amrita had picked up her cup and taken an enormous sip of tea. She choked and started coughing. 'Sorry! That went down the wrong way!' Nandita patted her back and gave her a glass of water. Amrita smiled shakily. 'Thanks darling. Of course I've heard of him. Starling, eh? Sounds impressive.' Oh god, when was this nightmare going to end? Amrita wished desperately that she would wake up in a minute and the world would be right again. But Nandita was continuing inexorably.

'Yeah, he's quite the big shot. Shanti was telling me, just the other day, that he has a stunningly beautiful wife, someone from the royal family of Bikaner. Apparently she…'

'Nandi, let's not digress… get back to your story,' said Amrita gently.

'Okay, Sunil Mehta of the gallery knows Mr Sabarwal really well, and introduced me. He had actually heard of me, can you believe that? We got talking and I told him about my aspiration to work in Mumbai.'

'And he offered you a job, just like that? How odd!' Amrita raised one delicately shaped eyebrow in disbelief. Inwardly, she was seething, fighting to control her raging emotions. Nandita's dream of working in Mumbai… A job in Sabarwal Associates! It was as if events were unfolding so fast that she was about to be swept away by a tidal wave, with no control over where she was going. And Nandita…she had been so unhappy that she had to do this behind her mother's back! Had she really been so selfish that she had let her daughter feel so trapped? Was she really one of those limpet-like women, who had built her world around her daughter and was not willing to let go? When had the independent, self-sufficient woman in her turned into this possessive, helpless, clinging creature?

'Obviously not!' said Nandita, cutting into her mother's reverie. 'We made an appointment to meet the following week when he was in town again. He looked at my portfolio, made some calls and checked me out too. I'm sure he's spoken to several of my clients and associates by now. He's certainly no pushover. Actually, he told me he loved my work on the Panchsheel project.' She tossed her head back and added with a mischievous laugh, 'Who knows, maybe he checked me out with Simi Aunty, and she's the one I owe this job to!'

'Simi may be an insatiable socialite, but I don't think she wields too much influence in professional circles beyond the sporting world!' replied Amrita, her voice devoid of emotion. She put down her cup and sat up straight in her chair. 'Nandi, are you sure this is what you want? Mumbai?'

'Why are you always so hyper about Mumbai? You've never even been there, Aai!'

Amrita thought it wise to ignore that. 'Once you take this step, your life is going to change completely.'

'I know, Aai. That's why I have to do it. You do understand, don't you?'

'Yes,' said her mother expressionlessly. 'I understand better than you think.'

She's opening up a Pandora's box, thought Amrita, and there's nothing whatsoever I can do about it.

CHAPTER FOUR
Mumbai, December 2012

Aryan Rai pushed aside the sheaves of drawings and sketches on his desk, distinctly unhappy with the way things were progressing. Nothing about the drawings and plans inspired him. They were good, probably very good, but not superb. Aryan only understood excellence. His eleven-year stint with the exceptionally premium Starling Group of Hotels had made him discerning enough to demand the very best, whether it was from his staff, his managers, or as the case was right now, his suppliers. He was trying to be patient but deadlines were whizzing by without being met, and the new all-suites Starling Lotus that was to come up at Worli seemed like it was going open considerably later than anticipated. October was almost a year away, but a soft opening looked possible.

A lot had changed in Mumbai and in the rest of the world since Aryan had accepted the responsibility of opening the first Indian Starling. The business environment in the country was more competitive than it had ever been. Most international chains were opening new properties at lightning speed. Starling Lotus had to be better than all of them—that was the mandate his bosses had given him. It was, without doubt, an ambitious project. Not slated to be the largest hotel in Mumbai, it was instead aiming to be the most luxurious. At thirty-four, Aryan was one of the youngest general managers in Starling Hotels to be entrusted with overseeing a project of this magnitude from scratch. Over the three years he had spent at the Starling Orchid in Shanghai, he had proved that he had an indisputable talent for managing new hotels and setting lofty benchmarks with an impeccable eye for detail. He had made the Shanghai property such a success that the management had seen him as an obvious choice to head their very first hotel in India. It was an opportunity he had welcomed, because Aryan thrived on anything that presented itself as a challenge. And frankly, he had had enough of Shanghai. China becoming the new hub of the hospitality industry was all very well, but one could not really date Chinese girls forever, and no one in the large expat community had particularly taken his fancy.

Aryan had always been the brightest kid at school, making the top grades so effortlessly that his teachers saw, early on, how he was constantly restless for more. His immediate family and friends had been taken by surprise at his decision to enter, of all things, the hospitality industry. He had seemed like the ideal candidate for a dazzling career as a neurosurgeon or even a NASA scientist. But Aryan had flummoxed everyone, including his mother who knew him best, by heading to Cornell to study hotel administration, and had graduated with his customary first-class honours. Cornell University's School of Hotel Administration offered the finest collegiate programme in hospitality management, and Starling Hotels had been quick to grab this most promising new graduate. Aryan's career path had been predictably meteoric, and his chosen career fitted him as well as his perfectly cut suits.

He picked up the concept board for the proposed Japanese restaurant at Starling Lotus. Frowning slightly, he dialled a number on his cell. 'Rajeev? Good morning! It's Aryan Rai.' He sounded more cheerful than he felt. 'I've gone over the new drawings again, and I have a couple of issues to discuss... Yes, this afternoon? Great see you then. Bye!' It was going to be more than just a couple of issues, he thought grimly.

Aryan Rai was what is known as, with not-so-affectionate derision, an ABCD, or American Born Confused Desi. Born and brought up in Chicago, this was the first time he was actually living in India, if one did not count the childhood trips to Indore to visit his grandparents. And even those infrequent holidays came to an end when his grandfather died and his grandmother agreed to move to Chicago. Holidays were spent, instead, visiting South America, remote areas of Africa, Bora Bora, Iceland or wherever Aryan's eccentric but adventurous parents felt like going, at the spur of the moment. Aryan had been fifteen years old when he'd made his last trip to the wilderness with his incorrigible parents; after studying the bio-diversity of the Amazon rainforests and contemplating 75,000 types of trees and 150,000 species of higher plants, he had finally rebelled, and decided that he preferred the comforts of the civilized world. His father, Sam Rai, was a botanist as well as an amateur journalist and wildlife photographer. He wrote occasionally for *National Geographic*, *Conde Naste Traveller* and *Time*, and more recently, serious content for websites. His mother, Gitanjali, taught modern history at the University of Chicago, and Aryan always considered her the saner of his two parents. While he had loved the visit to a breathtaking atoll in Micronesia, he was eternally grateful that she had drawn the line at a walking tour of the Luangwa Valley when he was ten.

Aryan still had memories of sitting at his grandmother's feet in the old rambling house in Indore while she made hot jalebis and told him the story of the Pandavas and Kauravas over and over again. The house was huge, with a number of sprawling rooms arranged around a central courtyard, and he was surprised that nobody had a designated bedroom except for his grandfather. There were piles of mattresses stored in one corner, and he could simply help himself to one and spread it out anywhere he liked. Aryan loved putting his mattress out on the long verandah, along with two of his older cousins. He'd spent hours in that verandah every afternoon, shaded by the dense banyan trees. When the rest of the household napped, he read the piles of *Amar Chitra*

Katha comics that his grandfather had deemed necessary for his 'Indianisation'. While the romantic warriors and gods from India's rich mythology had fascinated him, he never identified with them as comfortably as he did with the Hardy Boys and Nancy Drew. He had come to the conclusion, long ago, that he was essentially American in every way that counted. So although he was definitely American Born, there was nothing Confused or Desi about him.

Starling Hotels looked after their general managers well. Aryan lived, by Mumbai standards, in complete luxury. A spacious, three-bedroom apartment overlooking the Worli seaface had been fitted with expensive contemporary furnishings by an eager young interior designer. 'Elegantly appointed' is how the brochures would have described it, had it been a hotel suite. Normally, thirty-four-year-old GMs were married, often with children, but Aryan lived alone in this opulent pad. He had once come very close to getting married. Alison had been everything a man could ask for…a perfect ten, actually. Until he had discovered that he was not ready to commit to one woman just yet. In fact, the prospect scared him silly. Gitanjali Rai had been slightly relieved when the wedding plans were called off. Alison was not, she had always known, the girl to make her son happy. *Too accommodating by far, if you ask me*, had been her constant refrain to her husband Sam. No will of her own, her son would have been bored in no time, she'd predicted, but never communicated her misgivings to her son. Alison had moved on very reluctantly, and Aryan had, over the years, become fairly fond of his bachelor status. He was not really on the look-out for a wife. Life had too many possibilities, he had decided, to waste time getting married. He had, in fact, after the drought period in China, met a few interesting women in Mumbai, and had no dearth of dates who wanted to show him Mumbai's much-hyped nightlife.

His thoughts turned back to the problem at hand. Rajeev Sabarwal. Supposedly the best in Mumbai, highly recommended and a specialist in hotel design. Maybe that was the problem. Sometimes, specialists got so used to doing things a certain way, they lost the fresh perspective required for an utterly exclusive project like Starling Lotus. The decision to use a local architectural firm in tandem with the Singapore one they always employed had been hotly debated at the head office in Chicago, but it had been done because Starling Hotels wanted someone who was familiar and comfortable with the way things were done in this part of the world. So far, the concepts for the interiors of Starling Lotus that Sabarwal Associates had presented had been adequate, but not inspired. Aryan knew that adequate just did not exist in the Starling vocabulary. Nor in his own. Starling Lotus was going to be their flagship hotel in India, and it had to be every inch as sublime as every other Starling across the world. More, if anything, because the bar always needed to be raised. He wondered how much time Rajeev himself gave to any individual project. He knew that four assistants were working on the Starling assignment, only one of whom Aryan had been impressed with. He was not looking forward to the meeting this afternoon with too much enthusiasm.

Rajeev Sabarwal had promised him that there was going to be a new addition to the team working on Starling very soon. About time too, he thought. The new recruit was coming in with heavy recommendations and high praise from Rajeev, and Aryan had been promised that she was just the right person to turn this project around. Well, thought Aryan, the poor girl had a lot riding on her shoulders, and he was going to be her severest critic. If she could live up to his expectations, it would be nothing short of a minor miracle. So the unknown Nandita Dharkar, he reflected, had better be something out of the ordinary.

CHAPTER FIVE
Mumbai, January 2013

Nandita looked at the chaos around her and had a brief panic attack. How was she going to sort all this out in a day? Mr Bhandari had, with plenty of nagging and threats, finally managed to get the lease signed, and had given her the key to 7B on Saturday morning, the weekend before she started work at Sabarwal Associates. She had no desire to deal with household problems once she started her new job, and was determined that she would somehow get through it all before Monday morning.

With all her suitcases and boxes in by noon, she was surveying the confusion and wondering where to start when her doorbell rang. Nandita's smile was as bright as it was fake when she opened the door. Kulwant Singh, dressed in an embroidered silk kaftan, stood bearing a dish of steaming food. From the aroma, Nandita guessed it was biryani.

'Hello beta! Welcome to Sea Breeze. I thought maybe bhook lagi hogi, so I brought some food for you!' she said chattily. 'No time to cook and unpack also, no? You must be hungry, hai na?'

Nandita was touched by the gesture, and murmured a graceful thank you. Looking past her neighbour, she noticed that a young man was hovering uncomfortably in the doorway, not sure whether he should enter. He was probably in his late twenties, and had a slightly superior look about him. Tall and lanky, he was dressed in a baggy pair of Guess jeans and a faded NYU sweatshirt. His hair looked like it was seldom combed, and shaving was obviously not a daily event for him. On the whole, she thought, the effect was not unattractive.

Nandita smiled uncertainly at him, and Kulwant turned around.

'Oh, Tushar, come in, *aa jao*!' she cried genially. 'Nandita, this is Tushar. Remember I told you, paying guest? Tushar is a writer. Advertising wala... Tushar, meet Nandita. From Delhi. Not married!' She turned to Nandita. 'Tushar is also not married.'

Nandita tried not to laugh and glanced quickly at Tushar. He was not embarrassed; obviously, he was used to Kulwant's style of introduction.

'Kulwant Aunty thought I could be of some help to you. Unpacking or whatever.' His tone sounded doubtful and she felt a bit sorry for him, being saddled with something he had obviously no interest in doing.

'Thanks, but I'm fine. I wouldn't dream of imposing on you anyway.'

'What impose-shimpose!' said Kulwant indignantly. '*Yeh koi baat hui*! What are neighbours for, I say. Young girl, living alone, new to the city. It is our duty to help. *Hai na, bete?*' She turned with a look of challenge to Tushar.

'If you say so, Kulwant Aunty. If you ask me, I don't think Nandita here looks like a damsel in any kind of distress. In fact,' he added, sizing Nandita up audaciously from under his lazy eyelids, 'she looks particularly capable of fending for herself.'

Kulwant gasped at his impertinence and was about to tick him off in no uncertain terms, but Nandita's amused laughter stopped her. 'He's right, you know, Kulwant Aunty.' She glanced at Tushar. 'Thanks for the vote of confidence!'

'Not at all,' he replied, eyes twinkling. He casually glanced at the contents of the box full of CDs. 'Music lover, eh?' He flipped through the discs without so much as a 'May I?'

Tushar never needed permission to pry into people's affairs, and took liberties with such charming élan that no one had actually objected yet. Nandita didn't either, so Tushar flipped through her belongings quite unselfconsciously. Nandita intrigued him, and her arrival at 7B was a welcome change in the status quo at Sea Breeze. Maybe they would become friends, and he could spend a few evenings here listening to Supertramp and Pink Floyd in peace, leaving Kulwant to enjoy her 'orinjuice' in solitude. Kulwant genuinely believed nobody knew that her evening beverage was liberally laced with gin, but in truth, every resident of Sea Breeze was aware that Kulwant was an alcoholic. Tushar felt sorry for the lonely lady and indulged her in many small ways. His own family lived in Bangalore, and he was not particularly close to either his parents or his married sister. Living with Kulwant suited him just fine...after all, which of his pals in paying-guest rooms could look forward to the maternal care that Kulwant lavished on him?

The voluble lady, meanwhile, settled herself comfortably on the beige couch and proceeded to bring Nandita up to speed on who she might find interesting company in Sea Breeze. 'There're the Chowdharys, of course. Nice Bengali couple, she's from Calcutta and he's from Mumbai. Works at HSBC bank, doing very well. Drives a Honda Civic. Shonali is looking for a job now. Pretty girl. Then the Kulkarnis on the tenth floor. She makes prawn pickle for us, delicious!' She gave a hearty chuckle. 'Last daughter got married in June, but she comes to stay here often, bechari. Husband is a pilot, keeps flying off. Sometimes Paris, sometimes London. Always bringing presents for the in-laws, lucky people. Arushi Puri, of course, you have met, she lives with her brother and his wife. Arushi is very smart, works for some hotel in sales. Out every night...'

Tushar intervened in his lazy drawl. 'Kulwant Aunty, I think you have educated Nandita enough for one morning. Can we leave now? She obviously has to unpack, and I really have to finish some work by tonight, otherwise I'll lose my job. And I won't be able to pay you rent!'

Nandita threw him a grateful look, and shepherded the reluctant Kulwant out of the couch. She turned to Tushar and said, 'I would love to offer you coffee, but I haven't set up the kitchen yet!'

Tushar smiled enigmatically and replied, 'Oh don't worry, I'll take that coffee at a more convenient time... After all, what are neighbours for?' He left with a sly wink, bearing the reluctant Kulwant with him.

By 7.30 in the evening, there was some semblance of order in the apartment, and Nandita took a break to make herself a cup of green tea.

She looked around her. She had managed put her own mark on the little flat, with the few personal belongings she had brought with her from Delhi. Her clothes, and more importantly, her shoes had taken up far more space in the bedroom that she had envisaged, and she had ended up filling the closets in the guest bedroom as well. Even though she owned several bags, her fetish was shoes. She had dozens of pairs of pumps, sandals, boots, chappals and flats, in every type of leather and colour, with lots of gold and silver thrown in. These she arranged reverently in individual shoe bags, labelled carefully for instant recognition.

Nandita had forfeited her extensive library of bestsellers, but refused to leave behind her CD collection. She loved popular music and popular literature, and counted David Baldacci, Tom Clancy, Ken Follet and P.G. Wodehouse among her favourite authors. She had no time for more intellectual literary and musical pursuits, and had shocked the jilted Gaurav Mathur by confessing an aversion to Beethoven, Dostoevsky and the existential literature he favoured. Now, she popped a disc into the music system and began to relax to the soft, mellifluous crooning. Who needed Tchaikovsky when you could have Dido!

Nandita hooked up her laptop to the cable Internet connection. She had not checked her email or her Facebook account for a couple of days now. There were a couple of emails from her clients in Delhi, which she replied to immediately, tying up some loose ends on projects she had completed. A long email from her college friend, Natasha, who was now married and living in New York, was a welcome surprise. Natasha's move had wrenched Nandita, and for a while, the errant David could not be hated enough for snatching her friend away. She read the mail at a leisurely pace, savouring the pleasure. Natasha had been caught in such a whirlwind of activities herself that she had barely had any time to keep in touch. Obviously, the firangi husband was keeping her busy. Nandita smiled indulgently as she read Natasha's humourous account of life in New York... her friend was clearly enjoying herself. Maybe marriage was not that bad a deal after all. Even Shanti was blissfully happy with her Varun-plus-eleven. She thought about Gaurav, and wondered... no, she couldn't possibly have done it.

Nandita went to her wardrobe and pulled out an old jewellery box. She extracted a pale blue folded sheet of paper, weathered with age. Sitting on the edge of her bed, she read the letter again, from start to finish. For probably more than the hundredth time, she reflected wryly. Its contents, as always, made her feel restless and sad.

Nandita had chanced upon the letter about four or five years ago, purely by accident. She had been cleaning out her treasure chest, a big jewellery box made of carved walnut wood, which had once been her mother's. Nandita had, like a magpie, collected and preserved every trinket her mother had ever given her, including a small silver heart that she had worn at the age of five, and a beaded bracelet that Amrita had told her would ward off all those shadowy figures that scared her at night when she was alone in her bed. All these treasures, along with other relics of her childhood, were stored in that wooden box, and had been there for years. Amrita would have been astonished if the contents of the box were revealed to her now. She had no idea that her daughter was so sentimental. She would have been even more astonished, and also very frightened, if she knew that Nandita had found that letter under the parchment paper lining of the box.

When Nandita had read the letter for the first time, shock had prevented her from understanding its actual contents. Subsequent readings had shed more light, and there could be no mistaking the meaning. She had, with difficulty, kept her discovery from her mother. Amrita would not want to discuss this with her daughter, that much Nandita was sure of. So she kept it hidden in the box, hoping to discover its secrets. Now that she was in Mumbai, she felt instinctively that she was one step closer to discovering the identity of the writer. She carefully put the letter back into its hiding place in the box.

Suddenly, she felt hungry, and realized that the biryani had been eaten hours ago. Nandita decided to walk to the local Subway and pick up a sandwich. Pulling on a pair of jeans and a pale blue kurti, she picked up her enormous silver tote and emerged from 7B for the first time that day.

Saturday evening had brought crowds of people to Carter Road, and she was wondering which direction to set forth in when she bumped into Arushi, this time in purple track pants, jogging back into the building. 'Hey! You're the new girl in 7B, right? Have you moved in yet?' Arushi asked breathlessly.

'Yes, actually I have, just this morning,' replied Nandita. 'How can you run in such a crowd? This place is like a mela!'

'Oh, I run anywhere!' said Arushi. 'It's an addiction with me. Where you off to?'

'Looking for somewhere to pick up a sandwich... I haven't really got my kitchen organized yet.'

'A sandwich! Not on your life! I am meeting some friends for dinner and then later, we're heading to this big vodka launch party; why don't you join us! Should be fun... c'mon, it's Saturday night!' Arushi brushed a strand of bleached blonde hair away from her sweaty brow. Her eyes were sparkling with the exercise, and she exuded good health and energy. She was, Nandita guessed, one of those enthusiastic, inclusive people who took everyone under their wing instantaneously.

Nandita was about to refuse, pleading exhaustion, but changed her mind and said yes. This was an opportunity to meet some new people, and she thought that now was as good a time as any to start getting settled in Mumbai. She went back into the building with Arushi to change.

Nandita chose a pale green chiffon dress that had been Avantika Puri's gift to her when she had left Delhi. It was a simple, straight-cut dress, embellished with a scattering of Swarovski crystals towards the hemline. Avantika told her that she had chosen the colour especially for Nandita, as it would look 'mind-blowing with those cat eyes of yours!' Nandita decided to accessorize the dress with a pair of Manolo Blahnik shoes in dull silver, studded with rhinestones. Might as well go all out, she thought, it was her first party night in Mumbai. Suddenly she found herself looking forward to the evening. Mumbai, here I come!

CHAPTER SIX
Mumbai, January 2013

Aryan was just not in the mood to party. The day had been a bitch, he reflected with a grimace. Saturday was meant to be the winding down day of the week, a chance to relax before Monday dawned with a fresh set of problems. This Saturday had been the kind of day that he wanted to get over with as quickly as possible, head home, pour a stiff drink and pass out in blissful oblivion. But Rajat was being insistent about the big bash at a suburban bar tonight, which would probably be the usual squeeze that Rajat habitually dragged him to. He would have loved to say an emphatic no, but Rajat was not the type you could refuse, emphatically or otherwise. It was much easier to give in, as Aryan had learned from experience. He also knew that he could not disappoint Anjali, since this was something her company was organizing. Anjali and Rajat Gupte had been the first real friends he'd made when he came to Mumbai six months ago. They were a grounded young couple, and Aryan genuinely enjoyed their company. They lived in the same apartment building, and had bonded over many evenings spent at home, just the three of them, with no social veneer to impede the friendship. Anjali had adopted him as her protégé, and had made it her mission to get him to feel at home in the Mumbai party circuit. He resigned himself to another glamour-filled evening. Might as well have a date for the evening if he had to go, he thought, and after a moment's hesitation, dialled Mohini's number.

The evening started on an inauspicious note, with a ridiculous traffic jam at Mahim Causeway. There was a huge jatra on the side of the causeway, and hundreds of people were queued up to partake of its merriment. Aryan could see a few giant wheels and endless colourful stalls. Even 10.30 on a Saturday night was like peak hour, and the Mercedes inched its way painfully forward on the narrow arterial road. Aryan was trying to unwind with some soft James Blunt playing on the car stereo, but apparently Mohini had other ideas. She saw the long drive as enough time and opportunity to start on the where-are-we-heading-with-this-thing and my-biological-clock-is-ticking conversation.

Mohini was an attractive thirty-two-year-old relationship manager with a multinational bank, but the only relationship on her mind right now was the one she didn't actually share with Aryan. He was maddeningly non-committal about their dating, though she had begun to take it all quite seriously. Aryan was definitely marriage material. Successful, focused on his career, and more importantly, good-natured and great company. He was of average height, but well built, well groomed, and had the kind of pleasant good looks that were reassuringly ordinary. Mohini was wary of overly handsome, self-obsessed men. But unfortunately, Aryan had made it perfectly clear from the start that he was not looking for a committed involvement. Of course, that meant nothing. Men could be made to change their minds. She was hoping that he would at least consider a commitment not to date other girls, if not actually think about marriage. Not very wisely, she chose to bring it up at the end of Aryan's mind-numbing day. It was akin to bringing it up in the middle of the exciting finish of an India–Australia T20, or in Aryan's case, a Chicago Bears game. Aryan, in fact, was dating other women, though he enjoyed Mohini's company and spent a lot of time with her. But he now began to perceive the hazards of paying her too much attention.

'You must have some idea of what you're looking for in a relationship, Aryan,' she said with incredulity. 'I mean, where exactly do you see us a year from now? We can't be in the same stagnant place.'

Aryan tried to speak patiently. 'Mohini, I've never given you the impression that this is a relationship. I enjoy being with you, we have a good time, and I've told you from the start that not much more is going to come out of this.'

'I'm not saying that you've made any promises. But that can change. We know each other much better now, the relationship has to develop and grow in some direction, surely?' She was almost pleading, and Aryan felt uncomfortable. He had no desire to hurt her, but she had to know that she was assuming a situation between them that did not exist. He had told her that he dated other women, and had made it perfectly clear that this was not an exclusive liaison. Mohini was the one who had initiated the sexual part of their association early on in their friendship, and in those euphoric days she had made no attempt to tie him down. So where was all this commitment stuff coming from?

By the time they pulled up outside Olive in Pali Hill, he was through trying to couch things in a soft, inoffensive manner, and dangerously close to being brutally honest. Mohini made matters worse by clinging on to his arm in a possessive, proprietary way as they entered the noisy, crowded confines of the bar.

The event was a typical Mumbai Page Three party. Aryan was getting used to seeing the same couple of hundred faces everywhere he went. He had befriended a few of them, but on the whole, he still remained on the periphery of Mumbai's party crowd. He had connected with much of Mumbai's expat hospitality industry crowd, and was happy with his slightly off-beat social life. He had no real desire to see his picture in *Bombay Times*, even though opportunities presented themselves frequently.

The Olive bar was packed, and it took a while to get one of the many colourful drinks doing the rounds. He would have loved an ice-cold beer but that was obviously not happening at a vodka launch party, so he took the plunge and picked up a couple of super dirty martinis, handing one to the still-clinging Mohini. She was obviously doing the he's-my-property-lay-off routine, and he was too tired to protest. He shepherded her to the back of the bar, where he spied Rajat and Anjali waiting for them.

'You made it, I see,' Rajat grinned. 'You sounded like death when I spoke to you!'

Aryan smiled and gave Anjali a warm hug and kiss. 'You look sensational, honey. You should wear red more often.' Anjali laughed and blushed. She worked for the company that was launching the vodka and was really delighted that Aryan had made it tonight.

'You've been working too hard, Aryan. You need to relax a bit.' Anjali turned to Mohini. 'Hello, you! It's been a while!'

'Yes, work has been hectic for me too. Not been out much. You, on the other hand, seem to have a rather social working life!'

Anjali acknowledged this with a pretty shrug, and they began to catch up on the usual harmless gossip about common acquaintances. Aryan looked around, and picked up his second drink, this time a Scubatini Oceanic martini. The blue curacao looked cool and inviting.

Rajat raised his eyebrows. 'That's pretty potent stuff, you know.'

'Yeah, and they go down much too fast! Oh, what the hell. Might as well make a night of it!' Aryan looked around, observing the display of skin, and was once more struck by the ingenuity of designers who managed to use the most miniscule amount of fabric to create these delectable articles of clothing. He watched the many attractive women preening at the bar with an appreciation enhanced by the heady feeling of alcohol induced well-being. For the first time since he woke up that morning, he found himself relaxing.

He could have been in any bar in any part of the world, he thought. This could be Shanghai, Chicago, Berlin or Melbourne. The music was the same, the people dressed the same way and the same drinks were being served at the bar. And the conversation was the same. He tuned in idly to snippets of banter around him. *The sensex is rock bottom, man, my portfolio is so bloody screwed! Who thought that the sub prime crisis will affect India, boss, we are de-linked from the global economy. Arre yaar, do you know Pankaj is splitting up with his wife? Hey, just look at that bag Nayana is carrying, I mean, is she totally colour blind?* People were the same everywhere.

Mohini moved away finally, spotting some friends of hers across the bar. Anjali looked at Aryan speculatively.

'She's getting serious about you, Aryan,' she told him in her usual blunt way. 'I gather you don't feel the same way, so maybe it's time to give it a break.'

'I've realized that. It's not like I led her on, you know. Don't look so disapproving.'

'Oh, I'm not saying you did. Just wondered if you knew. Men are a bit dense about these things,' she said, with a superior air that made him laugh.

'And women know it all? You'd certainly like to think you do. Ok, I'll lay off Mohini. There're other fish in the sea.'

'You're incorrigible,' she replied, lightly smacking his arm. 'I see no reason why you don't think about settling down.

Especially when you have the ideal example of Rajat and Anjali Gupte to inspire you!'

'I wouldn't hold my breath, if I were you,' he said, handing her a fresh drink.

Rajat appeared again, cheerfully chiding Aryan. 'You trying to get my wife drunk *again*? Shame on you!'

'Anju doesn't need any help. We all know that!' Aryan gave her a big grin. Anjali's drinking abilities were a constant joke between them. Rajat bore his wife off to meet an old school friend and Aryan turned around and faced the other side of the restaurant. He picked up an appletini from a passing waiter bearing a tray with the most confusing profusion of cocktail glasses. About to take a generous gulp, his attention was caught by a girl in the corner of the room, and he froze in mid-action.

She looked like she was in her early to mid-twenties, taller than her companions, and dressed in a soft green chiffon dress that completely dramatized the deeper green of her eyes. Her luxuriant curls were black with tantalizing red highlights, and hung down to her waist with careless abundance. There was no come-hither skin display, but she stood out from the crowd of little black dresses and blonde-hair-out-of-a-bottle around her. Aryan had never quite understood why the Mumbai girls were so shy about their beautiful black hair. This one, though, had sheer magnetic presence. Somehow, she was different, didn't quite fit in with the surroundings. Aryan was mesmerized. He stood rooted to the spot, trying to memorize the way she looked, in every tiny detail. His eyes hungrily took in every feature, every nuance. The delicate arch of her eyebrow, the creamy perfection of her skin, the nose that was a fraction too rounded to be classic, the mouth that was just a little too wide for beauty, the figure that was too curvy to be fashionable. He was brought back to earth by Rajat, who spoke into his ear from behind.

'Can't introduce you, yaar, don't know who she is!'

'That's a first! Will introduce myself, thank you,' he replied. The girl was accompanied by a bunch of people who were not really close friends, he could tell. Mohini came up to him and grabbed his arm, pulling him back to the bar. The green-eyed girl glanced at him just then, and looked away. For the next thirty minutes, Mohini kept him occupied, introducing him to some friends, and he could not slip away without being rude, but his attention was elsewhere.

An opportunity presented itself a while later, when he saw the girl step outside into the garden area. Excusing himself, he followed her out into the welcome coolness of the night. Outside, it was almost as packed with people, and he couldn't locate her for a couple of moments. Suddenly he spotted her near the exit, with her cell phone out, making a call. He loitered in the doorway, thinking that it would have been an ideal time to pull out a cigarette, but he didn't smoke, so he waited as casually as he could, picking up a crantini from a passing waiter that was obviously meant for someone else. He was beginning to feel a little lightheaded after recklessly downing four or five martinis in a short space of time, and as he turned around to look at the exit again, he bumped into someone clumsily, and felt the contents of his glass lurch forward. He looked down and saw a green chiffon dress soaked in scarlet cranberry juice, and a pair of accusing green eyes looking straight into his.

Up close, she was even more mesmerizing. Not beautiful in the classic sense, he thought, but he felt as if all the breath had been squeezed out of his chest. She was about to move away, so without thinking, he caught her arm.

'Hey, sorry about that. Are you ok?' he said sheepishly.

'Yes, I'm fine. Could you excuse me?' She tried to free herself and move past him towards the restrooms. He pulled her closer to him, tightening his grip on her. He felt like he simply couldn't let go, even though he sensed her desire to get away.

'Actually, no. I've been wanting to talk to you all evening.' He sounded obnoxious, even to his own ears. 'Let's you and me go quietly somewhere and have a drink.'

She wrenched herself free and moved inside. 'Actually, let's not!'

They both saw that Mohini was watching this drama from the bar in complete disapproval.

'I can't imagine why you would presume I want to have a drink with you. And in case you are too drunk to realize it, your poor deluded wife is waiting for you at the bar.' The voice was cold and sliced through his alcoholic haze like a searing knife through butter. She turned abruptly and disappeared into the back of the restaurant.

Aryan was not sure what just happened. He had never, ever, made a drunken pass at anyone before, and now, he had done it at a time when it really mattered. He had no idea what had come over him and caused him to behave in such an uncharacteristically boorish manner. He had to find out who she was and make it right. He could not bear the idea that she must think him a loathsome, ill-mannered loser. But it was too late. He couldn't find her anywhere, and by now, it was too crowded to even move around the restaurant. She was gone. He definitely owed her at least an apology, to say nothing of a laundry bill. He thought about the damage, and ruefully decided that it would have to be a new dress. The only problem was, how was he going to find her?

CHAPTER SEVEN
Mumbai, January 2013

Sabarwal Associates was located inside one of the new plush buildings at Bandra Kurla Complex. It occupied a spanking 6,000 square feet of opulent but tastefully decorated space, and Nandita realized that Rajeev Sabarwal believed in showmanship. The haughty Parsi receptionist thawed when she learned that Nandita was the much-awaited new recruit, and condescended to rise from her throne behind the reception to personally lead Nandita into the hallowed inner portals of Rajeev's office. That morning, Nandita was dressed in her usual choice of working attire—low-waisted skinny black jeans from Mango and a fitted white cotton shirt that hugged her contours deliciously. This she had embellished with an elaborate silk vest, cut to show off the slim curve of her waist. Make-up she kept to a minimum during the day, with clear lip gloss and a single coat of mascara giving her incandescent eyes all the enhancement they needed. Nandita received a fair amount of curious stares as she followed Khurshid through the office, and she was a little amused.

A bright-eyed, plump young woman with pin-straight re-bonded shoulder-length hair wearing a short, short red skirt passed by in the opposite direction, and flashed Nandita a big, saucy grin that revealed deep dimples in both her cheeks. Without being beautiful, the girl was a bombshell, oozing sex appeal. Her dark eyes shone with mischief and Nandita blinked, momentarily dazzled by the vision of colour that was juxtaposed against the sober corporate backdrop. Nice, she thought. Definitely won't be a dull moment around here.

'That's Tara,' said Khurshid, in a frozen accent. Obviously, she didn't approve. Nandita stifled a desire to laugh.

To actually get to Rajeev Sabarwal, it was necessary to negotiate two possessive secretaries, a personal assistant and a thick, acid-etched glass door that opened into a swish office appointed with elegant Italian furniture from Milan. Rajeev Sabarwal rose cordially to greet Nandita. His long, lean face was wreathed in smiles as he welcomed her, and Nandita had the feeling of being received by a head of state. In his soft, well-cultivated voice he welcomed her to Sabarwal Associates. Nandita took a quick look around the room. It was large and dim, lit with tiny bright spotlights that focused only on the desk and the various pieces of art that were displayed. There were several paintings on the deep red wall, interesting installations, antiques and curios aplenty; too much to take in all at once, she thought. The vast leather and glass writing table was immaculate, with every article neatly in place. The royal wife from Bikaner made her presence felt in a series of exquisite silver filigree frames, and she was as beautiful as Shanti had described.

Rajeev Sabarwal was decidedly a self-proclaimed aristocrat, Nandita decided. The whole look of the room was carefully put together to proclaim old money, class, artistic patronage and sophisticated taste. Nandita knew that Rajeev's brother, Himanshu Sabarwal, had started Sabarwal Associates. The mantle of ownership had fallen on Rajeev's shoulders after his brother's death. When he had been alive, Rajeev's elder brother had been the star of the show, with his flamboyant style and pathbreaking design ideas. Both brothers came from humble beginnings, and had risen to the top with sheer talent. Rajeev,

Simi Aunty had told Nandita, had used every measure he knew to gain an acceptable status in society, collecting the trophy princess wife along the way to add to his credibility. The persona he had created for himself was that of a born aristocrat, and it worked amazingly well with his pedigree-conscious clients. She had heard that Rajeev had trampled on various people during his climb to fame, that he was manipulative and hard. Somehow, she couldn't believe it... he seemed like a gentleman, a man of integrity. Following the death of his brother, he strove to make Sabarwal Associates a household name in this city, with several landmark buildings to his credit.

Seated across his desk was an elegant woman in her mid-forties, dressed in severe black pants and a rose pink satin shirt. Her lush auburn hair was swept up into a high ponytail, calculated to achieve a rather youthful look, which, upon closer inspection, was belied by the faint yet unmistakable lines around her eyes. Large diamond and emerald drops hung from her ears. Glossy, over-jewelled and over-confident, thought Nandita, just the kind of combination that was impossible to please. She was assessing Nandita with undisguised candour.

'Nandita, meet Sabiha Khan, a close friend of my wife Pallavi. I've just been telling her about you. Sabiha and I are discussing her new office for the fashion magazine she is about to launch. It's a beautiful old building in Fort, and her own office is luxuriously large. Sabiha wants something different, not the usual spare, minimalist look that's going around nowadays.'

'We were thinking that the already existing high ceilings, exposed beams, rugged stone walls and arched doorways lend themselves to that charming Tuscan rustic look, but that's not really me.' Sabiha shrugged nonchalantly, and Nandita sighed. One more society wannabe *me* in search of herself? This particular woman looked like she would only feel at home on an antique

French Louis XVI chair. She listened to Sabiha ramble on for a bit about individual style and the need to express one's personality through one's surroundings, but couldn't hear a single concrete idea come up.

Rajeev Sabarwal interjected with soothing remarks at appropriate moments, and Nandita sensed that he was waiting to see how she would handle the situation.

'Oh absolutely, Mrs Khan.' Nandita leaned forward, feigning interest. 'You simply have to make a style statement at first glance, that's really important. I think, and I have to say the thought struck me as soon as I saw you, that for someone as individualistic as you, it can't be just a regular classic look. I was wondering, since it's an older building, why don't we go totally art deco? Like, chequered flooring, lots of chrome and glass, high gloss lacquered finish, white leather, rosewood and ebony, wall sconces and you know, those lovely nickel lamps with blown glass shades. Mirrors with geometric motifs, and woody chevron accents in the lacquered panels. I haven't seen that done recently.'

Sabiha was intrigued. 'That sounds interesting, Nandita. Can I see some references?'

Rajeev intervened swiftly. 'Of course, Sabiha. I'll have an assistant put together some stuff for you. Maybe we can meet again sometime at the end of the week?' Travel schedules were discussed, planners consulted and the next meeting was fixed up to everybody's convenience. Sabiha Khan departed a happy customer, and Rajeev turned apologetically to Nandita as he closed the heavy glass door.

'Not bad, Nandita! But I'm sorry, I didn't mean to get you into that literally the minute you got here. She's a school friend of Pallavi's and it becomes really difficult to snub her. Married a really wealthy man, and now that her kids are grown up, she's had this magazine brainwave. She's got her teeth into it like a terrier. Not stupid, our Sabiha, but can be annoyingly persistent. Anyway, I have put Tara on the job, and all you will need to do is supervise at a distance.'

'Oh, that's fine. I've dealt with dozens of Sabihas in Delhi.' Nandita's attention was caught by several beautiful cast bronze sculptures in one corner of the room.

'You have a great eye, Nandita,' said Rajeev as he observed the direction of her gaze. 'Those bronzes are by a young artist from Tanjore, terribly talented. We have just commissioned twenty-five large works for the Gurgaon hotel from him.'

'They are stunning,' she said. 'The finish, the patina, it's so unusual.'

Rajeev Sabarwal looked appraisingly at her.

'Are you going to need time to settle in, or can I throw you into the deep end? I have some fires that need to be put out urgently.'

'Oh, the deep end for sure. I'm itching to get started!' Nandita was, in fact, fired with enthusiasm. She had wrapped up her assignments in Delhi by mid-November, and had taken a month off to make the transition to Mumbai. It had been several weeks since she had put her mind to designing anything new, and she was more than ready to get started.

'You may be getting into more than you bargained for. But we need a fresh perspective on this one, and as I said, you have a really good eye.'

Nandita sipped her tea and looked at him with eager anticipation. He tossed a sheaf of papers towards her, and cleared his throat before he started speaking.

'That's the brief for the interiors of the suites at Starling Lotus. I told you earlier that we are working in tandem with the Singapore architects for the design of the hotel—they have taken over some of the public areas and the restaurants, but they have decided to let us handle the interiors for the banquet areas and suites. Starling Hotels always use a local look and flavour for their suites, but then again, it can't scream India. It has to be a sort of chic Westernized ethnic, if you get the drift. It's all in there...' He indicated the sheaf of papers. 'We have done some work on it, but I'd rather you didn't see that; just start afresh with the basic floor plan.' He looked at her squarely. 'The GM of the hotel is a bit unhappy with the way things are going, and I've done a big sell job on you. He wants to meet you in person before you start. So make sure you familiarize yourself with that stuff before he comes in. The meeting is at 12. Think you can do it?'

'Of course I can. Can I meet the other designers on the project before the meeting?'

'Not right now. Just focus on the brief for today, and you can meet them later. I am putting you in charge of the suites exclusively for now, and you can have all the assistants you need later. We need to get the concepts approved ASAP—we're really behind on schedules. Aryan Rai, who is the GM here in India, is very clear about what he wants, and I think the meeting with him will give you a fair idea how to start. I suggest you work in the conference room for the time being, and we can get you settled in your office later this afternoon.' He sounded a bit edgy, and Nandita got the impression that this Aryan Rai was proving to be a difficult customer. She was surprised and quite gratified that she had been put on such a big project on day one, but wondered why she was being kept away from the rest of the team before a crucial meeting. She was not nervous about the meeting itself. She had tackled several big clients with bigger egos and knew exactly how to manage them. After her design skills, people management was her special talent. The assignment itself was challenging, and the uber-luxurious hotel would provide her ample opportunity to showcase her flair. The unknown Aryan Rai would soon be eating out of her palm, she reflected with a trace of smugness.

The conference room was, thankfully, better lit than Rajeev's office. Nandita settled herself into a comfortable leather chair with another cup of tea and picked up the notes Rajeev had given her.

In the hotel world, she discovered, 'luxury' could mean unique, individual, exceptional service, elite clientele, spectacular settings, impeccable service, profitability, or all of the above, simultaneously. The hotel's job was to sell sleep, so the bed, above all else, must be comfortable, followed by an efficient bathroom. The aesthetics had to come after the comfort angle had been taken care of. She was engrossed in the brief when she heard the door open behind her. Khurshid's cultured voice floated in.

'Please come this way, sir. Miss Nandita Dharkar is waiting for you. I will inform Mr Sabarwal that you are here, and send in your black coffee immediately.'

She glanced at her watch and saw that it was almost one. Aryan the ogre evidently did not set much store by punctuality. She rose and turned around to greet him, and froze midway through putting out her hand. Heavens! This was Aryan Rai! There could be no mistaking the brown eyes that had looked at her so covetously on Saturday night. She did not know if she was more discomfited or stunned, but he certainly looked like he had been socked in the jaw.

The memory of the icy cranberry martini being poured down the front of her dress came rushing back, along with the memory of the familiarity with which he had held her close. She grew hot with embarrassment. He looked very different this morning, she realized in a haze of confusion—sober, respectable and very natty in his pale grey Armani suit. They both said nothing for a few stunned seconds, but it was Nandita who recovered first.

'Aryan Rai? *You* are Aryan Rai?' She said it as if his name was a bad word, a nasty surprise.

He put his hand out at the same time that she snatched hers back instinctively. He covered the awkward moment by saying smoothly, in his American accent, 'Guilty as charged. So it's Nandita. Pretty name. I'm really sorry about the other night, and your dress…as a matter of fact…' Aryan never had a chance to finish his apology.

'Please don't mention it,' Nandita cut in quickly. 'I'd rather forget the whole thing, actually.' She hesitated. 'In fact, since it seems that we are going to be working together, I'd like to just keep it totally professional… I mean…' Her voice trailed off in acute embarrassment.

'You've made yourself perfectly clear,' said Aryan in an even tone, his polite, pleasant demeanour changing perceptibly into frostiness. 'I have no intention of forcing myself on you again, so don't flatter yourself.'

Nandita felt a flush of anger rise immediately, and was forced to check herself because Rajeev Sabarwal chose that inopportune moment to enter the room.

'I see you have met each other,' he said genially. 'Aryan, Nandita is the one person with the perfect credentials to work on this job… I must tell you that she has gained quite a reputation for herself in Delhi, and we are really pleased that she is now part of the Sabarwal Associates team.'

'That's fantastic. I look forward to seeing what she can do for us,' replied Aryan with a faint trace of sarcasm that only Nandita detected. She was appalled that the beginning of her first meeting with her first important client had been such an unmitigated disaster. What are the odds, she told herself in frustration, that Aryan Rai should be the idiot from the bar that night!

Now, sitting in the conference room, she had to admit that after the onslaught on Saturday night, he was not paying much attention to her. After she had made her stay-away-from-me speech, he had adopted an indifferent, impersonal manner and begun his briefing session without any pleasantries. She had seen him watching her from the bar that night almost as soon as she had entered the restaurant, and since she had assumed that he was with his wife, she had been very put off by the blatant attention. Mohini had, for her part, been giving Nandita the hands-off look with venom. What was she supposed to think? He was definitely attractive, she had known that even then, but she was uncomfortable about the way he had stared at her all evening, and then waylaid her in the doorway. The cranberry martini had been the absolute limit, and she had readily assumed he was just some inebriated loser. Today, she was seeing a completely different man.

As she listened to his deliberate, measured tone, she realized that Aryan was clear about his company's objectives. 'People are more aware of what they want these days. The hotel needs to give a unique experience, something different. Designers design what they think is luxury, which is not necessarily what the paying customer wants.' He turned to Nandita and posed a hypothetical question.

'If you were a guest at Starling Lotus, what would you expect your 800 dollars a night to buy you?' Nandita had to think about that one; she had never been a guest at any of the exclusive Starling properties, and while she had stayed at numerous comfortable, even upscale hotels, she had never experienced the kind of obscene luxury that the Starling Hotels were famous for. She was about to venture a reply when she saw that Aryan was not really waiting for an answer, for he moved on smoothly.

'The feeling of being welcomed like royalty? The impossibly comfortable bed with its soft pillows and 500-count Egyptian cotton linen? The super-premium bathroom amenities, the fluffy towels and the giant sunken Jacuzzi tub? Silk hangings, original art on the wall, Italian marble on the floor, rich fabrics, sexy colour palettes? Or the discreet, personalized, impeccable service standards? All of the above, right? Nandita, it's about the interplay between the décor, service and cuisine. It's the whole experience for the guest. You have to focus on the guest. Do you realize, the simple fact of being in an aesthetically delicious atmosphere tends to hugely enhance your self-worth. You revel in belonging to this exotic world, and for the time you stay with us, this world belongs to you. That's the experience we like to give our guests at Starling.'

In spite of herself, Nandita was impressed by his passion. He was obviously very good at what he did. She was conscious of having judged him too harshly, too soon. That was not like her; usually, she thought, her first impressions were bang on. Who knew this Aryan Rai would turn out to be so...well, let's face it, he was getting more interesting every minute. He was also very appealing, she decided. Sexy, even. His clean-cut face was not precisely handsome, but something about his style and general air was very engaging. But she showed none of these conflicting emotions on her face...not for nothing was she Amrita's daughter. As he spoke, she began to get a clear picture of what was required of her, and was genuinely enthused to be a part of the design team on the project. Aryan was the kind of client she had always wanted to work with, clear, lucid, concise and wholly knowledgeable about his subject. She hoped the unfortunate beginning would not be an impediment to their working relationship. It was a dream project, and she was anxious to be able to perform to the best of her potential.

'Nandita, why don't you take Aryan to the Taj for lunch, and continue your meeting there? I would have joined you, but I have to meet another client right now,' suggested Rajeev.

'No, I have to be back in office,' said Aryan, without even a glance at Nandita. 'I think she has enough to get started. When do you think we can see the first concepts?'

Nandita was astonished to find herself feeling faintly disappointed, and a little piqued that the lunch had been so pointedly dismissed. She decided she would be equally impersonal and businesslike, and began to work out some schedules with Rajeev. The ultimate snub came when Aryan took his leave, exiting the room with a cordial goodbye to Rajeev, but not even acknowledging Nandita's existence. How dare he! She fumed inwardly. Of all the rude, obnoxious men, Aryan Rai had to be at the top of the list!

CHAPTER EIGHT
Mumbai, February 2013

Abhimanyu Menon was planning a birthday party for his son. In all the twenty-one years of Prateek's life, his father had never done so. But now that it was a landmark year, Abhimanyu felt he was required to do something special. Prateek was finishing his last year of undergraduate studies at the London School of Economics, having spurned the offer from Harvard, his father's alma mater. Prateek loved London and found that its comparative proximity to home gave it a distinct edge over anything Boston had to offer. Abhimanyu was not complaining. He got to see his son more often now than ever before. His wife Kamini had taken custody of Prateek at the age of seven, when their divorce had been finalized. It had all been very civilized, no rancour, no strident mud-slinging, just a cold legal settlement that had sliced the family bloodlessly into two. Abhimanyu had never blamed Kamini for leaving him. He had given her enough reason to, god knows, and he acknowledged the fact with a heavy burden of guilt that hadn't diminished over the years.

The marriage had been an arranged one, approved and sanctioned by both families. Abhimanyu was thirty at the time, and Kamini only twenty-four. But unlike so many other similar unions that ended up being happy, theirs was doomed from the start—a marriage without communication, without passion, without substance. Kamini knew from day one of her married life that she could never compete with the ghosts of Abhimanyu's past, or make a distinctive place for herself. Sadly, she would never be the most important woman in his life. She was dimly aware when she married Abhimanyu that there had been a relationship in the past that had, for some unknown reason, never fructified into marriage. That was common enough, and it hadn't really bothered her much. What she hadn't known until after she was married was that Abhimanyu would never be ready to move on. She discovered this bitter reality not long after she took the pheras, but still used every ploy she knew to get close to him, in vain. Even after Prateek was born, nothing changed. She tried to push her way past her husband's kind, polite indifference, but failed to succeed in breaking through the wall he had built around himself. He was always attentive, generous to a fault and supportive of everything she needed or wanted, but she knew that was universal, and not especially for her; he was that way with everyone, even his colleagues at work. Eventually, inevitably, she began to look for solace outside her marriage. The most painful cut came when she finally announced that she was leaving him for another man, because even that did not appear to faze him. She realized, agonizingly, that if he was at all crushed by her departure, it was only because he would miss Prateek.

Abhimanyu had watched her struggle with a deep sense of regret about his own inadequacies and pain at her valiant efforts to make the marriage work. Kamini was an innocent, pliable girl, and she had tried every possible way to adapt to his lifestyle, his likes and dislikes, his moods and his whims. The more he blamed himself for the failure of the marriage, the more he knew that it could be no other way. Her decision to leave him came as a huge relief, more so when he realized that she had found a man who would love her the way she deserved. He did not want to be guilty of ruining someone's life. His only regret when she left was the loss of Prateek.

Abhimanyu had not contested the custody of the child, and unflinchingly let Prateek go with his mother. It was the least he could do for her, after all. But he missed Prateek very much, and the sporadic weekends that they spent together did not compensate for the heartbreaking absence of his son from his daily life. When Prateek was sixteen, Kamini moved to Australia with her second husband and daughter and Prateek chose to remain with his father. Kamini had been reluctant to let him stay, but capitulated in the end, because she saw that it was what Prateek wanted. Now, all Prateek's frequent trips home from London were made to visit Abhimanyu, and finally the father and son had grown close. Prateek never asked his father what had gone wrong in the marriage, but even as a child, he always knew that the void in his father's life was a deep, painful one. At twenty-one, he was as much in the dark as ever, and had still not managed to pierce through his father's reserve about the past.

Abhimanyu pondered the birthday question. Should it be a weekend in Bangkok for all of Prateek's close friends, or a huge bash at a Mumbai nightclub? Or should he just leave it to Prateek to plan it himself? He was thrilled that Prateek would be home for good in May. His son had made all kinds of plans for the future, but none of them included staying on in London. Most of Prateek's friends, noticed Abhimanyu, were planning to return to India. That's where all the action was, after all. Gone were the days when the sole objective after completing graduation was to try and land a job in the US or the UK. Kids today were so focused. Abhimanyu himself had stayed on in Boston to work for a garment manufacturing company after his graduation, then moved on to California and later to Columbia to complete his MBA. It had been almost nine years spent in America by the time he had returned to India for good. He was happy that he had made the decision when he did, or he'd probably never have come back at all. His lonely father had been delighted by his return, but Abhimanyu had shocked him by refusing to join the family business. Making windows for cars did not excite him, he had told his father kindly but firmly. Eventually, his father had retired and sold the business, making Abhimanyu and his sister far wealthier than they had ever dreamed of becoming. When the old man died, Abhimanyu found himself in the happy position of never having to put in a day's work if he chose not to. However, he did choose to work, and made no drastic changes in his lifestyle. He was not a gambler by nature, so he invested his crores in safe, unadventurous ventures, secure in the knowledge that Prateek would always be taken care of.

Abhimanyu knew that life had been good to him and he could not really complain. But the truth was that the one thing Abhimanyu had really wanted badly in life he never got. So eventually, fate had played strange games with him; he had everything, but he had nothing.

Abhimanyu was pondering this quirk of destiny when his secretary popped her head in through the door.

'Mr Sabarwal is here to see you. Can I send him in?' The question was rhetorical. Rajeev Sabarwal was already inside the office before she finished speaking.

'Since when do I have to be screened by your secretary?' he asked with mock severity. Rajeev and Abhimanyu were old school buddies from Mayo College. 'Next you will be telling me to make an appointment to come see you. Don't let this CEO Asia Pacific bit get you all worked up…you're still the snotty brat from the back bench in the classroom, as far as I am concerned.'

'Snotty is something I never was,' replied Abhimanyu, mildly amused. 'You, on the other hand, were the grubbiest boy in the dorm.' Both men were in their early fifties, but the lingering memories of their wild schooldays were never more alive than when they met each other. The Sabarwal brothers and Abhimanyu had been inseparable as boys. Abhimanyu was a privileged boy from a wealthy family, while Rajeev and his brother had been put through the elite school by a benign godfather, as their own parents had lacked the means to pay for a fancy education. All three of them had had plenty to prove in their own way, and the post-college years had been spent in focused climbing of the professional and, in Rajeev's case, social ladder. It was only after Rajeev's brother Himanshu Sabarwal's death that the two men had found each other again, and this time they did not allow the friendship to slide.

'Now that we have the formalities out of the way, how about a drink? It's past seven, and that bottle of Glenmorangie you keep in your drawer is itching to come out.'

Abhimanyu obediently brought out the Glenmorangie, along with two heavy-bottomed squat glasses. 'Just a splash of water, right?'

The ice came in immediately, leaving Rajeev to suspect that it had been kept ready and waiting.

'What service! I take it you make a daily habit of sitting here and downing the malt in the evenings?'

'Nonsense. I knew you were on your way, you old fraud. All this preparation was for you!'

'I'm flattered. May as well bring on the dancing girls too... make an evening of it,' said Rajeev with a grin, waving his hand dramatically.

'Shame on you! I thought you were here to discuss serious business,' Abhimanyu reproved.

'Yes, but you've been so coy about getting to the point!'

The multinational pharmaceutical company Abhimanyu worked for was building a new research laboratory outside Mumbai, and even though it was not Rajeev's specialty, Sabarwal

Associates was pitching for the business. The facility was going to include a Bio-Safety Level 3 lab, which meant that Rajeev would need to employ outside consultants to advise them on the standard norms for designing a high containment building. It was new and uncharted territory for Sabarwal Associates, and Rajeev was hoping that the head office of Ve Pharmaceuticals in New York would approve their bid. The state-of-the-art facility was to be built in an environment-friendly fashion, and the multi-million-dollar project would be a challenging one for Rajeev.

'How soon are we likely to get the decision from your bosses across the Atlantic?' Rajeev asked Abhimanyu.

'I already told you, they will go by my recommendation. Why are you getting so antsy? Have some patience. How's the Starling thing going, by the way?'

'Excellent. My new colleague Nandita has outdone herself. The girl is undeniably talented, and Aryan has not said a nasty word to anyone after she got started on the job. I've decided that if your lab job comes through, she will work with me from scratch on the design. She has that knack of grasping a brief and translating it into design concepts that work, both functionally and aesthetically. She's...she's like a breath of fresh air in the company. Of course, Niranjan has his knife into her, but I guess that's to be expected.'

Abhimanyu poured another round of the Glenmorangie. He swirled the golden liquid in his glass and looked at Rajeev in amusement. 'I can't remember the last time you praised someone so unreservedly. When do I get to meet this paragon?'

'Oh, as soon as we sign the contract for the lab project!' laughed Rajeev. 'She is so busy with the hotel right now, I don't think she even takes a break for lunch!'

'Slave driver,' said Abhimanyu severely. 'You should be ashamed of yourself.'

'Ah, but will you complain the same way when it's *your* work that's getting done, without lunch breaks?'

'You'll find out when we get to that stage. Meanwhile, I suggest you do your homework on BSL3 labs.'

Rajeev inclined his head. 'So what kind of research are you planning to do in this fancy lab of your anyway?'

'Tuberculosis,' replied Abhimanyu. 'Do you realize, Rajeev, every year, over one million people die of the disease, while eight million people develop active tuberculosis? Presently, one-third of the world is infected. It's a tremendous challenge.'

The two men fell into a clinical discussion about the logistics of the lab design. Abhimanyu was very impatient to get the project started, and intended to make the lab the most modern facility in the country. He had decided to see this project through and then bow out of Ve Pharma to take a sabbatical and travel for a while. In the years after the break-up of his marriage, he had put most of his time and energy into work, but of late, he had really begun to feel the need to switch off and recharge himself. He had never come close to marrying again, though he had enjoyed a few relationships of convenience with women who were not looking for marriage either. He had mentally made a list of places he would visit, maybe some of them with Prateek. He had not discussed this plan with anyone, partly because he had no one to discuss it with, and partly because he liked the idea of keeping it to himself. But first, he had to see this project through. And if he could use his old friend's expertise to do it, so much the better. He had a comfort level with Rajeev which would make everything so much smoother.

Outside, it grew dark, and the offices of Ve Pharma were soon emptied of all staff. The incandescent lights of the spanking new mall opposite Abhimanyu's Worli office grew brighter and on the roads, cars were crawling at a ridiculously slow pace.

The evening traffic of Mumbai became predominantly northbound as the city headed tiredly home after another long day at work. Later that evening, when Abhimanyu was being driven home in the privacy of his sleek blue BMW, he pulled out a photograph from his wallet. He looked at it as if mesmerized, and allowed his mind to drift back into the past.

CHAPTER NINE
Mumbai, March 2013

Nandita quickly finished putting on a fresh coat of lip gloss and tied up her long curly hair with a black velvet ribbon. She was late for a dinner with Arushi, who was meeting her at a new bar in Juhu. There had been no time to go home and change, so she had to make do with a hasty freshen-up in the elaborately sexy powder room at her office. As she emerged, it was rather obvious that she was not heading home, which caused her colleague Monica to eye her with speculation.

'Hot date, Nandita?'

'Yes, with a girlfriend!'

'Yeah, right,' sniffed Monica. 'How come you get to have all the fun and I get to go and do math homework with the kid?'

'The joys of motherhood not all they're touted to be, eh? You should have stayed happy and single, Monica!'

'And have to worry about going out on dates? Or rather, not going out on dates! No, thanks, all that stuff's too much stress… I'm happy to go home to my safe and adoring family and dog!'

Nandita laughed and waved an airy goodbye. She walked past Niranjan Kulkarni's office and saw him glance up. He did not bother to acknowledge her, let alone say good night. Nandita strode on uncaringly. She was feeling amazingly exhilarated today. All her weeks of hard work had gratifyingly culminated in a complete and unanimous approval of all the suite designs for Starling Lotus. The high level team that came in from Chicago to view the designs with Aryan Rai had been openly impressed, and she was amazed to see how graciously Rajeev Sabarwal had let her take all the praise and credit.

It was the kind of high she had experienced in the past on a much smaller scale. The magnitude of this project was beyond anything she had done before, and she now understood why Rajeev Sabarwal had the reputation he did. His guidance had been impeccable throughout, and he had been able to stimulate Nandita into producing some truly stunning work. Having worked largely alone for the last few years, she realized the value of working with someone whom she could bounce ideas off, especially a person who could enhance her creative talent exponentially. The rest of the Starling team at Sabarwal Associates was a mixed bag, she reflected. A couple of them were tentatively supportive, some openly hostile, while Tara, the sexy young designer, was blatantly admiring. The problematic one was the aforementioned Niranjan Kulkarni, the senior-most architect employed by Sabarwal Associates, and Rajeev's chief designer. Niranjan had taken an instant dislike towards Nandita when the Starling project had been removed from his custody and handed over to the new girl. He had practically declared open war on her, and she saw now why Rajeev had been so reluctant to introduce her to the team on day one. On the whole, he had been a deterrent, she concluded. Insecurity, jealousy and resentment had been the key factors that were evident from day one, and she had been treated like a pariah from the outset. Rajeev's wholehearted support was what had kept her morale high, and in the end, she thought triumphantly, she had won.

Aryan had been privy to the entire presentation before the arrival of the powers that be, and for the first time since the ill-fated meeting on her first day at work, his glacial attitude towards her had thawed ever so slightly. She had realized that he was looking at her with something that might have been respect, and for some unfathomable reason this pleased her. As for Rajeev, he had been as proud of her as a mentor of his protégée, while he watched her make her presentation with satisfaction.

The suites were going to be the most luxurious Mumbai had ever seen. Each one had a private lobby that led into a spacious lounge adjoining an absurdly large bedroom, replete with a walk-in wardrobe and a full gourmet kitchen. There was a mini spa with a personal multi gym. Nandita had made ingenious use of the spaces and optimized the available area brilliantly. The furniture was contemporary, yet uniquely Indian in its ethos, and the wall, timber and fabric finishes complemented each other perfectly. All this would work in tandem with the legendary service protocol that Starling Hotels excelled in. She presented her ideas with conviction and passion, not realizing that she made an unconsciously pretty picture in the process.

Rajeev had taken Nandita out for a celebratory lunch with the rest of the team. Several beers down, the hostile component of the team had dropped their guard slightly, but not Niranjan. It was clear that Nandita was the heroine of the day, and there was way too much praise being directed her way for his liking.

Nandita's induction into Sabarwal Associates had, apart from the Niranjan clique's animosity, been fairly smooth. She had befriended Monica Rao, a talented woman who was looked up to as one of the most reliable people in the office. Monica never missed a day's work and always completed assignments on time, quietly and without fuss. She could permanently be depended upon to find quick solutions to knotty design problems. Tara, the mini-skirted nymphet she had encountered on her first day, was the exact opposite of Monica—unpredictable, impulsive and exuberant. Tara was the entertainment quotient in the office, with constant tales of her highly eventful love life, her practical views on others' problems and her hilarious agony-aunt solutions to everything. These were directed impartially to every member of Sabarwal Associates, including Nandita. Tara loved Google. She googled everything, from how to apply mascara properly to how many egg whites it was safe to eat in one day. She exasperated the overworked and harassed Monica by telling her to take time off to do pranayam breathing exercises to calm down, and stunned the Tamilian secretary by teaching her how to make her idlis fluffier. Nandita assigned all research work to Tara, who took it as a personal compliment whenever she was asked to google anything. Her sense of dress very much offended the straight-laced Khurshid, but Nandita was amused by the short skirts and tight blouses that the buxom Tara favoured. She flaunted her sexuality without trying too hard, and somehow escaped looking cheap. Nandita thought she was refreshing, and loved listening to her slightly bizarre views on life—she'd never met anybody quite like Tara before. Street smart, savvy, but far from intellectual, Tara had no illusions about herself.

'I know I'm not brainy yaar, or all intelligent like you,' she had confided to Nandita over a cup of mocha latte. 'You know so much about so many things. All that reading-sheading, books and stuff is not for me. I prefer to live life through my own experiences, rather than other people's. I am not even looking for the kind of professional success you and Monica and Niranjan work for. I just live for the day, man. Take it as it comes.'

'What's wrong with that?' Nandita had asked her. 'You don't have to make it sound like an apology. I admire the way you are; it's not easy to be so detached from the future. I think your attitude is great! And who's to say that your way is not more "intellectual" than anyone else's?'

Nandita, working for the first time in an environment with other people around her, was finding it an interesting experience.

The buzz of sharing ideas, the interaction with other creative minds, was very much to her liking.

If it were not for Niranjan's venom, she would have found Sabarwal Associates the ideal workplace. Oh well, she thought, to hell with him and his hang-ups. She would not allow him to ruin her day, but looked forward to her evening with Arushi.

Arushi and Nandita had become good friends over the last couple of months. Arushi was energetic, outgoing and ever ready to party, and often bore Nandita off to enjoy the various bars that dotted Bandra and Juhu. The two had bonded over many Bloody Marys and vodka martinis, and exchanged life stories. Nandita had been really glad of the company. She missed Shanti and Natasha acutely. Arushi was not a replacement, but in her own way, had endeared herself immensely to Nandita. Hell, a girl needed her girlfriends. Arushi's impetuous and spontaneous nature was a perfect match for Nandita's more measured and practical approach. It was the first time in Nandita's adult life that she had grown so close someone she'd not known for long or since childhood, and it was a novel experience. They lunched together, shopped together, shared work problems and boyfriend angst.

Nandita had watched with incredulous amusement at how deftly Arushi juggled three potential boyfriends—a systems analyst, a professional diver and an airline pilot, all of whom, conveniently, were frequent travellers, and never around to step on each other's toes. While Arushi blissfully dated all three impartially, Nandita got the impression that they were a smokescreen for someone else, because Arushi never actually did anything but have an innocent friendly drink or meal with any of them. She did, however, have some unexplained absences, which occurred every now and then, but she brushed them off whenever Nandita questioned her too closely. Then, one afternoon last month, after a long Saturday shopping session raiding Linking Road in general and Mango in particular, the two girls were replenishing their energies with steaming mocha lattes and pecan brownies when Arushi's cell phone rang.

She looked at the number on the screen and glanced guardedly at Nandita before she answered, almost in a whisper, 'Hey. I wasn't expecting you to call today. Aren't you in Alibaug?'

She listened for a couple of seconds. 'No, go ahead. I can talk.'

This time the conversation at the other end was considerably longer. All Arushi did was to listen in numb silence, and Nandita watched her as she paled perceptibly. She appeared to be in shock, but she made no reply. It was as if she did not trust herself to speak. Nandita waited for her to finish, in an agony of suspense. She had never seen Arushi look like this.

Arushi let the phone slide down in a daze. She had still not spoken a word. Nandita took the phone gently from her hand and spoke into it, 'Hello? Who is this?'

The caller disconnected abruptly, to Nandita's astonishment. She put her arm around Arushi, who had by now collapsed, shaking with dry sobs. There was only one other person in the coffee shop, who was trying to look disinterested in the drama that playing out. Nandita threw him a scorching look and turned her attention back to her friend.

'What is it? What's wrong?' she demanded urgently.

Arushi's only reply had been to sob harder and say indistinctly, 'Take me home, Nandita.'

Home they had headed, to Nandita's house, since Arushi did not want to face her sister-in-law's inevitable queries. Over the course of the evening, the sad, predictable story had come out in bits and pieces, with Nandita listening in alternating rage and sympathy. Arushi had been seeing a man at work, her boss, who was not only married but also not planning to change his situation. It was the classic syndrome and Nandita wondered for the hundredth time how women managed to get themselves into the same damn trap again and again. It was a story that never had a happy ending, yet it was played out in every city, in every office, and it was inevitably the girl who came out shattered and bruised. She was aghast to hear that the cad had actually called Arushi on the phone that afternoon in the café to break it off, saying his wife had found out and that he dare not continue. On the phone! She could have slapped the cowardly Ashish Kataria right there and then. He was really sorry, blah blah, he had mouthed all the platitudes, but Arushi was crushed.

'Arushi, surely you didn't think he was going to marry you?' Nandita asked, a little brutally. She thought that a little practicality would be good. 'They never do in such situations, you should have known that.'

That had been over two weeks ago, and since then Nandita had been determined to cheer Arushi up. Arushi was ambushed by frequent attacks of grief, and had spent a lot of her evenings at Nandita's, when both of them talked late into the night. Talking was Arushi's catharsis, Nandita realized, because she had kept this clandestine relationship hidden from everybody she knew for two years. Arushi was, in a way, relieved it was over, because she had known deep inside from the start that it was going nowhere. But she had been so acutely involved, so dependent and so charmed by her lover that she did not have the strength to break it off on her own. Now that he had ended it so callously, with a single telephone call, Arushi was grateful that the decision had been made for her, that it had been taken out of her incapable hands.

Tonight, as her rickety taxi wended its way between the rickshaws, pedestrians and cows at Juhu Chowpatty, Nandita contemplated her own lack of love life. She had been too busy to think about it for the last couple of weeks as the Starling assignment had kept her mentally occupied, if not actually glued to her desk twelve hours a day. But, she thought, her single status was not really bothering her right now. There was too much happening on the work front, she was still absorbing this megapolis called Mumbai and life was abundantly interesting. She tried not to dwell on the question of Aryan Rai. He intruded upon her thoughts more than she liked, and had a habit of making her restless and uncomfortable. His indifferent demeanour had begun to distress her intensely, and she had to keep reminding herself that it was she who had asked him to keep his distance. But he didn't have to take her so literally, did he? Men were so daft. Of course, she had always been equally distant and professional, never giving him reason to suppose that she wanted it any other way. She repeatedly found herself wondering what he did in the evenings, whether the possessive Mohini was still hanging around his neck, with whom he spent his time and, most of all, whether he ever thought about her. She doubted it, when she remembered her cold rebuff. He probably thought her stuck up and frosty, and had moved on to warmer pastures.

She arrived at the bar on this sombre note, and made her way to an outside table under the polite chaperonage of a chatty manager. There was no sign of Arushi yet. The manager fussed around, pulling out the chair. Would she have a drink while she waited for her friend? No? Some iced mineral water perhaps? He hoped she would enjoy her evening!

Nandita finally got rid of his obsequious attention, and sank into a comfortable all-weather wicker chair, finished in a matte navy blue and upholstered in cream silk. The outdoor area comprised a raised wooden deck, which was practically on the beach, and Nandita could see the white crests of the waves crashing onto the darkened shore. The breeze was cool, and palms rustled in abundance. A long bar covered the length of the deck on one side, adorned with glass barstools. There was a tantalizing aroma from the wood-burning pizza oven, and Nandita realized that she was very hungry. She had barely eaten at the celebration lunch—she had been too elated to think about mundane things like food. She was toying with the idea of ordering a thin and crispy pepperoni pizza when Arushi arrived in a flurry of activity, followed by the manager and two waiters escorting her. Arushi managed to make an entrance every single time. She was dressed rather soberly for a change, in a long dark dress, which gave her slender body a severe, forbidding look. Her bleached hair was pulled back in an austere chignon. Evidently, Arushi was not in seductive mode tonight.

'Where's my cosmopolitan?' She demanded. 'You mean you haven't ordered a *drink* yet?' The two waiters hastened forward to rectify the situation. Drinks were ordered, and the pepperoni pizza as well.

Arushi looked around. 'Nice, huh?'

Nandita cut the pleasantries short. 'Ok, out with it. You're obviously bursting with some kind of news.'

'How the hell did you know? Omniscient, as usual. Ok, here goes. I quit my job today.'

Nandita's eyebrow went up. It was an effective trick she had learned from Amrita. 'Lovely. So, I'm paying for dinner?'

Arushi laughed, but looked serious. 'I couldn't take it anymore, Nandita. I cannot, *cannot* look at his face every morning and act as if nothing has happened. I need to get out of there.'

'I think it's the best thing you could have done. Screw him. I hope he never finds anyone even half as efficient as you.'

'Elegantly put, my friend. I was thinking about applying to Starling for a job. I have heard that they are putting together a local sales team soon.'

'That's a great idea! Do you want me to speak to Aryan Rai?' Nandita spoke his name so self-consciously that Arushi, as self-absorbed as she was at the moment, noticed immediately.

'Oye! What's going on here... Are you not telling me something?'

'There is nothing to tell,' replied Nandita in the tone of one who rather wished there was. 'He barely knows I exist, other than as someone who works on his design team.'

'Rubbish,' snorted Arushi. 'I guarantee you he pretends not to notice because you've been such a hard-assed bitch. Speak to him about me by all means, it will give you a reason to call him!'

'Right! I'm not exactly pining for him, you know. Besides, I have Tushar to keep me entertained. He comes down to my apartment to hang out, every opportunity he gets, poor guy...I think Kulwant can be quite a handful to live with.'

'She's a freaking busybody, and a drunkard as well.' Arushi was disgusted, not mincing her words. 'She spreads all kinds of rumours about people, just because she has nothing better to do. But Tushar! Please, babe, he is not the guy for you—he's so up there, Nandita. He lives in his own world. He thinks he's much too good for us lesser mortals.'

'Oh, I'm not saying he's the guy for me, nothing like that. He's just sweet, that's all. He keeps bouncing his ideas for campaigns off me. I find that interesting. I've never been exposed to advertising or creative writing before. He seems talented.'

'Possibly, I don't really have much time for him. Before you came along, I kept the Sea Breeze population at an arm's length... too much grief!'

Nandita knew what she meant. In Mumbai, people lived in apartment buildings in such close proximity that everyone seemed to know what everyone else was doing. As far as she was concerned, it was too much information, but the likes of Kulwant thrived on the comings and goings of their fellow residents, and even fell to gleaning information from the maids and drivers.

An ageing not-so-successful actor passed their table just then, with a rather young girl draped on his arm.

'Arushi! How are you doing! Not seen you for a while...'

'Hey, Sandy,' she replied, not very enthusiastically. 'I'm great! You?'

He put his arm around the girl in a proprietary manner. 'Meet Sheena. *Very, very* up-and-coming star!'

Arushi blinked. 'That's nice,' she said. As the two moved away, both Arushi and Nandita burst into giggles.

'So there are degrees of up and coming!' said Nandita.

'Poor Sheena. I wonder what garbage he has promised her. He's a real has-been.'

'Forget Sheena. I'm dying to tell you about my presentation today.' Nandita recounted the happenings of the morning and as she spoke, she reflected on how much satisfaction she had derived from her first success in Sabarwal Associates.

Before long, the bar began to fill up, and there were what seemed like a hundred people milling around, in couples and groups. Laughing and chatting, they soaked up the sea breeze with their drinks in their manicured hands. Arushi amused Nandita by pointing out minor celebrities, spicing up each person with a hilarious anecdote or an abridged biodata. Nandita was particularly intrigued by a young woman dressed in an unbelievably slinky red dress, exuding personality and confidence.

'She's a tarot card reader,' Arushi told Nandita, noticing the direction of her gaze. She cupped her chin in her hands and leaned forward on the table, her eyes sparkling. 'Raima Baig. I've heard that she's pretty amazing with her predictions. She helped my friend Suzy out of a horrible mess last year, and Suzy swears by her. Would you like to?'

'Would I like to what, Arushi? You jump from one thing to another like an impatient bumblebee, honestly!'

'Consult her, silly. You know, peep into your future.'

'Are you nuts? Never. Suppose it's something awful?'

'It is something awful. I see Tushar approaching from behind you. What the hell is he doing here? Did you tell him?'

'Of course not... But babe, this is a bar, why shouldn't he be here? And he's not awful, give him a break!'

Tushar did stop to say hello, but to Nandita's relief, he did not join them. She didn't want a sulking Arushi on her hands.

Nandita took a contented look at the unbelievable buzz around her. She felt like she belonged, she was comfortable with Mumbai, and she reflected in wonder on how much had changed in the last four months. Above all, she finally felt a deep sense of fulfillment. Life couldn't be more different from Delhi, but as she kept assuring her anxious mother on the phone, it couldn't be better. Aditya also questioned her from time to time, less anxiously, wondering if she was happy in her new life. She was able to reassure him happily...life was good!

'So lets make career plans for you, darling,' she told Arushi brightly. 'By the way, how did your snake of an Ashish react when you told him you were quitting?'

'He was just sad, more than anything else. The thing is, Nandita, he really does love me. I know he does. He just feels too guilty about leaving Payal. She's a bit of the helpless type.'

'Arush, DON'T! Do NOT go down that road! He is playing both of you and wants the best of both worlds. How can you let yourself get fooled? Grow up, babe!' Nandita was emphatic, but her words made little impact on Arushi. She persisted. 'Arush, my mom's closest friend has been in a relationship with a married man forever. She's almost fifty now, and he's never leaving his wife. All those wasted years! You're worth so much more than this!'

'I'm not going back, if that's what you're worried about. Let's plan my career, by all means!' Arushi shook off her momentary despondency with lightning speed. 'What about that absolutely edible-looking hunk in the far corner? I think I could fancy him.'

Nandita laughed. 'Babe, that's Ranbir Kapoor, and I very much doubt he is even looking at you...but I would say you're on the right track!'

'Hmm...and of course, if I do get that job at Starling, it will mean the sexy Aryan is fair game. Unless, of course, you want me to lay off? If you say so, I will!'

'You're incorrigible! Do what you like, from what you've told me about the man, you'll be at the end of a very long queue indeed!'

CHAPTER TEN
Mumbai, March 2013

Tushar was struggling with his ideas, on the brink of a major breakthrough, but not quite there yet. Kulwant was having a rummy session at home with eight garrulous ladies, so he was stretched out on Nandita's living-room couch, in search of some peace and quiet, working on concepts for the new perfume, Karisma, that his agency was pitching for. It was the proverbial do-or-die situation—if they didn't manage to win the account, his promotion to creative director was a pipe dream. His vice president had made it quite clear that the onus was on him, and he knew he could certainly not depend on his art partner, Zack, to produce anything concrete in such a short space of time. Zack froze when there was a crisis. The best thing was that if he got the promotion, he could work with some of the senior art directors, who were much more proactive than Zack. The product was very high-end and the reams of research produced by the client servicing team had shown that their particular target audience was so used to buying designer perfumes from abroad that an Indian entrant had to be especially well positioned in the market to be taken seriously. Most beauty and fashion products that had been launched recently were for the young and yuppie lifestyle, but the team working on Karisma had decided to target an older, more sophisticated demographic and psychographic profile.

He rose restlessly and went into the kitchen to fetch a beer. It was Sunday afternoon and Nandita was messing around in the kitchen, making quesadillas. It was odd, but her exposure to cooking had been only towards exotic fare, and while she had no idea how to make daal and roti, she could whip up coq au vin or bœuf bourguignon in an instant.

'Do you have a favourite perfume? Something you identify with, something that says Nandita, something you *own* as yours?' asked Tushar, perching on the kitchen platform, very much in Nandita's way.

'Of course. I imagine every girl does. You'll have to move a bit, you're almost sitting on my grated cheese.' She rescued the plate of cheese and continued. 'Mine's BLV by Bvlgari. I love it. I even wear it at home, just to hang out by myself.'

Tushar stopped midway through opening the bottle of beer. 'You do? Cool!' A look of revelation crossed his face. 'That's it! That's what I want to do!' He gave a little whoop and hugged Nandita.

'What? Tushar, you've officially lost it now. Here, have a quesadilla, I think you need to be fed.'

'No, no, darling, you've just given me the best idea.' He took his beer and retreated swiftly to the sofa. He had barely sat down, though, when he bounced up and came back to the kitchen.

'Actually, I'll take that quesadilla. I'm too hungry to think properly!' He disappeared again and when Nandita peeped outside, she saw him scribbling furiously on his pad, his thoughts flowing with incredible rapidity. He barely noticed Arushi come in and Nandita decided to retreat into the bedroom with the quesadillas to give him some uninterrupted time to himself.

'He's made himself very comfortable,' commented Arushi as the bedroom door shut with a click. 'Honestly, babe, he's running wild in this house.'

'Oh, he's a nice guy, I like him. He feels happy coming here, and I don't really have to entertain him—he lies on the couch, listens to music and does his own thing. I gather Kulwant is entertaining her cronies today, so he needed to come here and work.'

'Yes, but he's so cocksure, and takes you for granted. He assumes he can just come and go as he likes.'

'Don't worry, I can put him in his place if I need to. He's harmless, bechara. Right now he's in the creative throes of dreaming up a perfume campaign.'

'Is he coming on to you?' asked Arushi disapprovingly.

'I don't think so,' Nandita replied with a laugh. 'Seems rather asexual, if you ask me.'

'Yeah, right!' Arushi sat on the bed and took a bite of the quesadilla. 'Ummmmm! Nandita, if this is how you cook, I am just dying to meet your mother!'

'Forget the quesadilla, you disgusting little foodie, tell me about the meeting with Aryan.'

'I told you already, babe. I got the job,' Arushi said indistinctly, her mouth full of food.

'Yes, but what did you think of him, what did he say? Don't be so obtuse.'

Arushi was anything but obtuse. She knew Nandita was dying to know everything that happened, and she was just trying her patience and teasing her.

'He was cute, he asked me to dinner, and I'm seeing him tomorrow night.'

'Arush, if you don't stop that right now, I will never feed you again, and you will never, *ever* meet my mother!'

This dire threat made Arushi capitulate. 'Ok, ok, chill! Seriously, he was fantastic. If I were you, I would thaw the cold war immediately and get on with it. I mean, what are you waiting for, woman? Guys like that don't fall out of the sky every day.'

'There is no cold war anymore. It's now a polite, formal, semi-cordial relationship. He actually smiles when he talks to me. Once in a while.'

'That could be called progress. Maybe. He did ask about you, you know. Can I have another one?' She gestured towards her empty plate.

'I though it wouldn't be long before we got back to the food. It's honestly incredible how you stay that size.'

'Running, sweetie, running. The cure to all ills!'

Nandita went out to refill Arushi's plate and found Tushar in deep contemplation.

'I think I've cracked it,' he announced. 'Tell me what you think.'

The campaign, he explained, would feature women the way they were, naturally. Not dressed for an evening out, not exquisitely made up, not styled to perfection. Just the woman, alone, in her own space. Maybe sprawled on a rumpled bed after an afternoon of lovemaking. Sweaty, lounging on a divan after a workout. Poring over a recipe in her kitchen, hands full of flour. But not ordinary women...these would be fashion icons, although not depicted in their public persona. Karisma, the perfume that lets a woman just be. All shot in black and white, and he even had the photographer picked out. He showed Nandita the copy concepts and waited for her reaction.

'I love it!' said Nandita. 'I'm sure your client will too. Have you thought about the women you want to use?'

'Older women...elegant style icons, eternally sexy and incredibly beautiful.' He was sounding more and more sure of himself as he fleshed the idea out loud.

Arushi emerged from the bedroom, wondering where Nandita had vanished. 'Hey Tushar, how's it going?' she asked.

'Good,' he replied tersely. He did not think much of Arushi's ability to judge his work, so he refrained from including her in the discussion. Tushar and Arushi existed in a chronic state of mutual disapproval.

Arushi herself was not particularly interested, and was happy to fill her plate from the kitchen and go back to the bedroom. She was thrilled with the new job at Starling, and really relieved to be rid of her irksome romantic entanglement. Now that she was out of it, she was incredulous about her stupidity. How could she have been so thoughtless and blind? Thank god for Nandita, she had been a real saviour. Arushi would never have made it without her. If her brother had found out, he would have been devastated. He and her sister-in-law treated Arushi like a daughter, and she could not bear to upset them in any way. With Nandita's support and coaxing, she had finally come out of her chasm and had begun to look at the world with new hope and renewed enthusiasm. She looked at herself in the mirror and saw that the shadows had gone from under her eyes, and she was back to being the fresh, pretty Arushi of the pre-affair days.

Nandita peeped in with two chilled beers and announced cheerfully, 'He's gone. You can come out now.'

Arushi gave Nandita a huge hug, on the brink of tears.

'Hey, what's going on? You ok, babe?' Nandita was bewildered by the sudden display of affection. Arushi was so impulsive, with such quicksilver changes of mood, one never knew what to expect with her.

'More than ok, thanks to you. I honestly have no words to say this, but you have been simply incredible.' Arushi almost choked on the words.

'Ok, if that's the way you feel, I know of a way you can pay me back.'

'Anything!' Arushi promised rashly.

'You have to come see *Olympus Has Fallen* with me.' Nandita knew Arushi hated seeing movies, especially action flicks.

'Sorry. Ask Tushar to take you. Or, your best buddy Niranjan. No, wait, ask Aryan…he'd happily take you anywhere.'

Nandita threw a cushion at Arushi, who collapsed laughing on the couch so recently vacated by Tushar.

Later, she thought about what Arushi had said. Maybe it was time to let things progress with Aryan…she *wanted* to get to know him, that was certain. She was very attracted to him—that was even more certain. And he? She would never know until she gave it a shot. After all, it was she who had drawn the boundary lines, and it was up to her to erase them. What the hell, she thought, there's nothing to lose really.

Later that evening, in a long, chatty phone session with her mother, she told Amrita that the last four months had felt like a year. 'So much has happened, Aai, and so fast. It's like being stuck in a whirlpool and just going with the flow.'

'That's all very well, Nandi, but you really have to be thinking of what happens next. You still haven't called Simi's friend in Malabar Hill—you know there is that MBA boy from London who is supposed to be meeting you. What's the harm? If you don't like him no one's forcing you to get married, but at least meet him, na?'

'Aai, you're sounding like Shanti's mother now. *Mi nahi kuthe mhante ahe.* I'm just too busy right now; I have no time to breathe. I will call, soon.'

'You are not too busy for nights out with Arushi, are you?' Amrita was sounding pettish, even to her own ears. 'I don't want to be one of those horrible matchmaking mammas, but Nandi, baby, you've got to get out and at least meet people. I hear Gaurav is seeing girls quite seriously, arranged types,' she added, rather irrelevantly.

Nandita giggled. 'Aai, you really are the limit. What does that have to do with me? Anyway, I promise you I will meet the London wala. Some Mehra, right?'

'Samay Mehra,' said Amrita, adding with a note of wistfulness, 'I don't want you to end up lonely like me, Nandi.'

Nandita was touched, and said gently, 'Was it that bad? You never seemed unhappy to me. If you were miserable, you hid it well, Aai.'

'Oh, never miserable. I had you, didn't I?'

'But you could have had more, if you had chosen to marry again. Things could have been different.'

'No. No, I couldn't.' The reply was final and as it had been in the past, Amrita refused to get drawn into any discussion about herself.

'So then if all else fails, I'll just have a baby too...then I'll be set!' Nandita quipped lightly.

There was a slight pause. Nandita was surprised; her mother was not prudish, and their conversations had always been open and easy. After a few seconds, Amrita spoke. 'Even that's not as easy as you think. You have to find a man to have a baby, you know.'

'Small technicality, Ma.' She changed the subject, sensing her mother's reserve. 'Let's just find you a man instead; you're far more marriageable than I am. If we put you out on the market, they will be falling over themselves to come woo you!'

Amrita gave up; there was no sense to be gotten out of her daughter that day. But Nandita *had* promised, and Amrita was hopeful that the MBA from London would pan out.

CHAPTER ELEVEN
Mumbai, April 2013

'Sharon, you can wrap it up for today. I don't think anyone needs to work late.' Aryan smiled at his secretary in a way she privately thought was irresistible. She considered her boss the most charming man she had ever worked for.

'Are you meeting Neil tonight?' he asked languidly.

Sharon had confided in Aryan about her new boyfriend and he had gently teased her all week. She blushingly said yes, they were going to a movie and dinner. She left, and Aryan leaned back in his large cushy swivel chair. It was all finally coming together, he thought. His hotel was beginning to take the kind of shape it needed to, and he was eager to see the project materialize as he watched. Aryan knew it was going to be his responsibility to set the benchmarks, raise the standards and ramp up the luxury factor, as far as the service ethics went. Style had to eventually translate into substance, and he had to be the one to see that it did. Now that the suite designs were finalized and work had started in earnest on the interiors, it was a load off his shoulders.

Aryan remembered that he was supposed to meet his friend Steve Walters for a drink that evening, at the Grand Hyatt. He was looking forward to a relaxing evening at his favourite bar. He finished the last of his emails in the car on the way to Vakola and left his laptop in the Mercedes with a sense of accomplishment. His phone beeped and he looked at the SMS absently as he ascended the stairs into the hotel. One message from Steve Walters. He opened the message and found that

Steve was going to be late—some last-minute work had cropped up. Would Aryan mind meeting a bit later, or should they just push it to another day? He was about to answer the message when he heard a familiar voice speak behind him.

'That's fine, Sabiha, we can take care of it even in your absence. I'll have Tara put in the finishing touches and send the samples across as soon as we get them.'

Nandita, here? He turned around quickly, and saw her standing on the porch behind him, saying goodbye to a vividly made-up older woman.

Aryan spoke easily. 'Nandita.'

She turned around and he saw surprise on her face. 'Aryan? Hi. Sorry, just give me a minute.' She exchanged a couple of words with Sabiha before the older woman drove off, and faced him again. 'That was one of my clients,' she said, a bit unnecessarily.

'I gathered. Are you on your way out?' he asked. 'Why don't you come in and have a drink?' He had no real expectation of her saying yes, but surprisingly, she hesitated for just a moment before she joined him at the stairs.

'Sure, why not.' They walked up the steps together. 'I was... I've been meaning to call and thank you for taking time out to meet Arushi,' she said.

Aryan was dismissive. 'That's not a big deal, Nandita. She's a good fit for us, and I am happy to have her on the team. I've hand-picked the local sales team myself—one can't be too careful about who is the public face of the hotel. I've always been very particular about that.'

'That's great. She's pretty thrilled about it.' Aryan was pleasantly surprised to hear the friendly note in Nandita's voice. She had actually agreed to have a drink with him, of her own accord? Well, what do you know? He had certainly progressed from persona non grata to person of consequence.

'How have you been? It's been a while since I saw you. All well on the work front?'

'Yes. Fantastic. Everything's going according to schedule. Haven't had time to breathe, though.'

'You need to have some R and R, then. How is Mumbai treating you otherwise?' As they walked, he dashed off a quick reply to Steve. *Postpone, for sure. Next week was good.*

Aryan was pleased at this unexpected opportunity to break the ice with Nandita. They had both been frosty and businesslike for several weeks now, and he was completely in the dark as to how he should proceed with her. He had been blown away by her presentation, by the content as much as by her. She was so talented, so composed and so confident. During the presentation, Nandita had had absolutely no idea that Aryan had been watching each nuance of her movements, and that every inflection of her voice was driving him absolutely crazy. It had cost him every ounce of self-control he possessed to keep up the cold war. She had been arctic with him, since the day they had met in the Sabarwal Associates conference room, and he had racked his brains to think of a way to apologize, but she had not presented him with the slightest opportunity to do so.

He was powerless whenever he saw her, and felt completely vulnerable. How did one ever get to this girl? She made him feel inadequate, and that was certainly a first. It was like she was put there to tantalize him, an object of desire that would forever be out of his reach. He had no intention of giving up on her, though, and was waiting for an opportunity to make her see how wrongly she had judged him.

Nandita told him that she would join him in a minute, and headed off to 'powder her nose'. Nobody she knew actually powdered their noses, but she could definitely use a fresh coat of mascara and lip gloss.

The bar was empty when Aryan arrived. He was dressed in his usual suit and tie, and looked fresh and groomed at the end of a long day at work. He had learned early on in his career that in this business, appearances counted for a lot, and he had made it a point never to be anything but perfectly turned out. He spent vast sums on his clothes and shoes, much to his mother's amusement. As a child, he had been perennially scruffy and couldn't have cared less if he was out in his pajamas. Now, his attire bespoke refinement and taste, giving him an air of elegance that added a distinct edge to his personality.

Aryan was a regular here and the waiters knew he began his evening with a chilled beer. He observed Nandita's arrival over the rim of his beer bottle. She walked with her head held high and just a hint of arrogance; he liked that about her, she was never apologetic about her blatantly striking looks. She was wearing a rust-coloured silk dress with a scooped neck, a straight shift that ended well above her knees. Her already long legs were lengthened by a pair of very high-heeled black patent leather pumps. He rose when she walked in, offering her the chance to choose where she would sit. She smelled divine, and he resisted the impulse to give her a hug and a peck on the cheek, which might have given been misconstrued…he was playing it very safe this time.

'You ok?' He smiled reassuringly, sensing her slight awkwardness.

'Yes. Do you usually hang out here in the evening?' She caught up her unruly curls and let them cascade over one shoulder as she sat on the tall bar stool, crossing her legs gracefully.

He sat down beside her. 'Sometimes. Actually, I am quite a bar person, I hate drinking at home alone.'

Nandita smiled. 'Do you have to do a lot of official socializing? I imagine it must be quite a drag.'

'Well, I'm new to Mumbai too, so I guess it helped me to get started with meeting people.'

He watched her place her order for a drink, smiling slightly as she ordered a cranberry martini. She read his thoughts, coloured a little and laughed. 'It *is* my favourite drink,' she said archly. 'But you didn't know that when you poured one down my dress, did you?'

'Of course I did,' he defended himself. 'I'm very selective about the drinks I pour on people. But I promise I will be very circumspect tonight. Besides, let me tell you, there's no better bar in Mumbai to have a martini than this one.'

They both laughed and the awkwardness eased immediately. He realized that this was the first normal social conversation they'd ever had, and was engulfed by a feeling of contentedness. He found it difficult to drag his eyes away from her face for more than a few seconds at a time and for the hundredth time, he inwardly marvelled at the effect this girl had on him.

'Are you even paying attention to what I'm saying?' Nandita asked softly.

'Of course I am!' He was actually engrossed in how the candle on the table was creating golden flecks in her green eyes, but he wasn't going to tell her so. 'You were telling me about Arushi. You're a very good friend, Nandita. She'll be fine with us, don't worry about her.'

'Are you enjoying Mumbai? I mean, after living mostly in the West, China, whatever, it must be a bit of a culture shock?'

He looked at her and replied enigmatically, 'Right now, I'd say I'm exactly where I want to be.' The waiter hovered expectantly, and Aryan ordered another beer for himself and a dirty martini for Nandita.

If she understood the context of his remark, she chose not to show it. 'I gather you hang out here a lot,' she said. 'They seem to know you pretty well!'

'Yeah. I like the place—it's never too crowded, and a great place to relax in the evenings. And they do perfect steaks. The one thing I miss being back home is the steak.' He glanced at her. 'My friend Rajat and I come here pretty often, actually... you know the guy I was with at the vodka launch?'

'Yes...with the really fair wife?' She paused, and said casually, 'The other girl with you, your girlfriend...'

Aryan interrupted quickly. 'Not my girlfriend. We went out a few times, but I'm not seeing her. In fact, I haven't met her since that evening.' He laughed easily. 'I guess you weren't the only one mad at me that night!'

Nandita laughed as well, and he became aware that she had finally forgiven him for that disastrous evening.

'It was a momentary aberration, I assure you. I'm not usually *quite* that badly behaved. I have no excuse, though. Unless...never mind!' He had been about to say that his excuse was that he had been completely bewitched by Nandita, to the point where he was not thinking straight, but decided that it would probably scare her off again. Obviously, even this time around, he was incapable of thinking straight!

She raised her eyebrow enquiringly. 'Unless what?'

'No. Not now. Maybe some other time I will tell you.'

'Coward!' She picked up a few peanuts and nibbled on them.

'Hungry? I could certainly do with some dinner.' He suggested they adjourn to the neighbouring Italian restaurant and Nandita admitted that she was actually famished.

'I've just remembered that I haven't eaten all day! Rajeev had me tied up in technical specs for a bio-lab today, and I've been at it non-stop.' She had not even touched the mouth-watering vada pav that invariably came into the studio as an evening snack.

'What kind of project is that? Sounds very specialized.'

'Oh, it is. Sabarwal Associates has never handled this kind of thing before, and Rajeev wants me to assist him on the project from scratch. It's a research facility that will house a BSL3 lab, very high containment. It's for Ve Pharmaceuticals. Rajeev has fixed up a meeting with the CEO, Abhimanyu Menon, next week, and there's tonnes of research to be done for it.' She swirled the remnants of her martini with her finger and picked up the last olive, popping it into her mouth. They rose and walked out of the bar towards the restaurant.

'I've heard Rajeev mention it...he seems very excited by the project. If he's asked you to work on it, he's obviously very pleased with your efforts. Have you ruffled many feathers among your colleagues? Niranjan, in particular. I've seen him look daggers at you, he obviously hates your guts.'

She shrugged wryly. 'Apparently, yes. He regards me as the interloper who has usurped his place and gotten ahead of the line, very much out of turn.' She tossed her head back defiantly as they entered the restaurant. 'It doesn't bother me, really. Obviously, I'd like him to cooperate, but this is the first time I'm actually working with a team, in an organization, and I'm learning how to deal with it on a daily basis.'

She's a fighter, thought Aryan. A fighter with aptitude and focus, and he admired the way she refused to be cowed in a hostile environment. He had watched Niranjan Kulkarni and the rest of the Starling design team from Sabarwal Associates ostracize her and try to put her down. It was an unpleasant situation to be in, and despite Rajeev's support, he was sure they managed to make her life as difficult as they could with their petty office politics. She had shown no signs of crumbling so far, parrying their thrusts with dignity and grace. But behind the façade she put up, Aryan could see a hint of vulnerability and the need to belong, and longed to protect her in whatever way he could. But he was a client, and had to keep his professional distance. He could not compromise the smooth flow of his project by taking sides in trifling office squabbles.

The menus arrived, and both of them lapsed into reflective silence as they chose their food. The restaurant was known for its thin-crust wood-fired pizzas, but both of them opted for pasta. Nandita selected the carbonara and Aryan decided on the marinara.

'Shall we have some wine?' he asked rhetorically, turning to the waiter and ordering it without waiting for Nandita to reply, 'We'll have a bottle of the 1990 Chainti Classico.'

'Do you remember all the good years for every region? I know you guys study all that stuff during your courses.'

'I wish I could say yes and impress you to bits, but no, only the region and the grape I really like. I like some Tuscan wines, but am more partial to the New World wines. I think French ones are sometimes a little disappointing.'

She leaned back and inclined her head. 'You seem to be deeply passionate about your work. Have you been with Starling for a long time?'

So she'd been watching him too, he thought with pleasure. 'Too long! I suppose you're right. Actually, I'm just very good at what I do.'

'Oh-o. Modest, huh?'

'Just stating a fact. Don't *you* know that you excel at what you do?'

'Yes, but I don't go around telling people so.'

'You don't need to. Your talent is patent.' He smiled at her. 'You are pretty exceptional, you know.'

She brushed off his praise, embarrassed, and asked instead about his life in the US. 'Have you never lived in India before?'

The wine arrived, was poured and pronounced potable.

He gave her a brief synopsis of his life, although he really wanted to ask about her. Nevertheless, he told her anecdotes of his bizarre childhood spent in the wilds of whichever part of the world his erratic parents fancied, which made her laugh endlessly.

Nandita took an appreciative sip of her Chianti and said wistfully, 'I would have loved to have grown up like that!'

'No, you wouldn't. You have no idea of the variety of creepy crawlies that can appear on your pillow in the night, to say nothing of the *boredom* of those long bumpy rides to nowhere. Or sailing down the Amazon at night, pointing your flashlight at the shores and seeing those beady orange alligator eyes staring back at you! Trust me, you were better off in, what was it, Vasant Vihar?'

'I guess. I never had a father to go camping with, so I don't really know what I missed.'

'Not that much, take my word for it!' He leaned back and watched her through half-closed lids. 'Ok, your turn now...come on, spill the beans.'

'There's not that much to tell.' She was interrupted by the arrival of the food, and both of them were hungry enough to suspend the conversation for a few minutes.

'Pasta all right?' Aryan asked.

'Nice. But not a patch on my mother's. I am spoilt silly as far as food goes. My mom is the best chef in the world.' She saw him look up in amusement, and said, 'No, really. She is in the food business and it's universally agreed in Delhi that Amrita Dharkar's Epicurean serves the best. It's that simple.'

'Wow. I'm impressed. Do you take after her?'

'Not at all. I can cook, but nothing to compare. Not even in the looks department. Aai's the beauty in the family,' she said proudly.

That did surprise him. He had been unable to take his eyes off Nandita all evening and here she was, calmly telling him that her mother was more beautiful than her. Either she was being unnecessarily modest, or her mother was indeed a paragon. Anyway, the question now was how to engineer the next date with Nandita. He filled her glass with more wine and settled down to watch her varying expressions in the flickering candlelight and listen to the gentle inflections of her voice as she told him about her life in Delhi.

'So why did you leave?'

Nandita rolled her eyes. 'I was dying to do something different. I was just so done with all the sameness. I can't tell you how happy I am that I did it.'

'And there's no boyfriend waiting for you back home?' He found it incomprehensible that a girl like her should be unattached.

'No.' She didn't elaborate and he forbore from pushing her, even though he was bursting with curiosity.

'Why architecture?' he asked, changing the topic.

'I always found it riveting to figure out how things take shape. I learned early on that historical civilizations are often known largely through their architectural achievements. Architectural monuments are cultural symbols, don't you think?'

'Never really thought about it, to be honest, but I guess you're right.' He seemed to ponder the question.

For Nandita, this was a new experience. The evening had started out as a quick drink at the bar, which she imagined would end before long. But it had played out quite differently, and she found herself drawn to Aryan in a way she had never been drawn to any man before. Gaurav Mathur had been a pleasant, comparatively mundane relationship, and could in no way measure up to what she was feeling now. Her earlier boyfriends in college didn't count; those relationships were for pure fun. Aryan stirred chords in her heart that she did not know existed. If she didn't know better, she would have thought she was falling in love with him. But wasn't she too smart to fall in love with an obviously commitment-phobic man?

CHAPTER TWELVE
Mumbai, April 2013

Khurshid, with a sense of self-importance, called Nandita from the reception. Didn't Nandita know that Mr Menon was arriving in a few minutes? Why was she not in Mr Sabarwal's office, where she should have been waiting for his appearance? Hadn't she told Nandita that Mr Sabarwal was going to be late, and she needed to field the meeting for a while on her own?

'Yes, yes, Khurshid, I'm coming! I need to approve these samples first, so that the veneers can be ordered. Just give me five minutes.' Honestly, that woman behaved as if the onus of running Sabarwal Associates rested only on her plump shoulders! In all fairness, Nandita thought, Khurshid had been very supportive of her from day one, helping her tide over some of the more unpleasant situations that the office politics had created. In addition, Nandita was always treated to lunchtime goodies from Khurshid's tiffin—Parsi delicacies like dhansak, prawn patia and sali boti frequently appeared on Nandita's plate. You had to be really privileged for that kind of attention from Khurshid. So she shouldn't complain. Nandita piled up all the assembled samples and called in her assistant.

'Sonia, please send this lot back, and we can go ahead with the ones I have marked in blue. Might as well place the orders today. As it is, we are on a tight schedule, so let's just move on quickly. What are you grinning about?'

'It's Saturday afternoon, Nandita. Do you even keep track of what day it is? I can only send these out on Monday morning. I hope you were not planning to come in to work tomorrow?'

Nandita smiled ruefully. 'I guess I'm just going quietly batty. When the people in starched white coats come to take me away, just make sure my laptop and iPod go with me; even in the mental asylum, I'll need those.'

'I'm willing to bet you're the type who cuddles your laptop when you sleep, instead of your stuffed toy,' said Sonia half-seriously. 'Honestly, woman, you need a break!'

'Right, tell that to Rajeev.' The phone rang. 'Yes Khurshid, I'm done. Oh, he is? I am heading there as we speak. Sorry, Sonia, got to run. You finish up and carry on home. I'll see you Monday.'

Ganpat, the canteen peon, came nonchalantly by and peered in. '*Tai, bhel magao tumchya sathi? Studio madhe magavlaya.*'

Nandita was famished, having skipped lunch. But she had no time for bhel now. '*Nako, mala ata vel nahin.* Thanks, Ganpat.' She mentally expressed gratitude to the absent Amrita once again for insisting that Nandita learn her native Marathi. In Mumbai, knowing Marathi made a huge difference. Especially if a cop caught you breaking a signal, she'd been told. She switched off her office lights, in accordance with the new rules laid down by Khurshid to conserve electricity, and headed towards Rajeev's office. Everyone seemed to have taken the afternoon off, including the dedicated Monica. Tara, she knew, had gone to Mahabaleshwar for the weekend with her current beau, a charming chef she had met at Seijo a couple of weeks earlier.

Nandita had heard a lot of good things about Abhimanyu Menon. She knew that he was an old friend of Rajeev's and was looking forward to meeting him. Khurshid was fussing around Rajeev's room when Nandita got there, offering snacks and beverages. Both the office assistants were missing this Saturday afternoon, so Khurshid was in her element, playing hostess. Nandita entered and found herself with a distinguished-looking man, tall, in his fifties, with curly salt-and-pepper hair. He was casually dressed in jeans and a pale pink linen shirt. He rose to greet her, his eyes widening slightly as she entered the room.

'Nandita? It's great to finally meet you! I have heard nothing but praises and have told Rajeev off for hiding you away all this time.'

'He has been keeping me buried under work, actually! Nice to meet you, Mr Menon. And I've heard lots about you too from Rajeev...especially about the last bench in the back of the classroom!'

'That's not very fair. I can assure you I have plenty of tales to tell you about *him*, but I'm too much of a gentleman to get started! And by the way, please do call me Abhimanyu.'

Nandita noticed he was looking at her rather intently. 'Those eyes of yours. Very unusual. You're an uncommonly pretty girl, Nandita.'

She accepted the compliment without embarrassment. 'The eyes are a family trait...I got them from my mother, and she got them from her grandmother,' she explained.

Abhimanyu's expression was inscrutable as he watched her fixedly. She sat down in one of the sleek Italian leather chairs. He inclined his head and rubbed his chin thoughtfully.

'Rajeev tells me that you have recently moved from Delhi. Do you have family there?'

'Yes, just my mother. I lost my father years ago.' Nandita got down to business.

'So, how soon are you going to be ready to brief us in detail on the project?'

'I hear you have already done a fair amount of research and preparation on BSL3 lab specifications. That's good, because you will be able to follow the brief more clearly, armed with all that information.' He paused and leaned across the table towards her. 'Sorry I'm staring, but you remind me very much of someone.'

'Maybe I just have a common face?' Nandita was convinced that he'd probably met her mother sometime, but wasn't going to bring that up now. Too many men were smitten by her mother for her to try and keep track of them.

Abhimanyu smiled, a little embarrassed. 'Certainly not. Quite the opposite, in fact. What's your mother's name?'

Nandita looked at him amusedly. 'Amrita. Amrita Dharkar. Do you know her?'

His face was unreadable. 'Perhaps,' he said noncommittaly. 'The name sounds familiar.'

The door opened and Khurshid appeared, followed by a peon bearing a silver tray with steaming cups of coffee and walnut brownies. Rajeev's royal wife from Bikaner had trained her seventeen-year-old daughter well, and young Ritika often treated her father's colleagues and guests to freshly baked cakes, cookies, brownies and biscuits for tea. If one thought about it, Nandita realized, the amount of snacking that went on in this office was positively sinful. The pizza delivery boys could find this place in their sleep, and the Udipi restaurant at the corner of the road did rocking business with the never-ending orders for medu wada and masala dosa that emanated from Sabarwal Associates.

The coffee was served, and Khurshid's bustling exit coincided with Rajeev's regal arrival.

'Oh good, I see you two are already at it. So Abhi, you finally meet my best-kept secret. Nandita, don't let him terrorize you, his bark is worse than his bite.' Unconsciously, Rajeev had a proprietary air about Nandita, and Abhimanyu could not help smiling.

'Yes, I finally met your paragon. You didn't tell me how charming she is. We've been having a nice chat waiting for you.'

Rajeev's arrival put an end to that conversation, and soon they were engrossed in a technical discussion. Nandita had done her homework well, and was able to ask the right questions and contribute to the discussion with sufficient understanding. Once again, Rajeev was proud of her quick, intelligent grasp of the subject. He could see that Abhi was impressed as well, and was pleased. It was very important to him that Nandita shine at her work, and be given every opportunity to grow.

The meeting ended late, and Nandita was mentally exhausted when she left. She had felt her cell phone buzz in her pocket several times but had not answered it, and finally pulled the phone out when she sank into the leopard-print seat of the dilapidated taxi. Four missed calls from Aditya! She rang him back immediately.

'Where's the fire?' she asked. It was so good to hear his voice. She had been too busy the whole week to even call him.

'I'm in your city, honey.' There was a note of excitement in his voice. 'Heading to your house from the airport, but I'm not sure where I should go in Bandra.'

Nandita was immediately roused from her fatigue. A quiver of anticipation ran through her. 'In Mumbai! Oh, that's fantastic! I can't wait to see you! Ok, I'm on my way home right now, will probably get back before you.' She gave his driver precise directions and then instructed him to put Aditya back on the phone.

'*Zara jaldi chalao*,' she commanded her own cabbie, impatient to get home now. 'So what brings you to Mumbai? Some new venture as usual?'

Aditya chuckled into the phone. 'You may not believe this, but I'm shooting an editorial for a new business magazine that's launching next month. It's a feature on the ten top businesswomen in India.' He reeled off a few names and Nandita was surprised. Obviously, her friend was taking this photography thing seriously. She was happy for him—it looked like he had finally found his calling. They continued to chat till her cab pulled into Sea Breeze apartments.

Nandita quickly removed all the extra stuff dumped in her guest room and had just finished putting fresh sheets on the bed when the doorbell rang. Aditya had brought large quantities of baggage with him, which didn't shock her. He was hopeless at packing and along with what was necessary, always carried a few things he *might* need, and several things he would never need. The two large suitcases and all the photography equipment barely squeezed into the tiny bedroom. Finally, he was free to give Nandita a massive, crushing hug. She was too excited to notice that he held her a little more closely and a little longer than normal.

He released her with a quick kiss on her forehead and surveyed his surroundings critically. 'A bit cramped, eh, Nan? Nice, but on the tiny side, I'd say.'

'Yeah, right! This is not rich playboy Aditya Arora's Panchsheel mansion in Delhi. It's working girl Nandita Dharkar's apartment in Mumbai. And let me tell you, I earn the money to pay the rent, if you have any idea what the concept of earning is!'

He looked aggrieved. 'I'm not a playboy, Nan. For your information, I am currently without a girlfriend, and I do know what earning is. Simi Bua has refused to let me touch any income from my dad's investments for one year. She thinks I need to learn responsibility. She's being very cussed this time.'

'And rightfully so. I wish she had done this five years ago. I have new respect for Simi Aunty.'

'Oh, go to hell. I thought you were on my side.'

'I am. You're just too blinkered to see that. Anyway, let's not fight about this again. At least, not right now. Give me all the goss from Delhi...how's Shanti doing? Happy with the Khanna khaandan?'

Aditya sat on the squishy armchair opposite the balcony. 'Busy making pickles the last time we spoke. The raw mangoes were beckoning, and it seems all the pickles in the Khanna house are still made at home. And Varun's youngest nephew has broken his arm, so everyone is in a tizzy.' He stretched his legs out with a tired sigh. 'Let's have a drink before the serious gupshup.'

Nandita had already made tea, but she abandoned that and produced a bottle of chilled white wine.

'This ok to start with?' She opened it and poured out two glasses, thinking that she would not have dared to serve this brand of wine to someone like Aryan. But Aditya was not knowledgeable about wine, he normally drank vodka.

'Sure. Whatever. You go first,' said Aditya, eyeing Nandita searchingly. 'Has Mumbai been everything you hoped for?'

'Oh yes, and so much more!' Nandita needed no encouragement to launch into a recital of all that she had experienced and how much she was enjoying her newfound freedom. As Aditya watched her, he noticed the subtle changes that had come over her. Confident she had always been, but now there seemed to be a new air of assurance, a sense of purpose, and above all, a contentment he had not seen in her for a while. She looked genuinely happy, and he was relieved. He had pushed and goaded her into taking this step at considerable personal loss to himself, and even though the decision had been hers, he felt responsible for her. He always had, in most situations, seen himself as her protector, unconsciously taking on the mixed role of the father, brother and husband she didn't have. He listened to her enthusiastic outpouring with a tiny smile lurking on his lips, occasionally interjecting with his customary sarcastic comments.

'So tell me more about this Aryan character.' With his usual acumen, Aditya had zoned in precisely on what Nandita had wanted to avoid discussing. How did he do it, she wondered. Maybe it was just that he knew her *too* well. 'You like him, it's evident.'

Yes, she did like him, didn't she? She had been trying not to admit to herself exactly how much she liked him. Trust Aditya to force her to confront her deepest feelings!

After the impromptu dinner at the Hyatt, Nandita had been unable to get Aryan out of her mind. He was great company, had a tremendous sense of humour and had made her feel very special. She found that he was constantly in her thoughts. It was apparent that he was quite taken with her, but she did not want to be another scalp in his belt, another Mohini or whoever the rest of his fan club comprised. He had called a couple of times after the dinner, but she had been genuinely tied up and the casual date had not yet been repeated. She was supposed to meet him sometime next week to do the rounds of a few of the art galleries in town, as he had expressed an interest in starting a small collection of contemporary Indian art. Nandita was familiar with the work of most of the younger crop of artists, and had promised to give him a guided overview of what to buy. She was looking forward to spending time with him again, but did not know how to reply to Aditya's question.

'I am not sure what to say, Adi. He's a wonderful guy, but it's all very up in the air right now. I would love you to meet him. Like, give me a male opinion, you know.'

Aditya realized that Nandita was far more infatuated than she would like to admit. He let it pass, and changed the subject to Delhi gossip, regaling her with tales of Shanti's domestic bliss and news of other common friends. Shanti's cousin Sheetal had dropped the unsuitable college sweetheart, and was now engaged to the highly eligible Rohit Agarwal, much to the family's delight. The most interesting news for Nandita was that Gaurav Mathur was getting engaged, apparently to a girl from Saharanpur. That tickled Nandita endlessly; she wondered how the poor girl was going to deal with Bach and Kafka. Aditya himself was off women, he told her. Too many transient relationships had left him disinterested and jaded, and he was now focusing on work instead. Nandita watched him as he spoke, thinking how impossibly good-looking he was. He was one of the hottest men she knew. Pretty amazing in bed too, she remembered wistfully from their dating days. No wonder there were women galore! Aditya never seemed to have to work to hard at finding female company. Disinterested and jaded, eh? *Well, we'll see how long that lasts*, she thought amusedly.

Amrita's business was flourishing, and her mother had just catered at the Kapoor family mega wedding with tremendous success, Aditya told Nandita proudly.

'Her new thing is Peruvian Japanese food. She has been experimenting and I get to be the guinea pig quite often. Don't look so sad, Nan. She's fine. In fact, she's enjoying her independence as much as you are. She's finally expanding the business and getting out a bit.'

Nandita had gathered as much from her conversations with her mother, but was happy to have Aditya confirm it. Through all her excitement of being in Mumbai and loving her new life, she had been plagued by a gnawing sense of guilt. Amrita was obviously not shattered by Nandita's departure. She should have known it; her mother was made of stern stuff, and was not the type to crumble easily.

'And you remember that guy, Rohit Dev, who wanted to interview her for his lifestyle show on some channel or the other? He's becoming rather persistent with his calls, not for the interview, but because he is nuts about your mom.'

'And he'll have as much success as the rest of them,' said Nandita calmly. 'There's been no dearth of men, Adi, but she just won't bite.'

'Oh, by the way, she said I should make sure you go meet some London guy, who Simi Bua is trying to set you up with. Should I just tell her you are otherwise inclined?'

'Blast! Samay Mehra. I completely forgot about him, and I promised Aai I would call.' Nandita was annoyed, and Aditya laughed.

'Don't worry, we'll tell her he was just not your type.'

'Fat lot *you* know about what my type is!'

'Well, I know what isn't, and trust me, Gaurav Mathur certainly wasn't your type, from any angle! And you'll be surprised at what I know about you, dearest Nan!'

Nandita shrugged. 'Thankfully, all that is history. But Aai worries so much. Says she doesn't want me to end up like her: alone.'

'You won't be alone. If no one else comes up to scratch, I'll marry you. We were pretty good together, weren't we?'

Nandita threw an accusing look at him. 'You're drunk. Good? We fought like jungle cats!'

'Yes, but when we made up...fully worth it!'

Nandita coloured. 'You're no genteman, Aditya Arora, to have brought that up!'

Aditya laughed. 'I haven't forgotten, Nan, and please don't say you have!'

Nandita did not answer, because she would not admit to him that she rembered every last detail of their wildly passionate sexual encounters. That was all over now! She changed the topic. 'Tell me about your assignment—how did you manage to land something this big so soon into your rounds of the agencies?'

'Are you surprised? I do have the gift of the gab, and though you may not know this, some talent as well!' Aditya launched into a witty description of his encounters with the agencies and their creative heads.

By 1.30 a.m., the second bottle of wine and at least half a bottle of vodka had been consumed, along with several platefuls of kababs from Karim's. Nandita had endured a really long day and fell asleep on the couch practically mid-sentence, so Aditya had to carry her to her bed.

CHAPTER THIRTEEN
Mumbai, May 2013

Nandita leaned back in her chair, stretching her aching muscles. She had been sitting in her office for twelve hours straight, hunched over her computer, too engrossed to notice how much she was straining her back. The BSL3 lab design was consuming her. At Abhimanyu's formal briefing session, he had explained that in a BSL3 facility, design plays a significant role in safety. She knew that labs such as these were used for handling organisms which could be highly infectious and potentially life threatening. Because the agents manipulated at BSL3 were transmissible by air, particular attention had to be given to air movement. The design was complicated and highly rigid specs had to be incorporated.

Nandita was all admiration for the dedicated people who worked with these high-risk viruses. It required a lot of tenacity and focus, and when she studied the protocol to enter the lab, the decontamination, the bio suits and all the paraphernalia that went into working in that environment, she was even more impressed. The Centre for Disease Control and Prevention, Atlanta, and WHO had set up stringent guidelines governing the design and use of high containment labs, and Nandita was learning more and more as she worked on the Ve Pharma building designs.

Rajeev was liaising with Nandita on the initial layout of the building with the help of the consultant who had been called in from Germany. As a result, Niranjan Kulkarni was now an openly declared enemy. He had not minced his words when he told Nandita that he would do everything in his power to have her removed from the bio-lab assignment. She was initially distressed by his hostility, but when she thought about it rationally, she decided her best course would be to ignore the threats and keep working. She'd find a way to sort him out somewhere along the way. She had managed to evade his barbs during the Starling design days and wouldn't lose her cool now.

Niranjan had a little coterie around him, who made life difficult for Nandita in small, subtle ways. She was too proud to even concede that it was irksome, and annoyed the perpetrators even more by acting supremely indifferent to their petty politics. Niranjan had, in reality, no reason to feel threatened by her, Nandita reflected. He was handling one of Sabarwal Associates' biggest clients, and had just finished supervising the building of a small township around a steel-producing factory. What possible reason could he have to grudge her the Ve project? Maybe he just disliked her. Well, too bad, that was his problem. Her colleague Monica had her own reading of Niranjan.

'He's just a big bully, Nandita,' she had said unequivocally. 'Don't let him get you down. He's like one of those swaggering two-bit political thugs who believe that they are genetically superior to the rest of us.'

Monica had an opinion on everything, which was usually very blunt and delivered without any euphemisms. She was short, round and comfortably ordinary-looking. Nandita usually found her judgment bang-on, and was happy that she had at least one outspoken, unbiased friend she could rely on in the organization. Some of her other anti-Niranjan allies were not as vociferous in her defense.

'I don't intend to let him affect me,' Nandita had replied. 'But what's the deal with the rest of them? It's like his word is law, and they all fawn around him like he's some freaking movie star!'

'Oh, he's great company when he chooses to be! They all hang out at various bars after work, and I hear he has a fantastic sense of humour—when he gets going, he can have you laughing your guts out.'

Nandita found that very hard to believe, having only seen his vicious side. But it was true that he seemed to be fairly well liked amongst his subordinates.

Tara had her own advice to offer. 'You need to sit down with him in a one-on-one discussion. He is really not such a bad guy, Nandita. But you know, before you came along, he was Rajeev's second-in-command here, and you have changed all that. You've infused a certain amount of freshness into this place, and he feels threatened. He has invested twelve years into this company, and he is seeing his position being eroded by a young upstart who has waltzed in out of the blue.'

'Is that how you see me too?' asked Nandita, a little hurt. 'A young upstart?'

'Of course not, you idiot. But I'm telling you how *he* sees it.' She regarded Nandita shrewdly. 'And you have to concede, being young and beautiful comes with its disadvantages. People mistrust you only because they assume you use your looks to get ahead. Plus,' she added, with devastating candour, 'it doesn't help that Aryan Rai was not too impressed with Naranjan, but seems to have quite a soft corner for you.'

Nandita flushed in annoyance. 'That's nonsense.' But she saw Tara's point.

'By the way, I came across a great source on the net for some Erte serigraphs... do you think Sabiha would approve? A couple of them would look fabulous on that recessed wall behind the desk.' Tara had changed the subject adroitly, but left Nandita with enough food for thought. She tried to focus on Erte, but kept seeing Niranjan's sneering face instead.

Nandita rose and stretched again, too fatigued to sit in her chair much longer. Strolling out of her office, she encountered

Ganpat happily circulating a bright pink cardboard box filled with pedhas. Grinning, he offered her the box, and she helped herself, raising her eyebrows enquiringly.

'*Mulgi zhali*,' he pronounced with satisfaction. A daughter, after three sons in a row, was apparently the cause of the celebration. Times were obviously a-changing— normally such broad smiles were, in Ganpat's milieu, reserved for the birth of a boy.

The two secretaries outside Rajeev's domain were chatting with gay abandon. Obviously, Rajeev was out. Nandita overheard snippets of conversation, focused largely on the exorbitant cost of tuition fees that both were shelling out to put their children through the SSC exams. This was a favourite topic, which came up almost as frequently as the antics of the saas and the bahu on prime-time soaps on TV. She lingered by Monica's desk to exchange a few words.

'How's the Seth residence coming along?'

'Don't even ask! The teenage son wants every gizmo ever invented to be incorporated, to say nothing of a king-sized bed and, get this, a full drum set. But the mother has bought the most humongous Husain painting for the only available wall, so that leaves no room for anything else…'

'And I thought I had problems! Good luck to you, sweetie, you need it.'

'They'll come around,' said Monica cheerfully. 'They always see reason, sooner rather than later. Let's see. How's the lab going?'

Nandita shrugged. 'Well enough. Too many rigid specs to stick to. And very time-consuming. I'm all jangled nerves right now.'

Niranjan passed by just then and nodded to the two girls. 'It's nice to know that some of us have so much spare time that we can gossip in the office. Great going, girls.' He moved on superciliously.

'He's impossible!' hissed Monica.

'Screw him,' said Nandita grimly, resorting to uncharacteristic vocabulary. 'He's not worth getting antsy about.'

There was a bustle outside and Nandita saw that Rajeev was back in the office.

'Hey,' she said as he walked towards her. 'Where've you been?'

'In my office,' he told her brusquely. 'And bring Niranjan.'

Nandita and Monica exchanged glances as he left abruptly, Monica emitting a low whistle. Obviously, something was in the air.

Nandita went to look for Niranjan and conveyed the summons to him. They both headed for Rajeev's office.

Rajeev was on the phone when they entered, and he motioned them to sit.

'Yes. Yes, yes, I understand. I will see you tomorrow at 3. Bye.'

He hung up and looked at both of them, his usually calm countenance visibly ruffled.

'They have asked me to pitch for the business,' he told them, still unable to believe the audacity of the builder. '*Pitch*! As if we're some newbie outfit which needs to prove itself.'

Nandita gathered he was talking about Sunville, the mill redevelopment project that was up for grabs in Parel. It was an assignment that architectural firms were waiting to get their hands on. Sunville was a multi-crore project involving the redevelopment of acres and acres of prime city space into an upscale residential and commercial complex, with cinemas, malls, restaurants, a spa and a luxury hotel. Unlike others in the city that had come up piecemeal, this was going to be planned from scratch and was Rajeev's dream project.

'I had almost decided to tell them to take a walk, but it's just too tempting. It's going to be pretty gruelling…are you two game?'

'Of course,' said Nandita, while Niranjan nodded grimly.

'Ok, we start work immediately. I will brief both of you together this evening, and we'll take it from there. We need to present our designs next month.' 'Who decides?' Niranjan asked curtly.

'The builder. A man called Naresh Patel. There's no question of not getting this job, I've been pursuing it for months.' Rajeev was emphatic.

'I can handle this on my own, Rajeev. I'm sure Nandita has too much on her plate with the whole Ve Pharma job,' said Niranjan, actually managing to sound sincere.

Nandita opened her mouth to protest, but Rajeev pre-empted her. 'Niranjan, I said both of you. Please don't let anything, and I mean *anything*, come in the way of getting this job. Do I make myself clear?'

Niranjan nodded, but did not look particularly chastened. On their way out of Rajiv's office, he cast a sneering look at Nandita and said, 'Don't get too comfortable here, Nandita. I am going to have you out sooner than you can guess.'

Nandita went back to her office and sat down in front of her computer. Niranjan's venom unnerved her. Why did he dislike her so much? She sighed, settling down in her chair. She would be working late again tonight, she guessed. The deadlines were crazy, and she had taken much longer over the bio-lab design than she had expected. The last few days had been a tremendous strain for her. Along with the mounting pressures at work, there was the task of entertaining Aditya. After three days of having him in Mumbai, Nandita was exhausted. His insatiable desire to party till the wee hours had not abated with his diminished bank balance, and she found it impossible to keep up with him.

Aditya had shot his businesswomen feature with so much sincerity that Nandita was forced to believe that he had finally decided to take something seriously in his hitherto flippant life.

Not only had he done a fairly competent job, he had decided to stay on in Mumbai for a while to source more work. The end result was that Aditya was now the newest resident of 7B, Sea Breeze Apartments, much to the disapproval of Kulwant Singh and, to a much larger extent, Tushar.

Kulwant had, predictably, voiced her disapproval. 'Beta, it doesn't look correct. What will people say? Unmarried girl like you, and some strange boy coming to stay with you? Doesn't look nice.'

Nandita had replied, in slightly quelling accents, that Aditya was not 'some strange boy', but a close family friend. There was no question of his not staying with her. Kulwant had refused to be cowed down. *'But beta, log kya kahenge?'*

'Kulwant Aunty, people should learn to mind their own business. How is it any concern of anyone else's? It's my flat, and my problem,' Nandita had snapped, all out of patience with the well-meant, though unwelcome advice.

Kulwant had tried to explain about decent societies and the unwritten rules of social conduct, but Nandita had brushed her aside firmly. Tushar had not said anything, but was sulking jealously. Aditya's presence in 7B had naturally hampered his own coming and going, and the fact that Nandita was on obvious terms of intimacy with Aditya rankled uncomfortably.

Nandita was too busy at work and with entertaining Aditya to have time for Tushar's ruffled feelings. She resolutely put all of that out of her mind and returned her attention to the computer screen. Now, how exactly was the ducted exhaust air ventilation system to be fitted? She rang Ganpat in the pantry and asked for some tea and the remnants of Ritika's freshly baked ginger cookies that had arrived that morning. As she applied her mind to the problem, the outside world faded away and Nandita was lost in her own space.

CHAPTER FOURTEEN
Mumbai, May 2013

Aditya and Arushi met on a Monday, the seventh day of Aditya's arrival. Arushi had been out of town on work during the frenzied first days of Aditya's appearance in Mumbai. The hectic travel schedule her new job at Starling entailed was exactly what she needed after the lull she had experienced, and she came back from Hyderabad with her mood uplifted, her face glowing with a sense of purpose.

Meanwhile, having decided that Mumbai was the place for a budding photographer to be, Aditya had been looking for an apartment of his own. He had concluded that it was unfair to Nandita if he just piled on her indefinitely. While he was not usually concerned about people's opinions, he had picked up some not-so-pleasant vibes from the residents of Sea Breeze and he would not stand for any aspersions cast on Nandita. He had been talking about looking for a reliable house agent, much to Nandita's mystification.

'Why bother, Adi?' she had asked. 'I love having you here!'

'You need your privacy, honey. And I don't want your neighbours pointing fingers at you. That Tushar character thinks he owns you, by the way. He was interrogating me the other night, big time. As for that Kulwant woman, she is just the nosiest creature I have ever encountered.'

'Oh, I would put her on par with your Simi Bua. Tushar's ok, though. He's a bit possessive about me, god knows why.'

'What on earth gives him the right to be anything close to possessive about you? Nan, you surround yourself with some pretty strange people, I have to say.'

'I know. Take yourself, for example!'

He laughed. 'See? That's what I mean. But don't you dare classify me with that supercilious Tushar. Seriously, Nan, I need to look for a place.'

Nandita relented. 'Ok. I will summon mucchad Pawan Bhandari. He's quite efficient actually, if you ignore his single woman bias.'

'Why, did he also give you a hard time? I think you arouse a protective instinct in the strangest of men.'

'That's crap. It's not protective, it's just being a bloody busybody.'

Aditya had agreed to meet Nandita's mustachioed broker, resigning himself to hostile looks from the neighbours till something suitable came up.

After a particularly long night of drinking and partying, he had woken up late that Monday to find that Nandita had already dragged herself to work. Having made himself a cup of strong coffee, he opened the classified pages of *The Times of India*, going to the Accommodation Wanted section. He wondered whether Simi Bua would be impressed with his new dedication to his work and let him have some of his family fortune. Or would he be renting purely on his earnings as a photographer? That did not amount to very much, as yet. He would have to slum it out a little bit, if that was the case.

He heard a key click in the front door and was surprised, wondering why Nandita was back at 11 a.m. He was destined to be even more surprised, because it was not her but some other girl, freshly showered and smelling of shampoo, dressed in tight tracks and strappy top, looking the picture of energy and good health. And quite lovely too, thought Aditya, still woozy from the previous night. Whoever she was, she seemed to be quite at home, he thought, walking in with a key as if she owned the place.

'Oops! I'm sorry, I didn't realize anyone was home.' She smiled cheerfully as Aditya put the newspaper down.

'Evidently,' he said in amusement. 'Do you make a habit of breaking into people's houses unannounced?'

'I'm not breaking in,' Arushi replied, very much on the defensive. 'You will notice that I have a key. It's not as if you are the "people" of this house, anyway. I should be asking you what you are doing here,' she added with a challenging look of mischief.

'Temporarily, I *am* the people of the house. Aditya Arora, Nandita's friend from Delhi.' He was still lounging on the couch in his shorts, making no attempt to get up. Arushi was quite taken with this indolent, handsome Aditya, tousled and very boyish in his tee and boxers, gazing appreciatively at her through half-closed eyes.

'Oh, I should have guessed! She talks about you all the time. I'm Arushi. I live upstairs.' She looked around. 'She's not here, is she? I need to borrow a pair of shoes. The yellow Prada ones,' she added irrelevantly.

'Arushi.' Nandita had spoken about her. 'The one who works at Starling?'

She looked gratified that he knew about her. 'Yes. Actually, I'm just back from a week of travelling and have taken the day off. You're a photographer, right?'

He nodded in the affirmative and asked casually, 'Want some coffee?'

The yellow heels were forgotten, and coffee turned into breakfast, which melded seamlessly into lunch. Neither knew the first thing about cooking, but Nandita had all the home delivery numbers sellotaped on the fridge, and they had ample choice. Aditya was amused by Arushi's energy, enthusiasm and zest for life, and stared with amazement at the amount of food she put away in the space of a few hours.

They chatted about everything, from the state of the nation to the state of Arushi's shoes, and Arushi never took her eyes off him for more than a few minutes at a time. In the space of a few hours, Arushi had heard about Aditya's nascent foray into the photography world, and Aditya knew every last detail of Arushi's new job, including her views on Aryan Rai. They spent the entire day chatting like old friends, getting more comfortable with each other with every passing moment.

When Nandita came home that evening, she found Arushi sitting cross-legged on a fluffy cushion on the floor, with Aditya leaning over her from the couch, engaged in deep conversation. The pair appeared to be on great terms with each other, and were making themselves cosy over a bottle of her best wine.

'Off women, eh, Adi? Am I missing something here?' she asked with interest, surveying the scene critically. 'When I left my home this morning, it was not the den of vice it appears to have become.'

'Not *vice*, Nan,' Arushi protested, peeping at her provocatively. 'I came in this morning to borrow your yellow shoes, and found Aditya here, all alone and really bored. I was just being neighbourly.'

'This *morning*? Are you serious? You two have been at this all day? Adi, pour me some of that wine too. I'm brain dead.' She flopped down on the big armchair, kicked off her shoes and looked at both of them sternly. 'Don't you kids do anything for a living?'

'Don't listen to her, Arushi, she's always cranky when she's tired,' smiled Aditya, who had risen from his prone position, carelessly flicking Nandita's cheek. He poured a glass of wine and handed it to her.

'Exactly. Which is why I intend to have an early night,' she said smugly, taking a deep sip and, turning to Arushi, 'And you, my friend are going partying with Aditya instead of me.' She tucked her feet comfortably under her legs, took another sip of her wine and sighed contentedly. Who would have thought that a reprieve would come in the form of the delectable Arushi?

'And that's supposed to be a punishment?' asked Arushi incredulously.

'Yes. If you've done it six nights in a row and worked like a dog the whole day every day, it certainly is.'

'Ok, ok,' said Arushi demurely, casting a look at Aditya from under her lashes. 'I'll take him out tonight. What are friends for?'

The evening had obviously been very successful, but Nandita had been too passed out to hear Aditya tiptoe in at 3 a.m. Arushi had taken him to four different clubs and bars before they had ended up eating kabab rolls on the street after 2, when no restaurant was open. The evening had ended in a long stroll down Carter Road, with the warm sultry breeze for company.

From that night onwards, Aditya and Arushi seemed to become an item. Actually, in retrospect, Nandita should have known it would happen. Arushi was on the rebound, ripe for a new relationship, and Aditya seemed like the heaven-sent opportunity. Aditya may have claimed to be celibate, but it was not in his restless nature to be without a woman by his side, however transient the liason might be. Nandita was not sure that it was a 'relationship' for Aditya, but they both seemed to be enjoying themselves. However, there was no saying that this would last longer than his usual whirlwind affairs.

Over the next few days, it seemed that she saw practically nothing of Aditya. She had initially been grateful that the onus of entertaining him had fallen to Arushi's lot instead of hers, and she could concentrate of one of the toughest design challenges she had faced in her career. But now she was a little hurt at Aditya's complete absence. She was usually asleep when he came in, and he was asleep when she left the house in the mornings.

Luckily, Aryan Rai had also been occupying her thoughts, and had been calling her on a regular basis. After the ice was broken during the impromptu drink and dinner, he had tried to get her to meet him again, putting her in a dilemma. She couldn't help remembering Arushi's tidbits of information on his free and easy ways with girls, and despite a strong inclination to accept his persistent invitations, she had allowed wiser counsel to prevail. Her perennial excuse of too much work was wearing thin, however, and Aryan was not a man to be so easily avoided. Last week, he had managed to pull her out of office in the afternoon to go with him to see an art show at Kala Ghoda.

'You know Nandita, if Rajeev Sabarwal really makes you work as long and hard as you claim he does, he should be sued for unfair labour practices,' he had told her on a half-serious note.

Having no answer, Nandita had capitulated. The expedition, as it turned out, had consisted less of art viewing and more of coffee and conversation.

'You are a complete fraud,' Nandita informed him, sitting in the Shamiana at the Taj. 'Why did you put on this big art show act if all you wanted to do was have coffee?'

'Because it was impossible to convince you any other way, remember? Would you be sitting here if I'd invited you for coffee?'

She looked confused, and he continued relentlessly, 'And please understand, I am running out patience for these silly excuses. Would you care to explain why you are so reluctant to have a damn drink with me?'

'Hardly reluctant, Aryan. I'm sitting here, aren't I?'

He rolled his eyes and shrugged. 'Under duress, you'll admit. Tell me, do you like movies?'

'Love them. And yes, Aryan, I would love to go for a movie with you.'

'I haven't asked you yet,' he pointed out.

'I know. *I'm* asking you,' she replied with a look of reproach.

He leaned back with an amused expression on his face, his eyes instantly crinkling into a smile. 'Now that should go down in history as a first!'

The movie idea had been a success, and Nandita had enjoyed his company as much as ever. The next day she took Aryan to Avantika Puri's fashion show, which Avantika had absolutely insisted she attend. It was Avantika's first individual showing in Mumbai and turned out to be an extremely well-attended affair. Aryan was treated to an unadulterated viewing of Mumbai's glitterati, dressed in dazzling couture, sailing in with as much confidence as the models did on the ramp. A bevy of photographers chose the well-known faces to waylay for a quick posing session, so that the next day's society papers could discuss who wore what, who came with whom and more importantly, who left with whom. Aryan and Nandita did not fall into the movers and shakers' category, but made a striking enough couple to be avidly clicked by the enthusiastic paparazzi.

'Do you do this kind of thing often?' he murmured, his air faintly condescending. They passed a svelte young socialite clad in delicately clinging aubergine chiffon, sipping a champagne cocktail, holding forth on the superiority of the new Prada bag over the Gucci one to a bored audience of fellow society queens.

'Not at all,' she replied, surprised at his attitude. She'd never thought him to be a snob. 'Avantika is one of my clients from Delhi, so it was unavoidable. For the most part, I think couture is a high level, carefully planned conspiracy to make women feel wretched about their bodies and the contents of their wardrobe.'

He laughed. '*You* are not one of those women at all. I think your body is particularly delectable.'

She glanced at him to see if he was teasing her but he looked perfectly serious. 'I guess I can never be the model type. I think that kind of skinniness is abnormal. The ones who are not bulimic are on cocaine, and that's the way they stay so thin.'

Some of the more honoured invitees headed towards the sponsored enclosure to join the tight but happening squeeze for drinks, while those not invited to partake of this privilege tried to appear unconcerned. Aryan was about to comment on this particular style of apartheid when a jingle of bracelets caught his attention. Avantika had spotted them at that moment and come over.

'Hey Nandita! You made it!' She gave Nandita a quick hug and told her to come to the after-party. 'I have no time to chat now, but I'll see you there, ok?' She shepherded them into the already packed bar area and disappeared into the crowd. Aryan and Nandita ruefully allowed the serious-looking man at the door to slide on the lime green wristbands that proclaimed their invitee status and manoeuvred themselves to the bar to get a drink.

'I think she must have had at least twenty-five bracelets on her arm,' said Aryan in awe. 'How can she stand that jingling?'

'Style, my dear, anything can be borne as long as a statement is made,' replied Nandita, laughing. 'Did you ever read *Little Women*? Remember the phrase "Dear me, let us be elegant or die!" That's what it's all about.'

Aryan confessed that he had never read *Little Women*, but when he looked around he agreed that the statement was amply justified. One young fashionista had a tiny purple-and-pink feather stuck to the corner of her eye, while another was encased in a shimmering lamé dress that was so tight and so short, she could barely walk, let alone even think of sitting. Neither Aryan nor Nandita were too familiar with the Mumbai party crowd, and were able to amuse themselves watching the absurdities in play around them without any pangs of guilt.

The show started late but the audience didn't seem to mind. Nandita thought the clothes were magnificent, and the enthusiastic applause suggested that the Mumbai glitterati thought so too. By the time it was over, neither was interested in the after-party.

Exiting surreptitiously so as to escape Avantika's notice, they headed out as quickly as they could through the crush of photographers and media. Aryan took Nandita to the Thai Pavilion for dinner. As they walked into the restaurant together, she spotted Abhimanyu at a corner table, with an older couple. She took Aryan's arm and went up to say hello.

'Nandita! It's good to see you!' Abhimanyu stood up and shook hands with Aryan, and looked at him speculatively. 'Aryan, finally. I've heard a lot about you from Rajeev, and from Nandita, of course.' Nandita blushed.

They chatted for a few moments, then Aryan steered Nandita to their table. 'He's a good-looking man,' he said, as soon as they were out of earshot. 'Seems very fond of you. And what has he heard about me from Nandita, by the way?'

'Nothing in particular. You just cropped up in the conversation a couple of times. It's not like you're constantly on my mind, you know,' she added acidly.

'Cat,' he replied with amiable good humour. 'You may as well admit I am and be done with it.'

CHAPTER FIFTEEN
Mumbai, May 2013

The offices of Ve Pharmaceuticals were long overdue for an overhaul, thought Nandita. This dark wooden panelling was like something out of an old Hindi movie. Abhimanyu's office was just a slight improvement on the décor outside, and she stepped in with a mildly critical air.

'Don't be so snooty, Nandita. Everyone doesn't have Rajeev Sabarwal budgets to style their offices,' Abhimanyu said admonishingly as he observed her reactions.

'I'm not being snooty. All this dark wood depresses me. I'm a light and sunshine kind of girl.'

'I'll keep that in mind and have our next meeting at the beach,' he replied meekly.

'Stop being defensive. All we need to do here is pull out the panelling and paint the walls white. And add some art and some pictures. See?' She noticed a photograph of an impish-looking boy on the desk. 'Is this Prateek?' Abhimanyu had spoken about his son to her, and Nandita knew that his mother had remarried.

'That's my boy. Handsome devil, isn't he?'

'Very. How's the birthday stuff going?'

'He wants to do it in Goa. The list is growing longer every day, and I've given up trying to coordinate. My efficient Preeti has taken charge.'

'Efficient she certainly is; she guards you like a dragon. It's practically impossible to get you on the phone with all her cross-questioning. Where is she today, by the way?'

'Come down with a viral. Ok, where's the fire?'

Nandita had requested this long-overdue meeting to go over some budgetary problems she was facing, and to make some decisions regarding choice of material. Since all this had a direct bearing on the design aspects of the job, it was imperative that it be sorted out immediately, and since Abhimanyu had been in Bangalore for the last week, Nandita had had to wait. Abhimanyu tackled each issue point by point, effectively and efficiently, as a result of which the meeting was over in forty-five minutes.

'Wow. I had thought that this was going to take the better part of the afternoon.' Nandita was agreeably surprised.

'If you crave my company so much, you can come with me to my next meeting,' said Abhimanyu half-seriously.

'Really?' Nandita laughed. 'Who are you meeting?'

Abhimanyu named a top Bollywood actor who was the current rage of Hindi cinema.

'Right!' said Nandita disbelievingly. 'He's invited you for afternoon tea.'

'Actually, he has. Why don't you just come with me?'

Nandita was too intrigued to say no, so she accompanied Abhimanyu, ignoring the pangs of guilt that she eventually decided she need not feel, considering how many hours of work she had been putting in over weekends. Sometime during the drive towards Bandra, she became aware that Abhimanyu was telling the truth and they were indeed headed to the screen idol's house.

'You know, Nandita, Preeti is going to immolate herself if she finds out I took you with me. Please make sure she never does, because she would have worked a month of Sundays to be allowed to come on this visit!'

'I won't! But do tell me why we're going. It's not like he's your drinking buddy or something, is it?'

'He's not. But he's a big philanthropist, and is spending large amounts of money with us on charitable programmes to provide medical treatment to AIDS patients. He doesn't like it to be generally known, but he sponsors the families of the patients and works with us on providing the medications. He's heard that Ve does cutting-edge research on TB, and wants to work with us on that as well. That's what today's meeting is about.'

Nandita was deeply moved. The star in question had a public persona that completely belied this humanitarian aspect of his nature. How little one actually knows about anyone, she reflected. We judge people by their exterior, and take pleasure in denouncing someone as flighty or promiscuous or saintly, little knowing the actual truth. Even Abhimanyu, she thought. She had taken him to be the suave, witty, socially prominent friend of Rajeev, but as she got to know him, she had seen the more serious side of his character and had become extremely fond of him. She knew that he took particular notice of her, and though she wondered why, it did not strike her as odd or unnerving. She enjoyed his company and had spent time chatting with him on many subjects that had nothing to do with the building of the Ve lab. Abhimanyu had spent hours with Nandita in the briefing stages and she felt very comfortable working with him. Now that he had stopped quizzing her on her green eyes, he treated her with professional respect tinged with friendly teasing, much in Rajeev's own manner.

The meeting with the Bollywood hero was overwhelming for Nandita. The star value of the man was not in the least overrated, she decided. He was every inch the charming, charismatic hero of the screen. He pledged staggering amounts of money to Ve Pharmaceuticals and, in answer to Nandita's question, explained that working with an NGO meant too much press and publicity. He preferred to do it this way, because he was not doing it to impress anybody. Ironically, to Nandita, that was the most impressive part.

Abhimanyu insisted that he wanted to drop Nandita back to Sea Breeze, since they were already in Bandra. Nandita was now comfortable enough with him not to find this odd, but could not for the life of her figure out why he spent so much time with her. He was always circumspect and though he teased her often, she did not find it lover-like in the least.

'You are a strange man, Abhimanyu.' She looked at him curiously. 'How is it that *you've* never remarried? You've been alone for a long time, haven't you?'

'Well, not alone, precisely. There have been women. To tell you the truth, I never met anyone I really wanted to marry.'

'Never?'

'Can you believe it? I think I'm just a polygamous guy.'

Nandita laughed. Somehow, Abhimanyu as the philandering playboy was an amusing picture. As the car pulled in to Sea Breeze, she invited him upstairs. Abhimanyu got out of the car to say goodbye, but refused the offer of a slightly more palatable cup of tea. He gave Nandita an avuncular hug and a kiss on her cheek, and got into the car. Aditya happened to have arrived a few minutes earlier, and was watching this scene critically from a few feet away. He accosted Nandita as soon as she entered the building.

'Who was that? Appeared mighty familiar with you. Can't have been Aryan, because he looked too old. Unless your Aryan is an older man?' The elevator arrived, and he ushered her in with alarming formality.

'Don't be silly, Adi. Of course it wasn't Aryan. And anyway, I'll thank you to remember that he's not *my* Aryan. This was Abhimanyu Menon, CEO of Ve Pharma. You know, the biolab project I am doing.' They reached the seventh floor and she opened the door, kicked off her shoes and looked at Aditya, her eyes sparkling as she sank on to the couch. 'And you'll never guess who I just met!'

She recounted the essentials of the visit briefly and waited for his reaction.

'What I want to know is, what is this bio-lab guy doing, taking you to his meetings and dropping you home? And *why* exactly was he kissing you? He is your client, Nan. Much older than you. What can his interest in you possibly be? Has he tried to pull anything? Does he come on to you? I have seen enough of these fatherly guys, they get you to trust them and then move in for the kill.'

'Aditya Arora, are you mad? He *is* my client, and he's perfectly circumspect, for heaven's sake. What on earth has got into you? I'm telling you I went to the King's house, and here you are, droning on about poor Abhimanyu!'

'Screw the King! "Poor Abhimanyu" is not as poor as you think. You may be twenty-nine, but you are very naïve, Nan. He has more than a common interest in you, that's evident... and you have to admit that I am a very good judge of people. *And* I am usually right about such things.'

Nandita saw that Aditya was genuinely upset. She gave him a hug and said in placating tone, 'I know you're very perceptive, and that you mean well, but can I be allowed to make my own mistakes sometimes, if I *am* making a mistake? Which I don't believe I am. He is a thorough gentleman and has no designs on me. I'm very sure of that.'

Aditya grinned ruefully. 'Arre yaar, I guess I'm a bit hot-headed when it comes to you. It's just a habit. Can't have any guy buzzing around you like that. Be careful, ok baby?'

'I will. I promise not to get seduced by him. But where's Arush?'

'Some spinning class. Decided she's getting fat.'

'Oh god, not again! Now we'll have her demanding fat-free salad dressing and skimmed milk.'

He laughed. 'It won't last long. That girl has the appetite of a horse.'

'By the way, her sister-in-law called me today. She was asking me a zillion questions about you. You seem to have made a favourable impression, but she was just checking you out.'

'Tell her to chill. What business is it of hers?'

'Of course it's her business. She sees Arushi hanging with you 24x7, and she is supposed to express no interest in who you are? You see me with Abhimanyu one time and you get hysterical about it...and you're not my sister-in-law!'

'Ok, ok, I get your point. But I'm not an evil lecherous old man preying on girls half my age.'

'Oh, you're impossible! So how is it going with her, anyway?'

He shrugged. 'She's fun...I guess we're having a good time. She's showing me the city.'

Nandita felt a pang of jealousy. *She* was the one who should be showing Aditya Mumbai, it was *her* city now. And he was enjoying it with Arushi instead. She shook off the feeling. Why should she be jealous of Arushi? She needed to stop feeling possessive about Aditya.

'Good. There's so much to do here!' Nandita forced herself to sound enthusiastic.

'I know! So tell me what's brewing on the Aryan front. You've hardly spoken to me in the last few days!'

Nandita gave him an exaggeratedly surprised look. 'I wonder why? I mean, I'm always around, aren't I?'

'Are you mad at me for neglecting you?' he asked gravely.

'Not at all, I enjoy being ignored by my best friends. Seriously, I myself have no idea what's brewing. He calls me every night, keeps asking me out, but I am not jumping into this. I need some time.' She twirled a lock of hair around her forefinger, a habit she had formed as a child when something bothered her.

'What for? I get the feeling that you're definitely nuts about him, from what I can see. So where's the hitch?' Aditya helped himself to a large apple from the dining table and bit into it. He was watching her closely as she thought this over.

'You make everything sound so simple. It doesn't work that way in the real world.'

'That's a load of crap and you know it.' Aditya put the apple core down and looked at Nandita disbelievingly. 'You either like the guy or you don't. It *is* actually as simple as that!'

'Spoken like a true man. Never spare a thought for the consequences.' Nandita threw her hands up in resignation.

'Consequences happen whether you like them or not, Nan, you can't plan them or avoid them. It's not about Aryan or any other guy, it's about you and what you want. You know, I've never seen you with a guy who deserves you. If he is the one who is destined to make you happy, why not?' He retired to the kitchen to look for something more substantial than an apple, and came out a few moments later with a bag of masala chips. 'Shit, Nan, there's nothing to eat in the house. Screw Aryan, why don't we go to China House for dinner tonight?'

'Don't be rude. Aryan is in Bangalore for a couple of days. Actually, I want to lie in bed and be a couch potato, or do I mean bed potato? You guys go on. I'm really tired and I need to do nothing.' She yawned and stretched in a languorous, feline way.

Nandita was actually looking forward to watching some mindless chick flicks and switching off completely from everything and everyone. Aditya offered to stay home with her that evening, but she suspected that meant Arushi would stay too, and she would be forced to be a third wheel in their date. She convinced him that it was not necessary at all. He and Arushi should go out as planned and let her vegetate in peace.

She heaved a sigh of relief when the door finally closed behind him and Arushi, who was showing a dangerous inclination to partake of the vegetating with Nandita. She changed into her favourite yellow pajamas. Instead of a movie, she decided to start on the new season of *Suits*, which the enthusiastic Tara had given her just yesterday. Nandita enjoyed the racy legal shenanigans of Mike Ross and Harvey Specter, so she felt quite happy to get into bed with a huge bowl of freshly popped butter corn and the DVD remote in her hand. As the credits began to roll her cell phone rang, and she cursed aloud. Then she saw that it was Aryan calling.

Nandita had met Aryan several times since the dinner at Thai Pavilion, largely for work, and often in the restrictive company of Rajeev Sabarwal. He had got into the habit of calling her every night, and she loved the lengthy phone conversations with him. It was so much easier to exchange confidences with him when she couldn't see the expressions on his face. Aryan had a disconcerting way of reading her mind, so she could never get away with evading issues when she was face to face with him. As it was, he was convinced she was avoiding him, and she had to admit to herself that this was partially true. He had stopped pretending to be circumspect with her and was openly pursuing her now. But how could she just give in to this unpredictable guy? Was it even going to be possible to resist his steely determination to get her, one way or another? He was the kind of man you did not say no to, but probably should, for your own safety.

She answered the phone. 'You back?'

'And hello to you too! No, I'm not, but I miss you. I'm calling from my very lonely room in Bangalore.'

'Lonely? You? Come on, do you expect me to believe that?' She switched off the TV and lay back on the pillows.

'You'd prefer to think that I am sitting here with a pack of girls having some wild orgy?'

'No, no, not a whole pack! One at a time is more your style.'

'That's my cat!' He laughed appreciatively. 'You've just decided that I'm some martini-spilling low-life who flits from woman to woman, having indiscriminate sex without so much as a pause to take a breath. I mean, it's true that I did flit occasionally, but that doesn't make me some perverted womanizer. Come on, honey, do you really think that's who I am?'

Nandita could think of lots of things that Aryan was, but she wasn't going down that road. She had no intention of getting into a casual relationship with a man who had the power to occupy her mind and heart the way Aryan did. How was she going to cope when he 'flitted' on, leaving her to pick up the mess? And mess there would be, that was for sure. Besides, he was her client. Wasn't there supposed to be some kind of taboo? But late at night, lying in bed and having protracted conversations with him about everything from her paranoia of lizards to his fetish for steaks from Spiaggia in Chicago, she realized that none of her objections would matter eventually.

'I have no intention of telling you what I think of you. Your ego would never be able to stand it.'

'Someone should have warned me about you. But I love you the most when your catty claws are out. I'm not going anywhere, Nandita, you may as well know that. I'm not giving up on you so easily.' His teasing tone had suddenly turned serious, and Nandita's heart skipped a beat.

'When are you back from Bangalore? There is a new show opening at Jehangir Art Gallery that I want you to see. And yes, I *will* go with you.'

'In that case, it's a date. I'm back tomorrow afternoon, can we have dinner?'

'Actually, I have to meet a client from Dubai with Rajeev tomorrow evening for a dr—'

Aryan interrupted, his voice suddenly arctic, 'Don't even complete that sentence. I don't want to hear it. Nandita, you can't avoid me forever. If you'd rather I don't call you at all, please say so, but don't play these childish games with me.'

'I'm sorry, I really am, Aryan. I'm not playing games. It's just that…I can't get involved with you in the casual kind of way you seem to expect, it's—'

'*I* seem to expect? How the bloody hell do you know what I expect? I call you every fucking morning and night, I am ridiculously patient with your flimsy excuses, I control my behaviour around you so that I don't scare you away, I've been insanely crazy about you since I laid eyes on you, and you're talking to me about *casual*?' He sounded furious and Nandita could barely comprehend what he was saying.

'Aryan, I…'

'Forget it. Just forget it. I can't get through to you at all. You're the…'

'Aryan, please listen to me,' she pleaded. 'I am honestly not playing with you. I don't want you to stop calling me. I want you to call me morning and night. I want you to be patient, and insanely crazy, and all those lovely things you just said. What I don't want is to be just another Mohini in your life. I don't think I could bear that.' There was a hint of tears in her voice.

'Nandita, you're a fool. I never knew you could be so blind. Mohini was nothing to me, even she knew that.' There was a faint noise at the other end. 'Are you crying?' he asked apprehensively.

'No. I'm eating popcorn. Lots of butter and chilli flakes. And before you bite my head off again, I do have a meeting with the client from Dubai tomorrow.'

'Ok. Point taken. I'll call when I land in the afternoon. But please let's not have this Mohini crap again, and *please* stop carrying on as if I am Casanova reborn. Deal?'

'Deal,' she whispered.

'By the way, did you go check out the site this morning? Is everything on schedule?'

Nandita was only half focusing on the conversation that followed. Insanely crazy, he'd said. *Insanely* crazy? Aryan wasn't the insane type. In fact, he wasn't even very romantic, she thought. Instead of whispering sweet nothings, he'd called her a fool, and blind. Men were incomprehensible. But Aditya had been right as usual. He had seen it much more clearly than she had. What was wrong with her? She prided herself on her people skills, her ability to judge her peers. But in the case of Aryan Rai, her feelings had been too deeply involved to be objective. Nandita Dharkar, you are losing your touch, she told herself. And after the highly emotional exchange that had just taken place, she was still not sure where exactly they stood with each other.

CHAPTER SIXTEEN
Mumbai, May 2013

The busy lane off Colaba Causeway was riddled with hawkers, pedestrians, cars, urchins and tourists. Nandita decided to give up on the taxi and walk the rest of the way. She had been told that Indigo would be packed on a Friday night, and it seemed to her that the case had been fairly understated. Nandita had never been to the restaurant at night, but had enjoyed a couple of very satisfying lunches there. Aryan had got back from Bangalore two days back, and been insistent on the phone about dinner tonight. He had informed her that it was *not* a date, lest she should think of another excuse. He had invited Rajat and Anjali, and it was just a friendly evening out, so could she please not pretend she was working late *again?* Nandita had told him that she would not have minded it being a date, but Aryan retorted that it was too late for that; he had already invited his friends. Nandita had heard enough about the Guptes to feel like she knew them and was looking forward to the evening much more than she had let on to Aditya and Arushi.

She took forever to get dressed. It was all very well for Aryan to say it was a casual evening out. Men were so blasé about clothes and Aryan, she thought, looked his elegant self no matter what he wore. Particularly in those well-cut suits he favoured. She spent an agonizing hour in front of the mirror, discarding one outfit as too eager, the other as too don't-carish, the third as too come-hither and a couple as plain tarty. A slim-fitting grey satin dress with a high front and practically no back was thrown aside as too formal. She cursed Arushi mentally for being out gallivanting with Aditya when she should have been here to help her friend in this crucial hour of need. Eventually, Nandita settled on a slightly flared wine-coloured dress in crepe silk, with cutaway shoulders, which fell in soft folds around her hips. She wore no jewellery; a pair of very high black stilettos and a black patent leather clutch were her only accessories.

Negotiating the short stretch between the main road and the restaurant—that was tucked away in a by-lane—on her spiky heels on a bad pavement took all her concentration, so it was only when she arrived at the gate of Indigo that she noticed Aryan standing and watching her unsteady progress with warm amusement.

'I told you to let me send you the car. Why do you have to be so dammed independent?' he said in response to her quizzical look. He gave her a prolonged hug, and suddenly and unexpectedly kissed her, right in the middle of the narrow gate. Nandita felt as if she would melt, all sensation in her body coming to a complete halt except for the feel of Aryan's lips. When he realized they were blocking the entrance squarely, he reluctantly let go and they squeezed their way into the buzzing bar area.

'Let's wait for Rajat at the bar...they're late as usual.' He steered her in the direction of a miraculously empty barstool. He was behaving as if it was the most natural thing in the world to kiss someone out of the blue as if they *belonged* to you, she thought, with a mixture of indignation and light-headedness. He turned and surveyed her appreciatively.

'You look amazing, by the way. Has anyone told you that you have the most mesmerizing eyes?'

Nandita was still weak-kneed and laughed a little unsteadily. 'No. Never. No one notices my eyes.' She took a deep breath and looked at him, barely able to control her voice. 'Aryan, don't do that again.'

'Why not?' he countered. 'Unless you don't want me to.'

Nandita was emphatic. 'I don't! At least,' she amended a bit lamely, 'not in full view of the doorman and thirty people in the street.'

'I'll keep that in mind. Is thirty people at the bar an acceptable audience?' He drew her close again and she pushed him away with a laugh.

'I'll think about it, but you need to get me a drink first.'

'Coming right up. Can I interest you in a new form of beverage tonight? The caiparojkas here are absolutely awesome.'

Nandita tossed her head back, a characteristic gesture that Aryan found very endearing. 'Why not? I'll try one of those.'

Before their drinks could arrive, Aryan spotted Rajat and Anjali and waved them over. Nandita was pleasantly surprised to see how warm they both were towards her. It occurred to her that Aryan must have spoken to them about her. This suspicion was confirmed a moment later when Anjali gave her a light hug and said that she had heard so much about her, and was looking forward to getting to know her.

'I can't imagine what he has told you. It's most intimidating to be judged in advance!'

'Oh, nice things, I assure you!' Anjali gave Aryan a playful nudge. 'I don't hear Aryan talking about anyone as much as he does about you.'

Aryan's eyes met Nandita's briefly, and he smiled at her in a way that made her quiver. 'You have to take everything she says with a pinch of salt. Anjali gets very carried away.' He leaned over towards Nandita, and said in a lowered voice, 'Having said that, I must admit that I do talk about you quite a bit!'

Nandita was aware of a rush of pleasure. She fluttered her eyes in mock disbelief and started chatting with Rajat, while Anjali kept teasing Aryan. The next hour flew by, and Nandita tried to go easy on the caiparojkas. She certainly could not keep up with Anjali, who had evidently a mind-boggling capacity to hold her liquor.

'No wonder you work for a booze company, Anjali. I bet one of the major criteria for hiring senior management is their ability to actually consume the stuff!' Nandita was all admiration.

'She's had plenty of practice,' said her irrepressible husband. 'I could tell you some stories of when we were at Michigan together during our undergrad year...'

Anjali interrupted unceremoniously. 'Aryan, you have to say something in my defense! They're just out to malign me. Sheer jealousy, I say.'

'From my side, it's jealousy for sure,' Nandita quipped. 'I would give anything to be able to knock them back like that.'

'Oh look,' said Anjali, momentarily diverted. 'It's Radhika. With a new man, no less!'

'Anju, screw it. Don't get into conversation now, she will just be never-ending as usual.' Rajat looked a bit apprehensive. It was too late for the warning, because it appeared that the never-ending Radhika was headed directly towards them, new man in tow.

'Anjaleeeee!' Radhika had a high-pitched voice, which rose several octaves in excitement. 'Daaaaarling! Where have you been, it's been ages since I saw you! So much to tell you, darling! Do you know that Vinita has *finally* found out about Ricky and Shanaya? She's mad as hell, and baying for his blood. And,' she dropped her voice, not so much for confidentiality as for effect, 'Ricky has *moved out*! Can you believe it? And the poor kids, they...'

Rajat interrupted, 'Radhika, I don't think you've met our friends, Aryan and Nandita?'

'Oh, cool! How come I haven't seen you guys around before? I know most people around town, you see.' She said it with a touch of pride.

'We're both fairly new to Mumbai; maybe that explains it?' Aryan replied, catching Nandita's eye and trying not to laugh.

Radhika eyed Aryan with interest, sizing him up with obvious curiosity. The new man fidgeted in the background, and Radhika belatedly remembered his presence. Before she could introduce him, however, the waiter arrived to announce that their table was ready, upstairs on the terrace. Thankfully, Rajat murmured an apology and they escaped, leaving Ms Never-ending to tackle another unwary acquaintance and pour out the saga of the philandering Ricky.

'She's unbearable,' said Rajat as they sat down. 'All that naatak. I can't understand why you encourage her, Anju.'

'Arre baba, I feel sorry for her. It must be awful to be abandoned by your husband for a floozy half your age, in such a callous way. Don't you see, she hides her humiliation behind the profusion of young men she parades, but this is not who she really is. Would you believe it, she actually spent a whole bunch of the money she got out of the divorce settlement to set up a trust to help abused slum women. She's not really a bad sort.'

'Does that give her the licence to behave in this ridiculous fashion wherever she goes? She makes herself a laughing stock.'

'I agree with Anjali,' Nandita said. 'Don't be so harsh, Rajat. Circumstances make people do strange things.'

Aryan looked at Nandita searchingly, as if he had detected something beneath the surface of that remark. He was right, as usual. Nandita was thinking of Arushi, and how she had embroiled herself in the unsavoury affair with her boss. That was not the real Arushi she knew. The real Arushi was the bright, lively, endearing girl who had captivated Aditya and had, in such a short space of time, become Nandita's dear friend.

Anjali and Rajat got up to say hello to a couple across the terrace who had been waving frantically, and Aryan turned to Nandita.

'How's Arushi, by the way? Is she enjoying the job? She's been travelling a bit.' Aryan proved once again that he could read her mind.

'She's great. She and Aditya have set a new record for the number of nights they can party into the wee hours. And I might as well be a part of the furniture, as far they are concerned. He needs to get to work, I think…they're maddening, the way they are right now.'

Nandita had watched, a little protectively, while Aditya and Arushi grew closer. True, Aditya was not sentimental, and she had never known him to get deeply emotional about any girl, but everything looked like it was going well. His shifty restlessness was still very much in evidence, but there could be no mistaking the glow that pervaded Arushi's entire being these days.

Aryan reached out and took Nandita's hand, holding it tightly. 'Do you miss him? It's hard seeing your best friend so absorbed in someone else.'

'Adi may be absorbed in anyone else, but he and I have always been the first priority for each other, Aryan. Nothing can ever change that. So yes, I do miss him, but I don't feel too badly about it. And anyway, I myself have…' She stopped short in confusion.

Aryan looked at her mischievously. 'You yourself have…?'

'Have been too busy to feel left out,' she replied smoothly. Of course, that was not what she had been about to say. But she was not going to admit to Aryan that she herself was too besotted by him to care what Aditya and Arushi were up to. How long was she going to be able to deny it? He was sensitive, intelligent, beyond sexy and altogether adorable. Perhaps she was being an absolute fool, but she couldn't shake off the thought of how speedily he had disposed of Mohini and the rest of his fan club.

Aryan laughed. He leaned forward and kissed her softly. 'Liar. And we now have to postpone this conversation,' he added, seeing Anjali and Rajat return.

'Has the wine arrived? Oh, you haven't even ordered it! You two are hopeless. Do you want us to move to another table, Aryan, and leave you alone with Nandita?' Anjali was looking from Nandita to Aryan, her expression comical.

'Certainly not,' said Nandita. 'You are not depriving me of the opportunity to hear the Michigan story that Rajat is obviously dying to tell. And,' she added triumphantly, 'We *have* ordered the wine, as you can see for yourself!' The waiter had arrived at this most opportune moment with a chilled bottle of chardonnay, as both women wanted to drink white.

Rajat started on Anjali's stories and, with his superb ability to recount an incident with embroidery and embellishments, reduced his audience to unmitigated mirth. Anjali didn't seem to mind all this fun at her expense, and the wine disappeared well before the main course arrived. The second bottle was ordered, this time red, and as Nandita watched Aryan lean forward to say something to Rajat, she suddenly felt an overwhelming sense of longing. She wanted this man. She wanted to belong to him. All she could think about was how it would feel to be wrapped up in his arms, her body entwined around his. All the Mohinis seemed immaterial suddenly, fading away into a blur of irrelevance. Nandita could not imagine why she had been concerned about any woman in Aryan's past. Nothing mattered, except for the sudden realization that her need for him superceded everything.

For once, it seemed that he was oblivious to what she was thinking. He was engrossed in what Rajat was saying, and Nandita felt as if she could keep watching him like this. Forever. She took a deep swig of her chardonnay, and was settling into a comfortably warm haze of well-being, when a cold voice spoke behind her.

'Well, hello, stranger! So you have not actually dropped off the planet, it would seem. It's been absolutely *ages!*'

Aryan looked up, his expression unreadable. The woman behind Nandita moved towards him and bent down to kiss his cheek. She was in her early thirties, Nandita guessed. Short, skinny, dressed in glittering black, she resembled nothing so much as a viper. She waved an airy hello to Anjali and Rajat and settled her venomous gaze on Nandita.

'Aryan, you do move on rather quickly! Surely it was someone else the last time?' Her tone was silkily insinuating.

Nandita smiled at the woman sweetly. 'Yes, it was...but Aryan has been quite busy since he dropped off the planet. And how could you possibly be expected to know? Surely it has been... absolutely *ages?*'

Rajat laughed outright at the ludicrous look of frustration on the woman's face. She cast a look of pure hate at Nandita, then spun on her heel and retreated.

'Aryan, please tell me she is not one of your exes,' said Anjali pleadingly.

But Aryan was looking at Nandita, and she at him. Anjali realized that they were, at that moment, unaware of both her and Rajat. There was warm laughter in both their eyes.

Aryan took Nandita's hand and pressed his lips to it. 'Thanks, sweetheart. I've never seen her so demolished. And no, Anju, she's definitely not one of my exes, as you so crudely put it. She tried, though, I'll give her that!'

'She looked like she could happily carve me into sushi. I don't think I even want to know who she is.' Nandita sniffed appreciatively as the chargrilled New Zealand lamb was placed in front of her.

'Oh, she needn't bother you,' said Rajat to Nandita, cutting his steak with surgical precision. 'Chandni is a socialite with nothing to recommend her except her dubious wealth and her unwelcome presence at every Page Three party.'

'This lamb is delicious...and goes so well with the Merlot. It goes against the grain to fuel your ego, Aryan, but I have to say you do know how to pick a wine.'

'My lovely cat's baring her claws again. Is this better than Mom's cooking, by the way?'

Nandita laughed. 'Once you have eaten Aai's food, you'll never crack this joke again, trust me!'

Aryan told Anjali and Rajat about Amrita's business, and Anjali was quick to recognize the name. 'Epicurean? Our company used them last year, in Delhi, when we launched one of our premium wines at a really select dinner party, and everyone was going ballistic over how brilliantly the pairing of the food was done. That was your mom, Nandita?'

'Yes,' she replied, pleased by the lavish praise. 'I think I remember that event. She went to such pains to plan the menu; she really loves that sort of thing. Aai's a food genius.'

'So when are you cooking for us, Nandita? Has anything rubbed off from your mom?' Anjali was always impressed with anyone who displayed the slightest culinary talent, since she herself possessed none beyond the ability to boil eggs.

Nandita was game. 'Whenever you want. It's not a big, stressful event for me, can be quite impromptu.'

The evening was warm and sultry, and the conversation veered around to the much-awaited rains. Monsoons were an event in Mumbai that neither Aryan nor Nandita had experienced so far. The arrival of the rain would be a welcome relief from the sweltering heat and humidity in the city, thought Nandita. She was used to Delhi heat, but not the muggy weather of coastal Mumbai. So much for dining al fresco—not the best idea at this time of the year.

Nandita was relieved to get out of the heat and into the cool comfort of Aryan's Mercedes. She was also pleased to have him to herself for a while; though Rajat and Anjali were great company, she wanted to be alone with Aryan.

Aryan instructed the driver to head towards Bandra, and settled himself with a bottle of beer he had carried out from the restaurant.

'I think I've had way too much to drink…that last glass of wine was quite the limit,' she told him, leaning on his shoulder comfortably.

'Clearly, I've created a monster. You were never into wine, were you?'

'Didn't know the first thing about it.'

He laughed. 'How's your week looking, by the way? Can your Dubai clients and bio-labs be abandoned for a bit?'

'Not really. Why?' She looked up at him enquiringly.

'Because,' he said carelessly, 'I would like to take you to Goa for my birthday.'

'Your birthday! When is it?' She was taken aback by the sudden invitation to Goa, with all its implications.

'The fourteenth. Yes, darling?'

Nandita didn't hesitate for even a fraction of a second. 'Yes. Yes, I would love to go to Goa with you,' she said.

Aryan's driver glanced into the rear view mirror just in time to see Aryan's head bend over Nandita's.

CHAPTER SEVENTEEN
Mumbai, June 2013

Nandita's level of frustration was rising by the day. Work had begun on the Sunville project, but Niranjan made sure that she was as peripherally involved as possible. The bulk of the major ideating fell to Rajeev, and Niranjan worked closely with him on the conceptualizing and the general direction the project would take. Nandita was left with the execution and supervision of the actual drawings. Inwardly fuming, she refused to engage in a power struggle with Niranjan, believing that it would do more harm than good in the given circumstances. Rajeev was out of the office more than in and appeared preoccupied; with the current pressure of work, she did not want to be on a tale-telling, complaining binge. That said, she was so mad at Niranjan that they barely spoke anymore. She was almost finished with Ve, and apart from a few small jobs in various stages of completion, there was nothing of importance on her plate. The resentment against Niranjan was building up, but she had absolutely no idea how she was going to tackle him.

As she sat at her desk one afternoon, Nandita was contemplating her plan of action when Tara bounced in, armed with a foaming cappuccino and an oversized muffin. She plonked down uninvited. She was dressed in a tight pair of jeans and a clinging top that displayed every curve of her plump, sexy figure.

Tara obviously had some new romantic angle in her life. Her shoulder-length hair had been cropped short and had a virulent orange streak going through the left side. What on earth was going on with her? Nandita did not have to ponder the question for too long, because Tara herself was bursting to tell all.

'He's a musician,' she informed Nandita without preamble. 'Cute, Nandita, unbelievably cute! French.' She bit into the muffin, and continued, her mouth full. 'Met him at the Blue Frog a week ago. He has the same haircut, with the identical streak, so we thought it would be fun if I did it too!'

'French, huh? Do you even know the guy, Tara, I mean, a week...' Nandita stopped. She and Tara were poles apart in their views on men and dating. Was there any point in saying anything?

'As long as you know what you're doing,' she said.

'I don't think I do, but I honestly don't care. I'm just nuts about him.' Tara was blissfully unconcerned. She never thought about the long run, the consequences, the logistics or any of that. Tara lived for the moment, grabbed whatever she wanted and learned to live with the consequences of her mistakes.

'Don't you ever feel apprehensive?' asked Nandita curiously. 'I mean, about getting in and out of relationships so easily? And with people you hardly know! There was that painter guy from Cal, and your famous Italian chef... God, Tara, I'm not a prude, but it would scare me shitless!'

'But that's the fun of it, Nandita! The adventure! Besides, I know all about Dominic. I googled his band the very same night that we met...his pictures are all over the Internet. Mmmm,' she popped the last crumbs of the muffin into her mouth and said wistfully, 'That was too good. Wish I had a doughnut!'

Nandita laughed and shook her head in disbelief. 'Why am I not surprised? You googled your *lover*? Is there anything you *don't* google?'

'No,' said Tara proudly. 'I mean, there's a whole world out there to explore, and the Internet's the easiest way. A friend of mine ate a bad oyster in Goa once. She called me in a panic, so I googled it. The solution, apparently, is to have three quick shots of vodka immediately. Which she did, and she was fine! A bit drunk, mind you, but who cares for that?'

Nandita couldn't stop laughing at this, and Tara was in the middle of another Google anecdote when suddenly, with no warning, Niranjan strode in. Without so much as a glance at Nandita, he addressed Tara coldly.

'Is there any chance that we can have the Nagpur drawings ready this afternoon? If you can spare some time away from your gossip session, of course.'

Nandita looked at him calmly. 'There's no need to be nasty, Niranjan. She's just having a cup of coffee.'

'You please stay out of my business, Nandita. Not all of us have the good fortune to be able to cosy up to our clients the way you do. Some of us actually have to work to get anything accomplished!'

'Would you care to explain that remark?' Nandita's tone was icy, because she would not show him how furious she was.

'Certainly!' he retorted, equally furious but less in control of himself. 'Can you deny that your client Aryan Rai is also your boyfriend? As is Abhimanyu Menon...you really know how to hook them, don't you? Is there any way that you can look at me in the face and tell me that your relationship with Abhimanyu Menon is purely professional? Do you think we are all idiots, Nandita, that you can pull the wool over our eyes? You think we will get fooled by that pretty, innocent face of yours?' His voice had risen, and by now there were several people outside Nandita's office, listening to his tirade in shocked silence. Her assistant Sonia looked like she was about to burst into tears.

Nandita herself was too stunned to speak. The insinuations, the venom in his voice, the public manner of his offensive, were more than she could comprehend. Tara rose quickly and murmured something to Niranjan, sweeping him away from the scene. The rest of the staff dispersed slowly, stealing furtive glances at Nandita's white face.

Nandita was shaking. How dare he confront her in this malevolent fashion? Who the hell did he think he was? Just because he was so abysmally insecure about his own position, he had no right to take off on her like that! Yes, she had formed personal friendships with her clients, but in no way did that mean that she worked less diligently than any of her colleagues. If anything, she did much more, because she had far more to prove. When she thought of the nights spent at the office, the hours of dedicated work, Nandita's eyes stung with angry, frustrated tears.

Such a raw unleashing of spite had not come Nandita's way before. She was unnerved to think that anyone could dislike her as much as this. She quelled her immediate instinct to pick up her bag and walk out of the building. She thought for a moment, then got up and walked into Rajeev's office. The outer room was empty, and so was his room. The peon clearing away empty cups told her that Rajeev was in the conference room. Nandita headed towards Khurshid.

'Who's at the meeting in the conference room? Any clients?' she asked.

Khurshid had also heard the row, and tried to remonstrate with Nandita. 'Look, don't get…'

'Khurshid!' Nandita was not to be swayed.

Khurshid sighed. 'No clients. Internal brainstorming on the Vashi project.'

Nandita turned and walked into the conference room. She opened the door without knocking, and deliberately left it open as she went in. She knew that there would be a small congregation outside in seconds, and she wanted everyone to hear.

Rajeev was in the midst of scanning some sketches that were being discussed. He looked up.

'Nandita. What's up?'

'Sorry to bother you, Rajeev. Just wanted to get something clear,' she said pleasantly, ignoring everyone else in the room. Monica, who was part of the team, was eyeing her apprehensively. 'In the last five months that I have been working with Sabarwal associates, have you ever had reason to be dissatisfied with the quality of my work?'

Rajeev was taken aback. 'Nandita, where's this coming from?'

'Please, Rajeev. Have you?'

'Of course I haven't. You are well aware that you have tackled two difficult projects in a most exemplary way. Why are you even asking me this?'

Nandita ignored the question. 'And in the rule books of this company, does it say anywhere who the staff can and cannot be friends with outside the office?'

Rajeev got up, thoroughly perplexed. 'No. There is no rule book. Will you please tell me what is wrong?'

'Oh, nothing,' she replied with a sunny smile. 'Just wanted to clarify those two points. For my benefit, and everyone else's. Sorry to barge in you like this.' She exited so quickly that the eavesdroppers outside had no time to disperse. She knew that the interchange in the conference room would be repeated to Niranjan in a matter of minutes, and that had been her sole intention.

Tara, who had been one of the eavesdroppers, followed her back to her room.

'Neat,' she said. 'Classy, efficient and to the point. You are one hard-assed babe, Nandita.' The admiration in her voice was manifest.

'I am not the type to crumble or lie down and offer myself as fodder for the likes of Niranjan,' replied Nandita matter-of-factly. 'And you can tell him that, if you like.'

'You're not suggesting that I am part of this attack against you?'

'No. I'm sorry, Tara. I'm still fuming. You don't want to be around me right now.'

Tara gave an injured sniff and departed. Nandita was about to get back to work when she was interrupted by Rajeev's entrance.

'Is it too much to ask what that was all about?' He didn't sound too pleased. Nandita felt a bit guilty, but did not apologize for her erratic behaviour.

'I don't want to tell tales, Rajeev. I suggest you ask Niranjan Kulkarni to explain.'

'Cut the bullshit, Nandita. I want an explanation from you, right now.'

She sighed and recounted the incident that had occurred earlier in full view of the staff. Her description was succinct and shorn of any embellishments. Rajeev's expression darkened, but he remained silent till she had finished speaking. He got up and walked towards the window, his back to Nandita. She watched him curiously, waiting for a reaction.

'I'm sorry you had to go through that, Nandita.' He came back and sat down heavily. 'Niranjan has an attitude problem, I've always known that, but he's indispensable to me right now. I'll speak to him.'

'No, no! Please. I'll handle this my way. I don't want you to intervene at all.'

Rajeev's face looked drawn. 'It'll be harder than you think. I'm going to have to be away for a while, and Niranjan will be running this place in my absence. You don't have to report to him, of course, but he will be the guy in charge.'

'Away? But…Sunville…how…there's so much happening right now! You never said anything.'

He raised his eyes and Nandita was shocked to see how strained he looked. 'Pallavi has been diagnosed with breast cancer, unfortunately in the third stage. Abhimanyu has a close friend who is an oncologist at Sloane Kettering, and I'm taking her to New York this weekend. I'm not sure how long I'll be away.'

Nandita was shell-shocked. 'I…don't know what to say, Rajeev. She's going to be fine. You're getting her the best possible treatment. Oh god, I'm so, so sorry to have piled my miniscule, stupid problems on you at a time like this!'

Rajeev smiled tiredly and replied, 'Don't be silly. I have enough faith in you to know that you will manage to work it out. I will be in touch with you over the Ve job, and anyway, you have it completely under control. It's Sunville I'm worried about. You'll have to work with Niranjan on that one, Nandita. You two are my best designers, and it's just a question of working on the plans exactly the way we've discussed.' He looked at her sympathetically. 'Try not to let him bother you. He's not really such a bad guy. It's just that someone with your talent, looks and flair is enough to make him insecure. He comes from a very different background, and is always wary of the more savvy competition. It's not easy for him to fit into the social mileu that people like you and I find very comfortable. That makes him defensive.'

'Let's not get into all that right now. You just focus on Pallavi, and we'll take care of the rest.' She leaned forward and laid her hand on his arm. 'If there's anything I can do, you just have to say it.'

'I may take you up on that. Ritika is going to be alone here with her grandmother, so if she needs anything, can I ask her to call you? She's very fond of you and really looks up to you.'

'Rajeev, you know I'd be more than happy to help!'

'Thanks.' He looked at her and stroked his chin thoughtfully. 'By the way, coming back to the speech that Niranjan gave you, I understand the Aryan bit quite well: just the way you two look at each other has been enough to set tongues wagging in the office.' Nandita blushed—she hadn't realized it had been quite so obvious. 'But,' he continued, 'what's the deal on this Abhimanyu comment? I can't believe he's been giving you the eye, that's not like him at all.'

'Rajeev, don't be absurd, of course he hasn't. How can you even think of something like that? But it's puzzling, nonetheless. He takes a lot of interest in me, and frankly, I enjoy his company. We're friends. I occasionally spend time with him. Is that so odd?' Her question was as much to herself as it was to him.

'Knowing Abhimanyu, yes, I think it's odd. He doesn't usually befriend girls half his age. Unless…' Rajeev had a puzzled frown on his face, but he didn't elaborate.

'I gathered that. Should I put an end to it? I don't want to; I'm very fond of him.'

'There's no need for that. I've known Abhimanyu for too many years to believe he is capable of any harm. He's the best friend a guy could have. He's been so amazing with Pallavi's cancer…just took charge and organized everything.' Rajeev's voice broke and Nandita felt a surge of pity. This must be the worst kind of agony for him, she thought.

After he left, Nandita began to wonder if Niranjan had been right. Her purpose of moving from Delhi had been clear; she wanted to move ahead professionally, to get out of the rut she had been stuck in for five years. Rajeev Sabarwal had given her a much larger canvas to work on, and from that perspective, her objective was on its way to being achieved. But had she screwed up somewhere? Let's face it; her personal life had also been in a shambles a few months ago. She had been a not-so-content single twenty-nine-year-old, jaded with men and relationships as she knew them. Then why should she feel any angst over Niranjan's taunting remarks? She was entitled to have both a career and a relationship with a man, and make a success of both. So what if that man happened to be her client?

She thought about what Rajeev had said about the social gap. He was right, of course. But Rajeev himself had surmounted that issue, years and years ago, when he had decided to overcome the same social gap that Niranjan was facing now. If it was so important to him, why couldn't Niranjan do the same? She shook her head in frustration.

Nandita had planned to meet Aryan at his house that evening, and she was somehow really glad of that. She did not want to spend the evening alone. The big showdown in the office, the dismal news about Rajeev's wife, the prospect of spending weeks with a hostile Niranjan heading things—it was all too much for one day. All she wanted to do was crawl into her pajamas and spend the evening with Aryan. Ever since the trip to Goa to celebrate his birthday, Aryan and Nandita had been spending every available hour together. The three days had been idyllic, and Nandita had never been happier in her life. Instead of staying in one of the deluxe resorts, Aryan had rented a quaint old Portuguese-style bungalow on the beach, just for the two of them. A young Goan couple had cooked and cleaned for them, so they actually never stepped out of their little paradise for the entire trip. In between endless bottles of beer and wine and languorous sex on the antique four-poster bed, they had sampled Rosie's prawn curry and pomfret rechado, and lain on the beach, watching the waves lapping their feet. It was three days that Nandita would not have exchanged for anything in the world.

As the taxi pulled into Aryan's building in Worli, Nandita's phone rang. It was Tushar.

'Guess what! The perfume campaign has been approved, we won the account!'

'That's great, Tushar, congratulations. I'm so happy for you. Does that mean your promotion is in the bag?'

'Without a doubt! Can we celebrate?'

'Not tonight, I'm not home. Can I call you?'

'Sure.' He sounded disappointed and Nandita felt guilty. She had been too busy to keep in touch with him over the last month.

'We'll do it soon. I promise. You take care.'

She got out of the elevator and rang the bell. Aryan's servant opened the door and smiled when he saw her.

'*Saab aya nahi. Late ho gaya*,' he said.

Nandita was not surprised. Aryan had been working late the whole week, in preparation for a visit from his bosses the following week. She kicked off her shoes and made herself comfortable. Aryan's apartment was impeccably furnished, but not, Nandita felt, reflective of its owner in any way. It was too proper, too perfect and lacked soul. When she had first seen the place, she had looked around to see if there were any clues to the personality of the man who lived there. No books, she had noticed.

'Don't you read?' she had asked in surprise. Aryan pleaded guilty. Not much of a reader, then. And movies? There were plenty of those. Spielberg, Brian De Palma, Quentin Tarantino, Ridley Scott...Nandita had approved wholeheartedly. She had rifled through his CD collection. If Nandita had been asked to choose the moment when she realized she was in love with Aryan Rai, she would have flippantly replied that it was when she found out there were no Mozart or Bach CDs in his house.

CHAPTER EIGHTEEN
Mumbai, June 2013

Nandita was seriously missing the array of culinary delights her mother treated her to every Sunday. As she didn't find opportunity or time to indulge in much home cooking, she had to resort to the efficient home delivery system Bandra had to offer. This particular Sunday morning, she decided to treat Aryan to a home-cooked brunch.

'Your mom has obviously trained you well,' he told Nandita as he watched her whisking cream. 'I can't wait to meet her. Maybe she can spoil me by proxy too.'

'Oh, you'll love Aai. She's the best. There's nothing she wouldn't do for me. I think she always made it a point to go that extra mile, to make up for my lack of a father.'

'And as a result, you never missed having a dad?'

'You know, it's true that she never ever let me feel deprived in any way, but honestly, Aryan, I did miss having my dad around. I never even knew him, and believe it or not, I don't even know what he looks like. She's not very communicative on the subject. I've tried so hard to get her to open up, but it pains her, so I just let it be.' Nandita did not mention the letter hidden in her jewellery box...she couldn't share that, even with Aryan.

'That's odd. One would think she would want you to know him, but then, I guess she has her reasons. You're lucky you have such a great relationship with her, Cat. Not everyone does.'

'You do, don't you? You adore your mom. More than anyone else in your family.'

'Yes. I guess that's because she and I are such similar people. Dad was always lost in his little world of science, but she was real, she could relate to my problems in the real world.'

'And your sister?'

'Sona is five years older than I am. She grew up much faster and was totally committed to her ballet. In fact, she never came with us on the wild Amazonian trips because she couldn't miss ballet. How I envied her…I pretended to develop a passion for soccer so I could stay back too, but Mom was not fooled!'

Nandita laughed. 'Poor little you! So Sona's passion for ballet goes that far back. How will she manage the ballet school with the third baby in tow?'

'By the time the baby comes, she will have her new manager in place, I'm sure she will be all set in a month or so. Sona is very organized. I hope it's a girl this time, both her boys have no interest whatsoever in dancing, much to her regret and to Dave's relief! He can't wait to get them both into Little League.'

'Well, if they were living here, it would be cricket. So I guess all little boys are the same.'

'Maybe if Sona had grown up here, she'd be an Indian classical dancer.'

'That requires an equal amount of commitment. I learned Odissi in school for four years, but it was too time-consuming, and I guess I lacked the passion.'

'You? A dancer? This I have to see,' laughed Aryan.

'It's not that tall an order,' she replied, poking him in the ribs. 'I was pretty good, I'll have you know!'

By this time, she was putting the finishing touches to the Belgian waffles and plating the Eggs Benedict.

'I'm starved…you know, working at Sabarwal has turned me into a monster! I can eat all day.'

'Yes, and it's showing on your waistline,' commented Aryan, baiting her for a reaction. She did not disappoint him.

'It is not! I am wearing the same jeans...'

He interrupted with a laugh and a hug. 'How quickly you fly off the handle baby...I'm kidding! Why are women so antsy and defensive about anything weight-related? I've told you a million times I love your body the way it is.'

'It's not about what *you* love,' she told him disdainfully. 'Why does it have to be about you? It's about how *I* feel about my body.'

'Yeah, right. I believe you... Hey, this must be Aditya.' Aryan was momentarily distracted by Aditya's sleepy appearance from his room.

'Good morning! Or rather, afternoon! What time did you get in last night?' Nandita asked amusedly.

'No clue, babe. Was too wasted to care! Hey Aryan...how's it going? Good to meet you, finally! Heard so much about you from Nan, I feel like we've already met before.' Aditya shook Aryan's hand and sat languidly at the dining table while Nandita poured him some freshly made coffee.

'Waffles? Toast?'

'Don't talk to me about food,' said Aditya, taking a tentative sip of coffee. 'I think maybe I drank a little too much last night.' His head went down on the table.

'You don't say? I'm amazed, that's so not like you!' she replied. 'Why do you have to party so hard, Aditya? Look at you, you're a mess!'

Aryan watched as she fussed around him, popping two Dispirins into a glass of water and persuading him to drink it. Aditya was a good-looking guy, he thought. Tall, lean and deeply tanned, he had an athletic, outdoorsy look that women would find attractive. Aryan was not surprised that Arushi had been so easily bowled over. As had Nandita been...she had told Aryan about their 'together' phase. Their relationship was obviously very strong to have survived the break-up.

When Nandita had assured herself that Aditya was ok, she poured Aryan a glass of chilled champagne. 'What's a good brunch without some champagne to wash it down?'

Aditya was tickled. 'Nan, Mumbai has changed you...you never cared about champagne before. Or is it Aryan's influence?'

Nandita laughed. 'A bit of both, I guess. Do you really think I've changed?'

'On some subtle, level, yes.' He looked at her reflectively. 'You've grown up, Nan. Suddenly, you're just all grown up.'

'So what was she like as a kid, Aditya?' asked Aryan casually.

'A handful. Socially inept but very stubborn. She loved being alone, and rejected most overtures of friendship.' He raised his eyebrows and looked at Nandita. 'Somehow, she accepted me. It was a lot of pressure being Nan's best friend.'

'Really? A loner? I find that so hard to believe!'

'True, nevertheless!' Nandita laughed. 'Poor Adi had a hard time catering to all my idiosyncrasies.'

'And now I'm paying you back by making you put up with mine!' retorted Aditya, pouring himself another cup of coffee.

'All that falls into Arushi's lap now. And she's happy to do it!'

Aditya threw her a quizzical look and changed the subject. 'What's the hotel business like, Aryan?'

'Right now, not such a happy place to be. I'm looking at a year-end launch, but with such an economic downswing, it's not going to be easy. There is an unbelievable amount of competition and choice in Mumbai today—it's a buyer's market. Most hotels are much lower on occupancy than last year. Plus, we are an all-suites hotel, and the luxury factor has been cut down by most companies, even though the worst of the recession is over.'

'But I would imagine that Starling will have its niche clientele, regardless of competition? Surely your brand is not subject to price consciousness?' Aditya asked.

Aryan took a contemplative sip of his coffee. 'You're right, Aditya, in a way. But ostentatious spending is not really in vogue right now. I'm just hoping that things will improve by November, or I might just be looking for a new job!'

'Rubbish!' said Nandita, heaping her fork with hollandaise sauce. 'You are married to Starling, irrevocably. You'll be the last man standing, if I know you.'

'Thanks for the vote of confidence, darling. I'll keep that in mind over the next few months, when I'm staring at my inventory of unoccupied rooms.'

'From what I've heard, hotel life is pretty much a twenty-four-hour job,' Aditya commented.

'I guess it can be,' answered Aryan. 'But I love what I do, so it's never been a problem for me.'

'He is very good at it, extremely so,' said Nandita, glancing at Aryan surreptitiously.

Aditya laughed. Aryan leaned across and kissed her. 'Your bias is showing, Cat!'

Nandita coloured and grinned, but refused to back down. 'It's not bias. It's all about passion. You have it, you know you do. If you can't feel passion for your work, it's the saddest situation in the world to be in.'

'Was that aimed at me, Nan?' asked Aditya half seriously.

'At *you*? Of course not, why would you think that?' She looked surprised.

'You never seem to think I'm worth much...you know, you're always lecturing me about passion and the need to do something fruitful.' This time he was dead serious, looking at her with an unfathomable expression.

'Yes, but...that was when you were spending all your time doing nothing. You know I meant it for the best, I was trying to...'

'No, Nan. You meant it as something that is lacking in me as a person. You've always told me that I lack passion, have no drive, no fire in my belly...' Aditya had put his cup down and was looking at Nandita unrelentingly. Aryan might not have been in the room, for all he cared.

Nandita was distressed. 'But you *are* doing something now, Adi, something you enjoy very much, and doing it so well. What have I ever said to make you think...' she broke off, too upset to continue.

Aryan looked from one to the other, and realized that he made a very bad third in this conversation. He got up and started taking the dishes back to the kitchen. By the time he came out again, it appeared as if the moment had passed. Shortly afterwards, Aditya disappeared back into his room, saying he needed to sleep it off. Nandita and Aryan were left facing each other.

'I'm sorry you had to sit through that, Aryan,' she said. 'I don't know what got into him; he's never ever been that vulnerable before.'

'Have you really been that critical of him in the past? He seemed to think so.'

'I don't know! Perhaps I have, and not realized how it affected him?' Nandita looked devastated. 'Of everyone I know, I can't think of anybody who has supported me more than Aditya. I can't bear that I should be the one to have hurt him.'

Aryan put his arm around her and held her tight. There was so much going through his mind, but he could not voice any of it to her.

CHAPTER NINETEEN
Delhi, June 2013

Simi Arora and Amrita Dharkar met every Wednesday evening at the Delhi Gymkhana Club for drinks and dinner. This tradition had been in place for the last twenty years at least, and it was something they never missed, unless one of them was out of town. The old colonial charm of the club had not changed over the years, despite the modernization efforts. Nandita and Aditya had grown up at the Delhi Gym, swimming, playing tennis on the well-maintained grass courts and eating the incomparably soft chicken sandwiches and crisp samosas. Amrita found that no amount of deluxe hotel dining could compare with the comfort level of the club, and she treasured these evenings with Simi as the one constant factor in their relationship. As Epicurean had grown, she had become busier, not finding much time for social pursuits, which suited her fine. Simi kept a much higher social profile than Amrita, who never made public appearances unless she had to. She had been lumped with her brother's company after his death, and had successfully managed to expand the business of seven sports shops to a chain of sixteen all over North India, and was now venturing into retailing at malls as well. It was certainly not something Simi had done out of choice. She had been on the brink of a successful and interesting career as a fashion stylist when her brother died, and she had taken over the sports stores under duress. Simi was a practical woman, not one to cry over spilt milk. Without dwelling on what could have been, she immersed herself in the world of sports equipment as if it had been her chosen career. In addition, she administered an ample investment portfolio with funds that had been left to Aditya by his extremely wealthy maternal grandfather. He would be the sole master of his wealth at thirty, and Simi hoped fervently that he mended his indolent ways in the two months that remained before he reached that age. It was a huge responsibility, and Simi often wondered if she had indulged him too much as a boy, to make up for his parents. She blamed herself for his lack of focus as much as she blamed him; her new ploy to cut off funds until he could learn to fend for himself had been a last, desperate strategy to motivate him to make something out of his carefree life. She hoped that he would take over the sporting business some day, leaving her free to do so many things she had wanted to but never could, in the past.

Simi's married lover had been a constant factor for several years now, but she managed her affair with such discretion that even the most censorious of Delhi tattles could not find fault with her manner of conducting herself. She had given up hopes of marrying the man a long time ago—there were too many family constraints related to business, and he would on no account allow his kids to suffer. Simi understood this, yet chose to pursue the connection, knowing there was no future in it. Now that the initial tumultuous passion in their relationship had quietened down, Simi and her lover had reached a stage of easy companionship, and she was more or less resigned to her fate. Amrita was the only person in whom Simi confided, and as Simi's closest friend, she was bound by a tacit agreement never to be judgmental or critical about the relationship.

Amrita and Simi had met when they were in school in Shimla. Though Simi was a little older, a series of circumstances had placed them in the same class in high school. Amrita had been around to pick up the pieces when Simi's first boyfriend broke her heart, and Simi had been the rock Amrita had leaned on when she came back from Bombay, devastated and desperately in need of help. Their Wednesday dates at the Delhi Gymkhana were just what they needed to shrug off the mantle of their responsibilities and exchange notes on current happenings. Neither of them realized quite how much they depended on each other, because each took the other completely for granted.

Simi walked into the club in pleasant anticipation of her evening. As she entered the refreshingly cool bar, she spotted Amrita perched on the barstool, her fingers drumming an impatient tattoo on the black marble counter. Amrita was looking absurdly youthful in a pair of white jeans and a pale grey kurti with delicate silver embroidery. Her long hair was caught up in a ponytail, and as Simi approached her, she saw that the usually sparkling green eyes showed signs of strain and sleeplessness.

Amrita jumped up when she saw Simi and the two women exchanged a warm hug.

'I won't ask if you are ok, because you obviously aren't,' Simi said bluntly. 'In fact, I've seldom seen you look worse.'

Amrita managed a wan laugh. 'What I love about you, Simi, is your brutal honesty.'

'Ok, out with it. What's bugging you?'

Amrita rubbed her cheeks tiredly. 'It's killing me, Simi. Nandita has walked into a time bomb from the past, and I live in dread of the day she finds out everything. She has to... something like this doesn't stay buried, you know.' Amrita's voice was unsteady and she sounded on the verge of tears. Simi didn't need to ask what 'something like this' was; the topic had been discussed any number of times in the past.

Simi called the barman. 'Can we have a glass of water, please?' She turned back to her friend. 'He won't really tell her, would he?'

'I've thought and thought about it, Simi. Sooner or later, he is going to tell her something.'

'Possibly. Amrita, look at it this way. Even if Nandi does find out, is it really the end of the world? She's your daughter, dammit, she will understand!'

'Never! She can never know such a thing about me.' Amrita's head sank into her hands in despair as she spoke. 'Oh Simi, what in god's name am I going to do?'

'Nothing,' said Simi briskly. 'Absolutely nothing. There's a good chance nothing will come out. All you have to do is to keep your cool, ok?'

Amrita looked at her friend, her eyes full of hurt. 'All I have to do? Simi, do you think I have any strength left in me now, to go through all this again?'

Simi was deliberately unsympathetic. 'You have no choice. None whatsoever. Come on, Amrita. Don't pack up on me now. Do you see me crumbling? I have spent the last seventeen years loving a man I can never call mine. It's the worst kind of hell to be in.'

'I know, babe, I know. But I'm not you. And you know I only survived all of this because of you.'

'Nonsense. You would have done it anyway. Give yourself some credit here. And it's not like you didn't make your sacrifice, and pay your dues.'

Amrita shook her head sadly. 'It's like some hideous, cruel twist of fate.'

Amrita gulped down the glass of water the waiter proffered and asked for another. Her mind went back to the moment Nandita had told her she was going to Mumbai to take up a job with Sabarwal Associates. She had known right away that some form of disaster was inevitable. She had raged against her wayward fate until she accepted that in one way, this *was* inevitable, and she had no power to stop it. All she worried about was how her daughter would judge her after all these years.

'How is Nandita doing?' Simi asked, judging it time to change the subject.

Amrita brightened perceptibly. 'Wonderful. Stressed, overworked, but you know how she thrives on that sort of thing. Seems very much in love with Aryan. The guy I told you about? He sounds lovely. Actually, I've spoken to him a couple of times.'

'American, isn't he? I mean, American citizen?'

'Yup. Sounds completely American. His parents live in Chicago. Nandi seems to be completely taken with him. She's changed, Simi. I hope everything works out for her.' There was a slight huskiness in Amrita's voice.

'She's a strong girl, Amrita. She'll be fine. We all are eventually, aren't we?'

'I guess. But I want her to possess her dream and live it to the fullest. I want her to have love, marriage, kids, all the happiness that I didn't… If she can have that, Simi, everything, *everything* will have been worth it.'

Simi gave her friend a shake. 'Will you stop being so lachrymose, woman? What on earth has got into you? Whatever has to happen will happen, no matter what you or I do, and you know what, it will be for the best. We've always lived by that adage, and we're not going to stop now, ok?'

Amrita tossed her head back defiantly. 'Ok. End of snivelling. Tell me about Aditya and the beautiful Arushi.'

'All I know is what I hear from you, what Nandita tells you. You know how reticent he is! I don't know how serious he is about Arushi. He's really not the marriage type, you know. Won't it be amazing if our two brats do finally settle down? I think it's pretty bizarre that they both go to Bombay and find themselves partners, both at the same time.'

Amrita raised her eyebrow in surprise. 'You know, you're right! I never thought of that. Who knows, Arushi may turn out to be what Aditya's been looking for. Maybe he will want to settle down, this time?'

'He hasn't said anything. He's working pretty hard anyway, and that's a first! If he sticks with in this photography thing, forget about anything else, I'll be so bloody relieved. I feel I have failed Bharat and Laila...he was left to my care and I raised him without a sense of who he is. I tried, Amrita. You know I did. I just don't understand what makes that boy tick.'

'Listen darling, you raised him to be an honest, caring and responsible human being. That's all that matters. He's been more than a friend to Nandi, and he does have strength of character. He'll find his niche, I know he will. Nandi says he is working harder than she has ever seen him work.'

'I hope you're right. Nandita understands him better than I ever will. Those two have uncanny insight into each other,' Simi said.

'Yes, they do. It's such a pity that their romance was fated to die...it would have been so wonderful if they had made a go of it. They are just so tuned into each other.' Amrita and Simi had discussed this often enough, but agreed that it didn't seem to be on the cards.

'Probably too much. Maybe they need this break to be with other people. Sometimes I feel Aditya has no other priority in life besides Nandi. He worships her.'

'Thank god he is finding his feet with his work. He really needed this badly,' said Amrita.

'Yes. Mumbai has been good for him, all things considered.'

At the mention of Mumbai, Amrita's troubles came back to her like a flood, and her face fell.

Simi saw the woebegone look and gently said, 'Should we order double vodkas?'

'I think so. I've never needed one so badly!'

Amrita sank back on the cushions, watching Simi order the drinks with extremely precise instructions about mixers and ice. What would I have done without Simi? she thought gratefully. If life had denied her love, it certainly hadn't denied her friendship.

CHAPTER TWENTY
Mumbai, July 2013

The rains had arrived in earnest after a hot and humid June, and Nandita experienced her first Mumbai monsoon with mixed feelings. The deafening downpour was incredibly glorious, and somewhat romantic, she thought, but getting to work was a nightmare. Although there had been no serious flooding yet, the already slow traffic crawled to a virtual standstill on some particularly rainy mornings, and she wondered how Mumbai survived three months of this onslaught. Almost everyone managed to be late on these days, arriving in office with a sense of accomplishment after having battled the forces of nature. News channels were predicting unprecedented high tides and major flooding in the city, and Nandita found herself wondering how much worse it could possibly get.

Work had not slowed down at Sabarwal Associates. The last report about Pallavi had been optimistic and upbeat, but Rajeev still had no idea when he was coming back. Meanwhile, she and Niranjan were galvanized, working against time to get the Sunville designs ready for presentation.

There was a bitter, uneasy ceasefire between Niranjan and Nandita; they managed to keep basic communication going, in order to get the work done. The usual cheerful demeanour of the staff was missing, though, and the atmosphere had taken on a slightly sombre cast. Tara, usually the life and soul of the party, was particularly downcast, and Nandita could see that it was affecting her colleagues as well. She had not been communicative, and Nandita guessed that the Dominic saga had come to its natural conclusion. Sitting in her office one Saturday afternoon, she decided it was time to have a chat with Tara.

Sonia had just brought in some drawings for Nandita's inspection, but she put them aside and said, 'Sonia, will you ask Tara if she is free to come in for a bit?'

'There's no point, she's just not talking,' said Sonia with candid certainty.

'Sonia, please.'

'Ok, fine, but don't say I didn't warn you.'

Tara walked in a few moments later, her expression distracted. Her hair was overgrown and untrimmed, and her usually immaculate French manicure was chipped. The joie de vivre was missing, as was the muffin/cookie/brownie she would habitually munch on.

'Tara. Sit. How's Nagpur going? Are you pretty much done with it?'

'Yes. Niranjan approved everything yesterday, and I just have to make some small changes in a couple of the drawings. Why?'

'I could use your help on the Sunville job. I'll clear it with Niranjan, of course.'

'Fine,' she said listlessly. 'Whatever.'

'Tara, cheer up! This is so not you.'

'I don't even know what's me anymore, Nandita. I'm in limbo right now.'

Tara chewed her lip, fighting back her tears. She paused for a moment, collecting her thoughts. 'Dominic wants to get married.'

Nandita was stunned. 'Married? But...isn't he some sort of live-for-the-moment, go-where-my-fancy-takes-me kind of guy?'

'He's willing to change all that and settle down, he says.'

'So where's the problem? You should have been in whoops, I'd imagine?'

Tara got up and walked around the tiny room, her face shadowed by uncertainty. 'I don't know if that's what I want, Nandita. I like him a lot, but to marry a man who is so, so different, live in France, leave everything I know here…I'm not ready for all that. And then,' she added self-consciously, 'there's Sameer.'

Here we go, thought Nandita. The plot thickens significantly. 'Who's Sameer?'

Tara came back to her chair, her face visibly animated for the first time since she'd entered the room. 'Sameer Raja is the son of a close family friend. My parents and his actually want us to get married. I know him pretty well, but it's this arranged kind of thing. He works as an account manager in an ad agency, and he's really nice. Nandita, it's all so familiar, a world I am comfortable in, and my parents love him. It's predictable and safe, and I am so bloody tempted!'

'Hmmm! What happened to adventure, the unpredictable, the high romance? All that stuff you thrived on? Take chances, jump into the fire?'

'It was great while it lasted. I've always known I can't go on like that forever. With Sameer, it's all very real, not my make-believe games. It's like I've finally gotten off the merry-go-round and I need to be still now. I think what made it all so adventurous was knowing that it didn't have to be forever. But marriage is forever, isn't it? I don't know if Dominic and I can be in that space. What would you do, Nandita? In my place?' Tara looked at her beseechingly.

'You don't need my opinion. It's pretty obvious what *you* want to do.' Nandita smiled.

'It is?'

'Oh, come off it, you fraud. Marry Sameer and be done with it. You have as much chance of being happy that way as any other. Poor Dominic may even be a little relieved!'

Tara's eyes shone softly. 'You think? Oh Nandita, do you really, *really* think so?'

'I really, *really* think so.'

'I wouldn't be some kind of selfish bitch, choosing comfort and security over true love?'

'But Tara, darling, you don't truly love Dominic, do you? If you did, you wouldn't even be looking at Sameer.' Nandita thought about Aryan...if she had to, wouldn't she give up comfort and security to be with him?

'Bless you, Nandita. I wish I'd talked to you days ago. You've made—'

Niranjan Kulkarni walked in just then and Tara froze, remembering the last time the three of them had been in there together. Surprisingly, he was not here to make another scene.

'Nandita, can you spare an hour or so? There's a crisis on the Vashi project and I want you to sort it out. Monica will brief you.' He was abrupt and to the point.

Nandita was equally short. 'Sure. And if it's ok with you, I'd like to rope Tara in on Sunville.'

'Rope in whoever you want, we're running very short of time. Tara, whatever your personal crisis is, I hope Nandita has helped you to sort it out. We need all hands on deck, and we need you to be a hundred per cent here.' He disappeared as quickly as he had come.

Tara gulped. 'My personal crisis! How dare he! As if I've not been giving my all to the job these last few days! He's such a prick!'

Nandita sighed. 'I can't wait for Rajeev to get back. But you *have* been distracted Tara, that much is true. Do you realize how much you motivate people around here with your infectious, enthusiastic attitude? Just get back to being who you are. Listen, let me get done with Monica and then we'll have you start on

Sunville. While I'm gone, just go through these files on my laptop, it'll give you an idea of what's been happening so far.'

As it turned out, Monica's troubles took much longer than an hour to sort out, and Nandita was brain dead by the time they'd finished. She told Tara that Sunville could wait till Monday morning, and headed out of the office with the feeling that she could not even look at another drawing that day.

Anjali had bought tickets for a play that evening, and the four of them were supposed to be at NCPA at 8.30. Rajat was planning to meet them there, since he worked at Nariman Point. It was already almost seven, so she decided to go straight to Aryan's house. It was raining and the traffic was ghastly as usual, and it was past 7.30 when she arrived. Instead of going to Aryan's flat, on an impulse she pressed the lift button for the fourth floor and rang Anjali's doorbell. There was no way Aryan would be home yet. The maid let her in, but there was no sign of Anjali. Nandita assumed she was changing and made herself comfortable. After a few moments, Anjali did not appear, so she got up and knocked on Anjali's bedroom door.

There was no reply, so Nandita opened the door softly and peeped in. Anjali was lying diagonally across the bed, curled up in a foetal position, moaning in pain. Nandita was beside her in a flash, cradling her while she looked frantically around for Anjali's cellphone.

'Where does it hurt? Is it your stomach?'

'Yes…spotting…call my gynaecologist, Nandita.' Anjali was clutching the phone in her white hands, and Nandita gently pried her fingers apart to take it out.

'Abhay Kelkar?'

'Yes…' She went into another spasm of pain and Nandita quickly checked 'K' in Anjali's contacts and found the doctor's number. 'Hello, Abhay? This is Nandita, Anjali's friend…she's in a really bad state.' She explained the situation as best she could and begged him to come immediately.

'I'll be back in just a sec. Anju, hang on, ok?'

She ran out and asked the maid to bring in a hot water bottle and a cup of tea, and was back as quickly as she went.

'He'll be here soon, don't worry.' She put a pillow under Anjali's feet and called Rajat, briefly telling him what had happened. 'You have to get home as soon as you can. Please.'

Anjali's cramps eased slightly with the hot-water bottle, and a few sips of tea seemed to revive her a little. She was extremely distraught, though, and held on to Nandita's hand helplessly. 'I've already lost one baby, Nandita, I can't lose this one too! Rajat will be devastated!'

'Shhh! You won't lose the baby. It's going to be ok.'

'I didn't even realize I was pregnant. I've been so sick the last couple of days, and now this! I hadn't said anything to Rajat; after what happened the last time, I wanted to be sure. Nandita, please pray for me!' She laid her head on Nandita's lap and seemed to doze off, and Nandita let her rest.

The doctor arrived half an hour later, together with Aryan, and Nandita felt a surge of relief. Anjali, already so fair, was looking dangerously pale. Aryan came in and gave the wan Anjali a reassuring squeeze, but the doctor requested both Nandita and Aryan to wait outside. They retired to the living room, and Aryan called Rajat to let him know the doctor had arrived, and not to worry. He knew Rajat must be in an agony of suspense.

The doctor summoned them inside after what seemed like hours, but was only about fifteen minutes.

'I'm certain she *is* pregnant, but I'll have to run some tests. I don't think she's having a miscarriage. All the same, I want her under observation for tonight, given her history. I'll arrange a room at Breach Candy Hospital, and we'll take good care of her. Where's Rajat?'

'I'm here,' he said, walking into the room swiftly just then, his face ashen. He went straight to the bed and leaned over Anjali, gently stroking her hair. 'You ok, baby? Still cramping?'

Anjali smiled tiredly. 'No, I'm ok. But Abhay wants to admit me to the hospital for one night.'

Rajat turned to the doctor, who had become a good friend over the last two years.

'Thanks for being here so quickly, buddy. *Kai karaicha ata?* Breach Candy?'

'I'll organize the room, don't worry. She'll be fine, Rajat, and I'm going to do my best to save the baby this time.'

Rajat's expression changed to one of such tender concern as he sat beside Anjali that Aryan and Nandita left the room to give them both some privacy.

'I don't think we should go to the hospital with Rajat, we'll only be in the way, and Abhay seems to have it under control. What d'you want to do?' Aryan asked Nandita.

'I think,' said Nandita, not really listening to what he was saying, 'that I am really not into this whole baby thing! Is this what one has to endure?'

Aryan looked at her in amusement. 'Not everyone does…I've heard it can be perfectly normal.'

She chuckled. 'Right! No seriously, I never thought of myself as the maternal instinct type, all gooey about babies. There's just too much angst associated with parenthood.'

'So what's wrong with that? It's natural enough, isn't it?'

Rajat came out of the bedroom, looking immeasurably relieved. 'Nandita, I can't thank you enough for taking care of Anju the way you did. I honestly don't know what to say.'

Nandita put her arms around him. 'Don't be silly, Rajat. It was nothing. Just make sure she takes it easy now and follows Abhay's instructions implicitly.'

'You bet. Listen, the evening's still young—you two go on and do something. Abhay is going to the hospital with me, so I won't drag you along.'

After they had said bye to Anjali and Rajat, Aryan took Nandita to his apartment. Nandita smiled to herself as they walked into his living room, and Aryan asked her what was funny.

'Today was my Good Samaritan day. I helped Tara make a life-changing decision; I bailed Monica out of an electrical mess and held Anjali's hand through her crisis. Quite a bounty of karmic dues paid, I should say.'

Aryan put his arms around her, kissing her neck. 'That's very uplifting. I think you should keep at it. I'm feeling in desperate need for attention, how about taking care of my crisis too?'

Nandita smiled. 'And what might your particular crisis be?'

Aryan slid his hand inside her shirt. 'Apart from the obvious one, I think I have an irresistible urge to get married. Will you, Cat?'

Nandita pulled away, not knowing whether to be shocked or to laugh...of all the blasé proposals ever made, this had to be the worst. It was not as if she had not thought about this question, or anticipated its coming. And in her mind, even if the setting she'd imagined had been much more romantic, the answer had always been an instant yes. But here, now, in real time, she could not bring herself to say the words. She had no doubt she loved Aryan, that she wanted to be with him, but marriage somehow seemed so final...she needed time.

'We don't have to discuss it now... Cat, it's ok,' said Aryan, sensing her hesitation immediately. He was terrified she was going to say no.

'Aryan, it's not as if I don't want…'

He cut her short with a kiss. 'It's ok, baby. I think that little scene with Abhay and Anju today made me realize that I'm kind of ready for that…with you. No pressure. Ok?'

She nodded. No pressure? Of course it was pressure! It was a huge decision, and she so badly wanted to be able to say yes. Nandita found it hard to fall asleep that night. What was wrong with her? Wasn't this what she had always wanted?

CHAPTER TWENTY-ONE
Mumbai, August 2013

Sunville, as a project, was larger than anything Sabarwal Associates had ever touched and Nandita was not surprised that Rajeev was so keyed up about it. There was obviously not going to be enough time to get into detailed designs, but they were to present concepts and sketches to the project head, Naresh Patel, in three weeks. She and Niranjan had realized what a dire responsibility it was to finish all of it in Rajeev's absence. What would they have done without the Internet, Nandita marvelled. Rajeev was in constant touch with them to keep the work flowing at a brisk pace. He scrutinized every detail of every sketch and plan sent to him, reverting with feedback on the minutest of design flaws or discrepancies. It was exhausting work for everyone concerned, and certainly not the ideal way to conduct a task of such mammoth proportions. But in the given circumstances, it remained the most viable choice.

Sunville was one million square feet of a textile mill that had shut down long ago, like so many others in Mumbai. It would now be redeveloped beyond recognition. The current winning formula was a combination of residential and commercial space, but Naresh Patel wanted it to be on a scale and style so far unprecedented in Mumbai. Such projects had been built piecemeal, till then; often without a coherent thread of design style to tie the whole look together. Sunville was going to change all that. The plan was to include two thirty-storey apartment buildings, a high-end shopping mall and a wealth of entertainment and leisure facilities, including a multiplex with twelve screens, a restaurant court, a fast food court, a supermarket and an organic food mart. It would also have a luxury hotel, a spa and a sports club.

The Indian middle class had risen in financial status, and with the advent of the BPO culture, younger people were flush with extra cash. Shopping was the new mantra and malls the new places of worship. The Indian economy had certainly felt the effects of the global economic slowdown, but things were looking up once more.

Rajeev had conceived the Sunville mall itself on international lines, a themed extravaganza that would have five zones modelled on international cities including Paris, Las Vegas, London, New York and Shanghai. The mall's atrium courtyard would be flooded with sunlight, comfortable seating and abundant foliage to create a relaxed yet vibrant shopping environment.

Rajeev had envisioned the twin residential towers in the style known as structural modernism. A two-storey recreation and club area was to connect the sister towers. The entire concept was on a scale unprecedented in the city so far.

The Ve project was now in the final stages, ready for execution, and Nandita was focusing all her attention on getting Sunville on paper as a finished concept. Niranjan was as cold and hostile as ever, but the pressure of work was such that neither had the time or energy to bicker, and they managed to work with reasonable understanding, if not actually in harmony. More than half the staff of Sabarwal Associates was involved in this presentation and not much else was discussed. Monica was the only senior designer who was not on Sunville, as she was fielding the rest of the jobs that were in various stages of completion.

Niranjan had glowered at Nandita today because she had come in late to work, but to her surprise, he'd said nothing. Anyway, she thought, she was more than on schedule with her part of the work, so he could sulk all he liked. Anjali Gupte's Satyanarayan puja had held her up; it was something she had really wanted to attend. Since the time Anjali's pregnancy had been announced, Anjali was taking it easy at home, and her mother had driven in from Pune to look after her. The puja was Rajat's idea, much to Nandita's surprise.

'It's just something we do when anything good happens—it's our way of saying thank you to the powers that be,' Rajat had told her with simple humility.

'Oh, I'm not questioning it. I've grown up with this; my mother does it every year.'

Nandita had dressed in a pale pink and silver chanderi sari with jasmine flowers in her hair, intricate pearl and silver earrings, and a small silver bindi on her forehead. Aryan had raised his eyebrows in disbelief on meeting her, followed by open approval; he had never seen her dressed so traditionally before.

Nandita enjoyed the puja very much. It took her back to her childhood, with the familiar, reassuring sound of Vedic verses being chanted, and the intermingled fragrance of the agarbatti, sandalwood paste, camphor and chafa flowers that lulled her into a sense of cocooned security. She had always been drawn to Sanskrit shlokas, and found they produced vibrations that created a very powerful effect on the listener. She chanted some of the familiar ones along with the pandit in a low, melodious voice. The pandit was a young man, well-educated and quite familiar with English. When he realized that Aryan was not even faintly following any of the proceedings, he went out of his way to explain them. He kept pausing to explain the various customs and actions in English, even telling Aryan which websites to visit for more information. Aryan participated in his enthusiasm with good humour, even asking a couple of questions, which highly gratified the young priest.

'Satyanarayan is a form of the lord that is considered an embodiment of truth. This puja is conducted to ensure abundance in one's life, or along with an auspicious occasion. In this case,' he said, beaming at Anjali, 'the happy occasion is yet to come!'

Anjali's mother Sarlatai was highly disapproving. 'This is some new-age bhadji,' she whispered to Rajat. 'Computer and all, he has!'

Nandita stifled a giggle, and thought it wise not to tell Sarlatai that her mother Amrita performed this puja on her own with the help of a CD, thereby dispensing with the services of a pandit altogether. It would probably have been too blasphemous for Sarlatai. Anjali's mother lived in the last century and had no desire to step into this one; she was comfortable with the way things had been thirty years ago. Nandita thought that if she wanted to stay connected with her daughter and, more importantly, her grandchild who would be born into a world different from hers, she would have to learn to accept, if not understand, the leaps modern technology had taken.

Nandita watched contentedly as Anjali and Rajat piled hundreds of tulsi leaves on the small silver baby Krishna idol until it had all but disappeared from sight, while the priest recited the one thousand names of Vishnu in his strong, vibrant voice.

The puja ended with the aarti and the delicious sheera that was the mandatory sweet, offered first to the lord and then to the rest of the attendees. It was traditionally prepared with equal amounts of semolina, sugar, milk and ghee, Nandita explained to Aryan, and flavoured with cardamom, saffron, banana and tulsi leaves.

'Everything has to be in a measure of one and one-fourth, even the banana,' she informed him.

'I'm so impressed with you girls,' Aryan said to Nandita and Anjali. 'How do you know all this? All those complicated Sanskrit prayers, the traditions, the correct way of performing the rituals. I know you've grown up with it, but look at the two of you!'

Sarlatai had whipped up a delicious Maharashtrian vegetarian lunch that morning, which was to be served at 11.30 to accommodate everyone who had to rush to work. The pandit declined lunch, saying he had another puja to perform elsewhere that morning. He was given his remuneration in the form of substantial cash and a few material things like a 'shirt-piece' and a dhoti. Sarlatai was of the opinion that it was way too much. In her day, she informed them after the man had left, a couple of hundred rupees was all that was given.

'No wonder he can afford a computer and all that. You people spoil these fellows!' she grumbled. 'Anju, you should have just given that sari which Atya gave and you don't like, what was the need to buy new?'

Rajat looked expressively at Anjali, and she quelled him with a light smack. 'It's ok, Mamma, don't fret so much. And anyway, I gave that sari to my maid.'

Sarla-tai was horrified. 'Your *maid*? It was nice silk, how could you! I could have given it to your cousin Atul's wife, and said it was from you.'

Anjali shuddered and steered her mother into the kitchen. 'Why don't you warm up the lunch?' She came back, smiling resignedly at her guests. 'Sorry, I just can't seem to curb her zeal for economy. Something about that generation and the Pune upbringing.'

'I think she's got the right idea,' said Aryan. 'I would have loved to see that priest dressed in a sari.'

'After all the trouble he took to keep you entertained and in the loop, I think that's mean,' Nandita told him severely.

'Yeah, he was kind of cool. Are we getting that much hyped lunch, or not? I'm late for two meetings.'

Anjali disappeared into the kitchen and Aryan seated himself at the table expectantly.

Most of the lunch would have been alien for Aryan six months before, as he had never been treated to a traditional Maharashtrian meal before he met the Guptes. Today, he enjoyed the poories and potatoes, shrikhand, masale bhat, stuffed brinjals and peas with coconut. Sarlatai kept anxiously urging her daughter to sit and rest, and Anjali was obviously trying to be patient with her mother.

'I know she means well,' she confided to Nandita softly, 'but I really wish she wouldn't. She's driving me nuts!'

'I'm glad she is. At least you're forced to follow the doctor's orders. I know you, Anju, the moment she leaves, you'll be back to your frenzied life.'

'I won't, I promise you. I'm determined to have this baby, Nandita. And,' she added mischievously, 'if I can give up my alcohol, I can do anything, right?' They both laughed; it was a source of amusement to all of them that Anjali's legendary drinking sprees had come to a temporary but complete standstill.

Aryan rose, making it a point to wish Sarlatai before he left. Nandita told him she'd help Anjali clear up and then go.

'By the way, Cat, don't forget to give me your passport and sign those visa forms today,' he said.

'Passport? Where are you guys going?' asked Anjali.

'To Thailand, on my way to LA and Chicago. Nandita will come back when I go on to the States.'

'Aryan thinks I need a break. And besides, he's going to be off for fifteen days in the US,' said Nandita. 'Might as well make the most of him before he goes missing in action!'

'You lucky girl. I wish I could go with you! I'm grounded for a while, Abhay says.'

'By the way, Aryan, can we push the date down by a couple of days?' Nandita asked. 'I need to be here for Aditya's exhibition—he's participating in some group photography show.'

Aryan hesitated. 'It will mean two days less of our holiday, because my Chicago meetings are already set, Cat.'

She looked contrite. 'I'm sorry, Aryan, but I really can't miss this. I promised.'

Aryan looked like he was about to say something, but changed his mind.

'Ok,' he replied brightly. 'I'll figure it out.'

Nandita was not even sure if it was going to be possible to leave for a few days, but she was hoping that Rajeev would be back by the next week. Pallavi's cancer was in remission and the prognosis was looking good. Aryan had insisted on gifting Nandita this trip, as a birthday present and a break from her gruelling schedule of the last couple of months. And besides, Aryan would be in the States for a couple of weeks at least, so it would be nice to have a few days with him before that. As it was, things had been a little awkward since his unexpected proposal…she had still given not him a reply.

Nandita was turning thirty in September and for once, she didn't have that familiar feeling of age creeping up on her while she was not watching. Life was going exactly the way she wanted, and she couldn't have been happier. If Sabarwal Associates won the Sunville job, it would only add to the overwhelming sense of accomplishment she had acquired over the last few months.

CHAPTER TWENTY-TWO
Mumbai, September 2013

'Oh, there you are, finally! I thought you were going to ditch me!' Aditya was visibly relieved to see Nandita walk into the M Art Gallery in Kala Ghoda where the Photographer's Guild exhibition was being held.

'I said I'd make it, didn't I?' Nandita was breathless from running up the stairs.

'Yes, but I kind of thought Aryan would whisk you away to Thailand...he seemed a bit peeved about you juggling the dates. He's not coming?'

'Oh, he'll get over it,' she replied, giving his arm a squeeze. 'No, he's not, and anyway, I am looking forward to spending this evening with you, so it's fine. Now let's go see this famous exhibition of yours!'

Aditya led Nandita into the crowded exhibition space. It was filled largely with photographers and people from the advertising fraternity.

'I can't tell you what a nobody I feel like here, Nan. They are all renowned photographers with years of fantastic work to their credit. They've given space to only three or four newcomers, and I just lucked out being one of them.' They passed a group of chattering press photographers, one of whom waved to Aditya.

'Lucked out! Rubbish! I'm sure you've earned your place here. So what if they're all famous, you've been taking pictures since you were seven! That has to count for experience, surely?'

Aditya laughed. 'Only you could come up with that! Thanks for being so loyal, Nan!'

Nandita started her inspection of the displayed photo art, helped by Aditya's guided commentary. He pointed out the famous participants, explained their specializations, and demystified some of the techniques used. She was fascinated, never having been exposed to art in this particular form before. She began to have a deeper appreciation for why Aditya was so besotted with his new career. He had always been a keen amateur photographer, but she had never actually paid much attention to the pictures he took. She was just so used to seeing him with a camera around his neck that she didn't give much thought to it. Come to think of it, he had never offered to show her his work. That seemed odd, now that she had seen how much it meant to him. They had shared so much else, how come he'd never wanted to share this side of his with her before?

His own work formed a small part of the entire exhibit, but by the time she came to his section of the gallery, she realized what a big deal it was for him to even participate in this event. She felt an intense surge of pride in him, realizing for the first time that he possessed depths she had never even guessed at. Aditya seemed to have found his niche, his rhythm and in the bargain, himself. Just as he had taken pride and joy in her successes in the past, she now had the opportunity to revel in his. She stepped forward to study one of his works closely. It was an unusual angle of a girl's head, shot from behind, showing the nape of her neck and her back, and a few strands of curly hair that had escaped from her hair band. The sunlight caught the highlights from the curls as they cascaded down her bare, shapely back. It had been shot at the beach, but the composition was too graphic to be called a portrait. Suddenly, she gasped in pleasure.

'Adiiii! That's me!' She turned to him, wide-eyed and excited. 'When did you shoot this? I never even knew! It's absolutely beautiful!'

'In Goa...remember, the summer we all went there for Natasha's birthday?'

'But you never showed it to me. Do you have any others?'

He looked a little sheepish. 'A few. I'll show you sometime.'

'Sometime? What's that supposed to mean? C'mon, Aditya, I want to see them!' She peered a little closer to observe the details of the picture.

'Hey, Aditya! Great work, man! Good to see you got your spot in the limelight!' Nandita turned around to see a middle-aged bespectacled man hugging Aditya.

'I should actually be thanking you for your support, Karan,' replied Aditya. 'You were one of the first to give me the opportunity to get into the business.'

'Yes, I'm still waiting for my beer on that one. But aren't you going to introduce your lovely girlfriend?'

'Sorry...Nandita this is Karan, one of the finest creative directors you'll meet. And Nandita's my ex-girlfriend, not my girlfriend!'

Karan raised his eyebrows quizzically, and looked at the picture of Nandita on the wall. 'That has to have been taken by someone who knows her inside out...it shows, man!'

'He does know me inside out...we're childhood buddies,' quipped Nandita. She shot Aditya a surprised look. He had never, ever, introduced her to anyone as an ex-girlfriend.

Karan laughed sceptically, and the conversation turned to work. Soon, he moved off to greet another acquaintance, and Nandita took Aditya's arm.

'What was all that about?' she asked with raised eyebrow.

'Why? It's true, isn't it?'

'Yes, but, you've never really said that before. Is that how you think of me? An ex-girlfriend?'

'I think of you in many ways, Nandita. Let's just say that that's one of them.'

She was inexplicably pleased by his reply, even though she did not understand exactly what he meant. An 'ex-girlfriend' somehow sounded more exotic and desirable than a 'best friend'. She didn't stop to wonder why it was important to her that Aditya should find her desirable.

'Let's go get a cup of coffee before any more people want to hijack you. It's been forever since we've had a chance to sit and chat,' she suggested.

'Cool. I'm ready to ditch this place...been here all afternoon.'

They strolled across to a small coffee shop at the corner of the road. Settling down with a latte and a muffin, Nandita looked at Aditya appraisingly.

'I won't say I didn't think you had it in you, but I have to admit I'm quite blown away by what I've seen today,' she said. 'And hugely, *hugely* proud!'

'That's a first, coming from you...never thought I'd hear you say that to me!' Aditya replied lightly.

Nandita had not forgotten his little outburst at the breakfast table with Aryan present. 'Have I been *that* critical of you, Aditya? Honestly?'

'It's not so much what you've said, probably more your attitude...it's like you always thought I wouldn't amount to much.' Aditya bit into his sandwich.

'If I'd thought that way, I would never have pushed you the way I did, you know that. It's just...I knew you were capable of so much more than you were doing. Haven't you done the same for me, over the years?'

'I guess...anyway, for what it's worth, I'm glad I've finally made you proud of me!' He smiled at her, but she could not guess what he was thinking.

'Why is it that I've never seen any of this stunning work before? Goa was years ago, you've obviously done much more since then. I hadn't a clue how good you are! Why, Aditya?' Nandita tried to keep from sounding hurt, but some of her feelings crept into her voice.

Aditya raised his eyebrows. 'Were you ever interested?'

Nandita was surprised. 'I would have been, if I'd known! I mean, you never once indicated...you never let on how much all this meant to you. I thought it was just...'

'I know,' he interrupted. 'You thought it was just another passing fancy, that I was not capable of taking it seriously. That's why I kept you away, deliberately. To be honest, Nan, I was too scared you'd trivialize the whole thing. I needed to believe I was good at *something*.'

'But I would never have done that, you must know that! Adi, why are you saying these things? You've been such a huge support in my life; I would really like to think I have been there for you too. Are you saying it's always been only about me?' Nandita was flabbergasted.

'Of course not! No, Nan, that's not what I'm saying at all. It wasn't you, it was me and my insecurities. You've always been there for me, no strings attached. I'm not blaming you in any way, please don't think that.'

Nandita took a deep breath. 'For a moment there, I thought... Anyway, never mind. I got to see your fantastic show, and it was a really pleasant surprise. Now when do I get to see the rest of it? All the stuff you've been hiding from me?'

Aditya smiled. 'When you're back from Thailand. So you're off tomorrow, for sure?'

'Yes...looking forward to the break. It's been a madhouse at work.'

'Aryan seemed a bit low about something the last time we met...he was quite uncommunicative. Is everything ok? Is he pissed at *me* for some reason?'

Nandita hesitated. 'No. It's not about you.'

'Then what?' he persisted.

'He's asked me to marry him,' she said baldly.

Aditya put his sandwich down slowly.

'Marry him? And you said...no?' Aditya was incredulous.

'I...didn't say anything, Adi. Just asked for some time. I know I should be ecstatic, going nuts with joy, etc. but something's stopping me. God knows I wanted this, always thought it would be perfect, but...' she shrugged despondently.

Aditya's face was a mask. Nandita waited for the outburst, where he would try to persuade her that it was the right thing to do, that she was just being silly and that Aryan was the perfect guy for her. But he said nothing.

Both of them drank their coffee in silence for a while. Aditya seemed to have forgotten his sandwich and was lost in some remote world.

Nandita was the first to resume the conversation. 'So, what do you think?'

'About what, Nan?' he replied evenly.

'About...come off it, Aditya, you know exactly what I'm talking about!'

'If you're talking about you and Aryan, I think you should make the decision yourself...I can't help you, Nan. No one can. That should be obvious even to you.'

'You're the only one I'd ever ask this question to, Aditya. It's not as if I'm asking everybody's opinion.'

'That's not fair, Nan, neither to Aryan, nor to me.' Aditya did not elaborate, and his tone was so forbidding that she decided it was best to let the topic drop. She had been hoping that a heart-to-heart chat with him would clear her mind a little, as it always had in the past, but she realized he was not going to be dragged into this one. Men had such curious codes of conduct, she thought. She would never be able to understand the way their minds worked. Why on earth would it be unfair for Aditya to have to discuss Aryan? Absurd.

CHAPTER TWENTY-THREE
Mumbai, September 2013

The deluge of rain that hit the city was the worst Mumbai had seen this monsoon. Nandita arrived at Chhatrapati Shivaji International Airport amidst fears that the plane would not be able to land at all, due to poor visibility. She was thankful that Aryan's driver Mohan was waiting for her with the Mercedes, because finding a taxi in this torrential downpour was unthinkable. She cleared the immigration and customs with incredible swiftness, and before she knew it, she was on her way home. The streets were flooded with swirling muddy brown water, and pedestrians were up to their knees in it.

It was almost 9.30 p.m. when she had got out of the airport, and she judged that she'd be lucky if she made it home before 11. She leaned back against the luxurious leather upholstery of the car and gazed at the rain beating relentlessly on the windowpane. It was a miracle that she had actually made it to Thailand and back. Rajeev had arrived in Mumbai the day after she'd left, which was why she had been able to go at all. Aryan had taken Nandita to Koh Samui after a couple of days in Bangkok. She had been to Thailand several times, but not to Koh Samui; Aryan had persuaded her to try scuba diving, something she'd never plucked up the courage to do before. The white sandy beaches and the crystal-clear blue water proved too tempting this time, and she had succumbed. Aryan had been a certified diver since he was a child, so he helped Nandita complete a two-day introductory level programme and do two open-water dives in that time.

The fascinating, mesmerizing beauty of the undersea life she had seen had left an indelible mark in her mind.

Nandita had delightedly swum around all kinds of coral, butterfly fish and yellow-tail barracuda. The actual discussion of marriage had not come up again, but Nandita sensed it hanging between them like an unspoken barrier. Aryan had tried to be light-hearted and easy, but she knew he was thinking about her apparent reluctance to commit. She longed to discuss it with him, but as she had no idea what she was going to say or what exactly her problem was, she decided to let it rest till she herself was a little clearer about what she wanted. Their parting at the airport had not been a good one…she was awkward, he was distant, and both seemed eager to go their separate ways. Maybe this little time apart was exactly what she needed to sort herself out.

In spite of all this, the trip had fuelled her energy levels and she was looking forward to getting back to work. The Sunville presentation was coming up this week, so there was plenty of excitement in store.

It was past 11 by the time Mohan negotiated the rising waters and unbelievable traffic snarls, but at least the incessantly lashing rain was showing signs of abating as they pulled into Sea Breeze Apartments. Nandita found a note under her door to call Tushar; there had been a delivery for her that had been left at Kulwant Singh's house, and he was not sure when she was coming back. Delivery? Nandita was puzzled and called Tushar as she entered the house and turned on the lights.

'Hi, Nandita. I'm coming down, hang on,' he replied and hung up. Nandita left the door ajar and took her suitcase into the bedroom. It was quite wet, having been exposed to the downpour while being unloaded at the airport. She hoped the contents were not going to be as soggy as the exterior. She had bought some shoes in Bangkok that would certainly not take well to rainwater.

She heard the door slam and came out to see what Tushar had brought down. As she entered the living room, she gaped. Tushar was hidden behind a humongous bouquet of orchids over four feet high, with white, purple and pink sprays delicately arranged to resemble a cascade of flowing water.

'Came this afternoon, and the guy obviously couldn't cart it all the way back to wherever they came from. The liftman told him to leave it upstairs.' He gave Nandita a light peck on the cheek and looked at her quizzically. 'Aren't you going to read the card?'

Nandita was dazed at the spectacle of the fragile flowers held up on a backdrop of lacy white trelliswork. Could it be Aditya, she wondered? He was in Bangalore, and had already called and wished her, and a large chocolate cake from him had been delivered to their suite in Koh Samui. This was not Aditya's style at all. She opened the pale lilac card, and suffered another faint shock. Abhimanyu Menon! He had wished her a happy birthday, happiness, every success, and more in the same vein. Her mind was a blur. She remembered having mentioned that she had a birthday coming up, but *this*? Odd, to say the least. A bit over the top, wasn't it?

'Well?' said Tushar impatiently. 'Do I get to know who the secret admirer is?'

'Oh! It's...it's just a client. One of my clients...' It sounded lame, even to her.

Tushar's supercilious eyebrows went up disbelievingly. 'If you say so, my dear.'

Nandita saw that Tushar's possessiveness was in evidence once again. Though normally she could never bring herself to snub him, because of the deep-rooted insecurity she observed in him, tonight her patience was wearing thin.

'What is your *problem*, Tushar? Here, read the note, if you like. Abhimanyu Menon is the CEO of Ve Pharmaceuticals, and one of my clients, as I told you before.'

He sighed and sat down on the windowsill. 'Sorry, babe. It's none of my business. I didn't mean to insinuate anything. I'd better leave; you must be tired and ready for bed.'

'Good night, Tushar. And thanks, by the way!'

'Sure. Hey, before I forget, I'm meeting Probir Bhattacharya next Saturday, that photographer I told you about? For the perfume campaign. Still want to go with me?'

'Oh, yes, I'd love to. Aditya just raves on about him. I want to see his work. Saturday is good for me.'

He smiled, and gave her a pat on her shoulder. 'Cool. We'll go together. Take care.'

The next morning, Nandita was so swamped with work that the orchids were temporarily forgotten. Rajeev had encouraged Nandita to go on leave out of sheer guilt over the stress she'd had to endure in his absence, but he was more than relieved to have her back on the job.

'I hope you're well rested and relaxed, Nandita, because the shit's about to hit the fan out here,' he said, as soon as she walked into his office.

'First tell me about Pallavi,' she insisted.

'Her sister is with her in New York. The treatment goes on for another two weeks, and then she'll be back. The doctors are really hopeful that they got it out of her system; now we just have to wait and see. She'll be ok, Nandita. Pallavi's a fighter.' He sounded much more confident than he had been when he first broke the news to her.

'I'm so glad, Rajeev,' she said quietly. 'I hope everything continues to go well.'

'It will. By the way, I'm so proud of the way you and Niranjan have held it all together in my absence.' He looked as if he was about to say more, but Nandita stopped him.

'Thanks. Now fill me in on where we are, and how it's all shaping up.'

Rajeev smiled at her impatience and picked up the phone. 'Suman, get everyone on Sunville into the conference room, right now. We're doing a detailed review of everything we have so far.'

The morning went in a haze of activity, with the review meeting throwing up plenty of glitches and issues on the finer aspects of the designs. Rajeev tackled each one separately and in great depth. Nothing was going to be left to chance, Rajeev had decided. Naresh Patel would see just how much more competent Sabarwal Associates were than anyone else.

As was the custom, rumbling tummies were soothed with the arrival of coffee, cakes and cookies at regular intervals, and later Ganpat came to take lunch orders for those whose dabbas had not arrived because of the rain. No one at Sabarwal Associates was capable of working on anything close to an empty stomach, and Nandita had willingly slipped into this groove along with all the others. Post Tara's engagement to the as-yet-unknown Sameer, her mother-in-law-to-be had taken to sending her delicious home-cooked lunches, in an attempt to get her to stop eating all that 'nonsense fast food'. Tara continued to feast on muffins and pizza, but her colleagues benefited tremendously.

It was almost 4 in the afternoon by the time the marathon review session ended, and Nandita decided she could not put off calling Abhimanyu to thank him any longer. She dialled his mobile number, but it continued to ring, unanswered. She hung up and got back to her computer with the intention of spending a couple of uninterrupted hours at work. Less than five minutes later, her cell phone rang. Abhimanyu.

'Hi,' she said. 'Did I disturb you when I called?'

'I was on another call,' he replied. 'Are you back in Bombay?'

'Yes. Just calling to thank you for the beautiful flowers. I was...a bit overwhelmed!'

'I wanted you to be. Did you like them?'

'Yes, they were gorgeous, but so many of them!' laughed Nandita. 'Do you go overboard like this every time you send flowers?'

'Of course not! Only for you. Can I take you out for dinner sometime to celebrate?'

Nandita was stunned. Were Aditya and Tushar right? What was this about?

'Sure,' she said, buying time. 'Things are rather hectic now, but sometime soon?' She hoped her uncertainty did not show in her voice. She did not want to offend him.

'Cool. So how was Thailand?' How did he know? Rajeev, she guessed.

'Great. I learned how to scuba dive. At the ripe old age of thirty, I learned something entirely new!'

There was a short silence. 'Thirty? You look much younger than that, Nandita. I thought you were probably twenty-six or twenty-seven!'

'I wish! No, sorry to disillusion you, but I'm now officially hurtling towards my mid-thirties.'

'Nandita, I have a call coming in from New York, I'll talk to you later, ok?'

'Sure. Thanks for making my living room look like a hothouse in Singapore right now!' She hung up, feeling perturbed. She had been feeling uncomfortable about that bouquet since last night, and it seemed she was right.

Nandita settled down to work again with difficulty, and to her exasperation, was interrupted for a second time. This time it was Niranjan who came in, looking grim.

'What?' asked Nandita irritably. She was really in no mood for his histrionics right now. She was in a state of limbo after her holiday, and Niranjan and his peeves could wait until she had a chance to come back to reality.

'Can we talk for a couple of minutes?'

She was surprised; his tone was far more civil than it had ever been before. Was Tara's mother-in-law to be thanked for working this miraculous change with her divine prawn pulao? Or perhaps it was the coconut barfi?

'I want to apologize,' Niranjan said baldly. 'I never should have said all those things I did, I was wrong. You have more than proven your talent and your ability to work harder than any of us. I would never have managed to survive the pressures of the last month without you.'

Nandita was stunned into complete silence. For the life of her, she could not imagine what to say. Was this Niranjan Kulkarni? The same Niranjan who had abused her in front of the entire office? Who had tried every ploy to undermine her and make her life impossible for the past few months?

'I'm ashamed of my behaviour, but I'm not going to grovel forever.' This sounded more like the old Niranjan. 'Can we please put all this behind us and start on a clean slate?'

Just like that, huh? Nandita saw a trace of arrogance even in the way he apologized, and in the way he expected her to forget his viciousness and move on as if nothing had happened. But she was not vindictive by nature, and more than anything, she just wanted this ridiculous charade to be over. Niranjan was never going to be her best buddy, but if her working relationship with him was going to improve, it would save everyone a lot of time and effort.

'Yes,' she replied in a matter-of-fact way. 'Let's put it behind us by all means. Consider the peace treaty signed.'

'Thank you.' There was a glimmer of a smile on his lips as he nodded and left abruptly. Well, thought Nandita, that took care of that. The stand-off had ended most unexpectedly. Nandita knew that she now belonged at Sabarwal Associates in a way that she never thought she could at the height of her rivalry with Niranjan. It was quite a new experience, being a vital part of a team. All these years, she had worked on her own, not answerable to anybody, never having to pull her weight in a team situation. Had she been arrogant, she wondered? Perhaps she had. Maybe that was the side Niranjan had seen. Nandita had carefully cultivated the slightly superior attitude, the confident posture and the 'designer' aura that had worked extremely well with her socialite clients in Delhi, but she realized that such an attitude might easily have been misconstrued as misplaced ego in a professional team situation. In retrospect, Niranjan had not been so wrong in assessing her initially. But that did not make him less obnoxious, she reflected.

Nandita could not resist the impulse to call Aditya in Bangalore and tell him what had happened. Aditya was enthusiatic in his response. He had been at the receiving end of her constant complaints about Niranjan, and was as relieved for himself as he was for her that it was finally over.

With the Niranjan Kulkarni glitch ironed out, life was set to become much more pleasant at Sabarwal Associates. In fact, life was looking good from every perspective. If only she could make up her mind about Aryan's proposal, pretty much everything would fall into place.

CHAPTER TWENTY-FOUR
Mumbai, September 2013

Nandita looked around with genuine interest at the larger-than-life blow-ups of famous personalities, from the eighties till date. Movie stars, writers, painters, politicians and models adorned every wall in sight, some in classic black-and-white and some in delicately crafted colours. Obviously, Probir Bhattacharya was every bit as talented as she'd heard. As she followed Tushar into the large airy studio, she noticed that the blinds were opened to reveal huge picture windows. She remembered reading somewhere that Probir loved to shoot in natural light. His portraits had an elusive quality about them that was hard to define. But one thing was certain—he captured the essence of his subjects with sublime mastery, delved into their souls and brought out aspects of them that no other photographer had been able to. Ageing divas of yesteryear graced the studio walls, and Nandita examined them closely as they gazed back at her with their misty, kohl-lined eyes. Probir had been the czar of soft focus in the eighties, and had started a trend that was much emulated over the years, but the truth was that no one could do it quite the way he did. Nandita missed Aditya, thinking how much he would have enjoyed this visit.

She was so engrossed in studying the works that she did not see the veteran lensman walk into the room. When she heard Tushar greet him in a slightly deferential manner, she was amused. So the usually superior Tushar did respect some people! She turned around to be introduced and saw a pleasant-faced, clean-shaven middle-aged man wearing a crisp white churidar kurta. He looked at Nandita and suddenly stopped in his tracks, as if in shock. Before she could react, the moment was gone and he shook her hand warmly. 'Nandita Dharkar, eh? Lovely to meet you!' He sounded as if he meant it. He motioned them towards the fat green Chesterfield sofa, and himself sat on an elegant antique chair. Tushar didn't seem to have noticed anything unusual, and Nandita wondered if she had imagined that momentary astonishment on Probir's face.

Tushar broached the topic of the perfume campaign without making any small talk, and was about to pull out the layouts when Probir stopped him, and gently asked that surely Tushar was aware that he was largely doing editorial work now? He had stopped shooting advertising campaigns.

Tushar smiled ruefully. 'That's all very well, but the fact is, there will be no campaign without you. Three of our celebrity brand ambassadors have insisted it has to be you. I hope you change your mind when you hear who they are.' Tushar mentioned the names of an actress and social activist, a seventies' star who still reigned supreme as a dancer, and a celebrated model-turned-fiction writer. He went on to explain his concept of the campaign and the look and feel that the brand was trying to create. Tushar was genuinely enthused by his campaign, and was selling it as if Probir was a client rather than a photographer. All through his animated monologue, Nandita had the oddest feeling that Probir was paying more attention to her than to Tushar.

'All the ladies you named are good friends of mine. It will be probably be impossible for me to refuse!' he said, with a touch of humour. He had obviously heard everything. He glanced at Nandita again. She was beginning to feel a little uncomfortable, and the photographer sensed it immediately.

'I'm so sorry, am I staring? It's just...well, it's your eyes.' He averted his gaze from Nandita's face with difficulty and turned to Tushar. 'Why don't you leave the layouts with me, and I will get back to you? You know I work my own compositions out, so I hope there will be no half-baked art director telling me what to do.'

Tushar sacrificed the absent Zack without hesitation. 'Of course not, you have a free hand! Can we... Is it possible to get some tentative dates down?' Nandita was enjoying the spectacle of the normally cocksure Tushar being reduced to a schoolboy. He was obviously in awe of Probir, a professional many years his senior, and the undisputed grand old man of Indian fashion photography.

'Don't worry about dates. I'll liaise with the ladies in question, that's my problem.' Tushar rose to leave. Nandita was dismayed as she wanted to question Probir about his 'eyes' remark. First Abhimanyu Menon, now Probir! What was the big deal? One would think that no one had ever seen green eyes before. She knew it was not just an offhand compliment; her instincts told her there was more to it. She was wondering how she could prolong the visit, when Probir solved the problem for her.

'Nandita, will you stay and have a cup of coffee with me? I saw you looking at the photos on the wall, and I have some more to show you that I'm sure you will find interesting.'

She smiled her acceptance of the offer. 'Could we make that green tea instead? I haven't gotten into the habit of coffee yet.' She waved goodbye to a disapproving Tushar. Nandita knew that Probir was famous for his liaisons with models, but somehow, she couldn't imagine this soft, silver-haired man having any designs on her. Tushar was relieved to have convinced Probir to shoot his campaign and was not about to rock the boat now, but his anxiety was patent. Probir's gentle looks belied his completely philandering nature, and Tushar was certainly not happy about the impending tête-à-tête. However, he had clearly been excluded, so he said a reluctant goodbye to Nandita with a last glowering look. What could have possessed the girl, he wondered in exasperation on his way out.

'Nandita, are you new to Bombay? I haven't seen you around in advertising circles.'

'I'm not in advertising. Tushar's a friend, and I just came along because I'd heard so much about your work. I'm an architect, actually. Moved here from Delhi a few months ago.'

'Delhi? Is that your home town?'

'Yes. But I've always wanted to work here, and finally made the move after so many years.'

'I agree. Bombay's the place for young professionals. It's been called the city of dreams, an apt description.'

Nandita wanted to cut through the small talk, and get to the bottom of his strange reaction to her. 'Probir, what did you mean when you spoke about my eyes?'

The tea arrived and was served by a bent old woman, who looked at least eighty. Probir looked at Nandita without saying anything for a few moments. When he spoke, his voice was soft and wistful. 'I've seen those eyes once before…and I never thought I would see them again.'

Nandita was uncertain how to react. It was uncanny how Probir was almost repeating the same words Abhimanyu Menon had spoken to her. She had dismissed Abhimanyu's comments about her eyes as teasing, but now it all seemed like a creepy coincidence.

Probir got up and opened an antique roll-top desk that sat by the window. He pulled out a leather-bound folder that looked like it had seen better days. 'These are some pictures that I have kept for decades. Do you know, Nandita, I have spent over thirty-five years in this business? It's only once in years that a face comes along that absolutely blows you away, makes you understand what you are actually doing in this profession. I've seen very few faces like that, and this one was probably the most special of them all.' He placed the folder on the coffee table and gently pushed it towards Nandita.

She picked it up with mixed emotions—confused, curious and apprehensive all at once. She opened the folder and looked down at the picture inside and felt a jolt of lightning course through her body. Staring back enigmatically at her was her mother Amrita! A young, *very* young Amrita, tantalizingly beautiful, her head thrown back in laughter, her white neck rising like a swan out of a foaming lace collar. She turned the pages numbly and saw her mother again, and again. Amrita as the femme fatale, oozing attitude, her shoulders bared and hair coiffed into a sophisticated twist on top of her head. Amrita pouting provocatively, her scarlet lips seductive and sensuous. Amrita as an angel in white, soft, vulnerable and utterly stunning. Amrita in wicked, alluring black, a collar of diamonds glittering at her Audrey Hepburn-like throat.

Nandita rifled through the folder blindly, excited beyond measure. So this was her mother's big secret! Her mother had been a model! But she had told Nandita that she had never even been to Mumbai. Why? Why had she never, ever said anything? Nandita's head was reeling and she looked up at Probir, incapable of hiding her excitement. His eyes held nothing but sympathy.

'She's your mother, isn't she? It's not the facial resemblance so much as your manner, your way of speaking. And the eyes. I saw it as soon as I walked into the room.'

Nandita couldn't speak, but she nodded, still too dazed to react.

Probir spoke gently. 'You didn't know! She never told you about this? Her life in Mumbai?'

Nandita shook her head. There didn't seem to be anything to say.

Amrita had hidden this glamorous part of her life from her only daughter, treating her like an outsider? If Nandita herself could not fathom her mother's reasons for secrecy, how would he?

His next question was asked with hesitation. 'How is Amu... Is she well?' In answer to Nandita's surprised look, he said, 'I haven't seen or heard from her in almost thirty years.'

'She's well. She's great,' Nandita said mechanically

'We called her Amu. Amrita Kalyanpur was such a mouthful,' he replied. 'So her married name is Dharkar?'

Nandita leaned back in her chair, trying to quell her agitated pulse. Amrita Kalyanpur had a lot to answer for. She had lived with her mother for the last thirty years, but did she really know the woman? This radiant creature in the portfolio was looking at her with the eyes of a stranger and Nandita felt confused, overwhelmed with a burning desire to know more.

Probir saw her fighting with her emotions and decided to keep talking till Nandita had calmed down a little.

'She was ambitious, you know, focused, determined and poised to take the modelling world and Bombay by storm. I was just the star-struck young photographer who shot her portfolio, completely mesmerized by her beauty. Even a little bit in love with her, I daresay. Who wasn't?' In fact, as he further explained, Probir had been very much in love with her, and had been galvanized into shooting some of the most inspired portraits of his career. Several top agencies had clamoured for the first look at her pictures, and contracts had appeared thick and fast.

'But she gave it all up overnight, and the week before she was scheduled to shoot her first campaign, she disappeared without a word of explanation to anyone. It was tragic—all those contracts, all those assignments lined up, all came to nothing. She never called, never wrote. It was like she had just vanished.'

Nandita tried to focus. 'Her friends, family, none of them were contactable?'

'She had no family here, she was not from Mumbai. As for friends, I never really knew any of them. Later, I heard that she had married and moved away.'

Nandita felt more confused than ever. She tried to make sense of the facts, but managed to get nowhere. Why the secrecy? Why didn't Amrita just trust Nandita and tell her the truth? She promised to come back to see Probir again and left the studio with no clear idea of where she was going. She had no idea how long she walked or even where she was when she stopped to find a taxi. Amrita was her mother, her only family, the one solid rock she had relied upon, and the centre of her existence. How could it be possible that she didn't even know who this person was? And then the contents of the letter at the bottom of Nandita's jewellery box came back to her.

CHAPTER TWENTY-FIVE
Mumbai, October 2013

When Nandita had left Probir's studio, she had been in a daze. All she could think about was those pictures of Amrita...those unbelievably beautiful pictures. What a career her mother could have had! Obviously, even Probir had thought so. And she had given it all up to disappear quietly into anonymity! Of course, Nandita knew why Amrita had disappeared. The blue sheet of paper hidden away at home was the clue to why her mother had skipped town so abruptly. Nandita knew she just had to find the person who had written that letter. Was she one step closer to finding out?

Nandita did not have the luxury of too much reflection, because the Sunville presentation was a day away and activity at the office had reached a crescendo. It was an orderly, well-oiled frenzy, where each member of the team performed their given responsibility with robot-like efficiency and calm. But beneath the surface of Nandita's outward serenity there was a restless storm raging, which she concealed from everyone around her with a dexterity that rivalled her mother's.

The day of the presentation came and went so smoothly, it was almost an anticlimax. Naresh Patel was deeply impressed by the calibre of work presented and all but clinched the deal there and then. Rajeev, at his aristocratic best, aided by a grave Niranjan and a serious and composed Nandita, made a formidable squad, and Naresh came to the conclusion that the Sabarwal Associates' team was as professional as it was talented. Discussions and negotiations went on for the better part of the day, and at the end of the exhaustive session, the builder announced that he would let them know in a day or two. But Rajeev knew without a doubt that the job was as good as theirs.

There would be no celebration, however, until the news was official, and Nandita was able to leave the office early that evening. She headed straight home, not in the mood to hang around and discuss the day with the others. She knew that the post-mortem of the presentation would go on for at least an hour, and there was no way she would be able to participate with the kind of enthusiasm expected of her.

'You've been a million miles away, Nandita. For the past couple of days. Is everything all right?' Rajeev asked her as she prepared to leave office that evening.

'Yes, of course, everything's perfect.' She forced a smile. 'The presentation went so well!'

'Yes, but I get the feeling that there's more to it. Are things ok with you and Aryan?'

'There's nothing wrong, Rajeev, honestly. I've had a touch of migraine for a day or two, and it gets me down. Thanks for being concerned, I'll be fine.'

Rajeev gave her an openly disbelieving look, but let it pass. 'Just take the day off tomorrow. It's Friday anyway, and a nice long weekend will get your juices going again.' He hesitated. 'If you need anything, or just someone to talk to…call me, ok?'

Nandita accepted the long weekend suggestion gratefully. She needed some time to figure out what she was going to do. She left quietly without saying bye to anybody.

Her phone rang twice on the way home, but she ignored it. It was probably Tushar, bursting to know about her afternoon with Probir. He had called several times over the last two days and she had not answered. She had no doubt he would be on her doorstep later that evening. She would deal with him then.

Unconsciously, her fingers went to the miniature painting of Ganesh set in a silver pendant and suspended on a thin silver chain around her neck. It had been a present from her mother, given over ten years ago, at a time when Nandita was entering a new phase in her life. She was seventeen then and just getting into the National Institute of Design. Her mother had wanted her to study fine arts in London, at one of the best universities, and be exposed to the kind of educational facilities that she herself had never had. Amrita had never been too keen on the architecture angle and had tried to persuade Nandita to use her artistic talents in some other way. Nandita had rebelled against fine arts as well as London, extremely reluctant to leave Amrita alone in India. The friction between the two had continued for a while, with emotions running high on Nandita's side, and eventually it was she who had had gotten her way, choosing to go to Ahmedabad and study architecture. Her mother had presented the pendant to Nandita on the first day of college as a good-luck charm. The pendant was only a good-luck charm because it had all of her mother's love and good wishes wrapped up in it. Nandita carefully removed the pendant when she got home and put it away in the rosewood box. She then pulled out the blue sheet with the handwritten letter and unfolded it carefully. It was addressed, in a neat, formal hand, to her mother.

Dear Amrita,
I was upset when you refused to continue our conversation on the phone this morning. You have every right to be angry, but you must believe me when I tell you I had no knowledge of the real situation. I am truly sorry. But you know that this was not my doing alone... some of the responsibility must fall on you.

There is nothing that can be done now, but as I told you, I would like to be of financial assistance to you and the baby. That is the least I can do. Your anger is not justified, Amrita. The child is mine too, and though the onus of looking after him or her will fall on you, I should be allowed my share in some way. I have made the necessary arrangements and will be in touch. Please don't leave Bombay and deprive me of the right to know my child. As for the rest, trust me when I tell you that had I known how things were between you and him, this would never ever have happened. I hope you believe me, and will accept my help for what it is worth.

The letter was not signed. For the hundredth time, she wished she knew the name of the writer. The mention of the baby, which she guessed had to be herself, had shattered the myth of Manav Dharkar as her father. When she had first found the letter at the bottom of her mother's jewellery box, she had known instinctively that it contained something important. She never imagined that her dream of finding out more about her father would be fulfilled this way. But something told her to abstain from questioning her mother. It had to have been a painful experience for her.

Anyway, one thing was certain: the financial assistance had obviously not been accepted. Nandita knew her mother's earnings were what had kept their family of two afloat during her childhood. There were no other clues as to the identity of this man who was her father, but Nandita had always known that it had to be in some way connected with Mumbai. The visit to Probir's studio had proved her right. Obviously, Amrita had been pregnant with Nandita when she'd left Bombay in such a hurry. Her heart ached for her mother...how did an eighteen-year-old girl cope with something like that? Though Nandita knew that it would make her mother's life a living hell if all this came out, she still resolved that sooner or later, she would find out the truth. She had to know, she just had to.

Her phone rang again, and this time she checked to see who it was. Abhimanyu Menon. Nandita let it ring. She noticed that the two calls she had ignored in the taxi were from Aryan, and decided to call him back. Making herself a steaming cup of hot chocolate, she took the letter, went into the bedroom and sat cross-legged on the bed, dialling his mobile number.

'Hello?' The voice was not Aryan's. Not even male, for that matter, and very American.

'Hello. May I speak to Aryan?'

There was a slight pause, and the woman spoke again. 'Just a moment.' She was abrupt, almost to the point of rudeness. Nandita heard her calling out to Aryan in the background.

'Hello?' Aryan this time.

'Hello yourself. Sorry I missed your calls earlier...all well?' Nandita did not ask the obvious question, but Aryan chose to answer it.

'Hi, Cat. Finally! You've been pretty hard to get a hold of! That was Alison, by the way.'

Alison. His ex-fiancée. At eight in the morning?

'Just having a quick game of tennis before I head out to the hospital to see Sona. Where have you been...working too hard, as usual?' He sounded quite unaffected and she decided there was no reason to disbelieve him. She had not spoken to him for four or five days now, what with the time difference and both their schedules. Aryan had extended his US stay well into the fourth week, telling her that he wanted to spend some time with his parents and his sister, who had just had her third baby. Was Alison the real reason? Well, she wasn't going to jump to any conclusions. She lay back on the pillows, chatting with him about inconsequential things. She felt really far away from him, and not just in terms of distance. She could not bring herself to share the events at Probir's studio. A few minutes later the doorbell rang, cutting through her conversation, and she was relieved to say goodbye.

It was no surprise to see Tushar standing there, tapping his foot in irritation when she opened the door.

'Where have you been, woman? I've been calling you for three days!' He strode in and faced her accusingly.

'Save the histrionics, Tushar. I've been busy.' She was annoyed, for the first time, by his demeanour. He didn't own her, goddammit!

His expression changed. 'Don't get all stiff on me, Nandita. I was worried about you.'

'There was no need to be, you're not responsible for me.'

Tushar looked visibly crushed. 'I know that. I know you've got enough friends who look out for you, but I also know none of them are here right now.' He added in a bitter tone, 'Whether you realize it or not, I do care about you, Nandita. I thought we were friends.' He looked so hurt that Nandita felt instantly ashamed. She was taking out her confusion about her mother and her uncertainty over Aryan on poor Tushar, who had nothing but affection for her.

She sat down tiredly and looked at him with an apology on her face. 'I'm sorry, Tushar. Really sorry. I'm just in a very weird mood right now. Ok?'

'Let's cheer you up, then. Feel like a drink and dinner with me?'

Nandita considered her options. Sit at home, puzzling and wondering and driving herself crazy, or take her mind off everything and go out with Tushar? The latter, she decided, hands down.

'Sounds good to me. See you downstairs at 8.30?'

'Yes. That's perfect.' He left with a much lighter step than he had arrived with.

As it turned out, the evening out did restore Nandita's spirits a lot. Tushar was always an entertaining companion, and it did her good to listen to his anecdotes about life in the advertising world.

'The Karisma campaign has been like a turning point in my career,' he told her. 'Promotion aside, I'm working on one or two of the biggest brands we handle. Meera actually smiles and says "good morning" now, instead of brushing me aside like I was a buzzing bee waiting to sting.'

'Good for you. But I think you should snub the mighty Meera and work with one of the other art directors instead.'

'Nahi yaar, not on your life! She's the goddess of design, that woman. Whiny little prima donna, likes to be given solid bhav, but so bloody talented! I could never pass up the chance of winning an Abby, which is almost certain when you work with her.'

'What's an Abby?' Nandita asked.

'Advertising Club Bombay Awards. All those people who say they don't believe in awards and focus on what's right for clients are bullshitting. They all bend over backwards for awards.'

'So you think Meera's your ticket to an Abby? Don't short-sell yourself, Tushar. You're quite capable of doing it without any Meera leading you there.'

He raised his eyebrows, giving her his best fat-lot-you-know-about-it look. She shrugged and smiled. 'I think you should have more faith in yourself than in others, to get to where you want to be. That's all.'

'Maybe you're right. Look at you. Eight, nine months in this city and you've achieved it all.'

Nandita said nothing. Had she achieved it all? On the work front, yes, she had delved into hitherto unknown areas and was happy. But as far as the Amrita mystery went, she was no closer to solving it than before. And her love life was supposedly amazing right now, but why was she feeling a sense of disconnect with Aryan? Was it because he was thousands of miles away in Chicago? Or because he was playing tennis early in the morning with his ex-fiancée? She drained her glass.

'Let's get another drink.'

'Fine. After that, do you want to talk about what's bothering you?'

'Not really.'

The waiter came and took the order for their drinks. Tushar leaned back in his chair and watched Nandita through his lazy, half-closed lids. She seemed distant and he wanted so much to help, but couldn't think of what to say. Nandita looked at her phone again, and just that moment it rang with startling clarity. Aai calling. Nandita wondered what she would say. Impossible to act normal right now, she decided. She silenced the ringer and let it ring. When the lights stopped flashing, she turned the phone off.

'What was all that about?' asked Tushar, perplexed at her strange behaviour.

She looked up, smiling with effort. 'Don't you know that it's rude to take calls in the middle of dinner?'

'If you say so.' He lapsed into a moody silence, but she was too preoccupied to notice. The waiter appeared with their drinks, and Nandita came back to a sense of where she was.

'You never did tell me how your tea with Probir went,' Tushar ventured.

'It was cool,' Nandita answered equably. 'He showed me some of his earlier work, and we chatted about the changes in his style in the recent years. He's an interesting guy.'

'Very.' Tushar was dry. 'A lot of women seem to think so.'

'What is *with* you, Tushar? I can't imagine why you use that sarcastic tone with me all the time.' Nandita was genuinely puzzled by Tushar's comments.

'It's because I know what these guys are like. They look at women as objects to be used. I don't want to see you falling into that trap.'

'And you? Are you saying you're so different? You're so critical of Aditya, of Aryan, what makes you so different?'

He looked her straight in the eye. 'Lots. For one thing, I'm gay.'

Nandita blinked. Suddenly, everything seemed to fall into place. His lack of sexual interest in her, his distrust of the careless and apparently insensitive Aditya, his no-strings-attached affection, his cold relationship with his family...it all made sense now.

'Of course you are,' she said slowly, digesting his sudden revelation. 'I should have guessed, shouldn't I?'

'Can you... not talk to anyone about this, please?'

'Of course I won't, if you'd rather I didn't. But I don't know why you need to hide it.'

'Plenty of reasons. Kulwant Aunty, for one. How do you think she'll react?'

'I see your point. Do your parents know?'

'Can you doubt it?'

'I'm sorry, Tushar. It must be awful not to be accepted by your own family.' Poor Tushar, she thought. How lucky she was to have such a loving mother. But a secretive one...that was going to have to change.

'I'm used to it now. I'm living a double life and a lie and bloody mortified that I can't be honest about who I am.' His usual superior attitude had vanished, and Nandita saw a vulnerable young boy instead of the usually swaggering, confident man. And she had thought she had problems!

She did not switch on her phone that night. She did not want to speak or listen to anyone. She missed Aditya sorely, who was away on a shoot. If anyone could help, it would be him. As it was, she just wanted to sink into alcohol-induced oblivion, into a deep, safe and dreamless place.

CHAPTER TWENTY-SIX
Delhi, October 2013

Two of Epicurean's chefs were down with severe viral infections, and Amrita was refusing jobs faster than she could answer the calls. After the hugely successful twin weddings of the daughters of one of Delhi's biggest industrial families, Epicurean had been besieged by requests to replicate the same menu at other events. Amrita, harassed to the point where she had almost decided to leave everything to her manager and escape to Shimla for a few days, decided reluctantly that such a luxury was not an option. Her day had been insane, but for the first time in four nights, there was no event slated for that evening. If ever a woman needed to put her feet up and relax, thought Amrita with a tired sigh, it was she, and tonight was the night. She had made no plans to go anywhere, instead opting to partake of a frugal soup and salad alone at home.

Nandita had not called today, nor had she called for the past few days. Amrita put it down to a heavy workload. It was odd, but not worrying…if anything was wrong, she would have heard. Amrita felt for the hundredth time that she couldn't be grateful enough for the success and satisfaction her daughter had found in Mumbai. The fact that Amrita's own secrets were in extreme jeopardy was something she would have to live with. She had observed changes in her daughter that had made her proud, and at the same time a little wistful. Nandita had grown independent in a way she never could have while living with her mother. She had lost her naiveté, stopped accepting everything at face value and become just a tad cynical. Her world had become much larger, her views more decided and her personal and professional life seemed on track, thought Amrita fondly. If only it had been somewhere else, in some other space, things would have been perfect.

Amrita's mind drifted, as it often did nowadays, to a picture she had seen in the newspaper recently. He had aged well. Still good-looking, slim, suave. But the unruly black curls were now trimmed, and grey. The maturity only added to his devastating charm. Amrita had been unable to look at him for long. But she had cut the picture out and glanced at it almost every day. This weakness she never admitted to Simi, who would have ticked her off soundly.

This evening, she retired to her wicker chair on the lawn with half a bottle of Grey Goose and a bucket of ice. She made it a point never to drink alone, but tonight was an exception. The faithful Amar Singh had taken the evening off, so there was no one to cock a disapproving eye at her. The soothing sounds of Simon and Garfunkel filtered out into the garden and as the vodka went down, a little too smoothly, she felt her taut muscles relax. The sound of silence was suddenly pierced by the ring of the doorbell. Amrita glanced at her watch, wondering who could be arriving unannounced at 10 p.m. She got up and walked to the door, opening it just a crack to see who it was.

Bathed in the dim light of the antique lamp above the door stood Abhimanyu Menon. Abhimanyu Menon, in the flesh. Amrita opened the door wide and swayed unsteadily. Seeing his picture in the newspaper was not the same as seeing him in person, after three decades. He quickly stepped in and caught her.

Amrita recovered swiftly and disengaged herself. He looked at her for a full minute, completely bereft of speech. She was as beautiful, as ethereal and as vulnerable as she had been thirty years ago. Her long, straight hair still hung to her hips like a sheet of silk. Her still-slim figure was evident in the black jeans and black polo-necked sweater. And her eyes, those green eyes, still made him dizzy.

'Amrita.' The years rolled back and they both thought about their last meeting, the bitter way in which they had parted.

'Abhi, what on earth…how did you find…' She touched his arm as if to reassure herself that he was real.

'It's obvious, isn't it?' His voice was harsh.

'You've met Nandita.' Amrita's voice was numb.

'Yes, I have. Are you surprised?'

'Does she know you're here?' she asked apprehensively.

'No, of course not.' He looked expressionlessly at her, and asked in a barely controlled voice, 'Amrita, she *is* my daughter, isn't she?'

Amrita's face crumpled. 'No. No, she's not. I wish desperately I could say she was yours, Abhi.'

'Can we go inside the house?' he said gently, putting his arm around her and drawing her inside.

She nodded, not trusting herself to speak. They went out into the garden. Abhimanyu noticed the vodka bottle, but said nothing.

He pulled out a silver case and lit a cigarette with shaking hands. 'When she told me she had just turned thirty, I did the math…she has to be mine, Amrita!'

Amrita turned away to hide the tears that had welled up unexpectedly. How could she explain what she had done? What would he think of her? She used to think that nothing could be worse than telling Nandita the truth, but then she had never dreamed she would have to face Abhimanyu like this. Her mind drifted back thirty years, as it had done so many times in the past, and she wondered yet again what devil had prompted her to act as she had. There was only so much you could blame on drink and heartbreak. Let's face it, she had barely had one beer that night. Where had that instinct to throw all caution to the winds come from?

She faced him squarely. 'Do you remember the day we broke up and you left for Boston?'

'Yes, like it was yesterday.'

'I was devastated by everything you had said to me. You disapproved of everything I was doing, my modelling dreams, the prospect of my success...you hated my pictures even before I'd had anything in print. All those assignments, those exciting campaigns I was about to shoot for meant nothing to you. It was only about you, your plans, your aspirations. And you walked out on me. Just like that.'

'Amrita, you know that's not...'

She held up a restraining hand. 'Let me finish, Abhi. All that is history now. I was in a murderous mood that weekend, and unfortunately I chose to go to a party at Madh Island. I was foolish, in a wild rage, and... Well, I met someone there. It didn't last longer than one night, but the damage was done.'

Abhimanyu stared at her in disbelief. 'You got drunk and slept with someone! How could you?'

'I can't apologize anymore, Abhi. I've paid dearly for that foolishness for thirty years. I lost you, I lost my career and I lost out on a chance to make a normal life for my daughter. I've had to spin a web of lies for the world, and for Nandita, and I've hated myself for it.' She looked at him defiantly. 'I won't apologize.'

'Are you saying *I* pushed you into a meaningless one-night stand and ruined your life?' he shouted.

'No. Why should I blame you? I did what I did and I was responsible for what happened. But now you know why I never replied to your letters. I couldn't.'

Abhimanyu sat heavily down on one of the wicker chairs. 'Who was he? Manav Dharkar? The man you married?'

Amrita turned steely eyes towards Abhimanyu. 'There never was a Manav. He didn't exist. I couldn't have married anyone at that point. I just wanted my baby to have a father, so I changed my name legally and made Manav up. Dharkar was my Aji's maiden name. After Nandita was born, I moved to Delhi with my friend Simi's help and pretended to be a widow.'

'And that's how you've lived all these years...as a widow!' He was stunned. 'But you knew I wanted to marry you, Amrita. You could have found me somehow, surely?'

Amrita was calm. Suddenly, it had all become so easy. 'You wouldn't have wanted to marry me if you'd known...' She paused, and resumed after a moment, 'Let it go, Abhi. It's too much in the past now.'

'No. I think I have a right to know.'

'How? Why? What gives you the right? It's not as if you were there to help me. I was pregnant and alone at eighteen, and had to fend for myself. If it hadn't been for Simi, god knows what I would have done. So please don't stand there and be all moralistic, Abhi. I don't have to take that crap from you, now or ever!'

'Who was it, Amrita?' he asked quietly.

'Let it go,' she repeated.

'Ok, for the moment I will.' He turned away from her, too stunned to assimilate what she had said. He tried to remember some of the things he'd said to her during their bitter break-up and shuddered inwardly. She was right...he had been selfish and overbearing, sparing no thought for her feelings. Abhimanyu had never wanted to share his precious Amrita with the world, and had disapproved of the modelling career from the word go. He had feared that the glamour of the modelling world would take her away from him, but ultimately it was his own obstinacy that had caused their break-up. It was only now that he realized how much he was to blame for what had happened.

Amrita's voice cut in on his harsh reverie.

'But how did you know Nandita was my daughter? How was it that you came looking for me?' Amrita had had no idea that Nandita had met Abhimanyu in Mumbai, even though she was aware that he and Rajeev Sabarwal were friends. How could he have possibly connected Nandita with Amrita Kalyanpur?

'Do you think that's any big secret? It's beyond obvious to anyone who knew you well. When I saw Nandita for the first time, I felt instinctively she had to be your daughter. No one else could have given her those eyes. I asked her outright what her mother's name was, and she made no secret of it. I assumed Dharkar was your married name. We worked closely for months on a project together. As I got to know her, I could see more and more of you in her. My god, every time she laughed, it was like having you in front of me. I went out of my way to spend time with her and get to know her...I never dreamed she might be mine, until she told me that it was her birthday last month, and that she had turned thirty. Obviously, I did the math.' His face darkened. 'I had no reason to suspect there was another man.'

Amrita froze. He looked up apologetically. 'I'm sorry, I shouldn't have said that. But for all your suffering and pain, I hope you realize that you managed to make a mess of my life too.' It was true. She had managed to ruin his marriage to Kamini because no one could ever compare with her.

Amrita shrugged. 'It's history now, Abhimanyu. I had hoped that you would never find out, and that Nandita could go on believing in her mother's widowhood. You shouldn't have come.' Amrita turned away from him angrily. 'You should never have come!'

Abhimanyu walked into the house, found the bar and picked up a glass and a bottle of single malt. Amrita watched him, not moving an inch. It was surreal to have him wandering around her house like this. How many times had she fantasized about seeing Abhimanyu again? Every night, she thought, for the last thirty years. But not in her wildest dreams had she pictured him standing on her doorstep, strolling around her house, drinking her whiskey. He came back and sat down, pouring himself a large shot and filling his glass with ice. Her glass was empty, so he poured a fresh vodka for her as well.

'Why did he not marry you, Amrita? Why all these forced lies and angsts?'

'Marry a one-night stand? Who does that, Abhi?' She took a cynical gulp of her vodka. 'Besides, he was married.'

'Amrita! What were you thinking?' Abhimanyu was more bewildered than shocked.

'I wasn't. I was getting back at you for walking out of my life,' Amrita said coldly.

Abhimanyu looked at Amrita's set face and knew that this was not the time to discuss it. He would have to approach this slowly. He was burning to know who this mysterious man was, and why Amrita had chosen to disappear the way she had. But he would be patient. She would tell him sooner or later, he'd make sure of that.

CHAPTER TWENTY-SEVEN
Lakshadweep, October 2013

Aditya examined the sky critically. Contrary to his expectations, the shoot was turning out to be a particularly painful one. The weather had been relentlessly cloudy with choppy seas, the art director Nilesh was unpredictable and inconsistent, and the models moody and high-strung. He was in no mood to pamper the girls or indulge Nilesh, and he wished desperately for one day of good weather so that he could work like a dog and wrap this thing up. The ad was for a ceiling fan; of course, the creative content of the pictures had no connection whatsoever with the product. It was early days to get cynical about his newly chosen profession, but today, Aditya was all out of patience with everyone. Arushi had correctly gauged his mood early in the morning, and had chosen to arm herself with a book and retire to a far corner of the resort to be out of his way.

Though it was Aditya who had suggested that Arushi come along to Lakshadweep for the shoot, he was forced to admit she was a distraction. She was not in her usual sunny mood. She had been petulant and demanding, and some squabbles had inevitably arisen. Aditya had found it all a little unpleasant, and the two of them had tacitly agreed to keep out of each other's way. No mixing business with pleasure again, he decided.

'Looks like it's clearing up a bit,' said Naina, Aditya's assistant. 'Should we get everything into position, just in case?'

This had the effect of galvanizing the team into action, for the sheer relief of doing something constructive instead of sitting around and waiting for things to happen. The boat was already loaded with all the equipment, and the models were told to stop munching on lettuce leaves and hop aboard. In spite of the vacillating art director, Aditya had worked out the shots in his mind. It was his first underwater shoot, and he was determined not to make a mess of it. The key was to shoot from a lower angle, he knew. Shooting upwards would give him a stunning blue gradient background all the way up the surface, capturing the distinction of colour on flora and fauna.

As it turned out, the sun did come out in all its glory, lighting the surface levels of the water and lending breathtaking clarity to the photos. Suddenly, the miserable Lakshadweep experience turned into an avalanche of creative expression for Aditya, and he thought later that he had never enjoyed an afternoon more. Four hours of work turned the entire shoot around, and luckily the exasperating Nilesh was too delighted to say anything other than 'Rocking, man!' at regular intervals. This after days of cribbing about how things were dragging and no progress was being made. On the ride back to the resort, Aditya made a mental note never to work on a location shoot with Nilesh again.

Sitting on the edge of the boat, away from the rest of the group, Aditya luxuriated in the salty spray of the sea on his cheeks. Honestly, sometimes he wondered how he would survive this profession. Photography was definitely something he loved as an art form, but he was not sure how well he fitted into the advertising world. He would never know, of course, until he tried. It was better than taking over the family business, of that he was sure. He felt guilty about the burden that had been placed on his Simi Bua; she had been forced to make the family business her life, only for his sake. He would have to find a way to make her sell the sports stores and relax a little. He knew she would like him to settle down to his profession. He also knew that she was hoping something serious would come out of his relationship with Arushi, but…well, he was not going there today, he told himself.

Now that Aditya had finally moved away from his playboy lifestyle in Delhi, he figured that he did not very much like the person he had been. He had lived as shallow and worthless a life as he possibly could, almost deliberately drowning himself in the meaningless social whirl that surrounded him. If there was anything that he had done single-mindedly, it was promoting Nandita's career and making sure she got all the right breaks. Even that was redundant after she found her professional feet, and he had lapsed back into his indolent ways. But all that was changing, he hoped. He was genuinely enjoying his newfound profession, and was hoping that it would be a sort of redemption for him.

He needed to find an apartment as soon as he got back home. He needed his space and he needed some solitude. He was very much in Nandita's way… he had no right to take her for granted the way he did. Her being with Aryan had subtly altered the parameters of their relationship. Yes, he needed to move out as quickly as possible. In fact, it would be better for him if he moved out of Mumbai itself… Why not try and set up base in Delhi? Simi Bua would be happy, and he would better off too. It wouldn't be too hard to commute, he could travel to Mumbai as and when required; anything would be better than staying in Mumbai and having to…

'Hey, Aditya,' called Naina from across the boat, cutting in on his thoughts. 'I think we can have a celebration dinner today, with the work we managed to get done. You were fantastic out there!'

'Whatever you say…you're the boss!' he replied, saluting her.

Arushi later found Aditya supervising the packing of his equipment when she emerged from her hideout that evening.

'We're leaving?' she asked, surprised. 'Without finishing the shoot?'

'We *have* finished. It was amazing. Got some spectacular shots. Where were you all day?'

'Keeping out of harm's way,' she shrugged. 'You've been a horrible surly bear, you know. I was just giving you space.'

'I'm sorry, babe,' he said absently. 'I shouldn't have asked you to come with me!'

'Well, I wouldn't actually call this a holiday, but what the hell. We can always take another one somewhere soon, right?' Arushi stole a look at him. 'How about Goa for a few days as soon as we get back? Sounds good?'

'No, I've too much to do once we get back. I'm moving back to Delhi.'

'Moving back…' Arushi stopped, shocked and confused. 'Just like that? What about us?'

'Arushi, we've discussed this before, you…'

Arushi was about to interrupt when Aditya's phone rang. 'Nan! Was thinking of you today…had the most incredible shoot…underwater… No, no, we're done, I'll be back tomorrow. Of course…no, I'll see you tomorrow, as soon as I get in. No, no plans this week, I am very much in town… Bye, babe…see you.'

Arushi took up where Aditya had left off. 'And since we've discussed it before, you won't discuss it again?'

'Sorry, Arushi. That was Nandita…checking when I'm back in Mumbai. Look, I know it's a bit of a sudden decision to move back, but it's something that I have to do.'

'And don't think I don't know why you have to do it. You're such a bastard, Aditya,' Arushi said, fighting to control her tears.

Aditya looked at her expressionlessly. 'I'm sorry you feel that way, but I have no idea what you think you know.'

Arushi turned around and began packing her bag mechanically. The tears were flowing now, but Aditya did not notice. His mind was elsewhere. Nandita had sounded preoccupied on the phone. Something was not right with her; he knew it as soon as he'd heard her voice.

CHAPTER TWENTY-EIGHT
Mumbai, October 2013

Nandita reached for her fourth bottle of chilled beer from the icebox and opened it absently. Lying idle like a vegetable on her living room couch was taxing and the beers were going down rather easily. Aryan was back from Chicago but completely snowed under with work, and had little or no time for her. Aditya and Arushi were in Lakshadweep. Bereft of her primary sources of social life, Nandita had had, over the past few days, plenty of time to think. Her purpose in coming to Mumbai had been to move towards her career goals. To get out of the stagnant Delhi routine, to meet new people, to find new work. And yes, she also wanted to discover the secret of the letter and find the mysterious writer. The letter had originated in Mumbai—that much was clear to her. Was the writer still here? How could she even begin to track him? More importantly, would her mother want her to meddle?

There was no doubt that Amrita's life had revolved unequivocally around her daughter for the last three decades and whatever had happened before that was irrelevant; who knew what Amrita's constraints were? The truth was that she loved her daughter single-mindedly. So her mother had a few secrets in her past. Big deal. Wasn't *everyone* was entitled to that? Yes, but Nandita still wanted to know.

She would find out what had happened on her own, instead of confronting her mother. If Amrita wanted to stay under the radar, let her. Nandita would not force her to confess. But she sure as hell would get to the bottom of the mystery. As she sipped her beer, Nandita reflected that Probir Bhattacharya was a good place to start. Surely he must have known if Amrita had a boyfriend? She had been too stunned by the events of that afternoon to actually make any enquiries. That was it! That was what she needed to do. Nandita's lethargy vanished. She turned on her cell phone for the first time that day and dialled Probir's number, but there was no answer.

Nandita came back to her earlier train of thought. Who was in her mother's circle of friends back then? she wondered. Amrita had obviously come to Mumbai to try a career in modelling, and god knows she was more than cut out for it. Nandita was willing to bet that it was against her grandmother's wishes; she could not imagine her old-fashioned Aji sanctioning such a career back then. Aji had definitely not been a supportive mother to Amrita.

Amrita was ambitious, Probir had said, but she chose to give it all up. Probir obviously had no idea that Amrita had been pregnant. There was only Probir…he would know who the boyfriend was. She tried his number once again. The phone rang a few times, but no one answered. Disappointed, she hung up.

Nandita ate her takeout Chinese lunch without really tasting anything. Her thoughts were racing, trying to piece together the puzzle as best she could.

She really needed Aditya; surely he was done with Lakshadweep by now? She dialled his number impetuously. He was still in Lakshadweep! Yes, he was coming back tomorrow. No, he had no plans, and would see her immediately. She hung up, relieved. Thank god she could depend on Aditya.

Nandita decided that she had spent enough time ruminating over events that had occurred before she was born. Tomorrow was a more relevant day, and she was nowhere near close to finishing the design for the grand staircase in the main mall of the Sunville complex. Barely had she opened the laptop and located her file when the cell phone rang. She glanced at it, and grabbed it. Probir!

'Hey Probir! Sorry, did I disturb you, calling so many times?'

'Not at all, Nandita…always a pleasure to talk to you! How've you been? I thought we were going to catch up for lunch sometime, but you never did call,' Probir replied.

'I know…things have been a bit hectic. Probir, would you mind very much if I asked you a question? About my mother?'

'If I can answer it, Nandita, I will. Ask away.' He sounded curious.

'That day in your studio…you mentioned that you had never met her friends, but do you know if she had a boyfriend… Do you remember?'

There was a pause. 'Nandita, why don't you ask Amrita herself? Wait…have you not told her that you met me?' Probir asked.

'No,' she replied guiltily. 'I…there are reasons I can't. Please, Probir. Just tell me.'

He sighed. 'I don't know what you're up to, Nandita, but I would suggest you leave it alone. If Amu wanted you to know, she would have told you.'

'Probir! You promised you would answer my question if you could. Don't make me beg!'

'Ok. I don't remember him too well, as I only saw him a couple of times. They were dating almost since the day she arrived here from Shimla…she met him at the Bombay Gym with one of the ad agency friends.'

'And? Tell me more!'

'I don't really know that much more. They were together for about eight months, I believe. Amrita was trying to find her feet in the city, and get her portfolio done. By the time she had lined up her big assignments, the relationship was over. I believe he left the country.'

'Do you remember his name, Probir?' Nandita asked breathlessly.

'Yes. It was Abhimanyu. Abhi, she called him. Can't remember the last name. Nandita, where are you going with all this?'

Nandita drew a deep breath. Of course, how foolish of her… she should have known immediately! Abhimanyu Menon and her mother. It made perfect sense. His questions about her mother, his comments on her eyes, his more than normal interest in her… it all fell into place now.

'Nandita? You there?' Probir was concerned.

'Yes…yes, I'm here. Sorry, Probir,' she said quickly, breaking out of her trance. 'Thanks a lot, I really appreciate all your help. You've been fantastic.'

'That's all very well, but I do hope you're not out to make trouble, my dear. And by the way, if you ever decide to let your mother know about our meeting, I would give anything to get in touch with her again. Is she still…does she still have that…' Probir broke off.

'Yes. She does. She is still one of the most beautiful women you'll ever see.' Nandita suddenly wished from the bottom of her heart that Amrita could have had the career she had chosen for herself. She would have been absolutely sensational. Had Abhimanyu Menon been responsible for her failure? Or was it her father, the unknown letter-writer?

She cast her mind back to the wording of the letter…she knew it by heart after so many years. It did not sound like the writing of a man who was in love with her mother—it was too formal, almost clinical. Surely it couldn't have been written by Abhimanyu? The writer was her father…her father, who would not marry Amrita, and the least he could do was offer financial assistance. Abhimanyu had gone abroad, Probir had said. She recollected the last part again: '...*had I known how things were between you and him, this would never ever have happened...*' How things were between Amrita and whom? Abhimanyu?

CHAPTER TWENTY-NINE
Mumbai, October 2013

Facing a gruelling day, Nandita cursed herself for the weekend break she had taken. What had she been thinking? Indulgence, too much indulgence! She had been greeted with relief by Rajeev, amusedly by Niranjan and with outright delight by Tara, who saw Nandita as her mentor and guide, and therefore highly indispensable to her comfort, now that the wedding loomed large. Before Nandita could seat herself at her desk, swatches of fabric for the bridal lehenga were brought to her for approval. Did Nandita think the pink was too flashy? The beige and gold brocade was classier, but did she not think the pink was more Tara's personality?

'Go with the pink, sweetie, I can see your heart isn't in the beige one...and I, for one, wouldn't be able to bear to see you as a sober bride!'

Tara laughed. 'You have an uncanny insight into my mind, Nandita. I promise to be there for you when it's your turn to don the lehenga. Speaking of which, how's it going with Aryan? Any date set yet?'

'He's lost under a deluge of work right now, Tara. The hotel is opening in less than a month, and there are an unbelievable number of loose ends to be tied up.' As a matter of fact, she was still evading the marriage topic with Aryan, but she did not want to discuss this with Tara.

The trousseau discussions had to be put on hold as the grand staircase design could absolutely not be put off any longer.

Nandita resigned herself to some serious work and a really long day.

When Nandita finally unlocked the door to her apartment late that night, she was looking forward to getting straight into bed, but found her living room strewn with bags and camera equipment.

'Aditya?' Nandita did not have to shout, as the tiny apartment was compact enough for her voice to carry. Aditya's wet, tousled head appeared around the edge of the doorway.

'Hey you! Just getting dressed, be out in a second.'

Aditya appeared, clad in a sleeveless T-shirt and colourful shorts.

'Hi Nan! I've just had the most amazing time…got loads and loads to tell you!'

'Evidently! You're looking ridiculously browned.' Nandita gave him a hug. 'Where's your prettier half?'

Aditya turned away, picking up the clothes that were strewn on the couch. 'At home. Got a busy week coming up.' She thought she detected a hint of reserve, but decided she'd imagined it.

Nandita flopped into the big stuffed armchair and enquired what Aditya would like to drink.

'Considering the number of coffees I downed in that godawful airport café, I think I deserve a real drink…any beer?'

'As much as you want, thanks to Tushar. He insists on stocking up so that he never has to go without!'

'What, is he still haunting you?' Aditya was indignant.

'Mumbai has been rather thin of company, in case you hadn't noticed. At least Tushar was here.'

Aditya snorted. 'Tushar is company? What happened to your taste in friends, Nan?'

'Shut up,' she retorted.

Aditya eyed her critically. 'Nan, are you ok? What's got into you? Fought with Aryan?'

'No, no, it's not Aryan. Not that I've seen too much of him… he's busy launching his hotel!'

Aditya was curious. 'Really? What's with him? What was he doing in Chicago all this time anyway?'

'Bonding with his family and playing tennis with his ex!' Nandita's voice was nonchalant.

'Bastard! I didn't put him down as the two-timing kind at all!' Aditya exploded.

'There's no two-timing or anything, Adi. Don't jump to conclusions. Actually, I have something to tell you and I need your advice…you've been away too long! I can't believe I needed you and you weren't there,' she ended petulantly.

Aditya sat down and looked at Nandita. 'Why would you need me? There's Aryan, there's your dear Tushar and all else failing, your precious Abhimanyu Menon.'

She looked hurt. 'I don't deserve that, Adi. You know perfectly well that it's *you* I need in a crisis. There are issues that I would never dream of discussing with anyone else. It seems like suddenly, the person I trust most in the world has his own agenda and has deserted me when I need him!'

'Why, Nandita?' Aditya said, walking around the room. 'Why are you so upset with me? Because for the first time in my life I'm doing something for myself, and am not around to hold your hand? But that's what *you* wanted, right? You wanted me to get my act together, move on and make something out of my life. How do you expect me to do it while holding your hand through every crisis? I have no agenda, Nan. You need to be a bit consistent with what you want. Or is it something else entirely that you're taking out on me?'

Nandita looked at him, trying to decide what she was going to say. She certainly didn't grudge Aditya his newfound career and Arushi…or did she? She was not used to him not being there for her, and not being his first priority. Nandita took a deep breath.

'Ok, you're right. I'm sorry I piled on to you. Of course I understand that you need to do your thing. Actually, there *is* something else on my mind,' she said.

Aditya raised his eyes heavenwards. 'Thank you! Are you finally ready to talk? The suspense is killing me!'

'Don't be sarcastic with me, Aditya! I don't need that right now. The thing is, I found out some stuff about my mom that's freaked me out. She's got some huge past that she has told me nothing about, and it's unravelling bit by bit in front of me.'

The bombshell had its expected reaction, and Aditya had a bewildered look on his face.

'Nonsense, Nan! Amrita Aunty's life has been an open book all these years, for decades, even Simi Bua knows that! There *has* to be some mistake!'

'No, there isn't, I'm sure. I've known for a while that there is some big secret she's hiding. I found a letter, years ago, which I didn't tell even you about. She's kept something from me all these years.'

'But Nan, how? What did you find out?' Aditya asked, still shocked.

Nandita recounted the events of her visit to Probir's studio and what had transpired.

'That asshole Tushar! I might have known he was party to all this. He's a bloody meddlesome—'

'Cut it out, Adi! Come on, the poor guy has nothing to do with all this, and he doesn't even know. You just have your knife into the poor chap.'

'Ok, ok! So...obviously, you never asked your mom about any of this. You decided to figure it out on your own.'

Nandita flushed. 'I know it sounds silly, but I can't ask her. I just can't. There's no need to judge me.'

Aditya put his arms around her. 'I'm not judging you, baby. Just trying to figure out why talking it out with her was not an option...you two are so close.'

'It's just... I couldn't intrude, when she has kept her secret so perfectly for so long.'

'But what I don't understand is, why? What's the big deal if she wanted to be a model? It's no sin if she had some beautiful photos taken...even back then it wasn't,' Aditya said, puzzled. 'Whatever her secret was, I'm sure it wasn't this. Come on, Nan, it doesn't make sense.'

'There's more. The boyfriend Probir told me about? It's Abhimanyu Menon. He wasn't coming on to *me*, Aditya. It was all about my mom.'

The expression of comical astonishment on Aditya's face was enough to set Nandita laughing. 'See, I told you. I was always sure he had no designs on me!'

She went to her cupboard and extracted the blue letter, and handed it to Aditya. 'And this,' she said, 'is where it all began. Here, read it. I found it a few years ago, at the bottom of a jewellery box my mother gave me. It was hidden under the paper lining... I guess she had forgotton she'd put it there.'

As Aditya read through the letter, his eyebrows knitted into a deep frown. 'You've known about this for years? You never said anything, Nan.'

'I...somehow I couldn't. Anyway, we were not speaking to each other at the time I found it... Remember, after we broke up? I wanted to, later, but I was just too confused.'

'I can imagine. There's only one possible meaning here, Nan…but Amrita Aunty…I don't like to say this…'

'You're right, Aditya. Only one possible explanation. I owe my existence to a cad of a man who my mother couldn't, or wouldn't marry, and the whole story of my supposedly dead father is a lie.' She paused. 'Now you know why I won't ask her anything!'

'Hey, slow down, baby… We don't know that he was a cad… we don't even know what the circumstances were. I assume it's not the Menon guy?'

'I don't think so… Anyway, come to think of it, I've seen his writing, and it's quite different.'

'So what about Manav Dharkar?'

'Figment of her imagination, I'd say. I think Abhimanyu… you know, I think Abhimanyu's the other guy mentioned in the letter. Coming back to Manav Dharkar,' said Nandita, 'it *could* be him. But from the letter it's obvious they never married.'

'Hmmm. Let's get that beer, my brains are getting fuzzy with all this mental exertion,' said Aditya, and started towards the kitchen.

Passing the sideboard, he picked up a brown manila envelope and called out to Nandita.

'Hey Nan, someone's sent you a rather official-looking letter… looks legal. Like someone's suing you for something!'

'Oh yeah, that came by courier yesterday,' said Nandita carelessly. 'I haven't had time to open it. Make me a vodka soda while you're at it, please!'

'It looks interesting…let's see!' Aditya ripped open the thick envelope and pulled out a single thick sheet of expensive embossed paper.

'It's from some Vakil & Mehta. Solicitors.' He handed it to her.

She began to read, and a puzzled frown appeared on her brow.

'What is it, babe?' Aditya peered over her shoulder.

Nandita read the first lines aloud. *'Dear Nandita, This is with regard to the trust fund set up for you by your father, which will mature on your thirtieth birthday. His identity will be revealed to you in person, for reasons of confidentiality. You are the recipient of approximately Rs 7 crore, as per the current funds in the trust. Kindly visit our office at your earliest convenience to complete the necessary formalities.'* She sat down on one of the dining chairs carefully, her face expressionless. Both of them were bereft of speech. Eventually, Nandita found her voice, though it sounded nothing like her.

'Aditya, make that a *really* large vodka, please,' she said shakily.

CHAPTER THIRTY
Mumbai, October 2013

Nandita sat at her desk in her office at Sabarwal Associates, reworking the finer points of mall design. Given Mumbai's hot weather, the idea was to turn the entire lobby into a shaded courtyard, climate-controlled, but with natural light streaming in during the day. Complicated enough. What kind of glass would let in optimum light? It obviously needed to be laminated, tempered, super-strength glass with outstanding stress resistance properties. *Which crazy person leaves so much money to a virtual stranger, daughter or not?* At exactly which angle would light reflect off the inclined panes on a summer afternoon? *Amrita had not accepted anything, so he had left it all for Nandita. That would explain the absence of any photographs or personal history.* The glass...should it be tinted?

Nandita absently sketched an angled section of a skylight in the sloping ceiling. She wondered why Abhimanyu Menon had not married Amrita...why had they broken up? Her brain was reeling from the unanswered questions, and she realized that she needed to focus on her work. Ever since she and Aditya had opened the letter from Vakil & Mehta two days ago, she had been unable to think of anything else. The staggering sum of Rs 7 crore had not even begun to sink in yet; all she could think of was that she had to know the identity of her father. Aditya and Nandita discussed the new development threadbare until late in the night, without achieving anything other than an admirable degree of inebriation. Aditya was deeply inclined to take the next flight to Delhi with Nandita and let her talk to her mother once and for all. But by the end of the evening, neither Nandita nor Aditya had come up with any concrete ideas to deal with the situation.

Nandita now began to understand why her mother had been so secretive about her past. She was being protective, so she had kept her daughter away from Mumbai and the people in it. Thirty years ago, things were different and the prospect of a single girl, particularly one so young, having a baby, was practically unthinkable. Nandita's blood froze to think of what poor Amrita must have gone through, all alone at eighteen, without even her own family to support her. But she had chosen to give birth to her child, faced untold difficulties and raised Nandita without letting her even catch a whiff of what had happened. Nandita realized that her mother was indeed an incredible woman. She was not so sure about her father.

She thought about Abhimanyu and her mother's feelings about him. She had never mentioned him to Amrita, so chances were she was not even aware that they had met. What would her mother's reaction be to all this? For the life of her, Nandita would not allow Amrita to go through any more grief. Maybe she should just say nothing, and hope all this would just die down. Maybe Abhimanyu was not even interested in meeting Amrita again. It would complicate his life as well as her mother's. Now that the bio-lab project was in the execution stages, Nandita was more in touch with the contractors and builders than Abhimanyu himself. She had not met him for weeks and, surprisingly, there had been no calls either. All for the best, she thought, it was better to leave it alone. She did not want to upset Amrita in any way.

As for the unknown father, that was no big deal; after all, Nandita had spent thirty years without a father, so what was the need to have one now? She chewed the tip of her pencil and stopped sketching. No, that didn't work for her. Surely a man would *want* to be in touch with a child he knew was his? She couldn't blame him for wanting to know her…but did *she* want to know *him*? Nandita had not replied to the letter from the solicitors, not knowing what to say. Meeting the lawyers meant that she would have to meet the man who had set up the trust fund. Her father. How could she open up that can of worms, knowing she would devastate her mother in the process?

Nandita decided that it was time to go to Delhi and see her mother, she had been incommunicado for too long.

She had another problem to resolve—was she going to tell Aryan about all of this? She owed her mother the right to her privacy. Telling Aditya was a no-brainer, he knew everything there was to know about Nandita. It would be unthinkable not to tell him. Aryan was different…somehow it seemed wrong to talk about Amrita's deepest secrets with someone who had never even met her. Aryan knew there was something on her mind and had asked her repeatedly what was bothering her. She had had no answer to give. Moreover, their relationship seemed to have undergone a tangible change since Aryan's return from Chicago. He was very preoccupied with his work and so was she with hers, but it was more than that. There had been no sex and virtually no physical proximity since he had been back. Part of her missed it, but part of her was relieved. She was too ambivalent about her feelings to be her usual uninhibited self with him.

She was due to meet Aryan for dinner at the hotel that night. She was not particularly looking forward to it, simply because there were too many unspoken questions hanging between them that she was not sure if she was ready to answer. Right now, her mind was wholly occupied by the saga of her unknown father, the mysterious legacy and her mother's past. How could she communicate any of this to Aryan?

That night at dinner, Aryan broached the topic of their relationship again. They were sitting at one of the almost complete restaurants in the new Starling Lotus, where Aryan was conducting food trials with a few of his senior staff.

'Cat, you're miles away…do you want something to drink?'

'No, thanks. I'm fine. Sorry, just a bit distracted.'

'You're distracted a lot nowadays. Is everything ok?' He sounded a little impatient. Nandita couldn't blame him…she had been acting really weird lately.

The evening was awkward, and Nandita was glad when the rest of the team left. She needed to be alone with Aryan. They had not had much time together recently, and it was obviously telling on their relationship.

'Aryan, I'm sorry I've been so preoccupied. I promise I'll behave, ok?' She clasped his hand as they walked towards the lobby.

'That's not what's bothering me. It's us, Cat. Something's not right.'

'But that's because you've been busy, I've had work pressures…'

'No. I asked you to marry me, Cat. Weeks ago. Have you given it any thought?'

'Aryan, there's too much happening in my life right now. I can't think about marriage.' She felt guilty, but it was the truth.

'Like what?' he countered. 'Work? Assignments? Those things are irrelevant to what I'm asking you.'

'No, Aryan. There's stuff that… I can't…I can't really discuss with you.' She realized how cruel she sounded, but now she had said it.

He said nothing for a moment. When he spoke, his voice was harsh. 'Stuff you can't discuss with *me*. But you can discuss it with Aditya?'

She was taken aback. 'What do you mean by that, Aryan?'

He stopped walking and turned to face her. 'I mean exactly what I said.'

Nandita was baffled. 'But Aryan, you know Aditya and I...I mean, we go back so many years, and I tell him—'

'Exactly,' he interrupted. 'You tell him everything. You can talk to him about anything. He takes precedence over everybody in your life. Every bit of good news has to be shared with him first. His is the first shoulder you cry on. He is the one you turn to instinctively, no matter what, Cat. He's your go-to person, your first priority and always will be, right?'

'Yes. Yes! Aryan, I've told you this many times. It's never really bothered you before, has it?'

'It's always bothered me, Cat. How can it possibly not? You're obviously really anxious about something right now, totally preoccupied by it, and you talk to him about it, but not to me. What does that tell you about our relationship? More importantly, what does it tell you about your feelings for him? Clearly you're still in love with him, Cat. All these years you thought you and he were just best friends—that's rubbish. You're very much in love with him.'

The corridor whirled dizzily, and then suddenly everything stood still. Nandita couldn't breathe. What was he saying to her? She was not in love with Aditya! She couldn't be!

And right then, in a blinding epiphany, she knew it was true. Everything Aryan had said was a hundred per cent true. She had always loved Aditya, never loved anyone but him. What a blinkered, blinded fool she had been! She stared at Aryan blankly.

'But...I didn't realize...until you made me see... Aryan, I had no idea. I...how did you...' She stopped.

'When I watched you with him, it was evident. I desperately hoped I was wrong, but the more I saw, the more I knew. You and Aditya have the kind of chemistry that is impossible to miss.

Do you realize you couldn't even deal with the idea of him and Arushi? Your possessiveness showed every time you saw them together! As for him, it couldn't be more obvious how he feels about you.'

'But that's impossible! He's never given me the least indication of any such thing! Why would he not say it?'

'You have to work out those issues on your own, Cat. As far as I am concerned, it appears that you and I, we're not meant to be. I wish… But I've realized now that you will never love me the way you love him. He's in your system, a part of who you are.'

She tried to absorb the words as they came out. Yes, Aditya was a part of who Nandita was; she was incomplete without him, had always been. She had been in love with Aditya all her life. For a moment, she felt a surge of complete exhilaration, which was replaced immediately with despair. Aditya was with Arushi. She had lost him because of her stupidity. Aryan said that Aditya still cared about her, but how could that be? He seemed happy with Arushi. And there was Aryan…whom she had inadvertently caused so much heartache.

'I don't know what…' she began, but he cut her short.

'No, Cat. I've known this was coming sooner or later. It's one of the reasons I stayed away for so long. I needed to distance myself from you, and to give you some space to figure out your priorities. Don't worry, I'll survive,' he said with a wry smile. 'I just wish things could have been different.'

'So do I. Oh, so do I, Aryan.' She gave him a warm hug, and he held on to her tightly for a few moments. When he released her, he was matter of fact.

'I'll have Mohan drop you home…I'm working late tonight.'

She nodded mutely and headed out of the hotel, barely seeing where she was going. Suddenly, the world was upside down, and there was only one person who could set it straight. But Nandita was not sure if he wanted to.

CHAPTER THIRTY-ONE
Mumbai, October 2013

The week after her break-up with Aryan, Nandita threw herself into work with renewed vengeance. She put all thoughts of Aryan, Amrita, Abhimanyu and the lawyer's letter out of her mind. Most of all, she avoided Aditya as much as she could. It was very hard to be around him and remain normal. Luckily, he was out of the house a lot. She had no way of knowing whether it was work or Arushi that was keeping him busy, but she hoped fervently that it was the former. He had told her he'd decided against finding an apartment in Mumbai and was planning to base himself in Delhi, a fact she was profoundly grateful for. She could not possibly watch his romance with Arushi flourish under her nose. It would have been too much for her to take. She did not want to lose Aditya as a friend, but she needed some time to adjust to her feelings. Being single again felt very lonely, and though she missed Aditya terribly, she knew it was wisest to keep her distance from both Aditya and Arushi.

Sabarwal Associates had a new client—a businessman who was building a school. A state-of-the-art international school, which had to outshine every other school in the city. Rajeev had entrusted the task to Nandita, much to Niranjan's delight; schools were not his thing. The brief was lavish. Air-conditioned classrooms, audiovisual rooms, labs, an auditorium, a swimming pool and more. Nandita was happy to take a backseat on Sunville for a while—anyway, her part was mostly finished now. It was a relief to have something new to work on at a time she needed distraction the most.

She was reading through the school brief a second time when Monica bounced in, clutching a bottle of water.

'Nandita, can you unglue yourself from here? I desperately need a cup of green tea and some sane conversation. Any chance of half an hour of your time? Please, *please* Nandita. Those Trivedis are driving me nuts, and I need advice!'

'You're in a mighty tizzy! I'll come right now, if you like. I really could do with a break too.' Monica thought she meant the work, but Nandita was actually referring to her personal thoughts, which were in complete overdrive.

As they came out into the reception area, Nandita bumped into Tara, demurely clad in a deep magenta-and-gold temple saree, with an intricate bindi adorning her forehead. Before Nandita could express her shock, Tara laughed and proffered an apologetic explanation.

'Mother-in-law's Diwali present. Had to wear it.' She was looking considerably slimmer, and the ubiquitous cookie/ doughnut/ brownie was absent. Nandita concluded that Tara was finally beginning to heed her ma-in-law's advice to eat right.

'You look amazing,' Nandita told her. 'Whatever you are doing to yourself is working miraculously.'

'It's a diet I googled last month,' said Tara. 'I've lost four kilos already…and I think I've eaten my last doughnut for all of eternity! It's all about the mindset, you know. I want to wear this utterly fabulous backless choli that my designer has made, to go with my ghagra.' She sighed, and added, 'Who knew that being a bride could be so stressful!'

'Whatever you're doing, it's better than the agony Monica is putting herself through, with her spinach juice and bottles and bottles of salted lemon water. Mindset be damned, the poor girl is going berserk with hunger!' Nandita was not an advocate of drastic diets, and though Monica was now half her original size, she could see how much strain the diet was putting on her.

Monica laughed. 'Today it's amla juice, not spinach. And I'll have you know that it feels amazing to get those kilos off. Whoever said that good things come easy?'

'Better you than me. I would be suicidal if someone fobbed me off with that outrageously small portion of food you consume in a day. How is all the wedding stuff going, Tara?' Nandita asked.

'It's one mad rush of fittings and jewellery and event managers. My mother wants all kinds of crazy stuff, and my dad is happily indulging her. Sameer and I are just small voices in the background; it's basically the parents who are letting loose their fantasies. I'd always known that Indian weddings are not really about the bride and groom, but I'm now experiencing it firsthand! Neither of us minds, though, we are enjoying watching our families in action. They are all so happy that it's worth it! My whole focus is getting our apartment in Lokhandwala furnished. I'm just so excited about it.'

'You're really lucky you are not staying with the in-laws, Tara. Ankush and I stayed with his parents till Ankita was born and it was an adjustment for all of us. It's not that they're bad people, but there was just zero privacy and it drove me nuts!'

'My ma-in-law refused to have us, fortunately. She says having two women in the same kitchen never works. Though with her around, I'd never have needed to step into the kitchen, she's way too good a cook. And if I know her, we'll be getting a tiffin sent to us every second day. But you're right, Monica, I'm really grateful that we're going to be on our own. And Sameer's not your typical Indian husband, he's pretty good with household chores!'

Khurshid interrupted this exchange summarily. 'Nandita, Mr Cyrus Vakil is calling for you *again*. Why don't you just talk to him and be done with it?'

'No, no, I can't!' Nandita shook her head frantically, and Tara looked at her in surprise.

'What's with you?'

Khurshid was insistent. 'Nandita, this is the fourth time since yesterday. Just deal with it, whatever it is! He's obviously a lawyer, it could be important.' She handed Nandita the phone, and Nandita took it reluctantly.

All three women watched with open curiosity as she said a hesitant 'hello'. None of them could figure out what the conversation was about, because Nandita was talking in monosyllables, largely restricting herself to 'yes' and 'no' and an occasional 'of course'.

When she finally hung up, Monica's eyebrows were raised.

'Well?' The question was asked expectantly.

'Oh, someone just left me a fortune,' replied Nandita flippantly, and they all laughed.

'You wish!' said Tara. 'Like that would be the solution to everything!'

Niranjan walked in, talking on his cell phone. He gave them a disbelieving look, covered the mouthpiece with his hand and said, 'Gossiping *again?*' He shook his head and walked off, leaving Monica and Tara with a burning desire to box his ears.

Nandita wasn't really listening. She had agreed to meet with Cyrus Vakil the following day, as he had sternly informed her that she could not shrug off the responsibility of accepting her legacy. Her life was unfolding like the pages of a bestselling novel, she thought wryly...never a dull moment. She allowed Monica to shepherd her into the conference room, and resolved that at least for the time being, she needed to forget boyfriends, family skeletons and fortunes, and focus on the mundane task of designing the Trivedi residence.

CHAPTER THIRTY-TWO
Mumbai, October 2013

Nandita was not looking forward to the visit to the lawyer, but it had to be done. Who would have thought that her search for her father was going end in a lawyer's office? She fervently hoped he was not going to be at the meeting—she was not ready to face him yet.

Nandita walked into the building at Ballard Estate expecting a dark and dusty interior, as was the case in some of the really old Mumbai buildings. She was agreeably surprised to find that not only was it clean and airy, but beautifully restored. The walls gleamed softly with an eggshell-white matte finish paint, and all the woodwork was old but beautifully polished. The offices of Vakil & Mehta, Solicitors, were located on the second floor, and Nandita travelled up at an agonizingly slow pace in an ancient but serviceable elevator with shining brass fittings and teak-panelled interiors. Nice, she mused, trying to think about anything but the interview she was facing. The old-world charm of the building excited her professional interest, momentarily distracting her from the task at hand.

As she entered the office, she noted that it had probably been designed sometime in the middle of the last century, but was impeccably preserved. The formidable lady manning the reception desk was an older version of Khurshid, dignity oozing out of every pore.

'Nandita Dharkar,' Nandita announced more cheerfully than she felt. 'I have an appointment?' Might as well put on a brazen face, she thought.

'Of course.' The lady showed no change of expression at all. Butter won't melt in her mouth, thought Nandita.

She was ushered wordlessly into a cabin behind a heavy oak door, and stepped into a large office panelled with deep rosewood. Behind the enormous desk sat a tiny man who looked like he must have been at least eighty. Nandita was taken aback. The man she had spoken to on the phone was definitely much younger; she was sure she could not have been mistaken. This was not Cyrus Vakil.

The man rose to greet her, reading her thoughts. 'It was my grandson you spoke to on the phone, Ms Dharkar. I am the original Dinyar Vakil of this company. Of course, now there are several more. Confusing, huh?' He chuckled.

'Do call me Nandita,' she said, smiling. Suddenly she felt at ease. 'The original Vakil? Do you mean the founding partner?' She didn't dare ask how many years ago the firm had been founded. But the old man was most forthcoming.

'Of course! Back in 1952. Well before you were born, you know.'

Nandita sat down on one of the antique chairs. She fidgeted uncomfortably while her host went through the motions of ordering tea and biscuits. He then meticulously unlocked a drawer in his desk and pulled out a red legal folder, tied up with white tapes. Nandita wondered how many secrets that voluminous old desk held. Hers had certainly been well preserved.

'Well,' said the old man briskly, 'my grandson has already informed you about the legacy that has been left to you. A trust fund. It was a much smaller sum in the nineties, but some judicious investment by the trustees and managers has more than quadrupled it. You are a very wealthy young woman, Nandita.'

'Look, I'm not going to beat about the bush with you,' said Nandita brusquely. 'I have no idea of the identity of this benefactor of mine. Though I have been told that he claims to be my father. Does he think giving me all this money would make up for everything?' An edge of contempt had crept into her voice, and old Mr Vakil looked at her squarely.

'I'm not sure that I am the person who should be telling you all this. It's best you read the letter he wrote you.'

Nandita was shocked. 'He's written me a *letter?*'

The old gentleman tenderly extracted a long blue envelope from the file and handed it to Nandita.

'Yes. Obviously he felt, as you do, that some explanation was due.' He watched the emotions raging on Nandita's face and added kindly, 'If you like, I will take a little walk and come back after you have finished reading it. By the way, I think you will find that he identifies himself quite clearly.' He added gently, 'You should also know that the person who wrote this letter died about fifteen years ago. The legacy you are about to receive comprises all his worldly possessions.'

Nandita's eyes widened in shock. Her father had died without ever seeing her. As Mr Vakil exited the room discreetly, she slit open the envelope with numb fingers and unfolded the thin sheets within. She studied the neat writing, recognizing it as the same hand that had written the letter to Amrita...no surprises there. The writing was close and small, and she actually had difficulty reading. Everything looked blurred. Suddenly she realized that was because her eyes had filled with tears. She wiped the back of her hand across her eyes impatiently and began to read the familiar handwriting.

Mumbai, 28 August 1998
My dear Nandita,
I am guessing that today must be your thirtieth birthday, and I wish that you and I could be together to celebrate it. I had hoped to share this moment with you in person, but if you are reading this letter, it means that I am no longer living. The doctors tell me I don't have much time left, and my only regret is that I never got to know you…my only child. The fact is that I am your father, and have never been able to claim you as my daughter for a variety of reasons. Please do not judge me harshly until you know the circumstances.

I met your mother Amrita at a beach party at a time when both she and I were going through a strange phase in life. I had recently got married and was having a very hard time adjusting to a marriage that had been as hasty as it was unwise. Your mother, though I did not know it then, had ended a relationship with a man she loved very much…my friend, Abhimanyu Menon. If I had known this, what followed would never have happened. Abhimanyu was always closer to my younger brother and I had been out of touch with him for a while. I had no idea who Amrita was. That night was completely out of character for both Amrita and me, and the only good thing that came out of it was you.

To cut a long story short, Amrita refused any help from me and disappeared from Mumbai. I tracked her down in Delhi, where she was living as a widow, and without letting her know, I kept up with your lives. I watched you grow from a distance, and all I could do was wish desperately that I could claim you as mine. You were such a beautiful little girl, Nandita.

But I had no right to disrupt the peace that I hoped Amrita had managed to find. I have great respect for the way your mother has managed to get on to her feet and single-handedly brought you up. I feel bitter, however, with the realization that the reason she never could go back to Abhimanyu was me...she would never tell him about us.

I so wanted to get to know you someday, one way or another. Now, given the condition of my health, I know that is not going to happen. I am putting all the available funds I have in a trust for you, which you will get when you are thirty. You are the only family I have, other than my brother.

Please accept it with my blessings. It will come to you at a time when I hope you will be mature enough to understand the circumstances in which I am acting this way. Forgive me if you can.

With much love and may god bless you always,
Himanshu Sabarwal

Nandita did not realize how long she sat immobilized in the high-backed chair, staring into a vacuum. She was brought back to sense of her surroundings when the tea and old Mr Vakil made a simultaneous entrance into the room. She could not make conversation now; all she could think about was the revelations in the letter. Himanshu Sabarwal was her father! And Rajeev was her paternal uncle! He had obviously known...he must have deliberately come to Delhi, sought her out, set up the meeting at the art gallery to make it look casual and brought her to Mumbai to work with him. He made her a part of his life, and his company, for his brother's sake. She had relatives on her father's side, whom she knew only as her employer's family. Little Ritika, who looked up to her so much and who was so fond of her, was her own cousin. It was all unreal to Nandita—she felt as if she was about to wake up from a bizzarre dream. But Mr Vakil had plenty of prosaic matters to discuss, such as the transfer of the money from the trust fund. There was a pile of paperwork, which an assistant brought in, and Nandita eyed all the spaces where her signatures were required.

'Could we...may we please do this another day, Mr Vakil?' she asked. 'I'm not quite feeling up to it today.' Somehow, she just couldn't face any of this.

'Of course.' If Mr Vakil thought it odd that she was reluctant to accept all those crores, he certainly did not say so. He benignly saw her out, patting her shoulder with a fatherly air. 'You can come back whenever you're ready. The money's going nowhere.'

Nandita acknowledged this with a shrug and made her way out. She was due to meet her school client for lunch. She tried to figure out how much and in what way her father was to blame, and if the whole story *could* have played out differently. The more she thought about it, the more she could not fault him. Amrita had obviously been a willing party, if rather misguided. She wished desperately that she could have known Himanshu Sabarwal. But at least she finally knew who her father was.

And now? Things had changed. Abhimanyu was no longer married. He would be bound to seek Amrita out sooner or later. How would her mother react? And Rajeev Sabarwal. Should she confront him? Yes, she had to. She could not live a lie the way her mother had, and really, there was no need to anymore. She was sure that the telling of the truth would be a huge burden off her mother's shoulders. Yes, she had to talk to Rajeev. She would support Amrita through the ordeal that followed, if necessary. It suddenly struck Nandita that her mother must have been agonized over her decision to work for Rajeev in Mumbai. She must have known it was no accident and been on tenterhooks, wondering where it was all going to lead!

Nandita decided to fly to Delhi at the end of the week, in time for Diwali. She had to speak to her mother before she spoke to Rajeev. She would have to miss the festivities at the huge Diwali party that he held every year for Sabarwal clients, but that was unimportant. Her father's two letters were safely tucked into her bag and would make the journey to Delhi with her.

Nandita made her way into the crowded restaurant for her lunch appointment, not looking forward to it very much. The client was late, but that was to be expected. She ordered a glass of white wine (anyone could be excused for drinking in the middle of the day when the day had been like hers) and settled back to wait, resisting the impulse to pull the letter out again.

Suddenly, she heard a familiar voice and looked up quickly. Arushi was walking into the restaurant, on the arm of a man she seemed quite cosy with. Wait, wasn't that Ashish Kataria, Arushi's ex-boss and ex-lover? Nandita was sure it was him; Arushi had once shown her his photo on her cell phone. From the look on their faces, Nandita was not sure if there was anything 'ex' about the two. A second later, Arushi spotted her. Guilt was writ large over her face, and she stepped forward awkwardly to greet Nandita. Nandita turned her head away deliberately, and ignored Arushi. Arushi's face turned a deep red, and she fled from the room.

CHAPTER THIRTY-THREE
Delhi, November 2013

Amrita was planning the menu for an expat wedding. The guest list was small and exclusive, including as it did many consular heads and members of the diplomatic community. The couple had asked for a completely Indian meal, but she realized that it had to be toned to suit the foreigners' palates. She was thinking about experimenting with some of the milder recipes from the Rajput princely families, which she had gleaned from a Mewari princess she had befriended some years previously. The use of spices was subtle in most of these, and Amrita had, as was her style, added her own twist to the original recipes. Cashewnuts and almonds, along with fragrant apricots, found their place alongside tender meats and delicate spices in the list of ingredients. She planned to use traditional silver thalis to serve the food, to create the most authentic ambience for the type of cuisine. She needed to get her menu and tastings finalized by the end of the week, as the weekend promised to be action-packed.

Nandita had called the previous day to let her know that she was planning to be in Delhi, but Simi had dragged her to a leukemia charity event she was organizing, as a result of which Saturday night was going to be a write-off. The event was for a worthy cause and Amrita did not grudge Simi the time and effort, but it was really bad timing. Oh, well, she thought, Nandita would just have to come along with her. She could do her bit for the cause too.

Amrita was anxious to see Nandita, for more reasons than she would admit. There was no doubt that she had missed her daughter, and a weekend together was a very welcome proposition. But more than that, she needed to know what Rajeev Sabarwal had told her. There had been no doubt in her mind that Rajeev had come to Delhi looking for Nandita…it was no coincidence that she had so conveniently been offered a job at Sabarwal Associates. Part of her fumed at his high-handedness. She had told him categorically when he had called her fifteen years ago to tell her about Himanshu's illness, and then again about his death, that she wanted nothing to do with the Sabarwal family, then or ever. She was angered at his persistence, but at the same time, she knew that he was probably just doing what his brother had asked him to.

The bond between Rajeev and Himanshu had been very strong, Amrita knew. Even though Rajeev was the younger brother, he had always been the protective one. Himanshu had been the larger-than-life, charismatic, flamboyant figure who appeared to dominate Rajeev, but in reality, Rajeev was like the elder brother. Himanshu's turbulent marriage to a temperamental singer had not lasted. She had heard snippets from Simi's inexhaustible source of gossip that his personal life was ruined beyond redemption by the time he died of hepatitis at the age of forty-one. Beyond the initial stages of the discovery of Amrita's pregnancy, Himanshu had made no effort to stay in touch with her. She had severely rebuffed his offers of financial help, wanting to cut that part of her life out completely. She wanted no connections to her past, nothing that would ever link Nandita to anyone from that phase of her life. The struggle had been intense, but Simi had been her saviour, seeing her through it all. She had no idea that Himanshu had stayed abreast of what was happening with their lives, and had watched Nandita growing up from afar. When Rajeev had called to tell her that Himanshu did not have long to live, and wanted to leave his money to Nandita, she had understood, but was adamant about her refusal. She told Rajeev emphatically that Nandita would never, ever know about her real father, and that she never wanted to hear from him again.

Amrita did not blame anybody for the turn her life had taken. Not Abhimanyu, not Himanshu, not even herself. That night at Madh Island, Himanshu had been the means she had used to get over her break-up with Abhimanyu; she did not try to romanticize what happened, it was what it was. A one-night stand. There was no euphemism for that. He had been as vulnerable as she was, and the brief time they had spent together had brought a strange, indescribable balm to their bruised hearts...a temporary respite from painful reality.

And now, Abhimanyu had tracked her down through her daughter. Since the night he had landed up on her doorstep, he had called her several times. She had not told him about Himanshu, and he had not asked. In fact, he had not brought up anything at all from the past. He would call to chat, ask her what she was doing, or fill her in on his life. He was relaxed, charming and never once brought up any controversial topic. But Amrita knew he had not given up. Abhimanyu would pursue her till the truth came out, one way or another. She realized that she would just have to tell him, so she could put all of this behind her, once and for all. She would also have to tell Nandita...that was the part she was really dreading. She could not bear to think of what her daughter's opinion of her would be when she found out that she owed her existence to her mother's chance encounter with a virtual stranger. But tell her she would, whatever the consequences.

Meeting Abhimanyu had, not surprisingly, brought back a flood of feelings from the past. Their quarrel over her desire to stay in Mumbai for her modelling career versus his desire that she accompany him to Boston seemed so trite now. The arrogance of youth, she thought, and smiled to herself. At that time, the world was her stage, and she'd had no idea of the shape her future was about to take. But all said and done, life had been good. She had nothing to complain about; on the contrary, she actually had plenty to celebrate. The only guilt she felt was that she had lied to Nandita. And that was something she could remedy… Simi was right, Nandita would understand. And she deserved to know who her father was…she had a right to know.

Amrita waited for the weekend with a mixture of anticipation and dread.

CHAPTER THIRTY-FOUR
Mumbai, October 2013

While Amrita was wrestling with the problem of how to tell her daughter the bizarre story of her true parentage, Nandita was waiting impatiently for Arushi to join her for coffee. She had been summoned by Arushi with the plea that Arushi should at least be given an opportunity to explain. Based on what Nandita had seen, no explanations were necessary…Arushi was seeing Ashish Kataria again.

Twenty minutes later, Arushi arrived with her usual flurry of activity. In the first few breathless moments, her story came pouring out. Nandita was flummoxed.

'But Arushi, I simply cannot comprehend what you are saying. Ashish Kataria left you in the cruellest way imaginable. How can you expose yourself to that kind of treatment again?'

Arushi wrung her hands and looked abysmally guilty. 'I don't know, Nandita, it just happened. You know, it's been equally hard on me. He'd been calling me while I was in Lakshadweep and begging me to come back to him. I've always told you he loves me, he really does. I met him last week, and I realized that all those old feelings still exist.'

'But what about his wife? Is Payal not in the picture anymore?'

'Yes, but he's promised me he'll leave her if I go back to him. He means it this time, I know he does.'

'And Aditya?' asked Nandita coldly. 'He's just expendable, someone you used to get Ashish to commit to you? That's despicable, Arushi, and beneath you.' Nandita was more furious than she ever remembered being with anyone.

'It wasn't like that, Nandita, you have to know it wasn't. I care about Aditya. You've got to believe me.' Arushi was crying now, not caring that her mascara was running down her cheeks in ugly streaks.

'Bullshit! He was here conveniently for you to fill in the gap and wait for Ashish to come begging to you. You knew Ashish would be unable to see you with another guy. I'll never, ever forgive you, Arushi. You've treated Aditya in the worst possible way a woman can,' Nandita told her contemptuously.

'You don't know anything about it, Nandita…you won't understand!'

'Don't insult my intelligence with such trivial clichés,' scoffed Nandita. 'Look at yourself, Arushi. You're a pathetic mess. I wish I could feel sorry for you. I wish I could say I hope you'll be happy. But somehow, I know you won't, not with that cad you've chosen.'

'If that's the way you feel, Nandita, I guess you're entitled. Aditya has been your friend longer than I have, and you will naturally have his interests at heart. But somehow I believed that you cared about me too, and would see things my way.' Arushi's voice broke and Nandita was aware of a tiny pang of guilt. 'Nandita, you don't know the first thing about Aditya and me. I've never discussed it with you because I hoped he would change his mind. But just for the record, Aditya made it very clear to me from day one that he was not looking for a commitment. That was on our first date. And he repeated it often, with unnecessary finality. He said he liked me, he enjoyed being with me, I was cool, fun, etc., etc., but if it was anything long-term I was looking for, I should look elsewhere. Do you blame me as much now?'

Nandita was stunned. 'You never said anything! Nor did he...I mean, I know him inside out. He never breathed a word to me!' What was this new twist? What on earth was Aditya thinking? But, she thought, had he ever told Nandita that he was in love with Arushi? Had he ever shown the kind of infatuation that Arushi had? Never, she realized. Nandita had just assumed everything.

Arushi hesitated, about to say something, but she changed her mind and remained silent.

'There's something you're not telling me, isn't there?'

'It's nothing. Nothing at all.'

'Are you sure? I can tell you're hiding something!'

'It's just...' She stopped, looked at Nandita speculatively and shook her head. 'It's nothing,' she spoke lightly. 'He's not the marrying kind... It's like he just breezes through numerous girlfriends to keep himself amused. It'll have to be a really, really special girl to make him change his mind. Unfortunately, that wasn't me. He's a wanderer, Nan. He's not about to hang up his boots and be tied down to one woman. The very idea of marriage bores him.'

'But Arush, has Aditya actually *told* you all this himself?' she asked cautiously.

'Of course not, not in so many words. But some things are quite obvious to anyone who knows him well...except you, evidently. Damn it, for a while there I believed things would change, and that something was going to come out of the relationship.'

Nandita was silent. Judging by Aditya's past record, everything Arushi was saying must be true. Nandita had lost track of the women in his life after his break-up with her, and seriously doubted that even he remembered each one clearly. Why had she thought Arushi would be any different?

'Arushi, I am so sorry for everything I said. I had absolutely no idea. Please forgive me.'

'No apology required. The reason I told you was pure selfishness, I couldn't bear that you'd think badly of me, so I wanted you to know the truth. Aditya is never going to change his ways, unless...'

'Unless?'

Arushi waved her hand. 'Never mind, Nandita. You are lucky you have Aryan. You have no idea how lucky you are,' she said wistfully.

Nandita was quiet. She had not said anything about her break-up with Aryan.

Aditya will change, thought Nandita in panic, he has to. She would make sure of that. Nandita didn't feel like talking about Aditya to Arushi, so she reverted to Arushi's affairs. 'So, you're back with Ashish. I don't want you falling into the same trap again. You've not had very good luck with men, have you?' Nandita said.

'No, but this time it's different. Payal has got tired of his disinterest in her and I think she's ready to move on. Ashish may not be the ideal guy, Nandita, but he's the one I have to be with. It's my destiny,' Arushi replied matter of factly.

'Well, in that case, give the relationship everything you've got. I'm trying not to be judgmental here, so just help me out, ok?'

'Ok. Will you just meet him once? Don't form an opinion till you've had a chance to talk to him. Fair enough?'

Nandita nodded absently. Her mind flitted back to Aditya longingly. Their relationship had ended badly and they had never spoken about getting back together. She thought back to the Delhi days. Aditya had been through any number of women, but Nandita had been the only constant in his life. Did that mean anything, did it possibly mean that there was a chance for them? Did he feel the same way she did?

'Nandita, your phone is ringing!' Arushi's voice cut through her reverie.

'Oops!' She answered it. Aai! 'Hi, Ma! Yes, I'll be in Delhi Friday evening…it's an early evening flight… On Saturday? A charity event! Oh god, Aai, do we have to? Yeah, I guess you can't… Ok Ma, I can't wait to see you either! Bye, love you!'

Nandita hung up and turned to Arushi. 'So have you told Aditya?'

'Yes…on the flight back from Lakshadweep. He wasn't particulary heartbroken,' she said, a bit sadly. 'I did try to make a go of it, Nandita, I really did. But he just wasn't interested. One day you'll understand.'

Nandita kept quiet. There was nothing to say, really.

CHAPTER THIRTY-FIVE
Mumbai, November 2013

The city was a riot of lights, and the atmosphere unbelievably festive. Nandita had never seen anything like this in Delhi. Every street she passed was lit up with streams of tiny colourful bulbs and the pretty Maharashtrian kandeels. She loved the rows of identical orange ones that were put up in profusion in the chawls, lending a beautiful symmetry to the decorations.

Nandita was on her way to Tara and Sameer's pre-wedding bash at a Bandra hotel. Last year at this time, Nandita had been attending Shanti's wedding, and merely contemplating a change in her life in terms of shifting out of Delhi and her comfort zone. She had certainly not bargained for the kind of changes that had actually taken place, so many and so soon. In the last ten months, Nandita thought she had lived the equivalent of several years. How much had altered in her circumstances, how different a person she herself had become! It had all happened in a whirlwind that had carried her along at a pace she had never experienced before.

Her phone beeped for the seventh time in the last ten minutes, and thinking it was yet another Diwali greeting, she was about to delete the message without even reading it. Then she saw that it was from Tushar. Nandita felt a pang of remorse. She had been ignoring him and his calls, thoughtlessly preoccupied with her own issues. She opened the message: '*Hi Nandita. Just thot you shld know that I have brought Kulwant A to Lilavati Hosp an hour ago. Bad chest pain, looked pretty serious so didn't want to take a chance. Will keep you posted. T.'*

Nandita rang Tushar immediately.

'How is she? Have they diagnosed anything? Are you ok?'

'Hi Nandita. No, nothing yet. I'm at the hospital; they're running some tests. I think it must have been heart related.'

'Oh, the poor thing! Listen, I'm on my way to the Taj Land's End, so I'll drop in and see her. I should be there in ten minutes. Can she have visitors? I mean, she's not in the ICCU, is she?'

'No, no, you can come. She'll be glad to see you.'

'Ok, I'll be there in a bit. See you soon.' Nandita hung up and instructed the taxi driver to stop off at the hospital. She messaged Tara to say she'd be a bit late, briefly explaining the circumstances.

Kulwant Aunty was lying in bed looking pale and wan, but cheerful nonetheless, her indomitable spirit intact. She was delighted to see Nandita and insisted on trying to sit up. Tushar sternly persuaded her to remain as she was.

'*Arre, beta, Tushar nahi hota to mera kya ho jata*. He is like my son, the way he takes care of me.'

'I know,' replied Nandita. 'Tushar is really a rock you can lean on.'

The object of her praise looked a little uncomfortable and Nandita laughed.

'It's true, Tushar. You're a great friend, and I know that I don't value you enough. Kulwant Aunty, how are you feeling? Are you still in pain?'

'No, I'm feeling much better. So much fuss is being made over me! How can I feel sick!'

A nurse came in and told Tushar that he was wanted by the admin department for some paperwork.

'I'll be right back. Nandita, will you sit with her till I return?'

'Of course I will. You go on.'

She turned back to Kulwant.

'Aunty, has anyone called your son in Minneapolis?'

Kulwant looked away and said nothing for a moment. Nandita wondered whether she had asked an awkward question. After a couple of moments of silence, the old woman spoke in a tired voice, stripped of the usual buoyant note.

'My son is not interested, Nandita. His wife has never liked me, and they have not included me in their family for years. *Bhool kar bhi kabhi phone nahi karta, to ab kya meri halat poochne aayega.* No, Nandita. To me, Tushar is more like a son to me than my own Karan.'

Nandita was appalled.

'He doesn't even call you? When was the last time you saw him?'

'Pata nahi, maybe fourteen years?'

There didn't seem to be anything to say after this. At least Nandita could think of nothing. Her admiration for Kulwant swelled exponentially. The woman was strong beyond belief, she thought, to have borne all this with such good cheer.

'I have not told Tushar this, but I have made a will, leaving my house to him. He is all I have. And I know that his parents don't care about him, like Karan does not care about me. But he has been good to me, Nandita. Like a son, if not more. He thinks I don't know that he is…different. *Woh sochta hai ki main samajh nahi paoongi. Main boodhi zaroor hoon, par buddhu nahin.* I do understand, Nandita. He may not want to discuss this with me, but please tell him. I understand he is—kya bolte hain usko—gay. I don't care—he is still like my son.'

Kulwant seemed exhausted by this long speech, and her eyes closed gently. Nandita guessed she had been sedated, so she sat back and watched the old lady sleep. A feeling of warm compassion for Kulwant overwhelmed her. How wrongly she had judged the woman, she thought with regret. She had written Kulwant off as an old busybody, gossiping and interfering in the neighbours' lives. But under all that, Kulwant's heart was in the right place. Nandita decided that this should be a lesson to her to stop being judgmental about people. One never knew.

She heard the door open behind her, and rose quickly to warn Tushar to be silent. She motioned that she would come out.

'All sorted out?' she asked, stepping into the corridor and shutting the door softly.

'Yes. You'd think they'd try and simplify the procedure, but they just love their paperwork!'

Nandita shrugged. 'Hospitals! I better leave now, Tara will not rest in peace till I have checked her outfit and certified her fit to make an appearance!'

'Girls can be so silly. Thanks for dropping by, though, it meant a lot to me. By the way, some great news! I'm finally working with Meera…there's a pitch happening for a new dairy product brand, and we've come up with the most original and different campaign you'll ever see for butter! Abby material, whadya know!'

Nandita was delighted and gave him a warm hug.

'Surely you're not surprised? I can't think of anyone more deserving!'

She hesitated, and then continued, 'Tushar, Kulwant Aunty knows about you. She just told me. She is far more astute than you give her credit for. I think she has known all along, but she is not the old-fashioned woman you thought she was. She told me she loves you like a son, despite your being gay. She wanted me to tell you.'

As the initial shock faded from Tushar's face, he turned away so that Nandita would not see the tears in his eyes. She pretended not to notice and said goodbye quickly. She was conscious of a sense of relief that she would not have to worry about Tushar anymore…for some reason, she had always felt a degree of concern for the boy.

She got into another cab and headed to the hotel.

CHAPTER THIRTY-SIX
Mumbai, November 2013

Friday morning proved far busier than Nandita had anticipated. She had planned to take the day off so that she could squeeze in some time to shop for Diwali gifts for her mother, Simi Aunty and her friends in Delhi. Her hopes were dashed by a frantic call from Tushar. Kulwant Aunty had to be discharged from the hospital and brought home that morning, but he absolutely could not miss the dairy client's presentation...could Nandita please help out? She could hardly refuse his request, so she abandoned her shopping expedition and set forth to Lilavati Hospital. The discharge procedure, with all the accompanying red tape and paperwork, took up the better part of the morning, so it was almost lunchtime when Nandita finally got back home.

She had not bothered to pack—since it was just a weekend trip, she guessed it wouldn't take to long to throw her things together. Pulling out her overnight bag, Nandita began to fill it with the bare essentials. Since these comprised three pairs of shoes plus her trainers, and several shirts, her jeans, her track pants and two jackets (it would be cold in Delhi!), she found that there was no space for any actual clothes. There would be Friday night to cover, and then there was the charity benefit on Saturday...that would be a really dressy affair, and she needed at least two options to choose from, if not three. Who knew what her mood would be like on Saturday night? She abandoned the overnighter and pulled out a larger suitcase. A couple of evening dresses joined the heap of things now piled on the bed, along with two pairs of evening shoes. Make-up, accessories, toiletries… Goodness, it looked like she was going away for a whole week! Rajeev had told her she could have a couple of extra days off in case she wanted to stay on in Delhi, because November onwards there was going to be no leave in store for her at all. She had not even faintly betrayed to Rajeev that she was in possession of a legacy from his brother, or that she had even heard of Himanshu Sabarwal. All that would come later, after she had had a chance to speak to Amrita.

Engrossed as Nandita was in sorting her lipsticks and eye pencils into individual make-up pouches, she did not hear the front door open. She jumped when Aditya's voice sounded right behind her.

'Going somewhere, Nan?'

'What the…! You gave me a fright! What are you doing at home?'

'Shoot postponed…the set was all wrong and the production people are in deep shit. I'm glad, though, looks like you were about to slink off without telling me.'

'I'm not slinking anywhere…just off to Delhi for the weekend. Is it my fault that you're never home? I haven't seen you for ten days.'

'And there's no such thing as a cell phone, right? Why have you been avoiding me?' He was standing behind her, so close that Nandita's heart was beating treacherously fast. It was one thing to know that she was in love with him, but how did she proceed from there? She wanted nothing more than to be crushed against his body, to be kissed, made love to, feel his skin against hers. There was a tightness in her chest that she thought must be so obvious to him.

She moved away quickly, pretending to search for something in her wardrobe. 'Don't be a fool, Aditya. You are such a dramebaaz sometimes.' She spoke lightly, dismissing it as a joke.

'So Delhi, huh? You haven't told me what happened at the lawyer's office…any fresh clues?'

She sat on the bed and pressed her hands to her head. In all her efforts to avoid him, she had not filled him in on the meeting with old Mr Vakil and the identity of her father. 'Oh god, I haven't, have I?'

She rummaged in her bag for Himanshu's letter and passed it to him. 'It's self-explanatory.'

He sat next to her on the bed and read it slowly. 'Rajeev Sabarwal's brother… Wow.'

Nandita watched him as he read the letter again, even more slowly this time. His face, so recognizable in the past, suddenly looked interestingly unfamiliar. The shape of his lips, the curve of his smile…how had she forgotten the tiny dimple that quivered in his chin when he laughed? And the way his eyes crinkled when he was thinking…she resisted the impulse to reach out and touch his cheek. The memories of their exquisite physical closeness all those years ago came rushing back.

'So what now?' he looked up and asked her.

Nandita came back to reality with a jerk.

'I'm not sure. I'll figure it out when I get to Delhi.'

'Aryan going with you?'

'No.' She hesitated, not sure whether to continue.

'All ok there?' He raised his eyebrows.

'Actually, it's exactly as it should be.' He had not told her about his break-up with Arushi, so she saw no reason to be forthcoming about Aryan.

Aditya stared at Nandita for a few moments and she wilted under his gaze. It was not easy to lie to somebody who knew you so well. She stuffed the last shoebag into her suitcase, zipped it shut and spoke brightly.

'Have you had lunch? I'm ravenous. There's some lasagne in the fridge I can warm up.'

'Sure. Whatever.' He followed her into the kitchen and perched on the platform while she popped the pasta into the microwave and took out plates and cutlery.

The silence between them was strained. Nandita had no idea what was going on in his mind, and he didn't seem to be in a communicative mood. He toyed with the food on his plate disinterestedly, certainly a first for the perennially hungry Aditya.

'What time is your flight? I'll give you a ride to the airport. I have the hired car till the end of the week,' he said.

'Oh, you don't have to bother, I can take a cab.'

'It's fine, Nan, I have nothing planned. I was supposed to be shooting today.'

She smiled her thanks. 'I guess I should leave in half an hour or so…I just have a few emails to wrap up and I'm good to go.'

'Fine, gimme a shout when you're done.' He disappeared into his room.

The ride to the airport was even more silent. Nandita stole several surreptitious glances at him while he focused on the road. His stern profile revealed nothing. When they finally pulled up outside the terminal, he parked and got out of the car. Nandita stood beside him, not wanting to say goodbye. She hated the thought of any rift between them, especially when she was getting on a flight.

She turned to face him. 'Adi…'

Abruptly, he pulled her into a fierce hug that almost took her breath away. She felt his arms tighten around her body as he whispered into her hair, 'Don't worry, darling. Everything will sort itself out. Your mom's a tough woman…and so are you.' He released her quickly, his lips barely brushing her cheek.

Two cars were honking furiously behind them and Aditya gave them an acknowledging wave. With a brief goodbye, he got into the car and drove off.

Nandita watched the Honda weave its way through the maze of travellers and disappear down the ramp. He was gone. There was a lump in her throat, and a deep void in her heart. She stood rooted to the spot until a fellow passenger jostled her rudely. She was brought back to her surroundings, and in a daze, she turned to walk slowly into the airport building.

CHAPTER THIRTY-SEVEN
Delhi, November 2013

Simi's charity event was slated to be one of the most glittering affairs that Delhi would see. It was a cause that many people espoused, and plenty of celebrities, socialites and politicians were expected, along with a sprinkling of corporate types. Nandita was not wild about attending these parties, as she found the social set a little superficial, and such occasions brought out the worst in every wannabe socialite looking for a quick photo-op. Nonetheless, she made the effort to dress up. It had been a while since she'd attended a big formal event, so she actually enjoyed the process of choosing her dress, shoes and accessories.

Moving around her familiar bedroom, she luxuriated in the bliss of being home after almost a year. The heavy depression she had felt on the flight home had lifted as soon as she stepped into the house and met her mother. Temporarily, her troubles were forgotten and she and Amrita chatted late into the night, catching up on the last few months. The ghosts of Amrita's past were not brought up…Nandita wanted to enjoy her mother's company for a while, without any complications. Nandita's life was, however, discussed in detail, and Amrita was visibly distressed to hear about the break-up with Aryan.

'But why, Nandi?' she had asked in bewilderment. 'I thought everything was going so well!'

'It just didn't work out, Ma. One of those things. You don't have to be upset; I'm perfectly ok with it. He's a fantastic guy, everything any girl could want, but not for me.'

Amrita had refrained from commenting further. Ruthlessly pulling her brush through her tangle of curls, Nandita smiled as she recalled their tête-à-tête last night. She was so lucky to have Amrita as her mother—no pressure, no judgement and always plenty of support.

Amrita had gone on ahead to the venue, as Simi had put her on the organizing committee. Nandita drove there alone, making sure she left well in time to negotiate the Delhi traffic...she had no intention of being fashionably late at Simi's event, she'd never hear the last of it.

When she arrived at the hotel, she was amused to see the lineup of celebrities posing for photos even before they entered. The usual wealth of designerwear was on display everywhere. She moved quickly past all the activity in the foyer and entered the grand ballroom, and almost gasped in pleasure. The area had been beautifully decorated—everything was done in pale beige and gold, with yellow roses and huge golden bows on the chairs. The room was dotted with a quantity of round tables laid for ten people each. The place was still quite empty, and Nandita spotted her mother and Simi almost immediately.

She walked over to them. 'Brilliant décor, Simi Aunty,' she said, giving her a hug. 'It all looks gorgeous!'

Simi was delighted. 'Nandi! How fantastic that you are here. We've really missed you, haven't we, Amrita? You look lovely, as usual. Come, give me a kiss!'

Nandita laughed at the enthusiastic greeting.

'So how's my baccha Aditya doing? He's not very good about keeping in touch, but he did call me this morning...he's travelling madly, isn't he?'

'Yes...I really don't see much of him either. You shouldn't complain, Simi Aunty, you wanted him to get serious about something, and now he has.' Nandita found it hard to speak about him in this casual way.

'That's true, and I'm grateful for it. But I wish he would think about settling down too. I mean, if he gets married, then all my worries will be over.'

'Aunty! You're incorrigible! Take it one step at a time, na?'

Simi chuckled. 'You know me, Nandi darling. Always pushy and obnoxious.'

'Never obnoxious, Simi,' said Amrita fondly.

People were beging to stream into the ballroom, and Simi was galvanized into action. 'Nandi, our table is Number 3, go find it and sit down...I better go see what those ushers are doing, they're looking more lost than the guests.'

Simi hurried off, and Amrita was accosted by an acquaintance. Nandita wandered off in the direction of Table 3. It was empty, so she took a round to check the place cards, to know who was at the table with them tonight and how boring the evening was going to be. Dilip Chopra and Mala Chopra...old friends of Simi Aunty, she had met them before. Vinita and Aman Shastri. Never heard of them. Sayali Varghese, socialite! Motley crew. Amrita's name next to her own, then Simi's and the last one was Abhimanyu... What? Abhimanyu Menon? What the heck? Nandita's mind raced furiously...what on earth was he doing in Delhi, at Amrita's event, at her *table*?

She had no opportunity to accost her mother, as Amrita was escorting the Chopras to the table.

'Nandi, you remember Dilip and Mala, don't you?'

'Of course. I remember Mala as the benefactress who used to bring Aditya and me chocolates from her trips to Europe...and really yummy ones, at that!' Nandita greeted the couple warmly, and they took their places at the table.

'I guess we won't be seeing much of Simi at dinner. She's in her element when she's running around three places at the same time,' observed Amrita.

Mala Chopra commented on what a wonderful job had been done of the décor in the hall and in the general discussion that followed, Nandita was able to take a quick look around the ballroom to see if she could spot Abhimanyu. There was no sign of him.

She found a moment to catch her mother's attention. 'Ma! Abhimanyu Menon? What the hell is this? What is he doing here?' she whispered quickly.

Amrita was about to reply when Sayali arrived, flushed with the excitement of posing for the photographers outside. 'It's a madhouse out there,' she said. 'I haven't seen so much press at an event for a long time. Simi is to be congratulated, she certainly knows how to throw a party!'

Sayali knew everyone at the table and soon managed to dominate the conversation entirely. No one minded much, as all of them were absorbed in looking around to see which of their friends had made it to the event. Amrita was now avoiding Nandita's eye, much to her daughter's annoyance. There was no sign of the unknown Shastris. It was half an hour past the time the function was to begin. As if on cue with her thoughts, the lights dimmed and a suave compère asked everyone to take their seats. This would take another few minutes, Nandita knew. Still no Abhimanyu. What sort of game was her mother playing? She saw quite a few people she knew well, and some she knew only by sight. Spotting an interesting-looking woman in her fifties sporting a gorgeous kanjeevaram sari and enormous red bindi, Nandita was intrigued. She turned to Amrita to ask who she was, but Amrita was busy smiling at a silver-haired man approaching their table. As Abhimanyu neared, she rose to greet him. Amrita was looking particularly beautiful tonight in a flowing peach silk tunic with wide silk pants, and a dazzling choker of diamonds and pearls around her slender throat. Her long hair was worn in her signature style, loose down her back. The effect was obviously not lost on Abhimanyu, who was looking at her with open admiration. However, he said nothing and submitted to the introductions with his usual charm. When it came to Nandita's turn, her mother casually said 'Oh, Nandita, of course, needs no introduction to you, Abhi...you and she are already good friends, I believe!'

Nandita was indignant. How blasé her mother was being! Shouldn't she have mentioned something before? When conversation at the table had resumed, Abhimanyu addressed Nandita, a hint of amusement in his voice.

'You can stop looking so curious and surprised, Nandita. I told you when I first met you that I knew Amrita. Thanks to you, I've been able to get in touch with her again.'

'No, you never said you knew her. In fact, you were particularly vague when I mentioned her name!' Nandita was not going to let him off so easily.

Amrita had the grace to to look apologetically at her daughter. 'We'll talk about it later, ok?' she whispered.

The emcee was back on the mic. The speeches began, and Nandita's mind trailed off. Simi still hadn't joined them at their table. Most of the other tables looked quite full. Nandita was impressed with the punctuality shown by everyone tonight. Gloved waiters came around, pouring wine. Nandita accepted the white. She was surreptitiously watching her mother and Abhimanyu. They seemed, if not intimate, more than comfortable with each other. Nandita had no means of knowing that three nights ago, Amrita had finally divulged the whole story of Himanshu Sabarwal to Abhimanyu. While he had been extremely surprised, he had not shown his hurt to Amrita at all. Abhimanyu had decided, since the moment he had walked into Amrita's house the first night in Delhi, that he wanted her back in his life. He saw no point in raking up old issues...what was done was done, and Himanshu was no more. Abhimanyu was now pursuing Amrita in a quiet courtship, and she was not discouraging him in any way. But Nandita was blissfully unaware of these developments, and could only speculate from over the rim of her crystal wineglass. More speeches were made, followed by polite applause.

'Why don't they learn to keep it short?' whispered Nandita to her mother. 'How long does this go on?'

'Shh...don't be rude. This is the last one, I think,' Amrita admonished her.

Nandita heard the chair being pulled out beside her and turned in time to see Aditya slide easily into it. Aditya? Here? Her eyes were full of questions as she leaned across to receive his hug. This time, it was she who lingered in his embrace longer than usual.

'You never told me!' she whispered. 'Why didn't you say you were coming?'

'I didn't know myself until this afternoon. The set was still not ready, and I was tired of waiting around. So I just drove to the airport and took the first available flight.'

'All this trouble for a charity event? It's not like you, Aditya!'

The ending of the last speech produced a much more enthusiastic applause than earlier. Lights came on and conversation filled the room. After Aditya had wished everyone at the table, he looked at Nandita.

'I didn't come for the event,' he said softly. 'I came for you.'

Nandita's heart skipped a beat. Aditya had never looked at her quite like that before.

Amrita murmured something to Abhimanyu and rose. 'I think I'd better go and see what Simi is doing... I'm supposesd to be on the managing committee, but I've not managed anything so far.' She looked at Aditya and added, 'By the way, your bua is going to be over the moon when she sees you...she's really missed you, you know. And by Nandita's expression, so has she! Don't the two of you live in the same city? Same house, as a matter of fact?'

Nandita blushed and avoided Aditya's eye. Amrita wandered off, and in a moment or two, so did Abhimanyu. The waiter came around, pouring more wine. Sayali was not the type to stay rooted to one table through one evening, and got up to make her rounds before the first course was served.

Nandita grabbed the opportunity. 'You came...to see me? You saw me last evening, Adi.'

'Can we get out of here?'

Mala Chopra's voice cut into their conversation. 'How do you like your new career, Aditya? Simi tells us you've been doing some fantastic work.'

'You know Bua. She loves to exaggerate! I'm just trying to break into the field... it's not easy, but I'm enjoying myself.'

There seemed to be no way of escaping the Chopras, and it would have been rude to leave them sitting there by themselves. How could Amrita have abandoned her like that? Aditya continued the conversation smoothly, while Nandita just watched him. He looked unbearably good in his custom-made suit, and Nandita wondered why she had ever let him go. Why had they even broken up? It seemed like such a string of silly squabbles now. She wanted him back, more than she had ever wanted anything in her life. She forced her gaze away from his face and tuned into what Dilip Chopra was saying.

'And you actually worked with some of those new underwater cameras?' Dilip asked.

Aditya was about to reply when they were joined by Amrita, Simi and Abhimanyu. The first course was served, and there was a flurry of activity at all the tables. Simi came straight to Aditya and engulfed him in a huge embrace.

'I am so happy you could make it, Aditya! You didn't sound so sure when we spoke on the phone this morning!' She planted a big kiss on the top of his head and took the seat vacated by Sayali, who had apparently found somewhere else to sit. 'Bon appetit, everybody! And here's to seeing my two favourite young people back in Delhi...' she raised her glass.

A plate of shrimp salad was placed in front of Nandita. She ate it without really noticing. Suddenly, she felt Aditya's hand take hers under the table and clasp it tightly. She turned towards him but he was deep in conversation with Amrita, and paying no attention to her. She clasped it back, not looking at him either. In that unspoken moment, Nandita did not know what passed between her and Aditya, but one thing was as certain as could be: she and Aditya belonged together, and had always done so. It could never be any other way.

She leaned closer to him and whispered, 'If you've come to see me, why don't you talk to me?'

Aditya stood up and addressed the table generally. 'Nandita, there's someone here I really want you to meet... Can we be excused for a few moments, please?' Before anyone could say a word, he led her away from the table. They exited the ballroom and found a small alcove in the adjoining banquet area that was empty. Aditya pulled Nandita roughly into his arms without a word, and kissed her. In all her wildest imaginings, Nandita had not dreamt a kiss could feel like this. Her body felt like it was not her own, but a part of his. She melted willingly into the feel of his protective arms, and his familiar lips on hers.

When she finally pulled away, he cupped her face in his hands and spoke softly. 'There's just so much to say to you, Nan, but I don't know where to start. But before any of that, I just want to tell you one thing…you belong to *me*, ok? I should have said this years ago, baby, and spared both of us a lot of grief. I was a fool to let you out of my sight.'

She took his hands in hers. 'Maybe years ago we were not ready, maybe we needed to go through everything that we did… It doesn't matter anymore, Aditya. Anyway, start from the beginning…why did you decide to come after me? All of yesterday I was looking for some sign, some signal from you, but you were so cold and distant. I was so hoping that you had broken up with Arushi for the same reasons I broke up with Aryan, but you were painfully indifferent!'

'I couldn't do anything until I was sure you had broken up with him… I suspected from your behaviour that something was wrong, but you were so uncommunicative! I heard about your break-up from Simi Bua this morning when we spoke on the phone. I couldn't wait to get to you!'

She laughed delightedly and pressed closer to him. 'Who would have thought I would live to be grateful to Simi Bua! I was so miserable on the flight back home, I think I was in tears all the way here.' In a more serious tone, she continued. 'I have to thank Aryan from saving me from making the biggest mistake of my life…it was he who made me see…'

'No, my darling, I would have come to my senses sooner rather than later. I wouldn't have let you marry him, or anybody else.' He looked deep into her eyes. 'I can't believe what an idiot I've been…it was only when things began to get serious between you and Aryan that I realized… Oh god, Nan, when you told me he wanted to get married, I was so afraid that I had lost you forever!'

'But why didn't you say something? Why didn't you make me see sense? You knew I was confused, you knew I hadn't said yes…'

'Nan, we broke up the first time because you didn't think I was doing anything with my life. Let's face it; most of our fights were about me. I couldn't ask you to be with me again till I knew for sure that you thought I was worth something. But now I don't care about all that, I'm not letting you go anywhere, ok?'

This time, it was Nandita who pulled him towards her, and ignoring the amused stares of two waiters and people on their way to the restrooms, she made it clear to Aditya that he was everything to her, and she wasn't letting him go anywhere either.

CHAPTER THIRTY-EIGHT
Delhi, November 2013

When Aditya and Nandita made it back to the ballroom, the next course in the form of lamb chops had already been served. Too happy and excited to eat, Nandita picked at her plate. She watched Aditya from the corner of her eye, unable to quite believe what had just taken place. She felt like she had finally come home. The rest of the meal passed in a haze for her. She did not even notice how much attention Abhimanyu was paying her mother, a fact that would have been commented upon zealously by her in other circumstances. The evening began to wind down, and the Chopras took their leave, finally giving the group a chance to drop the formal conversation. Abhimanyu stayed, and Simi finally relaxed, now that her precious event had been successfully concluded. Soon, there was almost no one left, and waiters had begun to clear up…however, at Table Number 3, it looked like the party was just beginning. Simi called for a bottle of brandy to be brought to them.

'Can we make that a bottle of champagne instead, Simi Bua?' asked Aditya mischeviously.

'Why, darling, what are we celebrating?' asked Amrita.

He took Nandita's hand. 'Nandita and I are getting married.'

Not surprisingly, this announcement produced a medley of loud reactions and expressions of delight from Amrita and Simi. Characteristically, Simi was the first to speak.

'But how? When? The dearest wish of my heart, and you spring it like this!'

'Nandi, you said nothing last night...' Amrita chided her daughter, sounding so surprised.

Nandita broke in indignantly. 'Well, this is news to me too... he hasn't even proposed!'

Abhimanyu laughed. 'I like your style, Aditya.'

Aditya grinned, kissed Nandita and spoke. 'Will you marry me, you little spitfire?'

'That depends entirely on whether you have a ring to go with that shamelessly unromantic proposal,' she replied with a laugh.

'I do. Somewhere in the depths of her vault, Simi Bua has been saving my mother's four-carat emerald just for this occasion. For your green eyes, my lovely Nan!' The last part was whispered for her ears only, and Nandita felt tears spring into her eyes.

'Simi, all those years of our plotting and planning for these two have been fruitful...finally, they've seen sense. This is the most natural conclusion to your history together, though you've certainly taken your time about it!' Amrita said to the pair of them.

Several rounds of toasts were made, and Nandita felt she had never seen Simi Aunty look happier. Amrita was delighted too, but Nandita had unfinished business with her mother, and suddenly realized that now was the time to tackle it. After all, all the key players were there, except for her dead father.

Nandita looked at her mother. 'Ma, there's something we need to talk about. And since we are all here, I just feel it's the right time to do it. Simi Aunty and you, well, I know you have no secrets.' She glanced at Abhimanyu. 'I don't pretend to know what you are doing here, Abhimanyu. You haven't told me how you knew my mother, but by now I have a fair idea. So I guess all this involves you as well.'

Amrita looked at Simi and froze. 'What is it that you know about Abhimanyu, Nandi?'

'Aai, I don't want to cause you any pain or grief after all the years you've suffered already. But it's not necessary to do this anymore...you don't have to hide anything from me. You see...' she paused, unable to continue after seeing her mother's white face.

'Go on, Nandita,' said Abhimanyu. 'You're right, this does concern me and believe me when I tell you, I have nothing but your mother's best interests at heart. Unless,' he turned to Amrita, 'you'd rather I went away?'

She put her hand on his arm and shook her head mutely.

Nandita took a deep breath, looked straight into her mother's eyes and started. 'A few years ago, I found a letter hidden inside a jewellery box.'

EPILOGUE
Mumbai, January 2014

Nandita looked around with a mixture of pride and satisfaction.

'Not bad, eh?' she said to Rajeev Sabarwal, who was also looking slightly smug from all the compliments that had come their way that evening.

'That's an understatement. I think we pretty much bowled everyone over.'

'Does that mean that the next Starling in India will be ours too?' Nandita queried hopefully.

'I expect so,' he answered. 'By the way, Nandita, has Aditya finally decided about moving back to Delhi after you get married?'

'Yes, but I can still work for you on a project-to-project basis, can't I? I don't want to have to sever my connections with Sabarwal Associates.'

'Sever your connections? Nandita, even if the world doesn't know it, you *are* a Sabarwal. Trust me, you have every ounce of your father's talent and drive. Ritika has no interest in architecture, so you have to carry this company on your shoulders at some point. Besides, I've got used to having you around.' He paused and smiled at her fondly. 'You know, at first I came looking for you because that was what Himanshu had wanted, but now you're a very much loved member of my family. I was hoping that we could look at opening a branch of Sabarwal Associates in Delhi. Something you could spearhead and run for me…how do you feel about that?'

'It sounds absolutely heaven sent! Thank you, Rajeev...I would like that more than anything else!'

Rajeev gave her an awkward hug. He was not a very demonstrative man, but she knew that he had grown extremely fond of her. When Nandita had told him about the legacy from Himanshu, he assured her that he'd known about it all along. He was the one who had helped Himanshu set up the trust, and Nandita had been stunned when he revealed that he himself was the main trustee. Rajeev was absolutely insistent that she accept the money...he had no claims on his brother's wealth. But it was not until Amrita gave her the go-ahead that Nandita called Mr Vakil and signed the papers.

Someone beckoned to Rajeev from across the hall, and he excused himself. As he strolled off, Nandita cast another look at her surroundings. The enormous poolside area and the adjoining banquet rooms of Starling Lotus were filled with Mumbai's power glitterati. The entire hotel had been decked with rare flowers from all over the world, lending an aura of exotica to the already stunning décor. Huge canvasses of original art hung on the majestic marbled walls, and even the cynical Mumbai high net worth individuals who had seen and done it all were mesmerized by their surroundings. The patent luxury was not crass and over the top, but quietly elegant and tastefully understated. The guest list did not include the usual banal crowd of Page Three party animals, but a more select corporate profile, many of who ranked high on the Indian power list. There was no circus of pole dancers and Bollywood performing troupes; instead, the entertainment comprised a world-renowned jazz maestro, very much appreciated by the discerning invitees.

Aryan had recommended to his bosses that the launch party of Starling Lotus be small and exclusive. Ironically, the more discreet they tried to keep it, the more it became touted as the Party of the Season. The select guest list of 200 people could not be envied enough, and as was the usual style in Mumbai, many aspirants who were not invited simply pretended that they were, but could not attend as they were out of town.

Champagne, premium wines and malt flowed freely, and guests were treated to the finest creations from the three restaurants in the hotel that were headed by famous Michelin-starred chefs. Nandita spotted Anjali sitting by the pool with Rajat, wrinkling her nose in distaste while sipping from a glass of something that looked suspiciously like orange juice. She went up to her in amusement.

'Nandita, I can't take this non-alcoholic mocktail crap anymore! Can I not just have the baby and be done with it?' She was visibly pregnant now, glowing and healthy with plenty of rest. And no alcohol!

'Just a couple more months, babe, and you'll be good to go. Be patient. Are you tired?'

Anjali was about to reply when Aryan's voice sounded from behind Nandita.

'There you are! Feel good about all your hard work, Nandita?'

'I would say so, yes!' she said.

'You're looking well. And happy,' he added with a smile.

Nandita was wearing a short black Prada dress of upholstery fabric with a plunging V neckline. An antique silver choker was clasped around her neck and on her third finger, she wore an enormous princess-cut emerald, the engagement ring that Aditya had wasted no time in putting on her finger.

'How have you been, Aryan?' she asked.

'Pretty good, all things considered. You know it's been a madhouse around here the last few weeks.'

She wanted to know how he was on the personal front, but did not like to ask, with so many people around. Aryan moved away to welcome a new arrival.

She turned to Anjali. 'Anju, how is he doing? He puts on a façade for me, but with you, I'm sure he is himself. Is he ok? I feel so guilty about everything that's happened.'

'Don't be silly, Nandita, there's nothing to feel guilty about. He's fine. He misses you, of course. But these things happen, you know. Besides, there have been enough heartbroken women in his wake, and I think, in a way, it's good for him to know what the other side of the fence feels like. I always felt he lacked that sensitivity which is required in a successful relationship. Anyway, I hear Alison is pursuing him single-mindedly, and wanting to make a trip to Mumbai. So far, he hasn't taken the bait...he's too busy with work right now to think of much else.'

Nandita nodded slowly, not particularly reassured by Anjali's words. She changed the topic, speaking gaily, 'You're looking good, Anju, really glowing. How do you feel?'

'Divine,' replied Anjali, looking ruefully down at her baby bump, ensconced in a voluminous silk maternity dress.

Rajat and Nandita laughed, but Nandita spoke seriously.

'Don't worry, Anju, you're probably never going to look this beautiful again, no matter how skinny you become. Pregnancy is amazing!'

While Anjali made disbelieving eyes at her, Rajat squeezed his wife's hand.

'She's right, Anju. You do look kind of cute. But I would go easy on those cheese and caviar canapés, if I were you!'

'You're probably right, but they're way too delicious! Nandita, don't you dare get married until after this baby is born, I'll never forgive you if I have to show up at your wedding looking like a blimp!'

'I think I can safely promise you that, Anju. It will take my mother and Simi Aunty at least that much time to give vent to their enthusiasm. First it was a temple ceremony, and then it became a beach in Thailand. The last I heard, they were thinking small, intimate wedding in some palace in Bikaner.'

'And Epicurean will do the food? Fabulous!' Anjali helped herself to another canapé, and Rajat laughed outright.

'All she can think about, now that the sick phase is over, is food!'

'Seriously, Nandita, I know things didn't work out with Aryan, and I'm really happy for you and Aditya, but you won't forget us, will you? You know you were more to us than just Aryan's girlfriend?' Anju was being sentimental now, and Nandita hugged her.

'I promise I won't, Anju! Delhi's not that far away, you know...I will see you often!'

Nandita wandered around the pool area in search of Rajeev. She bumped instead into Arushi, accompanied by Ashish Kataria. Even though Nandita had by now met him several times, she was still wary of him. Trying to disguise the stiffness she felt, she greeted him awkwardly.

'Rather lavish. isn't it? I hear the suites are going to be hideously expensive. Aryan will have his work cut out for him in the next few months.' Ashish addressed his remark to Arushi after greeting Nandita with equal awkwardness.

'Oh, he'll manage. Starling spells luxury, you know, and people don't mind paying for the real thing,' replied Arushi confidently.

Ashish spied an acquaintance and moved away, and Arushi turned to Nandita quietly.

'Aditya not here today?'

'No, he had to be in Delhi for some work Simi Aunty wanted him to do. Besides, given the circumstances...'

'I guess,' said Arushi. 'It would have been a little awkward. Nandita, I just want to say, I'm really happy for you and Aditya. I mean, I've always known that the reason Aditya could never be with anyone else was you. I never said anything, but I always knew. That was the real reason I broke up with him.'

Nandita nodded. She did not want to get into this discussion with Arushi. Their friendship had changed. Nandita could no longer confide in Arushi the way she had before; there was a barrier that both of them felt but neither acknowledged openly.

Arushi was silent. Nandita had gauged over the last few weeks that given a chance, Arushi would have chosen to be with Aditya rather than with Ashish. But that was not going to happen. Her heart ached for Arushi, and she hoped fervently that Ashish would turn out to be a decent guy after all.

Nandita's own life was better than she had ever imagined it would become.

The night at the charity banquet had gone on till almost 2 a.m., when Nandita had told the story of her search for her father in the deserted ballroom. Amrita was unable to control her tears at the end of Nandita's story, and since it was the first time she had ever seen her mother cry, it had been a very emotional moment for Nandita too. But somehow, in the stillness of that incredible night, the secrets of the past were washed away and everyone present was grateful for second chances and new beginnings.

Nandita did not know what the future held for Abhimanyu and Amrita...they were taking baby steps towards building their relationship again. But for Nandita and Aditya, life had taken a full circle, and both of them were finally where they belonged.

ACKNOWLEDGEMENTS

My appreciation and thanks to:

Fahad Samar, who read, reread and dissected my manuscript, even though it wasn't really his 'genre' of writing. Thank you for all the encouragement, and all the lunches!

Roshan Abbas, for being my first critic and reading my manuscript in Suncity, where I'm sure you had more exciting things to do.

Alisha Shirodkar, for pushing me and encouraging me with your sweet, practical wisdom.

Siddhant Shirodkar, for just being Sid. You are immeasurably special.

Mahesh Shirodkar, who had no real contribution except wanting to pack me off to Goa for a sabbatical so that I could 'write in peace'. Peace for whom is what I wanted to know! That said, I could not have asked for a more wonderful husband.

My sister and fellow author, Madhuri Iyer, who didn't bat an eyelid when I told her I wanted to write, and supported me through the process.

Jankee Desai, Dilip Puri and Elahe Hiptoola, for taking the time to read my manuscript and giving me valuable feedback.

Kanishka Gupta, my literary agent, who got me three publishing offers in less than a month of submitting my manuscript.

Kausalya Saptharishi and Amrita Mukerji at Rupa, for all the guidance and help.

My lovely parents, Kunda and Nicky Nadkar, for always being completely supportive. You are the best.

www.ingramcontent.com/pod-product-compliance
Lightning Source LLC
LaVergne TN
LVHW021759060526
838201LV00058B/3161

9788129132697